A Dream of Steam

James W. Barry

A Dream of Steam

James W. Barry

For My Mother,
who taught me to read,
and who wore polyester pants
so we children could have lessons.

Acknowledgments

Anyone who has admitted out loud that he or she is working on a first novel has probably received a tight, pitying smile at some point; it's tough bringing a book to completion and publishing is even harder. People who might encourage you are either generous friends or secret sadists, but I think you can generally tell the difference.

I want to thank all of the people who read my manuscript, at its various stages, and provided helpful commentary, especially: Daryl and Lyndsay from *Wild Blue*, Bridget Arbour; Edith, Susan, and the Rehoboth Book Club; and Gina Ohrnberger, Trevor Schwellnus, Helma Hermanns, Boyd Hottenstein, Dave Bonney, and Esta Spalding.

I am grateful to my brother-in-law, Erik Ohrnberger, for his superb and cheerful tech support, keeping my computers running smoothly.

A good book needs a good editor. Thanks to Tyler Tichelaar for patiently working through every detail of this book with me.

Thanks to Larry Alexander for his superb layout.

My old comrade, Josh Payne, brought his talent, energy, and vision to the cover art.

Thanks to my family for their love and support. Lastly, and most of all, thanks to Corinna for her constant goodness.

TABLE OF CONTENTS

Book One

A Compromise

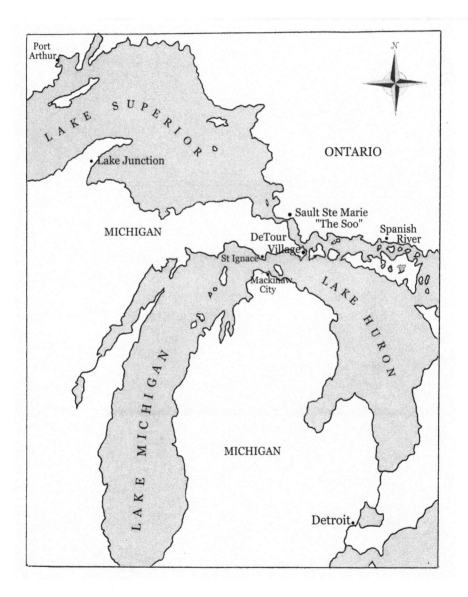

CHAPTER 1

August 14, 1891

I T WAS PERHAPS a trick of the calendar, but as he gazed at it, William McGrath realized he had somehow lost a day. It was clearly Friday, but he had been certain up until that moment that it was Thursday. No longer comfortably ahead, he now had to worry about falling behind. The jump forward of one day also meant that it was the fourteenth of August, an anniversary of sorts. Hard to believe another year has gone, he thought. He typically saved private correspondence for the quiet emptiness of his home, but today he felt compelled to attempt a letter during work. The mail was picked up from the general store at eleven o'clock, so if he hurried, the letter could be posted today.

The date and salutation were easy, but never gifted at writing personal letters, William held his wetted pen over the inkwell as he wavered over how best to begin. What string of words stood the best chance of reaching a woman where all previous approaches had failed? What new understanding could he tap to produce a letter she would want to read?

The pen dripped.

Old questions tumbled over fragments of happier phrases William had intended to write, until intrusive images of neglected tasks began flashing in his mind. He dipped his pen again, but when it ran dry for the second time, he was forced to acknowledge he was wasting valuable minutes. Left alone, his production problems on the mill floor would only become more pressing. He set his pen aside to go in search of Svensson.

"Are we running behind?" William McGrath asked Svensson, his mill foreman.

Svensson nodded and was about to reply when a sharp cracking noise caused both men to look around, trying to understand what had just gone wrong. As minor disasters go, a cracking noise couldn't touch the sharp punch of an explosion, or the heat of driven flame. No, a few splinters of wood had shot sideways, a shaft had fallen out of line, leather drive belts had sagged, and now the mill had convulsed to a staggering stop. Men looked up from their dying saws, all idly curious to divine what was the latest calamity to halt the machinery. In a former time, one might have guessed another child was caught in the main gear, but at the McGrath Brothers' sawmill, commonplace breakdowns were happening regularly, in a variety of forms, due to the machinery's age.

To prevent himself from interfering with his millwright, William McGrath retreated to the sweaty closeness of his office. He measured the floor in paces, six strides from his desk to the window, six in return. At thirty-four, William was a man who stood out in a crowd, partly because the human eye is drawn to motion, and driven by nervous energy, William was rarely still. But in addition, he had unusually dark red hair brushing his collar.

Now what would he do about *Genevieve*'s arrival? Counting silently, he stepped on every fifth pine board, not to any enumerative purpose, but merely as a subconscious routine developed while grappling with the complexities of running the family sawmill. Perched on the eastern tip of Michigan's Upper Peninsula, the mill offered him a series of little puzzles to solve daily, and these he could dispose of quickly and easily. Now and again, however, he would confront a real conundrum—what his father had called a "two pipeful"—but instead of smoking, he paced.

Today, the unwelcome return of quiet to his mill, and its implications, was cause for pacing. The absent racket of rolling logs, whirring saws, and chattering planer blades echoed hauntingly in his ears. Everything was stopped from the twelve-foot undershot water wheel down to the long carts used for trundling finished material into the stock yard, leaving twenty-six men trying not to appear idle.

A knock at the door halted his march.

"Yes, come in."

Boyle, the millwright, entered. His broad, wrinkled face bore unspoken bad news. "Well, Mr. McGrath, it's err...." He hesitated, mopping his brow, gauging William's mood while he tried to find the most appeasing phrasing for his description of the latest setback and its necessary repair. William's handlebar mustache didn't hide his hollow cheekbones but rather emphasized his sharp chin. He leaned slightly forward, which put Boyle on edge.

William sensed the man's mild distress. "Go ahead; tell me."

Boyle gathered himself. "The jam was caused by the overhead bearing splintering on the secondary shaft. It's broken outward in two places. The shaft went out of line and burst several of its gear teeth as well as some on the main gear until it jammed solid."

"I see, I see," William muttered impatiently through his mustache. "But this bearing was only installed two months ago."

"An unfortunate piece, I'm afraid, sir, but it must be pulled and replaced," Boyle said.

"No repair is possible? Not even temporary bracing?"

"I'm afraid not, sir," said Boyle, holding his ground firmly. "This kind of splintering won't allow it to knit cleanly, and we would be wearing out the end of the upright shaft on a rough joint."

William nodded unhappily. Boyle was right. It was a clear case of pay now or pay more later—however infuriating. This was one of the afflictions of a wood-geared, water-powered mill: water turned a wooden wheel, connected to a wooden shaft captured in wooden bearings, spinning wooden gears that transferred power through meshing wooden cogs. However strong, hard, and durable these elements might seem to the touch, in the end, they were only wood, and despite lubrication, subject to chipping, splitting, and wear, while in constant motion to render logs into lumber.

Boyle stood waiting until William completed his reflections and realized he must conclude the interview. "Do we have a new bearing block on hand?"

Boyle, ever competent, bobbed his head affirmatively. "It only needs final fitting to the end of the shaft, but with the other damage to the gear teeth, I'm afraid the mill won't be running until morning."

William had known he would lose the day's work; he nodded and said, "Pick a couple of men to help you; the others I'll send home early."

Boyle made his exit, leaving William to resume his pacing. Stopping to change blades on the saws was routine, but these time-consuming repairs were becoming more frequent as he tried to boost production using this old equipment. And the lost work hurt; William's brother's ship was due alongside the mill's loading dock any day now. As it was already August, it would be criminal to keep the ship waiting for cargo.

William glanced up at the walnut clock on the bookshelf over his desk and realized he had been pacing, fretting, and cursing for over half an hour—regrettably unproductive activity! His eyes dropped to his desk where his pen also rebuked him; he could have written the letter to his wife by now. But no, there was no use rushing that project. He stood still, closed his eyes, and pictured steam: steam boiling up from his insides; scouring, sanitizing steam clearing gummy passages and plugged pathways; live steam, venting pressure out of his ears, eyes, and nostrils. He exhaled a long, hot sigh, completely deflating his chest. Then, he imagined steam more practically: steam that built pressure in boilers, that pushed pistons driving iron wheels, powering a mill that could produce lumber at a mechanically guaranteed rate!

Another knock on the door interrupted his fantasy of steam.

"Come in!" he called. This time it was Svensson.

"We've just spotted *Genevieve* coming downriver," the confident old Swede said.

William grimaced. *Already?* he thought to himself.

"Thank you, Svensson. Let Boyle have who he needs; take a couple of hands to the pier and send the rest home. We'll start an hour early tomorrow."

It was embarrassing to be caught without cargo ready, but he decided he would go on the offensive. He had to persuade his brother, a traditionalist, to look forward rather than back. Thomas was unlikely to embrace steam passionately; he clung to his known world, secure in his ability to forge ahead in it. William had tried, without success, to convince Thomas to sell his old sailing ship and acquire a comparably sized steamship. It was 1891, for goodness' sake; everyone had steamships! A steamer, in William's mind, would reduce lumber delivery to a mathematical certainty, unswayed by contrary winds, or the lack of tugboats for river passages. Well, that was a separate argument. For now, he searched for the master word to convince Thomas that they must update the mill to steam power if he wanted to continue to fill his ship.

And as William considered persuasion, at the disabled upright drive shaft, Boyle caught a dangling thread from his sleeve on the tip of a fine splinter he had not noticed before.

Eventually, the river grew less narrow, and soon *Genevieve* was setting sail. The tug *Avenger* gave a loud hoot on her whistle, the tow line was dropped, and *Genevieve* sailed on her own through the final tree-clad, rounded humps of granite islands down to DeTour Village. A handsome gray barkentine, *Genevieve* was no ordinary lake ship; one-hundred-and-fifty feet long, she was rigged with three masts: foremast, mainmast, and mizzen mast, named from bow to stern. Four square sails spread across her foremast, and she was gaff-rigged on the main and mizzen. The last decade of the nineteenth century was an era of steamships, or alternatively, schooners, and *Genevieve* was numbered among the few square riggers actively plying their trade on the Great Lakes.

Captain Thomas McGrath surveyed the passing landscape of the river's edge. On watch as he was, Thomas stood tall and alert. Heavy labor in his formative years had given him sturdy limbs, and yet he moved with an economic grace from one side of the deck to the other as he watched the ship's progress: Canada extended east along the port side, and the United States ran down starboard, the St. Mary's River dividing the two nations.

The topaz sky poured a hot westerly breeze over *Genevieve* as her captain and mate prepared to take her alongside the lumber mill.

"So, Mr. Ringle, almost there now." Thomas ran a hand through his yellowed hair and began his checklist. "Fender boards rigged? Kedge anchor ready to drop? T'gallant and tops'l gear ready to run? Main boom topping lifts snug? Good. Mooring lines rigged? Grand."

Dennis Ringle, the young mate, had answered positively to each question, reassuring both men that they were indeed prepared for the upcoming maneuvers.

"All right," the captain continued, "we have the usual head to wind mooring here; we'll carry this tack south until we can easily point back for the pier. After the tack, we'll shorten sail." Dennis plotted his campaign against the sail area as the captain spoke. It would require fast work to strike five sails with a crew of eight in time to be ready for the final approach.

McGrath squinted into the sun, the crow's feet around his eyes screening excess light while he completed his plan. "We'll stand in on the port tack under easy sail, then drop the jib one ship length from the pier. As I bring her into the wind, square the lower tops'l and be sure the bow line and amidships spring are on in time to stop us from coming aft."

"Aye, aye, sir," Dennis answered, before going forward to coordinate the crew and inspect mooring line preparations. After his final round of checks, Dennis looked toward the pier, enjoying the last few minutes of calm preceding what would be a series of frantic activities until the ship was safely moored. He could identify the characteristic fists-on-hips posture and red hair of the captain's younger brother, who was positioning mill hands along the pier.

The barkentine tacked and Dennis flew into action, clewing up square sails to their respective yards and dowsing the jibs and staysails. As the distance to the pier diminished, the ship's bowsprit described a shallow horizontal arc, pivoting neatly and then slowing to a stop. Just over ten feet from the dock, weighted heaving lines were cast; the mooring lines snaked ashore, took hold, and *Genevieve* rested secure.

Thomas McGrath was pleased to be alongside. The unusual trip to Port Arthur had been tiring—a demanding mix of headwinds and fog. He breathed deeply, savoring aromatic cedar, spruce, and—king of them all—white pine planks mingled with the scent of Stockholm tar from *Genevieve*'s rig—the smell of home. Enough of the afternoon remained to get caught up with William and still be at his own table for dinner.

Here came his son George, walking quickly along the pier, looking a little rumpled. Thomas smiled at the sight of his boy and abruptly concluded his work on *Genevieve* so he could take up his responsibilities as mill owner and father.

"Mr. Ringle."

"Yes, sir." Dennis came aft.

"I've business to attend to. You can take it from here; furl sail, square away the decks, then warp the ship forward for unloading. Double up the mooring lines; then that will be all for today. We'll get the red pine out of her tomorrow."

"Aye, aye, sir," the tow-headed officer replied, gratified to be left in charge since this was his first season as mate.

Thomas stepped onto the pier, from the quarterdeck rail, and greeted George. After hearing some family news, Thomas dispatched him to inform his mother he would be home early. William strode forward after George had departed, and the brothers shook hands warmly.

"Where's all my cargo?" Thomas asked playfully, furrowing a tanned brow as he noted the paucity of stockpiles. William stiffened slightly but forced a smile.

"I have much of it stowed on the other side of the mill."

"Ah, good. Why over there?"

"It'll be easier to see than explain," William replied, before leading his brother up from the pier.

Some of the rosy glow of homecoming had dimmed for Thomas by late afternoon. The rest of his cargo on the mill's far side was, in fact, unsawn logs—something he had suspected. But with the mill inoperative, he was surprised William's sense of humor stretched to being cryptic about such matters. He sat in his chair, backed up to his erstwhile vacant desk, and half-listened to William hold forth on a favorite topic—the power of steam.

"So with the increase of power input, we can project...."

Thomas leaned back, fingers interlocked behind his sun-bleached head, and slipped from the mainstream dissertation into eddies of his own thought. Boyle's discovery of a crack in the upright drive shaft had brought on a more extensive repair than William had anticipated. Waiting to have *Genevieve* fully loaded would keep him alongside the pier longer than expected. This alone wouldn't bother him since the ship always needed some work on sails, rigging, pumps, and so on, but August was getting old, and soon, the west winds would blow harder every day. He wanted to complete his last run to Port Arthur, at the top of Lake Superior, as soon as could be and forsake that lake before the gales began. Well, he would enjoy the rare luxury of extra nights at home with Anne and the kids in high summer. The blueberry bushes were still bearing and perhaps the tomatoes would be ripe.

"...a gangsaw, without question, would thereby increase efficiency, adding...."

Thomas straightened in his chair, repositioning to ease the stiffness out of his lower back; at thirty-seven, he was feeling the early creaks. He took in the measured paces that carried William's wiry frame back and forth to the window as he continued his monologue. His brother had warmed to a fever of enthusiasm for increased production—something that didn't stimulate Thomas that much. Something impish awoke in him, and so, as his brother wound down, Thomas gave in to temptation.

"Once the gangsaw is going at quadruple speed, where will we get enough trees?" he asked as soberly as he could.

William's face flushed almost to the color of his hair.

"You think it's funny that we're losing money—that the mill's broken down again? We've already lost five days this year, and I'm not sure we'll be running tomorrow. Take a look at the books."

A short time later, Thomas conceded that the mill was becoming less than profitable. He asked, "How can this be? Have we really lost that much money this season? Perhaps we're overlooking something."

"Steam," William said, enjoying seeing his older brother at a disadvantage.

"What do you mean?" Thomas asked. "Is it something forgotten in your ledgers? Or are you saying it's the cause or the cure of our troubles? I don't understand."

"Many other mills have converted to steam. In a steam-powered mill, every board foot is produced at a lower cost due to greater efficiency of gangsaws, higher speed, and dependability. We've lost five days to breakdowns this season, and each of those days adds to our cost per board foot. When our lumber is sold, however, we can't pull in a better price than what our steam competitors offer. Look at this column." William indicated a row of numbers with his pencil. "For the last two years, price per board foot has dropped steadily. It will stop, but by then, we won't be able to compete!"

"I see," Thomas nodded wearily, "but we haven't got the money to buy steam engines and saws. I didn't know this was happening so quickly."

"This is what you find out if you stop to do the arithmetic. We'll need to borrow money to update the mill," William said.

Suddenly, Thomas felt very tired. He could hear the buzzing of cicadas outside in the early evening heat.

"Have you any whiskey?" he asked. William nodded and moved to the corner cupboard.

"I don't like the idea of going into debt; let's have a quiet drink and then head home," Thomas proposed. "It's getting late. I'll consider all of this, and we can talk more tomorrow."

William poured, anticipating victory.

Troubled by his discussion with William, Thomas hardly took notice of his walk home, but at long last, he looked upon his house, bathed in an evening sunshine that cast orange hues over all. His wife, Anne, stood waiting by the front gate, having been warned of his approach when he crested the hill farther up the road.

"Mrs. McGrath, are you out looking for something?" Thomas called to her.

"Yes," she replied. I'm keeping an eye out for my long lost husband, but I've forgotten what he looks like."

"How will you recognize him then, if he should happen by?"

"Well, he'll smell like an old ship, but otherwise, I'm counting on him to remember me!" she said.

Thomas gazed at Anne as he stepped through the gate. Her dark hair was tied back with an indigo ribbon that complemented her blue eyes wonderfully, and her loose summer dress did little to hide the firm figure beneath it. At thirty-five, he believed she was even more beautiful than when he had met her eighteen years earlier.

"Annie, I doubt your husband could ever forget you," he said. She laughed and kissed him, noting the taste of whiskey.

"Has your brother been keeping you from me?" she asked.

"Yes, I'm afraid so," he said. "He's after me again about buying steam engines; the mill's broken down at the moment. I'll tell you about it later."

Anne nodded and said, "Dinner's waiting. A cold plate tonight: roast beef and potatoes, pickled cabbage, fresh tomatoes, and bread baked this morning. The children are hungry," she added, taking his hand and leading him up onto the porch. "After they've been put to bed," Anne stopped and lowered her voice, "there's a cauldron of hot water sitting ready for your bath so we can retire early." She smiled significantly.

Perceiving her meaning, Thomas, for the first time that evening, anticipated beyond his dinner. As he went inside to be mobbed by his three children, he wondered how long repairs at the mill might keep him here.

Chapter 2

September 19, 1891

THE CREW STARED simultaneously at the red tug towing *Genevieve* toward Detroit, and the dynamic city she was bound for. Considerable excitement rippled through them as they anticipated shore leave on a Saturday night.

Genevieve was clean and the final staysail was almost furled. On the galley house roof, up forward, Dennis Ringle was directing two deck-hands, Mark and Risto, in the squaring of the course yard by lifts, and then after mooring alongside, it appeared that the day's work would be complete. Following that—Detroit—over 200,000 people of multiple origins, mingling and blending, loving and fighting—a place for urban adventure.

William was also pleased to see Detroit's skyline peeking out from behind Belle Isle. He sat in working clothes on the after starboard bitts with his elbows on his knees, hands clasped together and head craned up, monitoring the ship's approach. He could see one of the impressive new buildings under construction; a great deal had changed in the three years since his last trip.

"Where will we put in?" he asked his brother who stood next to the binnacle.

"Hopefully, in one of the slips, as close to Rivard street as we can get. We'll see what's open as we get closer. You can never tell from this far upriver," Thomas replied. A weak feeling of disappointment swept through William, instantly subdued by deliberately applied patience. He desperately wanted to get off the ship.

"Er, so you wouldn't hazard a guess at how long it might be until we're tied up?" His patience failed him after all.

Thomas noted the ferry starting out from Windsor and continued scanning the smooth river ahead for any potential trouble, while regarding his brother's red head peripherally. He was unused to having a passenger on his ship, and he never would have entertained such a question from any member of his crew. He took his time replying.

"You just can't wait to get ashore," he shrewdly jabbed.

"No, no, no—oh, not at all," William said, at a disadvantage for having his armor so easily pierced. "I—ah—was just thinking—perhaps I could buy you a steak dinner, time providing, of course."

"Well, that sounds fine. Let's see; it's a quarter past four. If there's an open berth, we could be snug alongside before the second dog watch, er—six o'clock so to speak."

"I see, I see." William's head bobbed thoughtfully. In truth, it had not been a bad passage. It had only taken two days. He had tried to read, but his mind wandered to his loan proposal; his restlessness would build and drive him from his cabin to the deck with nothing specific to do. He now keenly wished to stretch his legs on shore where he could actively pursue his purpose, unrestrained by the ship's operations, and be soothed by the offerings of such a center of culture, commerce, and industry.

Now, as *Genevieve* slid downcurrent, obediently tracking her tug, details of the city emerged. William could see men climbing the scaffolds that surrounded buildings under construction, slender iron light towers standing in extinguished repose until dark, cranes swaying ponderous cargo into and out of ships. Everywhere he turned, he saw motion; the activity pulsing possibility out onto the gray-green waters of the passing river—not alone for his mill, but also for a beckoning sliver of likelihood that somewhere in that cauldron of action was the opportunity to find a lost love.

CHAPTER 3

EDGAR FIELDGATE STANDISH sat at his mahogany desk, straining his square chin toward the left lapel of his worsted wool suit in an effort to end a spasm in the back of his neck. He could feel knotted muscle, drawn tight from his gray right temple down to the top of his shoulder blade, tweaking annoyingly—the corporal result of a trying day.

Edgar Standish had made a stellar success of almost everything he had put a hand to. As a young Eddie Standish, he had first taken work in a foundry where his height, muscularity, and vigor had made him indispensable. It had taken two years, a little cleverness, and a small compromise to his dignity (some minor boot-licking), to get promoted to foreman by the age of twenty. In this position, he had learned the art of casting iron, and by the time he had turned twenty-four, he had saved enough money to open his own modest stove-building shop.

Now a business owner, he began to insist on being addressed as Edgar by friends, and Mr. Standish by his few employees. Innovative by nature, he scorned boxy stove designs and sought to fabricate a higher standard of product, with better heat dispersion and convenient features for fueling, baking, and ash removal. Initially, his stoves sold only in Detroit, but as the railways stretched into the countryside, stoves traversed the iron road westward with new settlers. Finally, his stoves were offered back east, where they competed successfully with products from Albany and Philadelphia. Demand flourished. Edgar expanded, hiring an engineer who blended ores to improve flow when pouring and to obtain harder finishes—metallurgic negotiations that ultimately yielded near-perfect castings. He saw opportunity and developed a line of safes and vaults that were an instant success. Airtight when closed, his safes were advertised as fireproof and virtually impossible to crack.

Wealthy and accomplished at the age of thirty-two, Edgar courted the lovely Louise Beaulieu, a beauty from one of Detroit's older French families. She was taken by his vision, energy, and occasional tenderness, and after a year, they married. She brought not only charm, but distinction and social connection to the union. They were happy together and brought forth two children over four years: first, a girl, Beatrice, and then a boy, Paul.

Fortified now in a great house, with a large staff in his plants churning out the heavy work, Edgar gained a little in girth. His self-image became grander. He adopted the unusual middle name of Fieldgate, which he then chose to label his safes with. Although always strictly fair, by the time his hair was gray, he had become somewhat imperious and wished to distance himself from the hot grittiness of his foundry operations. With a small fortune amassed, and unready to retire, he decided to organize a bank and safe deposit company, outfitted exclusively with Fieldgate safes. The Industrial Bank of Detroit, therefore, opened on Griswold Street, with a capital of $70,000, and Edgar Fieldgate Standish—President.

It was only in the endeavor of raising his son that Edgar perceived a measure of failure. Paul had charm and his mother's handsome dark features, but he lacked most forms of capability and, perhaps, the desire to acquire them. Edgar had tried several strategies to form and educate the boy, but he seemingly often mischose, judging by the shortfalls from hoped for results. Nonetheless, Edgar had deep wells of determination, from which he drew buckets of fresh, cool resolve after any reversal of expectation for Paul's success.

Edgar took Paul under his wing at the bank with high hopes of giving him a profession. But now, after three years of tutelage on the job, it had only seemed to culminate in his currently twitching neck muscle.

"Fitzpatrick!" Edgar bellowed for his clerk.

A bespectacled, bald head with inquisitively raised eyebrows leaned out from behind the open door's mahogany jamb.

"Yes, sir," Fitzpatrick promptly answered in a rich baritone. Edgar looked at him for a moment before saying, "Send young Mr. Standish in."

"Right away, Mr. Standish," Fitzpatrick replied cheerily, and departed. Edgar had taken Fitzpatrick, his son-in-law, into his employ at the bank, but despite the younger man's clerking abilities and marvelously reassuring voice, Edgar had never warmed up to him. At family gatherings, he consistently addressed him as "Fitzpatrick," intimating that he would never shift in any direction from his status as clerk. Edgar doubted the man's abundant bonhomie and wondered whether his daughter had not been seduced merely by a golden voice. He thought she might have done better than to have married an insincere Irishman.

A moment later, Paul Standish stepped through the doorway, dreading the possibility of a lengthy and unpleasant lecture.

"You wished to see me, Papa?" Paul asked.

"Yes. Come in. Close the door."

Paul obeyed and sat in one of the red leather armchairs opposite his father.

"First of all, how often must I remind you that I am to be called 'Mr. Standish' at the bank?" Paul groaned inwardly; he had slipped again; this would not be a pleasant meeting.

"Yes, P—sir. I am sorry, once again, Mr. Standish." Somewhat mollified on this point, Edgar moved on to the issue he had summoned Paul for: "We have a list of discrepancies in our accounts with foreign bondholders." Edgar paused to see whether any voluntary elucidation would be forthcoming, but sadly, it didn't appear to him that Paul had any idea what might be amiss. For his part, Paul had learned that remaining dumb was far safer than conjecturing incorrectly and incurring his father's ire.

"It has taken me a portion of my day to unravel this," Edgar continued much aggrieved. "It seems that the exchange rate has been incorrectly applied on sixty-one accounts." Another expectant silence ensued, and as it drew longer, Paul realized it was imperative to explain the situation somehow. Feeling trapped, he ventured: "That sounds unfortunate. I'm sure I…."

"Unfortunate? Unfortunate! Fortune has nothing to do with it!" Edgar growled. "It is an embarrassment to the bank that we have misplaced fair sums of money for close to two weeks now. Do you have any idea how many dollars you have in limbo?"

"I would need my abacus and the ledgers to—"

"The total amount is $621.15," Edgar continued hotly. Paul tried to smooth it out: "Mr. Standish, if you would show me the bond accounts in question, I will make every effort—"

"No, blast it, no! We have the money in the vault—I checked; your payouts were too low." Edgar scowled, trying to settle himself down again while rubbing his temples. Paul brightened visibly, suddenly seeing a sunny avenue to wheel the conversation down.

"Oh, well then, everything should be properly settled in a couple of days; I'll simply arrange transfers for the compensatory amounts."

"Yes, yes, yes, you will, but you are not seeing the heart of the matter, my boy. Would you rather be seen as incompetent or corrupt?" Edgar asked.

"Incompetent, I suppose. I wouldn't wi—"

"*No*, you fool; that isn't the sort of question that's meant to be answered; you shouldn't want to be seen in either fashion!"

"Oh, I understand," Paul replied, and then gazed at a spot on the desk, settling into the dubious protection of chastened reticence, while still puzzling over his father's trick question.

It was plain to Edgar that Paul had not understood the lesson he was trying to convey, but he was equally sure that nothing would be gained by berating the boy further.

"We'll go over the entire list of corrections in the morning, and then I would like all of the affected accounts compensated by the end of the day tomorrow."

"Yes, sir," Paul swallowed, "but with sixty-five corrections, that could be hard."

"Sixty-one corrections. Good night."

With hasty stealth, Fitzpatrick slipped from outside Edgar's office door before Paul could leave.

CHAPTER 4

RISTO RETURNED TO the saloon's back corner carrying a pitcher of pale ale and two bottles of sarsaparilla from a spot farther down the crowded bar.

"Whew, Risto, just in time; we're almost dry," Mark said. Risto flashed his best smile back to his mate, entirely for the benefit of the two girls flanking him, and refilled depleted glasses.

"Ja, so looks," he said and drew from the vessel in his hand. *Genevieve*'s starboard watch was on duty, letting Mark and Risto ashore. Delighted with their luck, the duo had washed quickly, set off at once, and were now sharing their second pitcher of beer in the company of two fetching girls. Having stopped at The Swinging Rudder on Atwater Street, they encountered a gloomy crowd of sullen-looking men and bruised, desperate-looking women. They had summarily moved along until they had reached Franklin Street and happened upon an overfull, boisterous saloon with conversation and laughter echoing out through open doors. Squeezing inside, the noise had been loudly varied as glassware clinked, stools scraped the pine floor, and raconteurs strove to be heard in the long rectangular room. A thick covering of patrons coated the maple bar, keeping two men occupied pulling at beer engines and pouring from a collection of mirrored bottles lining the wall. Across from the bar, floor space was occupied by irregular pools of men and women enjoying their evening out.

Mark had infiltrated all the way to the brass rail near the end of the bar, next to four rather handsome young women in the company of two dapper men. After a short time, sipping casually at his ale,

Mark boldly made the acquaintance of Steven Nielson, the nearest man in the group, asking him his occupation while subtly joining his party. In a moment, Mark had introduced Risto, and Nielson, not wishing to be unmannerly himself, had shifted position to introduce the attentive young woman on his right.

"This is my sister, Elizabeth Nielson; next to her my wife, Alice; Elizabeth's friend, Martha Burns; and behind them, Tobias and Sarah Jenks." And so it was done; the shipmates mingled into the group, to be retained there on the strength of Risto's handsome Nordic features and Mark's gift for chatter.

A guitarist and fiddler began playing in the front corner of the saloon, opposite the bar.

"A dance, Mrs. Nielsen?" Steven invited his wife. Alice smiled, drew up the train of her gown, and took his outstretched hand. The Jenks couple followed suit, leaving Risto and Mark in the winsome company of Elizabeth and the pretty Martha, in pale yellow. Conversation flowed down happy channels, occasionally carried on in delightfully close proximity and loud voices, to compete with the enveloping din. Music filled the smoke-stained air as stately partners twirled time away, below gas lights and over beer-sloshed floorboards.

In through the back door of the saloon came a small troupe of rough-looking longshoremen, trailed by a well-dressed, corpulent man with a handlebar mustache. The last entrant appeared to be well known and important, for he was soon attended not only by the toughs he came in with, but many others besides. The bartender sent a whiskey sour to the corner where the gentleman held court, cunningly allying bystanders to his dim view of shipping companies as he distributed pay packets.

"Who's that?" Mark asked Elizabeth, discreetly indicating the gang boss with a stealthy jerk of his thumb.

"I've heard his name is O'Shea; he owns this saloon and others, but he's rumored to be organizing the lumber handlers into a union." Just at that moment, O'Shea said something about Mayor Pingree that brought loud murmurs from his audience.

The music had stopped, and as patrons arrived and departed, the clientele slowly shifted from skipping couples to small groups of shabby men, hectoring one another for some minor variation in their political outlook. As the evening's gaiety wound down, Elizabeth and Martha were collected by Nielson and his wife to be escorted home.

"It's been a delightful evening," said Mark, taking Elizabeth's proffered hand. "It would be nice to meet again; our ship is in Detroit until at least Wednesday." He'd had to concentrate so as not to slur his words.

"That would be lovely," agreed Elizabeth, and she passed him one of her brother's calling cards. "I'm at the library from nine until three-thirty each day, or you can find me through Steven's address."

Mark beamed as the group took their leave through the side door reserved for ladies.

O'Shea finally completed his harangue and departed through the back door, leaving his audience to break into smaller knots of discussion. As the crowd thinned slightly, Mark noted the deteriorating quality of the company and a more dominant smell of sweat and stale beer.

"Risto, maybe it's time to shove off."

Risto looked around. "Ja, so looks. One more and then go," he finally said. They moved to a spot farther along the bar and procured a final pitcher. After another couple of glasses and some one-sided conversation with Risto, Mark was replacing the pitcher when he accidentally bumped the glass of the man next to him, splashing lager over its owner. He happened to be one of the bigger longshoremen, and he responded with immediate violence.

"I'm sorry; I…. Whoooomphh!" Mark doubled over as the burly man's fist sank into his stomach, dropping him to the floor in pain. Not content yet, the unappeasable thug kicked Mark hard in the ribs and had his leg in mid-swing for a second hoof when his vision was suddenly interrupted. His foot touched down softly, harmlessly, on the floor, supporting him on weakened knees.

"What's wrong with me?" he wondered vacantly, and instinctively staggered to hold his balance. He put a hand out and found the bar as he began to feel fiery stabs of pain in his face. He heard the barkeep yelling: "You had better get outta here! Run—go now!"

Who's he yelling at? wondered the thug, and then gradually his vision cleared.

Risto, upon seeing Mark kicked, had delivered a hammer blow of a right jab to the thug's nose. He reached down for Mark, while the other man was stunned, and dragged him backward, keeping alert for a counterattack. Mark scrambled to his feet, astonished at the damage Risto had inflicted to the thug's face in one punch: his nose was now bent over to the right, splitting away the left nostril, which flapped like an obscene wing over his bloodied mouth and chin. Momentarily shocked, no one moved until the barman had started yelling at them to get out.

Risto quickly propelled Mark toward the rear exit to avoid passing any of the longshoremen. Once outside, they slammed the back door, and with three ferocious tugs, slid a rubbish bin through the stony dirt to block it from opening. Furious pounding broke open the door as the shipmates fled down the alley and into the night.

While Mark and Risto tried to evade a certain beating, across the city, in the back room of another of O'Shea's saloons in Corktown, cards took short flights to the hands of five players around a circular table.

"Gentlemen, it will be a five-card draw, jackpot and flush rules," said Sullivan the dealer.

John Fitzpatrick spread his cards, furtively looking over them to observe his opponents. As they, in turn, studied their cards, only this fellow Rafferty, across from him, gave away any sign of the caliber of his hand. Hardened by long play, the others displayed little personality whatsoever. Fitzpatrick took in what he held, carefully controlling his features so as not to betray himself.

Everyone anteed up and the drawing began. Rafferty's luck could be spotted in a draw. A poor actor at best, he gave what he hoped would be subtle, misleading twitches to his mouth, and now he looked very mildly pleased—a sure sign Fitzpatrick had but three competitors in this hand.

Fitzpatrick had played faro and chuck-a-luck, but with the jackpot and flush rules now widely played, he found poker a more invigorating game. It required iron nerve, outstanding self-control, and keen insight respecting one's fellow players' intent, all traits that he, John Fitzpatrick, knew he had. In early games, he wagered and won very little, but as he balanced play against the bluffing abilities of his opponents, he enjoyed some success and gained the confidence to move into a higher stakes game. True, he occasionally lost, which would have hurt deeply if he had to depend on his pay to cover losses, but losing fed the appetites of bumpkins like Rafferty who would surely give up if they weren't given something. He began to feel confident that he could clean out Rafferty tonight.

"What will you have, Mr. Fitzpatrick?" asked Sullivan.

"I'll take two," Fitzpatrick replied, very carefully modulating his marvelous baritone.

Chapter 5

HAVING EARLIER BOARDED a cross-town streetcar, William and Thomas were whizzing westward to the accompanying sounds of hooves on cobblestone and forged wheels scraping over aged iron rail. Pedestrians and bicyclists scattered before the horses' jingling bells, from the cobbled lane between tracks to the cedar block pavement that covered the rest of the street.

"You look tired, Thomas," William said loudly over the horse-drawn car's racket.

"Well, it's my watch below and I haven't had a nap," Thomas replied. Conversation stifled by road noise, he fell to staring vacantly at the blurred repetitive patterns of the cedar block paving, until random thoughts grew more whimsical, blending far-flung elements of present and past. He fought the overwhelming urge to sleep, feeling a vague shame in the idea, but with no activity possible, he sank into dreaming.

William took in the many changes to the city as his brother dozed. Many grand new houses had been built; numerous towers supported electric street lighting; and a general air of prosperity extended from the number of people riding bicycles down to the tar macadam pavement in the heart of the city. When the car approached their stop, William jostled Thomas. "Wake up; we're almost there."

Thomas opened his eyes and recognized his surroundings just in time to step off the moving car.

The brothers sipped whiskey while awaiting their dinners at a corner table, in a bustling French restaurant on Brush Street. Stretching to an uncomfortable length, a silence hung over the table between them. Thomas felt he must say something or the evening would render them a bit glum.

"William, you're very quiet tonight. You aren't worrying over our chances for financing, are you?"

"No, no. Our books are in order," William replied without making eye contact. His reply had been a little bit short, Thomas thought, not quite rude but terse. Something was nagging his brother. The men continued to nip at their whiskey, but now Thomas noticed that William was detachedly scanning the room and not facing him exactly. Turning to follow William's gaze, Thomas spied a stylishly dressed young woman, which inspired him to try a topic outside their usual range.

"It's rather charming to see that the bustle has dropped out of fashion again, isn't it?"

William realized he had been caught staring and smiled at Thomas. "Yes, yes, I think so."

"I've never liked all that reconfiguration of a woman's form; it makes them look like strange birds of some kind—cranes or plovers or…or…."

"…a carrier pigeon," said William, filling the gap with some spirit.

"Yes, you've got it exactly. Thank goodness that's gone for a while; we can appreciate the ladies for what they are."

"Yes, I suppose so," William said blandly again, and a shroud of silence was drawn over the table once more. It was then that Thomas identified the source of William's mood.

"You're looking for her, aren't you?" Thomas asked.

Four years earlier, William had come to Detroit to negotiate contracts with a number of railroad interests. While in the city, he had met a vivacious Italian girl who had a fire and verve that was a siren song to him. Never one to be shy, he had commenced a whirlwind courtship that kept him five weeks past his intended departure for home. After the fourth week, Thomas had been forced to intervene because the mill had begun to suffer the lack of a full-time master, and William had returned home dutifully to address the backlog of problems. In a few weeks, William had gone again, leaving his brother a note that only stated he would return as soon as he could. True to his word, he astonished everyone, returning in twelve days with the zesty Carmina on his arm as his wife.

Almost a year later, William arrived home one August night to a note saying only that she had left and wouldn't be back.

William's eyes snapped into focus on his brother. He thought of denial, but grimaced slightly and replied:

"Yes, I suppose I am. I didn't mean to tonight, but it happens all the same."

"You have been to this restaurant before."

"It was a favorite of Carmina's…back then."

"I see." Thomas nodded sympathetically, pausing before asking, "What would you do, or say to her, if you suddenly met now?"

William picked up the pepper shaker and regarded it as he rolled it between his thumb and forefinger.

"Not that it's really your business, but I don't know. I had always hoped for an explanation, or a fight, or something…final."

Thomas considered this. William had tried very hard, three years ago, to locate Carmina, haunting parts of Detroit she had frequented. As summer turned to fall, he had faced the bitter fact that if she were in the city, she refused to be seen. He returned home, spirits corroded, and threw himself into his work, coldly focusing on production.

Thomas, understanding something of obsession, proposed a course of action. "Will, I don't like to see you like this. Trade seats with me and I promise I'll tell you if she comes in." William reluctantly agreed to take the other chair, and when dinner finally arrived, he began to show a measure of relief. As the men tasted their meals, Thomas ignored William's earlier warning and decided to probe a delicate topic.

"I haven't asked before William, but would you marry again?"

"I'm married now," William countered quietly.

"I know, but would you get married again, assuming your current situation was ah…legally resolved?"

"You mean divorce."

"Yes."

William concentrated on cutting his steak, feeling slightly piqued at his brother's intrusive questions. After chewing a while, he said, "I would need to have her cooperation, and presently, that isn't forthcoming; otherwise, I think it would cost a heap of money."

Thomas cut open a roasted potato as he considered this and said, "In a long life, a little money thrown around is hardly remembered. The question I put is: Would you like to marry again?"

William looked directly at his brother. "I'm uncertain, Thomas. I have other plans now…. I want to see us quadruple production in the next two years; it will take time and effort, and I fear another woman would want something…else from me. I tried before, and look how well that turned out. I might not be good for marriage."

The words had poured out of him in a series of short bursts like water from a vigorously cranked hand pump, and there was William's constant theme, Thomas thought—production, always production. He worried his brother could no longer see life in any context outside of laying waste to swaths of forest.

"Perhaps this isn't the right time to consider your prospects while we are preparing to expand the mill, but it would be worth thinking on away from here. As for myself, I often think of other things; I consider possibilities that may never occur."

"Such as what?" William asked, annoyed, bored, and curious all at the same time.

"I sometimes think of taking *Genevieve* out to deep water again; carrying small cargos between distant lands; eating mangos and bananas in tropical ports."

William was shocked. "What do you mean? You wouldn't leave your family for so long. Or do you mean you want to sell out and move on?" Crow's-feet deepened around Thomas's blue eyes as he laughed quietly. He had stirred the coals in his younger brother's furnace once again.

"No, I don't mean to do either of those things—not now anyway." His smile faded. "What I'm trying to get across is that life holds out many possibilities to us, some we can't dodge, but often we can choose the ones we prefer. If your greatest happiness will come from quadrupled production, so be it. But if you want to get married again, the mill need not be a hindrance, not from my point of view anyway."

"You mean to sell our father's mill!" William said.

"Pa left it to us; it's ours now. If it serves us, we should keep it. But if it stands in the way of our prosperity—in any sense—life could be lived without it. We could choose other courses."

Having delivered this message, Thomas sought to lighten the mood. "This is a marvelous piece of beef. You have made a fine choice for dinner."

"Thank you, Thomas," William replied, glad to have the little lesson over with.

The return streetcar ride moved much faster later in the evening, depositing Thomas and William near the base of Rivard Street.

"It's getting cold, and it's rather dark and lonely down here. Why are the streetlights out?" William asked.

"The city has traded a view of the stars for this light; can you believe it? The lights are on, but they're way up there." The current theory on street lighting was to put the lights very high up, two or three hundred feet, to illuminate as large an area as possible. The effect was dim light for everyone. "This is normal; we'll adjust to it shortly," Thomas said.

"I don't like it; this part of town isn't the best."

"I know. I've survived it a number of times, though. Keep your head up; we only have a few blocks to go and we'll be back on board."

The brothers paralleled the river along Atwater Street at a good pace. As they crossed the railroad tracks near the old waterworks, they could hear some commotion coming from behind a workhouse on the pier ahead. After they passed the workhouse, the weak light revealed a figure pushing a struggling form into what appeared to be a large box or crate.

"What's that fellow up to?" William asked of Thomas as he slowed and pointed to the strange action in the slipway next to the pier.

"Oh, that's most likely the dogcatcher."

"Isn't it rather late to be rounding up dogs?"

"Perhaps he's extraordinarily devoted to duty," Thomas replied. "But most likely he's engaged in some work that doesn't show to advantage in the light of day, much like many others in this neighborhood."

William pulled at his whiskers as he contemplated this cryptic explanation and they closed the short distance to the slipway and possible dogcatcher; he knew little of dogcatchers and the various tasks of their occupation. The racket from the crate increased in volume and became distinct noises: barking, snarling, whimpering. *Thomas is correct*, he thought. *It has to be a considerable pack of dogs.*

At the quayside end of the pier, the meager light was still strong enough to show a dry sandy bottom four feet below the quay. Two rails stretched in twin convergent lines from the sand out into the river, only interrupted by a long flat railcar bearing the crate packed with dogs. William watched as the dogcatcher collected another dog from his nearby wagon. The struggling animal snarled and flailed, captured in a noose at the end of a short stout pole. The catcher deftly handled the pole, negating the dog's efforts toward liberty, propelling it inexorably down into the slipway and the crate.

"He's going to drown the dogs," William said dispassionately to himself.

"Yes, I'm afraid so," Thomas said. "This railway is often used to haul out small ships, but I've seen it used this way as well."

By now, William's eyes had adjusted to the comparative darkness, so he could see details of the iron-strapped cage that held the boisterous pack of frightened angry dogs. A crescendo of furious, hysterical barking rose as the efficient catcher dropped this last dog through the cage's top door. Fully loaded now, he slammed the grated door shut with a loud clang and bolted it; then he walked to a large winch at the slip's quayside end. William couldn't see exactly what the man was doing, but it soon became apparent he had released a brake of some kind because the car began to move very slowly down the slightly inclined rails to the quick tympanic klink, klink, klink of a tripped pawl riding over gear teeth.

The dogcatcher, perhaps because he was not without a heart, decided he could leave the car to roll to the stops at the end of the rail unattended. He untied his pony, mounted his wagon, and departed before his capture's inevitable demise.

William stood transfixed by the horror of death by drowning as he watched the cage's slow progression to the river. The dogs whimpered and howled, sensing their impending doom.

At this point, Thomas had seen enough. "Let's go, Will," he said. "No good can come of watching this." The cage picked up speed as the grade grew steeper below it, and although still moving slowly, it had doubled its pace. William made no reply and continued to stand, staring. He was deeply disturbed by the waste of life occurring right in front of him. Then a louder, longer, more heart-wrenching howl came from the cage.

William reacted. He couldn't let this happen; it was just too horrific. Without any plan, he tore down the four steps into the slipway and ran for the winch.

"Will! William, what are you going to do?" Thomas called after him. William had no answer—he didn't know himself. The winch was in the deeper shadow thrown by the quay, so he could discern only its form and the wire as it traveled from one end of the drum to the other, rapidly spooling out. He dared not try to feel a moving machine he could not properly see. He hunted around for a bar or something he might jam into a gear or throw the pawl with. He found a short piece of driftwood and poked it into the dark spot where he imagined the gear to be. The wood caught and flew back at him, glancing off his shoulder with a painful thud. He knew better than to try again. Thomas was close by now, having followed him into the slip.

"Will, you'll hurt yourself," Thomas said. "Come on; there's nothing for us to do here. This takes place all the time, whether we see it or not. You shouldn't interfere with local practices."

"This is awful!" William retorted. He leaned back from the winch and could see the black bulk of the cage silhouetted against Windsor's lights across the river as it entered the water.

Thomas grabbed William's arm saying: "William, think. What will you do with a pack of dogs? If you free them, the catcher will have them back here next week."

As the dogs began to feel the ingress of water, a series of frenzied shrieking howls rent the cool night air. William shook loose from his brother's grip and ran in pursuit of the sliding, sinking cage. Thomas retreated to the pier, having now decided to let the matter take its own course. He walked a short distance until he found a bollard to sit on while he watched the outcome of his brother's endeavor.

William boarded the rolling railcar as it became thigh deep in the river. Scrambling onto the top of the cage, he began a tactile search for the trap door the catcher had closed. Below his knees, he could now see the packed, writhing bodies of whimpering, swimming dogs as they thrashed, competing to maintain airspace over their heads. He slid his hands back and forth, systematically covering the iron-grated surface area beneath him. Hard iron edges bit into his knees as he moved about, and in his pain and desperation, he shouted out loud, "Damn it! It must be here somewhere!" Having reached the cage's far end, he speedily worked his way back to the middle where he knew the door must be. Water lapped against the roof of the inclined cage's low side by the time he at last found the bolted door. A surge of hope was slowly broken when, after some awkward wriggling, he had not managed to slide the bolt in any direction. Angrily, he beat on the end of the bolt with his bare fist, badly skinning his knuckles. Then he calmed himself and tried to think of how it might be stuck.

The cage was submerging. The door itself was underwater now. Through the cage's roof, the dogs' final terror welled up, soaking into William as thoroughly as the river around his legs. Luckier, or tougher, dogs pressed their noses against the roof at the up end of the cage while William, farther down, with his back to the river, felt bubbles rising in the water all around him. Probing with his fingers, he at last discovered a misalignment in the door, which trapped the head of the slide bolt. He wriggled the bolt again while simultaneously lifting the door. The bolt slid free, but now the cage was completely beneath the river's surface, so bubbles seethed all around him. He struggled, up to his waist in water now, and threw back the door, purged of any hope.

He leaned back and roared with frustration as the enormity of his failure bore down upon him. It weighed down on every part of him. He had failed. He had failed to save these poor beasts; he had failed as a husband. He was the operator of a slowly failing mill. This failure in an unequal contest against time and water crushed every opinion he had ever had of himself—he was a failure. Overcome with grief and self-pity, he wanted to touch one of the dogs, to apologize for his failure before swimming from the still-sinking cage. Reaching through the door, he realized with a start that there was motion inside the cage. Sharp teeth then sank into his forearm; recoiling from the opening in surprised pain, he dragged up a wildly terrified, medium-sized mutt in the process. Overjoyed, he reached in again, hazarding a second bite on the chance that he could bring forth another dog. Sticking his head below the river's surface, he reached farther into the cage and felt another dog moving. He grabbed and felt the animal push away. Grabbing again, he only encountered the stilled fur of expired dogs. He was under two feet of water now, out of breath, and assailed by a residue of fear from this lonely death cage. It was time to give up.

Thomas had watched the drama play out from the bollard on the pier. He had thought the contest decided when the cage had submerged and William had bellowed out in rage, but then William, the soaking conjurer, had fished out a living, spluttering, hacking dog, and trailed the animal back toward the sand. Thomas stood and was about to walk down to the slip again when he saw motion in William's wake.

Down in the slip, the dog that had bitten William landed, shook briefly, and immediately ran from the slip, disappearing into the night. Water streamed from William's hair, mustache, and clothing as he waded out of the shallows and sat heavily on the sand, exhausted, wounded, and shivering. Thomas came to his side.

"William, are you all right?"

William felt his dog bite and his knuckles. "I'm a little sore but okay."

"We should get to the ship, get you dry and warmed up."

William let his head hang forward. "I need a few minutes rest and then we'll go," he answered through chattering teeth. The truth was, more than anything, he needed a moment to collect himself. Why had he done this drastic thing? What did it prove? Now that the dogs were gone, he wasn't sure why they had mattered so much to him—but they had. He heard labored breathing coming from the water in the slip as Thomas remarked, "It looks like two more pups, bound for Detroit!"

Sure enough, two more dogs, a big one and one more medium-sized, waded into shallow water. Upon reaching hard sand, the larger of the two repeated the performance of the first escapee: shaking and taking flight. The second dog shook, snorted, and wheezed several times, but then it wagged his way over to William and commenced some frantic nuzzling and licking. As William reached out to pet the sodden creature, it began to lick and nibble his fingers.

Thomas got his brother on his feet. "Time to go, Will. No more delaying; you'll freeze out here. It seems you have a new pal; you did well. We'll be back on board in a few minutes as long as we make no more stops."

William allowed himself to be guided back to the ship, trailed by the friendly dog he had saved. Thomas smiled to himself, reflecting on the surprising turn the evening had taken. Perhaps there was some hope for William yet.

CHAPTER 6

September 21, 1891

WAKE UP, MARK; ten to four." Benjamin shook Mark's leg.

"Yeah, okay, I'm up," Mark whispered groggily into the stuffy darkness of the fo'c'sle. As Benjamin's feet trod the wooden ladder up to the deck, Mark shook himself awake, and then, surrounded by snoring men, groped for the clothing left at the foot of his bunk. Anyone who noticed the change of watch stirred slightly and immediately returned to sleeping. Most of the crew would sleep through any light disturbance but, paradoxically, were keenly aware of strange sounds—anything out of the ordinary.

Mark quickly pulled on shirt, pants, socks, leather boots, sweater, and a work smock before making his way up into the chilly morning air on deck to relieve Benjamin. When tied alongside a dock, *Genevieve* had one-man watches set, and on occasions when she swung to her anchors, a two-man watch was customary. Thomas McGrath's ship spent few solitary hours.

Mark enjoyed the morning watch best out of the night watches. Once Benjamin had gone below, Mark checked the mooring lines for chafe and sounded the bilges as a matter of routine. Having ascertained that all was well, he made a mug of hot tea and sat in the galley doorway. Now he could enjoy an hour of quiet in the still, chilly air with the comfortable illusion of ownership: that he owned *Genevieve*, the pier, and the city beyond at this early hour. *Certainly, I have it to myself*, he thought, as he sipped from his mug and contentedly awaited morning's gradual approach, while the ship and the city slumbered on.

Predawn twilight slowly unveiled the shadowy shapes that were *Genevieve*'s unloaded stockpiles, railcars, and the buildings farther out. Mark took the dim light as his cue to shovel some coal into the big galley stove, ensuring that it would be piping hot when Norman, the cook, started breakfast.

Norman was a sight as he commenced his work in a clatter of pots and pans. In the meticulous order of his well-scrubbed galley, Norman stood out as an anomaly: His stained apron covered a small potbelly that prevented his pants from riding at the waist. In consequence of this unfortunate pant position, the cuffs at each heel were badly tattered, one dragging some thread. The sole of one shoe had become separated from the main body, but he had masterfully solved this using six wraps of tarred marline with a single frap on each side. At his other extreme, thin gray hair coiled up from his head in disarray like smoke from damp tinder. Below intelligent brown eyes, a large hooked nose sat next to a raised scar running down his right cheek, and beneath the nose, thin lips jiggled an unlit cigarette up and down as he muttered the grumblings that were his morning exercise. In his youth, Norman had had a powerful physique, and traces of it could still be seen in his upper body; a deep chest sprouted two muscular arms ending in large meaty hands. All in all, despite his age and shabby attire, Norman did not look like someone to trifle with, and he knew it.

"Get me a full pot of water," Norman grunted.

"Okay, Norman." Mark took the pot Norman thrust at him. He carried it to *Genevieve*'s water tank abaft the galley house and began filling it. In the open lake, water was commonly drawn from over the side, but *Genevieve* was equipped with tanks from her deep sea days, and these were filled for use when in murky harbors.

Having filled the pot, Mark looked down and was startled by the unexpected sight of the dog licking the wetted deck where the pump had dripped.

"Gyughh!" he exclaimed while lurching away from the mutt, spilling more water in the process. The thirsty animal advanced and began lapping up the fresh spill.

"The dog surprised me again," he said upon his return to the galley.

"I know; bloody mongrel, he's become a fixture in my doorway," Norman replied. At this, the dog appeared at his post and began a steady surveillance of Norman and his activities. Mark looked at the dog in turn and admired its handsome makeup: he was mostly sable except for a medium-length black muzzle and a long black diamond between his upright ears. The ears tracked noises, consciously or unconsciously, swiveling independently while the dog's gaze remained fixed on Norman and the food. A mouthful of bright, white teeth was occasionally obscured by his panting pink tongue. He looked a little underweight, perhaps forty pounds, with a hint of promise that he might still grow into his paws.

"Well, he's friendly enough, and at least he hasn't come into the galley."

Norman snorted: "Make no mistake; dogs, they are all sly. He may sit for you or wag his tail for you, but all the while, he's plotting how to get hold of your breakfast before you do. He'll be in here in two shakes of a mare's tail if I turn my back on him." Suddenly, Norman was done with pleasantries.

"Fetch me some more coal. This bin is never as full as it should be. I can't be getting coal all the time and trying to put the captain's breakfast out, never mind food for that pup, his brother, and all of you who never fill this coal bin properly! Two-and-a-half buckets should do it—brimming full."

Mark could not recall a time when he had seen Norman refilling the coal box himself, but he took the bucket and nodded to him so as not to rile him up. On his way down to the coal pen in the forward part of the hold, he puzzled over his instructions: Why two-and-a-half buckets brimming? Why not three even buckets? How did one bring a brimming half-bucket? It seemed as though Norman purposely gave unclear orders and then went into a tirade if the wrong choice was made in completing them. It was probably best to bring the first two buckets absolutely filled, and the third one almost full, and hope Norman would be busy as the last bucket was emptied into the pen.

Mark carried the third bucket of coal up from the hold and approached the port galley door, stealing a glance around the doorframe to check whether Norman was looking. His heart sank as he locked eyes with Norman, staring straight back at him. In a bold attempt to recover and appear to be acting naturally, he stooped and said, "Go on," as though shooing the dog away. To his horror, he next saw the dog peering over the starboard galley doorsill—behind Norman. His acting was only making matters worse. It was all up; he decided to brazen the situation out. Stepping into the galley, he quickly dumped the final bucket of coal, but Norman wasn't fooled.

"How much coal are you trying to stuff into that bloody pen? I don't want it overflowing! I'll be tripping on spilt coal in here when the ship heels, burning myself. I—"

"Good morning, Norman!" a cheery voice hailed from the opposite door.

Saved! Mark was saved. William McGrath stood at the starboard galley door, diverting Norman's attention as only he could.

"Norman," William continued, "I'd like to get something for the dog."

Mark took a moment to make his escape and shifted quietly to the galley house roof where he could hear and see some of the expected byplay between the cook and his new opponent.

Norman spoiled for a fight, but he restrained himself somewhat since it was the captain's brother.

"Something. Something wet? Something hot. No, perhaps something dainty; lady fingers in cream, hmm? What is something?" he asked.

"Well, something left over perhaps," William answered, now feeling awkwardly defensive since he was asking a favor for a dog.

"Left over. There is nothing left over; I haven't served breakfast yet."

"Oh, I see, I see," William muttered, irritated by the cook's combative nature. He turned to leave. "I beg your pardon; it wasn't my aim, in any sense, to inconvenience you," he quipped, intending great irony.

Untouched, Norman shot after him, "In what sense were you here then?"

William continued along the deck on his way aft, followed by the dog, pretending not to hear so as not to be bested by the sharp-tongued cook. What truly irked William was that he had absolutely no say in the manning of *Genevieve*; Thomas alone owned and operated the ship; she was not a joint holding as the mill was. He could complain about the cook's behavior to Thomas, but he couldn't send him packing as he would have liked to at this moment.

Soon after the altercation between Norman and William, Mark woke the rest of the fo'c'sle and the day was properly begun. The crew ate a breakfast of porridge, bacon, and biscuits, and then prepared for the day's work. This day would complete the unloading of the hold with the help of some local lumber handlers, and see the ship warped farther aft so the crew could load general cargo for DeTour. Soon the pier bustled with activity; the crew emptied the hold, and Dennis Ringle singled up mooring lines for the upcoming move. Unnoticed by anyone in the crew, a couple of longshoremen, farther down the pier, displayed a keen interest in Risto as he passed planks to the lumber handlers on shore.

"That blasted cook of yours is insolent!" William said to Thomas over breakfast in the saloon.

"What's wrong now?" Thomas replied.

"He was incredibly rude to me. I wanted somethi…" He hesitated over the word that had started the argument with Norman, "some food for the dog, and he practically chased me away!"

"I've told you before: Leave him alone in the morning. He's getting breakfast out on time and it has to be on time. It doesn't matter when the dog eats."

"Okay, but he could be polite, given my position—he could promise to accommodate me later. Why don't you get someone less prickly?"

"I wouldn't think of it; Norman and I have had many years together; he's a good cook, and you can't know what that's worth until you've been without one. Lastly, he has some hidden talents; he's a good man in a scrape," Thomas said.

"A brawler—nothing more. Well, all right, but will you have a word with him? It doesn't help me to be made ridiculous in front of the crew."

"I will," said Thomas, "but in future, you will steer clear of the galley around mealtimes. Agreed?"

"Agreed," William replied, inwardly wishing for this trip's rapid completion.

An hour later, the workday was progressing well with the ship riding high on her marks, now fully unloaded. As the McGrath brothers prepared to embark on their business in the city, a scene unfolded that delayed their departure: Mark and Risto were assigned with two other deckhands, Eric and Benjamin, to help the few lumber handlers complete the stacking of *Genevieve*'s pine planks. The work was going smoothly until six longshoremen appeared from between the lumber stacks, wielding crude wooden clubs.

"Are you guys signed up with the union?" one of them asked the lumber handlers.

"We're just trying to make a living here, pal," replied a lumber handler.

"Run off," said the longshoremen's leader, a large menacing man with a swollen nose carrying some stitches. Knowing what they were up against, the lumber handlers walked away. Mark and Risto recognized these big, rough men as they quickly encircled Risto, dividing him from his shipmates. One of the longshoremen, without warning, delivered a cruel blow to Risto's lower back. He went down in a heap and the longshoremen closed in, issuing more body blows to the fallen man. Mark, although isolated from the others by the gang, reacted quickly; taking one of the planks they had been stacking by its middle, he swung it into the hostile pack of men. Benjamin and Eric grabbed planks likewise, Eric swinging like Mark, while Benjamin attempted ramming, stabbing motions with his weapon. Although their blows were light on force, they drew a few yowls of pain and successfully disrupted Risto's beating. The vicious men rounded on Benjamin and Eric before being outnumbered by *Genevieve*'s crew led by Dennis, joining the fight with oars, cant hooks, and iron belaying pins. Still on board, the dog barked constantly during a brief noisy clash, before the longshoremen turned tail to escape. Five of them raced past Mark, but the sixth, the thug with the broken nose, was intent on beating someone, and Mark stood in his path. Realizing his plight, Mark fled, commencing a frantic chase up and down the pier, between crates, boxes, and barrels, and through long avenues flanked by landed lumber. As the chase gathered momentum, *Genevieve*'s crew helped a very sore Risto back aboard and settled on the galley house roof, cheering Mark on as he ran his desperate race—sport like this didn't come up every day.

William leapt ashore as the racers came closer to the ship. "Stop this!" he shouted while blocking the hurtling longshoreman.

"Outta my way," growled the thug, easily knocking William down with a hefty shoulder smash to the chest. The younger McGrath got to his feet, dusted himself off, and returned to the ship's deck, shaken.

"We should take charge here," William said to Thomas. "I'll get your revolver."

"Good Lord, no. We don't want this to become a gunfight. The crew will handle this one way or another."

"Well, why don't they then?"

"Just watch; you'll see this end on its own. It's best to avoid getting involved in a fistfight unless it looks like they mean to kill each other." And with that, Thomas resumed watching the race.

Mark had gained some distance from his pursuer when he fetched up in a laneway that was closed by a barrier of longshoremen at the far end. Momentarily at a loss, he heard cries of, "Climb, Mark; climb, jump," from the crew, and he responded accordingly. He nimbly scaled a stack of planks, tipping a few into the lane below him in his haste. His pursuer was a heavier man, less fit and somewhat winded; he chose not to scale the lumber pile. Adopting Mark's own tactics, he picked up a fallen plank and began swinging it ponderously. Mark's island of safety became fraught with danger once again. The first two swings were slow and easy to jump, but he realized that other longshoremen would soon join in, and then he would be in serious trouble. As his tormentor faced away from him, following through with the third heavy stroke of his swinging plank, Mark ran and leapt for the next stockpile.

Four stockpiles divided the distance between him and the safety of the ship. Running the first one, he easily cleared the eight-foot gap, landing comfortably. Tearing along again, he could hear the labored pursuit of the man in the lane, below and behind him. He paused only long enough to gather himself for the effort of the next sprint and vault—he was almost to the ship. Once again, he made the leap, his toes finding the very end of the far stockpile. The crew roared approval from the galley roof and began to descend to help him aboard after his final jump. The dog stood with his forepaws on the amidships rail, ears forward, fully alert and barking.

As Mark raced along the boards, he suddenly knew he didn't have the spring in him for a last jump. He had no choice, however, and no time to think about it. He leapt.... It wasn't good enough, and he felt it instantly. He sank through the air, landing hard on his stomach, folded over the edge of the stockpile with his legs dangling down.

Ohhh, oh it's bad, real bad, he thought as he slid down the pile, turned, and leaned against it. And there was the longshoreman, slowing his pace now that he was sure of his prey, an ugly malicious grin undergirding his distressed nose, preparing to enjoy himself. The rest of his gang recaptured their courage and were not far behind. Mark watched their approach with dread.

Pain ran through his knees, thighs, and midsection; continued flight was out, so he must stand and defend himself somehow, but all he could think of was guarding his head. He hoped to see Elizabeth again, and he didn't want her to see him with a battered face. With a swallow, he realized he was fooling himself; he would be lucky to survive this fight, never mind see Elizabeth again. Where were his shipmates?

The broken-nosed man was almost upon him, and Mark was timing his moment for a kick, when something black and seemingly heavy sailed through the air and hit the brute a dull fleshy slap in the throat. Falling, gasping, to the work-worn boards of the pier, the man clutched at his windpipe, his eyes rings of panic. Mark looked incredulously at the object that had saved him. He only registered that it was a cast-iron skillet once he was in Eric and Benjamin's clutches and being propelled toward the ship. The safety of *Genevieve*'s wooden walls and his boisterous shipmates began to dull his pain.

"Marvelous jumping, Mark," said one after another, clapping him on the back. Risto, wearing a puffy eye, shuffled forward stiffly and shook his hand without saying a word.

"Where did the frying pan come from?" Mark asked.

"Norman slung it," Eric said. "He held us back so he could get a clear shot. Norman's thin lips pulled into a brief smile. "I must stay in practice. I was aiming a little higher; that should have skipped off his head like a flat rock across a pond."

Mark marveled at what hidden power lay in the cook's arm, allowing him to throw a twelve-inch skillet over seventy feet with such force and accuracy.

The twice-beaten longshoreman was helped to his feet and partially carried down the pier, his gang members throwing sullen scowls at

Genevieve's crew men whenever they faced in their direction. The crew in turn guffawed with delight at the outcome of the entire incident.

As the laughter died down, Benjamin said, "They'll think twice before bothering us again!"

Norman feigned a tight smile as he met Thomas's gaze down the long quarterdeck and whispered to himself, "I wonder."

Chapter 7

Departing the First National Bank of Detroit, William felt a little set back, but—no matter; he had planned for this possibility. He made an effort to revive his favorable outlook after the unsuccessful interview, but his taut, energetic gait showed that he had not.

Thomas matched his brother's speed with long strides over Gratiot Street's cedar block sidewalk. The blue sky admitted a late summer sun, bringing Detroit's bricks to exude a smell of warm dust. With their next meeting over an hour away and a scant three blocks distant, Thomas preferred not to overheat himself.

"William, we have plenty of time. Let's stop for some coffee and settle down before the next appointment." William flexed his right hand and grunted.

Leaving the second bank, Thomas began to see long wispy clouds introduced into the previously clear sky. Their second loan application had progressed further than their first; at least they hadn't been turned down flat. The bank manager had, however, offered them an atrocious interest rate—one's desperation might force the acceptance of it, but not sound business practice.

Thomas's earlier feeling of disappointment with their financing hitch took a swing toward ambivalence. If it didn't work, life could amble amicably down some other path or perhaps go on unchanged. On the other hand, his brother seemed to need this loan quite badly. He watched William fidgeting with his right hand as he had done intermittently throughout the interview at the bank.

"Will, what are you doing with your hand?"

"I—I can't feel two of my fingers, but where I can feel them, they give a horrible, rubbing, tingling feeling. This would have to happen today!"

"Well, when is there a good time to lose the feeling in your fingers?" Thomas asked.

"Never, I suppose!" said William. "But it's considerably distracting, today of all days, when we are trying to make a good presentation!"

"Stop fretting. It doesn't help matters to look agitated and desperate. Besides," Thomas softened his tone, "they'll likely get better in three days to a week. You probably injured them on the dog cage."

William held his tongue, reflecting a little resentfully that Thomas was probably right. He always spoke like he was right and, maddeningly, he often was.

Just prior to entering the Industrial Bank of Detroit, Thomas took in, once again, the changing sky: the white wisps in blue were drifting steadily eastward, being replaced by a solid shield of gray from the west. Wind direction was deceptive down in the city streets, but he thought it had shifted to the southeast.

"Third time lucky," he smiled bravely at William, opening the bank's paneled oak door and ushering him in.

Inside the bank, high above them, belt-driven ceiling fans whirred meaninglessly between corniced walls, for the warm air remained motionless at floor level. Business was conducted in hushed tones down a long row of tellers, stationed behind heavy etched glass and ornately carved posts. An impression was made that if one spoke aloud, the words would be swallowed whole by the bank before any sound could register. As William led the way to a wicket marked "Chief Clerk," Thomas tugged with a forefinger at his collar, struggling with a desire to loosen it fully and then remove his jacket.

Arriving at the chief clerk's wicket, William was greeted by a perfectly bald-headed gentleman with small, round spectacles.

"Good afternoon," the man intoned as he stood up from behind his desk.

"We are the McGrath brothers; we have an appointment with Mr. Standish," William said.

"A pleasure to meet you," the clerk said in a most pleasing baritone. He advanced outside of his counter to shake hands. "John Fitzpatrick at your service." After greeting William, he took Thomas's proffered hand into both of his own.

Thomas flinched inwardly; he hated the two-handed handshake from a stranger. It was the unmistakable mark of an imposter or, most often, a salesman. He felt an instant distrust of Fitzpatrick, simple and complete.

Fitzpatrick, probably noting this somewhere in Thomas's expression, addressed himself to William.

"Mr. Standish is just concluding a meeting; he'll be ready shortly. Would you gentlemen like something to drink while you wait? Coffee or tea?"

"Tea would be grand," said William, enjoying this small distinction.

"Nothing for me," was Thomas's response.

Finally seated in a plush red leather armchair, Thomas listened as William presented his proposed expansion to Edgar Fieldgate Standish. Despite the interview's importance, he couldn't lend it his full attention, especially when William spoke. His mind wandered to other problems: How had the crew earned the longshoremen's wrath? Longshoremen were becoming more troublesome at every visit, but the altercation this morning seemed terribly antagonistic—something greater than a disagreement over who should unload lumber. He hoped there would be no more serious incidents.

"…with the introduction of gangsaws into our mill we—"

"Who will you get your saws from?" Standish interrupted William.

"Bay City Saw, of course, we have pricing for—"

"What saws are you putting in the new mill?" Standish asked, jumping to his next thought.

New mill; William liked the sound of this. "We have priced two models of gangsaw—"

"Bandsaws are what I would use," Standish interjected. "They've got them all over the west now. That's what they're using in big lumber country."

"Well, ah, we do have some fat trees," William said diplomatically, and the conversation fell into different tree species for their size, qualities, and cash value, with Standish largely dominating the topic and William politely agreeing.

Thomas, left to himself, considered the weather: If the wind stayed in the southeast until tomorrow afternoon, he would likely have enough wind from this weather system to make above Port Huron with southerly or westerly winds, and then he could avoid the expense and bother of being towed upriver. He fervently wished now to get out of this stuffy, mahogany-clad office and back to his ship. This entire experience had become distasteful to him; there had to be some less extreme way—some means of achieving William's goals gradually with the cash and assets at hand. Try as he might, though, he hadn't come up with a workable scheme to date.

Standish fell quiet as he examined William's ledgers and other papers. William caught Thomas's eye silently, with a grin and arching russet eyebrows, plainly feeling that the meeting was going well. Thomas nodded non-committally.

"It seems your profitability is slipping. Has that not been so?"

Standish's question brought William back to earth; this was the point that had soured the last interview.

"Er, yes. Our projections at present show less profit than last year and 4 percent less than two years ago. This is precisely why we wish to expand: to give us the chance to compete in the marketplace with steam-powered mills."

"No doubt," Standish replied. "Competition is fine—drives forward progress, but what if you compete and lose on borrowed funds? How does an investor know he won't lose on this?"

William was not unprepared for this question. "We have a good number of steady contracts for…." Standish held up a hand and broke in: "Collateral was what I was getting at. You must secure the loan with stocks or bonds or, in your case, property. Do you understand? In this way, you are betting on yourself." The banker made up his mind. "I see this as a medium-risk loan, but I like you boys," he smiled patronizingly. "You remind me of myself at your age. I am prepared to offer you a two-year expansion loan at a fixed rate of 7 percent. There will be some conditions: benchmarks for expansion and disbursal of funds etc., etc. We can draw up the papers today and sign tomorrow if that suits?"

"Yes, of course," William readily agreed, forgetting to confer with his brother. Thomas shot him a sharp glance, but he decided to take the matter up with him outside.

"Excellent; check with my clerk for a time." Standish stood to shake hands, effectively dismissing them. "Until tomorrow, then."

Thomas's relief at exiting the bank was short-lived, marred by an undercurrent of unease below the surface of thought.

"We're almost there!" William said happily as they weaved their way into the afternoon crowd.

"Sure; it sounds…promising," Thomas replied distantly. William sensed his brother was working himself into a foul mood; he wondered why. They were on the brink of achieving the crucial first step: securing financing. It made no sense.

As they boarded a cross-town streetcar, each man pursued his own thoughts. While William began construction of the mill in his head, Thomas brooded indefinably. The city became oppressive to him. He felt an unreasoning anger toward the sweaty people crushed in around him, swaying with the moving car, and now he was stuck with returning into all of this tomorrow to sign this hideous deal at ten-thirty. How he detested the idea of going into debt! He would rather have been leaving Belle Isle astern by that hour as the warm front blew in.

He realized two things were bothering him: First, if the trouble with the longshoremen continued, someone from his crew could get badly hurt; secondly, but more immediately, the warm heavy air packed between bodies in the streetcar stifled him. How many of these people were pinched by debt and riding this car daily against their will? He feared debt would destroy any illusions he had of autonomy.

Catching Thomas by surprise, William frantically clanged the bell, signaling for a stop. He squeezed through the crowd toward the door and hurtled out abruptly, crying: "It's her! It's her!" and losing his hat in the process.

Thomas looked back in the direction William was running. He saw an attractively dressed brunette woman turning the corner into the side street they had just passed.

"Oh, brother," Thomas muttered to himself, believing the day couldn't possibly get any worse.

Chapter 8

T
HOMAS LAUNCHED HIMSELF out of the moving streetcar in pursuit of his brother, picking up William's lost cap as he went. If the woman turned out to be Carmina, he wondered what his brother could do or say. Carmina had clearly, painfully severed their tie, in his opinion. He had hoped, and sometimes even thought, that William could see beyond her, but he fully understood his brother's weakness in this regard. He quickened his pace to a run, dodging a cat and a man with a small child, as he approached the brick building on the corner where William had disappeared. Turning into the side street, he saw William's red hair bobbing wildly among other heads and hats a block and a half in front of him. He rushed to catch up.

The woman being pursued—Carmina, or someone else—heard commotion behind her, turned to see a very intent William, eyes locked upon her, running fast. She took off in an alarmed canter, her long skirts preventing full flight. The afternoon traffic, however, made top speed impossible for William, thwarting closure of the gap between them before she reached a two-story house midway down the street. As she climbed the six stairs to the doorway, William called after her, earning strange looks from the pedestrians he was struggling through.

"Carmina! Carmina, wait!"

She fumbled with the key in the lock, turning, pushing, pulling, turning again—turning the opposite way. As William approached the steps, something in the lock clicked and she swung the door inward. Then, in one smooth motion, all awkward panic forgotten, her hand turned and removed the key; she stepped inside and then slammed the door.

William fetched up against the closed door in time to hear the locks click into place inside. Held at bay still.

"Carmina, Carmina, please open up! Carmina, please.... I just want a few words; could that be so awful?" He waited a long time for an answer, then eventually:

"Carmina, please say something."

A voice inside finally said, "I don't know you; go away!"

Was it her? No, he thought. Despite their separation, William was sure he would have recognized her voice, and this was not it. Yet he was also certain he had seen her walking on the street. He hadn't imagined her, or had he? He had spent hours picturing a chance meeting where she accidentally bumped into him, and after some forgiving conversation, began to look at him as she had in the beginning.... No, he was almost certain he had seen her. But then, who was this voice on the opposite side of the door? Whoever she was reiterated more stridently, "Go away or I'll scream."

Out of the corner of his eye, William saw Thomas approaching at a fast walk, calling to him. "William, look out!" His right hand pointed up, fingers clenching William's abandoned cap.

Taken for a split second by the familiar sight of his tweed cap, he didn't react right away. Then a wooden box collapsed next to him on the stone landing, spinning broken staves and splinters out in many directions, some hitting his legs. He looked up in time to see a pair of feminine hands release an ancient chamberpot.

Scurrying down the steps, he was narrowly missed by a soft crash and small tinkling shards of broken porcelain. At a safe distance, he stood and faced the building, calling out: "Carmina, can't we please talk?" He marveled at the woman's duplicity; she must have had the window open and missiles ready to have ascended so quickly from behind the door to drop bombs on him.

Numerous onlookers had stopped by now to see this curious scene develop. Thomas clutched William's arm and, through clenched teeth, said candidly, "William, let's go. Obviously, you can't talk. Certainly not with whoever is in that house!"

"I can't leave. I must speak to her. I must!"

"Are you certain it's her? You had no more than a quick glimpse from a moving streetcar," Thomas replied.

"I got closer on the street," William said. "Almost certain," he continued a little doubtfully. "I have to stay and find out."

"Oh no, no, *no*. William, can't you see? This won't do; you've already attracted a crowd. Soon there will be police here, and then you'll be in trouble, explaining why you continue to harass this house's occupant."

"Harass? I'm just trying to start a conversation!"

Thomas paused, forcing himself to be patient while holding William's gaze. He then answered quietly, "You don't see how it looks from the outside; all of these people have just witnessed you chasing a lone woman down the street and her locking herself inside a house in fear." He nodded his head. "Think on that."

William glared at him while digesting his words. It had to have been Carmina, and yet the voice—he thought how it wasn't her voice. He was so close to finding out. Glancing up at the second floor window, he was just in time to see a figure pull back inside. Resignedly, he said: "Okay, Thomas; we'll go, but sometime very soon, I must find out who is in that house!"

"Take the address—we're going," Thomas replied.

Norman joined Dennis on the rail, aft of the pilot house, for an after-dinner smoke. This ritual occurred in almost any weather—alongside, anchored, or underway. Neither could remember how, or when, they had become smoking partners, but some time after Dennis had been promoted to mate, the habit had developed. Each man looked down the length of *Genevieve*'s deck and took a personal satisfaction from the peace of the moment: The dog slept quietly in the deck coil from the mizzen sheet; most of the up-bound cargo was securely stowed; a dinner of beef stew had been eaten—then cleaned up; and now some of the crew were stripped to the waist, scrubbing warm toil and stale sweat from themselves amidships, with hopes of going ashore. As Dennis tamped some shag tobacco into his pipe, Norman cupped his hands around a lit match and ignited the cigarette that had waited between his lips for the past few hours. A couple of pulls on the cigarette brought it to life and he asked, "The old man's not back, hunh?" referring to Thomas in the slang used by seamen for their captains.

"No," Dennis replied. "He must have been held up in town. Did you save them some dinner?"

"No, I gave it all out. In fact, I ate the last of it myself; I had to force the third bowl, but it was well worth it," Norman said with a self-satisfied grin as he patted his stomach.

"You are shameless." Dennis laughed. "What if they get back and want some grub?"

"Well, then, I'll knock something together in a hurry. I've got some fresh bread and tomatoes to get them started. But," he paused to take a pull on his cigarette, "if they haven't returned by now, then I don't think they'll be back for dinner. Mr. William doesn't prefer to spend a lot of time on board."

"I've noticed that," Dennis said contemplatively while finally lighting his pipe. A few short pulls set his bowl alight, and he pushed a sultry blue cloud out around him.

"I wish the old man would get back, though. I'm not sure about liberty for the men tonight."

"Oh, I think you could let 'em go; we're not leaving early in the morning. Go ahead—the captain won't mind," Norman said.

Dennis paused and puffed a few times, contemplating the advice and its source; Norman was capable of goading him into a regrettable decision just for fun. The cook took great enjoyment from the creation of a certain level of trouble.

"Tonight might be different," he said solemnly, then turned and looked over the transom. "There's a fellow, a lounger, just sitting on a bollard over there watching the ship. He's been hanging around for a couple of hours."

"Oh, really?" Norman leaned back to see—taking a fresh interest in his evening. "You're worried that he's reporting to the goon squad from this morning."

"Yes." Dennis took his seat again and relit his pipe. "If he were a Pinkerton man, he'd have a uniform, and he's been there too long to be up to any good."

"You're probably right, but the boys'll gladly take a small chance for a last run ashore in the city." Norman perhaps pursued compound mischief.

The two men sat in companionable silence while Dennis hesitated over the decision. He tapped the ash from his pipe over the transom and refilled it. "This is some nice tobacco. The new crop is in," he digressed. Norman concurred before returning to the main discussion.

"The lounger might just be put there for intimidation."

"But to what end?" Dennis asked. "What can they want from us?"

Norman chuckled. "They probably don't want the story of how they got licked this morning to travel too far! Those guys are most likely part of the 'enforcement arm' of their organization, and any story of successful resistance to them will hurt their reputation. That—and their feelings are hurt. Ha-ha."

"Hmm, possibly," Dennis remarked and pulled pensively on his pipe again.

The longshoremen had been strengthening as a group over the last few years and were making an effort to become a formal union in Detroit and across the region. Like many such movements, it wasn't without its physical persuaders who used indelicate forms of coercion.

"Young Mark is itchy to get ashore," Norman said. "He has a 'prospect.'"

"Norman! Have you no romance left in you?" Dennis chided playfully. "I've overheard him talking about this girl; he'll be inconsolable if he doesn't make it ashore tonight."

"I'm sure it'll be awful for him," Norman replied gravely, and he let the words dangle, adrift in the light air, while he sucked in and breathed out the last of his smoke.

Dennis stood up and looked down the deck's length before turning toward town.

"Well, I'm off the hook and you are on; the old man is on his way up the pier. He can decide about liberty, but you might have to cook another dinner."

"I'll be all right. We have plenty of good grub on board," Norman replied confidently and sauntered forward to the galley.

Arriving back aboard, Thomas brusquely dismissed any concerns that awaited him and ordered the ship warped forward so she would be ready for departure tomorrow, at the outer end of the pier. The crew set to work, grumbling a little over this additional task since they had thought the workday finished and had hoped for one last spree ashore. Contrasting the crew's demeanor and efforts, William happily patted the dog who greeted him with a wagging hind end and reciprocated enthusiasm.

As the mooring lines were doubled up and the ship put to rest again, Thomas sat down aft with Dennis to discuss ship's business and await his dinner.

"Everything stowed?" he began without preamble.

"Yes," Dennis said. "We'll take aboard twelve additional barrels of salt, which will be brought here in the morning."

"I see. Any more trouble today?" he asked next, clearly referring to the longshoremen who had loaded the ship.

"Nothing bad; they were a little surly, but not the same group we saw this morning."

"Hmm. Any idea how that fight started? I can't imagine it was because we off-loaded our own lumber."

"I'm not sure," Dennis said. Truthfully, he thought it involved Mark and Risto primarily, but he didn't wish to stir up more trouble. He moved on to the problem he had been considering prior to the captain's arrival.

"That fellow you passed has been sitting on that bollard since about four-thirty, and I'm afraid he's up to no good. I'd like to allow the men liberty tonight—they worked hard today—but there might be more trouble afoot."

Thomas looked silently out at the man on the bollard, wondering—not for the first time—whether this would be the last in a string of difficulties he had encountered today. When his silence had stretched to an elastic limit, Dennis ventured, "Perhaps we could occupy the man's attention while we swing out a boat and let the boys ashore from a spot upriver."

"I suppose we could," Thomas replied, "but I prefer a more direct approach."

Fifteen minutes later, Thomas and William were at the salon table quietly devouring a dinner of chicken, fresh bread, and tomatoes.

William chewed his food without great relish as he brooded over Carmina. Thomas brooded in turn over William, the bank loan, and the grim annoyance of the longshoremen problem, but he concurrently had the faculty to savor the tomatoes. Finished first, he wiped a cotton napkin across his mouth and went on deck to address the crew: "Listen, boys; we have some people in town who don't like us. If you go ashore tonight, I don't need to remind you to stay out of trouble. Stay in groups and get back to the ship early. If you venture out and stay out late alone, you are on your own. Everyone going ashore should be ready to leave in ten minutes." He then went down the pier with Norman to keep the sentry occupied, in the kindest way that circumstance and his cook's disposition would allow.

Chapter 9

A BIG MOON ROSE secretly in the east, unseen above the cloud-clad sky, and on nights during the full phase of the moon, whether clear or cloudy, the gas lights of the city's streets remained unlit. Detroit took up its evening routine in all other aspects: businesses closed, doors and windows shuttered, leaving only bars and restaurants to animate the warm heavy air. Then, night began to paint itself onto the cityscape, softly daubing darkness into twilit corners and alleys, and around buildings made vacant until morning. Children were read stories and tucked in while sleepy people drew curtains, confining the light escaping their rooms. As the restaurants closed and the bars let out, their lights were extinguished and night poured the blackness out into small pools, spreading, creeping toward each other, merging, and then creeping on again. Lovers snuffed candles and heads nestled into pillows, making ready for the next day's work; pools of darkness joined until night had accomplished a near blackness as the good people of Detroit went to sleep.

Finding his way through the urban darkness, Mark floated along Atwater Street, reliving his evening with Elizabeth. He recalled her bright smile upon receiving the few flowers he had bought her; he could still feel her closeness as she sat next to him on the bench in her brother's garden…. He remembered the smell of her hair as he had dared to kiss her, and he felt once again the thrill of her lips' light pressure, pushing upon his in return.

Arriving at the shore end of *Genevieve*'s pier, he began to come down from his rapturous cloud and felt the weariness of his long day sink in. He had been awakened before four o'clock this morning, and it was now well past midnight. Added to his twenty-one-hour day were the various small hurts left over from his fight (or flight) with the long-shoremen. He wanted, badly now, to be in his bunk.

Mark's feet found the railway track, and he measured his stride by the even interval of ties beneath the iron; the track ran the length of the pier so he could follow it safely to *Genevieve* and his bed. Being on the pier reminded him of his morning and Captain McGrath's warning to be careful, but surely, he was safe enough. It was late, but there was hardly anyone awake at this hour, and he was almost back on board. Just the same, darkness was unnerving, and the unseen worked on his imagination. His keen night vision, however, rather than imagination, brought to mind the presence of a dark figure, almost out of sight, lurking behind one of the plank stockpiles he had raced over that morning. Ducking down, he crawled behind some crates piled near the warehouse to see whether the figure would reveal himself as a crew member or someone more sinister. Five minutes passed and the waiting had shown him nothing. After five minutes more, his weariness began to hurt. Squatting behind the crate made his thighs ache; blood flow to his extremities became inadequate, providing a pins-and-needles sensation in his toes. He decided he would risk a quick move to a new position and begin working his way up the pier, toward where the ship was now berthed. Standing bent double, behind the crates, he momentarily allowed the blood renewed access to his legs. When it seemed fairly certain the other man couldn't be watching, he made his move.

Each footfall was made as stealthily as possible, landing carefully flat on each heel, rolling smoothly over the ball of his foot and springing off his toes. Mark made the short sprint to a lumber stack and squatted down once again on the less open side, looking out from behind the wood to see whether he had been spotted. Untouched by the breeze, he broke a cold sweat in the humid night air. After catching his breath, he began edging down the laneway with his back to the stockpile; reaching the corner, he turned to face the lumber and very cautiously eased his head around its rough ends. Shocked, yet not surprised, he could see the dark form of a man, not six feet away, peering slyly around the next corner, lying in wait. Quelling a small tremor of panic, Mark held still, holding his breath, eyes fixed on the back of the man's head. He realized there could be two men, or possibly more, since he thought he had spotted the first man farther down the pier. A minute went by in this way, then another. Mark, breathing as softly as possible, inhaled a vagary of the light breeze that brought the scent of stale tobacco, mingled with a hint of whiskey, into the lane. He knew he was smelling the man in front of him and fretted over his own scent. What if his odor should give him away? His heart was beating fast so he made a new effort to calm himself. Having washed scrupulously, prior to meeting Elizabeth, he wouldn't smell nearly as strong as the vigilante's tobacco. Reassured on that point, he kept watch on the man and leaned against the wood.

A little time passed with no change to the situation until Mark's fatigue asserted itself. He felt himself falling and came fully alert, gripping the wood in front of him. He hadn't actually fallen; he hadn't even moved—but he had been asleep for less than a second! Shocked at his body's betrayal, he determined he couldn't remain this way; he would have to move on—get to the ship, make one desperate run and jump on board. When he tried a covert glance around the stockpile, he saw his would-be ambusher was still there, peering around the corner periodically, and then turning around to nip at a hip flask that made the waiting bearable. Holding his breath again, studying the man, Mark closed one eye in order to focus through his fatigue, determined to move again. When the watcher turned to look down the pier, he would bolt for the next pile. In a moment, the man swigged a little whiskey and turned away. Mark opened his left eye and commenced a desperately exposed tiptoe only six feet behind his watcher. Coming close to his destination, he heard the man shuffle and expeditiously took cover behind the next lumber stack. He crept on, reaching the far end of the pile, and stood absolutely still, listening. No noise; perhaps—perhaps he had been missed! There was no time to celebrate; another man lay concealed somewhere ahead. Feeling calm now, he repeated his earlier actions, slowly craning his neck around the corner. As his eyes passed the plank ends, once again, he saw a man, now squatting with his back to the lumber. This time the man also saw him. Jumping up like a frog from his low position, the man made a swipe at Mark's head, but Mark had pulled back and fled.

"I got one over here," cried the man, hoping to gather some help.

It's all up, Mark thought, running for safety around the far end of the woodstack, then into the open, and making a beeline for *Genevieve*—nothing else for it. Running as hard as he could, he stumbled slightly as he encountered the railway track. Slowing down, he recovered, stepped carefully over the ties, and resumed his breakneck pace. When he heard his pursuer tumble over the tracks, he felt a surge of hope that he would make it safely aboard.

Then he was tackled. Tackled, dealt a couple of blows to the back and head, and then pulled struggling to his feet, an arm twisted behind his back.

"Who th'hell are you?" his assailant asked.

"Night watchman; let go of me," Mark said boldly. "I might ask your name and let you know you are going to be in some trouble."

"Night watchman, huh?" his captor sneered, unimpressed, as the other man approached them. "I think I might have seen you this morning."

The newcomer struck a match and held it up to Mark's nose, close enough to warm the tip. "Yes, this is the same boyo," he said, facing Mark.

"Thompson will love to see you!" he threatened pleasantly.

Mark's mind raced, desperately searching his tired, frightened brain for an effective counter-threat or any words to improve his situation. Thompson could only be the thug whose nose Risto had broken. Thompson's meanness would be unendurable, if not deadly; he must risk injury to escape these two men.

The dog barked on *Genevieve*, having detected movement out on the pier; it prompted Mark to rally help from the deck watch: he yelled as loudly as he could while stamping his heel down forcefully on his captor's toes. Kicking out forwards, he struck the other man's midsection, while trying to wrench free. Almost succeeding, he was free of his foe's grip for a moment, but in an attempt at flight, he careened into the man he had kicked and, suddenly, had powerful hands clutching his throat. The other thug soon found his arm again and torqued it around his back. This time, his assailant was far too angry to settle for mere restraint; he pulled and twisted in a manner that betrayed a studied enthusiasm in the art. The pain in Mark's arm increased as the give was turned out of his limb. As he fell to his knees, he knew with fleeting horror that his arm would be broken and he couldn't stop it. Crack! He thought he heard the pop from inside his body. Agony ripped from his arm to his head, and mercifully, he passed out. When he fell limp, the two men let go of him, dropping him with a thunk on the pier's worn boards. Savagely delighted with their work thus far, they further enjoyed kicking the unconscious young man, trying to do as much damage as possible without the bother of leaning over. Soon, they were winded, and then the noise of the ship's dog started to concern them since there seemed to be other motion over by the ship.

"Do ya think he's dead?" the arm twister asked.

"I doubt it; not yet, anyhow—no head injury," replied the other.

"Let's not take any chances. If he wakes up, he'll know us."

"Right-o. Grab his shoulders, I'll get his feet," agreed the other. They lifted Mark hastily and carried him to the pier's edge, dragging his limp arm underneath him at a perverse angle.

"So long, fella," said the arm twister. They rolled him into the river's burbling current with a small splash, and then slipped away into the deeper darkness.

CHAPTER 10

ARRIVING EARLY FOR work, Edgar Fieldgate Standish stepped down from his hansom and turned to dismiss his driver.

"Be sure to arrive promptly at 11:30 for my lunch pickup," Edgar instructed him.

"Yes, sir," the driver replied in a patient, neutral tone.

As Edgar turned again to unlock the bank's oak-paneled door, a chill, dewy breeze ruffled his short gray hair. Once he had gained the interior, he was surrounded with the pleasing aromas of paper, floor wax, and lemon oil rising off polished mahogany. After locking the door from the inside, he pocketed his key and strode eagerly toward his office. Passing his thick fingers brusquely over his scalp, he likewise combed through the tasks ahead and composed his busy day: he had to review Paul's corrections to the foreign bond accounts; the managing director of the Cross-Town Streetcar Company had requested a meeting; it was necessary to write an apology letter to the foreign bond holders (he felt it was prudent to handle mistakes personally); and there was the meeting with these lumbermen, the McGrath brothers, all before his luncheon with the chairman of the Chamber of Commerce.

Being early, Edgar expected to see few of his staff at work, so he thought it unusual to see no one inside his bank. Equally surprising, the great iron door to the main vault was ever so slightly ajar. It was a little bit early for opening the vault; the tellers wouldn't be here for another hour, so something seemed odd. Paul opened the bank following a precise timetable each morning; it was one of the few tasks he had never failed at. There was usually no reason to have the vault open so far in advance of the business day; in fact, there were many good reasons to keep it locked as often as possible. Edgar wondered whether Paul was in the vault, and why? Also, Fitzpatrick should be in by now. Edgar advanced to the vault.

God Almighty, if Paul can't even open the bank correctly, what will I do? Edgar sagaciously halted himself in that line of thinking. The worst thoughts always came to him first, he knew, usually based on scanty facts; the true situation was often something quite different. Perhaps Paul was working on an account that required a quick verification in the vault. But what could that be—the bond corrections? Paul rarely showed the kind of initiative that would induce him to feverish poring over accounts prior to business hours.

Having now traversed his foyer's length, Edgar passed through the swinging wicket in the counter and approached the great iron door. Just as Edgar reached it, the door swung open several more inches. Fitzpatrick emerged carrying an acetylene lamp in his right hand, and cradled beneath his other arm were a large ledger and a medium-sized brown paper envelope. Momentarily unsettled by Edgar's unexpected presence immediately outside the vault, Fitzpatrick felt his face go blank before his usual composure returned.

"Good morning, sir," he began with a warm smile, hoping to forestall questions with an air of normalcy.

Completely immune to Fitzpatrick's charm, Edgar gave a curt nod and demanded, "Why is the vault open so early? Where is young Mr. Standish?"

Fitzpatrick maintained a small, reassuring smile, inwardly grateful that he hadn't been asked who had opened the vault.

"I'm sorry, sir," he answered contritely. "Regrettable necessity. This ledger was forgotten in there yesterday. Mr. Standish has stepped out to the water closet."

Edgar was not to be satisfied so easily.

"Let me see." He held out his hand for the ledger, which Fitzpatrick duly gave him. Having received his ledger without taking his eyes off of his clerk, Edgar asked, "What's in the envelope?"

The blank look skimmed Fitzpatrick's face again, followed by a wounded expression that he should be mistrusted in this fashion.

"Why, nothing, sir," he said. Setting his lamp down on the floor, he made a dramatic show of turning the open envelope upside down and giving it a shake. "Nothing."

Edgar cared very little for Fitzpatrick's bruised feelings: He stepped over to the vault and peered inside; then, seeing nothing unusual, he swung the great iron door shut with a metallic thud that resounded with several muffled echoes within. Turning the wheel that locked the door, he simultaneously read the title on the ledger in his hands—foreign bonds.

"Why was this in the vault?"

Fitzpatrick looked at him unhappily and answered in a non-committal baritone, "I really don't know, sir. Mr. Standish was working with it yesterday."

Now Edgar was uncertain; was everything as it seemed? Had Paul opened the vault and sent Fitzpatrick to retrieve the foreign bonds ledger just before stepping out of the office? Or was something else happening here? Why was Fitzpatrick carrying an empty envelope? Finding out anything more by asking was unlikely, and he had to get on top of his day. He would have a more thorough look in the vault when Paul was back.

"Send young Mr. Standish in to see me when he has returned from his other—ah—business. I will be keeping this ledger for now," he said and continued the interrupted trip to his office.

By ten-fifteen, Edgar's intended program for the morning was knocked badly out of shape; he had taken three telephone calls while reviewing Paul's work, and consequently, it had taken longer than expected; the director of the Cross-Town Streetcar Company telephoned at nine o'clock to postpone his nine-thirty meeting until ten-thirty, but in the process, he had begun to discuss his business. Hampered by a scratchy line, it had taken Edgar several minutes to get rid of him. Now he sat in front of a partially written letter to his foreign bond customers that would remain incomplete until after lunch. A few minutes were needed to prepare for his meeting with Cross-Town Streetcar's director, and he would have to have Paul handle the agreement signing with the McGrath brothers.

"Fitzpatrick!" Edgar bellowed from behind his mahogany desk. His clerk leaned his bald head and shoulders through the doorframe, resting on the outside jamb.

"Sir?"

Fleetingly, it occurred to Edgar that his clerk looked mildly apprehensive.

"Give Mr. Standish the McGrath loan agreement and send him in."

"Right away, sir." Fitzpatrick smiled and retreated.

Edgar deposited his partially finished letter in a drawer and reflected, not for the first time, how difficult keeping a schedule had become since installing his telephone. It would save a great deal of time to have someone else answer the phone, but it was unthinkable to have Fitzpatrick any deeper into his business than he already was. It often irked Edgar to be in such close contact with his clerk, but as a son-in-law, he couldn't readily get rid of him without irrefutable justification. Fitzpatrick was tidy, efficient, smartly dressed (but not gaudy), punctual, and unfailingly well mannered. Paradoxically, it was Fitzpatrick's impeccable conduct that provided Edgar his misgivings; although he knew a man had little choice but to be pleasant to his employer, his clerk's mellifluousness struck him as insincere. It seemed the man's elaborate courtesy and pleasing voice were no more than a well-crafted cloak for some essential falsehood. He couldn't pin it down.

Paul knocked and entered, carrying a small sheaf of papers.

"Ah, good, here you are," Edgar began. "I'm running behind, and I'm double-booked. I need you to look after the McGrath agreement. Standard contract, all terms are in there; get it signed by the brothers. Any questions?"

"No, Mr. Standish."

"Okay, good; let me sign those." Edgar took the papers.

Once the papers were duly signed, Paul collected the agreement and made to leave the office when an afterthought occurred to Edgar. "Oh, Paul, one more thing."

Paul turned to face him.

"Why was the vault unlocked so early today?"

Paul didn't understand the question; he had opened the vault at eight-forty-five as usual.

"Early, sir?"

Edgar's face began to flush characteristically. "Yes, early; the vault door was open at eight o'clock when I arrived this morning," he said with diminishing patience.

Paul stood silently, trying to review his morning, when Fitzpatrick leaned his head through the doorway.

"Mr. Standish, your ten-thirty appointments have arrived."

"We'll come out," Edgar said, dismissing him.

"Be sure to open the bank on our timetable—I place a great deal of trust in you for this. Every detail is important in this business."

"Yes, sir," Paul replied, knowing that no other answer would do this time, but certain he had not opened the vault early.

Thomas felt bedraggled, and he wasn't sure he was hiding it well. After a broken night with only two hours sleep, he had risen, washed, shaved, dressed, and eaten. Three cups of Norman's coffee had braced him for the morning ahead, but his foul mood from the previous day had ripened into a discontented weariness that was more than physical. Sitting on a burgundy upholstered bench, he leaned back against the wall and regarded William, sitting kitty-corner from him in the bank's foyer. William, having slept much of the night, looked bright and fresh, and only subtly displayed agitation by fiddling with his numb fingers. Watching William's veiny left hand work his anxiety from the injured fingers on his right hand, Thomas wondered whether he couldn't refrain from this new habit. Considering asking him to stop, he finally conceived of an inoffensive slant: "Will, are those fingers bothering you?"

"Yes. I believe today they are worse. The tingly feeling is not easy to describe, but it's awful."

"Well, that's probably a good sign that they're healing up. Maybe you should leave off pulling them; it makes you look anxious. Is the loan worrying you?"

"No, no," William responded. "No, we almost have the loan in hand. It's not that." He now made a small effort; separating his hands, he placed them on his knees and forced a smile.

"Everything happens at once, doesn't it? I go for months at home moving logs into the mill—and out again, but in the few days we've been here, I've gained a pet dog while losing the feeling in my fingers for the effort, witnessed a concerted attack on your crew by the long-shoremen, have almost secured financing for a major mill expansion, accidentally spotted my estranged wife—"

"Possibly," Thomas interjected.

"I'm certain it was her," William said. "Survived a bombardment of household articles by her, and now there has been this terrible incident with Mark."

"Plenty of fun to be had in Detroit," Thomas joked without mirth.

The men lapsed once again into sober silence, each reviewing his memories of last night. Thomas had been awakened by the constant barking of the dog, but he had stayed in his bunk, letting Dennis Ringle get up to investigate. A moment later, the ship's bell had rung, sounding the alarm for all hands, signifying that something was badly wrong. Benjamin had been in the water, and Thomas knew, to his chagrin, that this circumstance was a result of his own impatience with the longshoremen's lookout.

He looked up from his reminiscence; here was this fake Fitzpatrick again.

"Mr. Standish is on his way out, gentlemen," Fitzpatrick said.

As Edgar approached, the brothers stood to shake hands. "Gentlemen," Edgar greeted them, "I must apologize; I have been double-booked for this hour. This is my son, Paul Standish."

Paul stepped forward, greeting Thomas and William with a firm handshake.

"Paul has my implicit trust and will complete our loan agreement with you." Having finished the introduction, Edgar wished them success, gave a quick nod, and returned to his office in the company of a short, fat man in a gray suit.

Paul gave a generous smile. "Right this way," he said, guiding them to his office.

Once seated in a small armchair, Thomas took a moment to look Paul Standish over; he was almost mature physically, with a slight frame that nicely carried his well-tailored suit. His facial features were proportioned to each other, producing a handsome assembly. Below his black hair, his skin was smooth with none of the fine lines showing about the eyes that come in the later twenties. His age might be twenty-four, and Thomas thought sardonically of how grand it was to have one's financial future put into the hands of a recently graduated schoolboy.

Paul cleared some paper from his desk and then laid out the loan agreement for the brothers to read.

"Please, gentlemen, pull up your chairs if you like. We have two copies for you to sign. One will remain at the bank, of course, and the other is for your keeping."

William pulled up to the desk, but Thomas took the papers in hand and leaned back in his armchair, letting his eyes wander over the document; it was two pages long and terminated the second page with spaces for signatures, dates, and a witness. Going over it line by line, everything was in accord with his expectations until he reached Clause 11, titled "Payment Upon Call." Even after reading it three times carefully, he was not sure he understood it clearly. He pulled his chair up next to William.

"Will, do you know what this is?"

"Not quite," William replied. "Um, Mr. Standish, can you explain this item here?" He pointed two-thirds of the way down the second sheet.

"Let me see," Paul answered. "Oh, that's part of what our pressman calls 'boilerplate.'"

"Boilerplate?" William asked.

"Yes, it's in most contracts that we issue, so the typesetters keep it in one big plate for the printing press to save time and repetition. Ha-ha. It's rather funny thinking of a pressman trying to avoid repetitive work." Paul smiled at his insight.

This revealing little joke confirmed Thomas in his thinking that Paul had never worked with his hands.

"I suppose so," Thomas replied, unamused. "Okay, but does it mean you—the bank—can just demand the money back at any time?"

"Well, yes, that is what it means. But it would be a very rare event, if it should ever happen. The bank must have a way to collect should it become overextended."

William realized Thomas's signing might hinge on this point, so he tried to steer the discussion. "And you say it's very rare?"

"Yes. It has never happened in all my time at the bank."

"All that time?" Thomas pretended astonishment; only William knew it for the unobtrusive ridicule it was—a sure sign his brother would not be soothed like a frightened child.

"Oh, yes, a very long time." Paul smiled.

Thomas didn't like the idea of taking such an open-ended risk, but he acknowledged that the bank couldn't just hand out money without some safeguards for its position.

His own position came to mind: William's behavior had become more and more erratic since arriving in the city, and his crew was caught up in a brutal feud with the longshoremen. This horrid loan business would have to start all over again if he didn't sign, and that would require at least two more days, if they could get another, better deal at all. That would be two extra days of port charges and trouble. Meanwhile, *Genevieve* was loaded, ready for travel, and there was a wholesome southeast wind to get them well-started upriver. By tomorrow evening, he might be out in Lake Huron and have a chance to rest. Another idea would be to walk out of the room, disappoint William, and cope with the consequences and acrimony. He shot William an inquisitive glance.

"Everything will be fine," William said, trying more overt reassurance this time; then he dipped his pen in the inkwell.

Thomas nodded, resigned himself to the idea, and clearly wrote his signature on both copies.

Chapter 11

"Um-buh, hello?"

Eric was interrupted from his work loosing the gaff sails, in preparation for departure, by a great lump of a man.

"Hello." Eric slid down the main boom topping lift tackle.

"I'm looking for Mr. Ringle."

Eric waved him aboard. "Come on, I'll show you to him."

Dennis considered the young man brought before him. Left by Thomas to replace Mark for the passage up the lake, Dennis had appealed to the ship's agent. The agent had said he had someone honest and hardworking; now, on short notice, this fellow had turned up. He was young and big, big in every way. His straw-colored hair sat in excess of six feet above his boots; he had broad shoulders, thick arms, and well-used brawny hands. Amply fed, he carried some weight in his midsection and had powerful, protruding buttocks above heavy trunk-like legs. He looked as though he could lift a cant all on his own. Carrying a cloth sack holding his possessions, it appeared he had come ready for work. Standing by the wheelhouse, Dennis interviewed him.

"What's your name?"

"Morris, Morris Roberts."

"Right, Morris. Have you worked a barkentine before?"

Morris's eyebrows pulled together as his mouth opened slightly, giving Dennis his answer.

"Sailing ship; have you ever worked under sail?"

"Uh, no."

"Have you worked in steamships, tugs?"

"Not really. I worked on something else."

Dennis thought briefly of what else there was. "It didn't have any sails, and it didn't have an engine. Were you on a barge?"

"That's it, a barge. Purty close, right? Barge—bargentine?"

"Barkentine," Dennis corrected him mildly. "No, it's different. So, you worked on a barge. Around here?"

"Yup."

"What did you do?" Dennis asked.

"Um-buh, usual stuff...moved things, tied ropes up."

"Can you tie knots? Make lines fast? Did you handle mooring lines?"

"I handelt the mooring line." Morris nodded his head proudly. "I don't know a lotta knots, but I'm a good learner."

Dennis wondered about that, but it was early yet. On first impression, the man looked to be what the shipping agent had said: honest and strong. No mention had been made of ability, experience, or smarts. Oh, well; as long as Morris took direction and got along with everyone, he would be some help on the trip home.

"It pays ten dollars a month—all found. Take your gear up forward; find Eric—he'll show you around. When the captain gets back, we'll settle things, as long as he approves.

Morris for the first time exposed his teeth in a large, homely, toothy grin. Large spaces separated his upper incisors; his lower teeth, also in roomy berths, angled out on different paths from each other, giving the impression of a clumsily built thresher. Pleased to have made it past the interview, he thanked Dennis.

"I'll do a good job. I will. Thank you for the work."

"It's only for a little while, as long as the captain says okay," Dennis temporized.

Morris was undeterred, nodding and smiling. He threw his bag over his shoulder and went forward. He had found a job.

Dennis watched him go, briefly wondering how the crew would receive Mark's replacement. A new man would feel the taint of his foreignness initially, and especially in these circumstances. The crew would be forced not only to work with him, but to train him in this case and, hardest of all, to live with him. Uninitiated in the ways of a ship, Morris would have some pointed instruction on the habits and customs of the fo'c'sle.

Looking over the port side, Dennis turned his thoughts back to his final preparations for sailing *Genevieve* away from the pier. With the strong southerly wind, the captain wanted to avoid the expense of scheduling a tug or workboat for pulling the ship against the current. The wind, though, even with full sail up, would not be enough to counter the force of the water pinning *Genevieve's* deep body to the pier. For this, the captain had left a plan: a very long heavy line—the warp—was to be run from the bow of the ship, across the slip to the corner of the pier immediately upriver from them. The warp would then be run around a bollard there, and back to *Genevieve*, making the bitter end fast at the amidships bitts. Once this great hempen vee was formed, from amidships—to the pier—to the bow, the windlass would crank out the slack and winch the ship sideways, upcurrent, buying the room necessary to sail free of the pier.

Dennis suddenly remembered he had left Benjamin in the lazarette, rummaging for small line. He descended into the salon and aft to the small compartment in the very stern, where spare line was stowed. Arriving at the "laz," as they referred to it, he found Benjamin struggling to free a very long coil of three-quarter-inch hemp line from a snarl of other ropes he had pulled up.

"That looks like a good one," Dennis said, coming to his aid. Wrestling alone with the line had left Benjamin frustrated, his outlook toward difficulty weakened by somatic hardship: he was wearing dry a pair of damp trousers, and he was running on very little sleep, both consequences of the incident with Mark.

"There are too many ropes back here; they aren't in order—every time I have to get something, it's a mess!" he complained.

At first affronted by the outburst, Dennis secondarily saw it for what it was. Besides, he was forced to agree that the laz had become a shambles of late; it had been badly set up by the old mate and, as yet, he had done nothing to improve it. Nonetheless, he couldn't tolerate too many comments implying criticism or it would be unending.

"At the end of this trip, you and I will set it to rights," he promised Benjamin firmly.

Benjamin clamped his back teeth together, bitterly realizing he might have bought into an ownership of the laz and its inherent difficulties of organization for the price of a few careless words. He decided to toughen up and get on with the business at hand.

Approaching *Genevieve*, Thomas noted with approval that the warp was run out and the sails had been loosed from their gaskets. The squares, now hanging in their gear, flopped back and forth in the stiffening breeze. Long curls of canvas waved erratically, occasionally giving a sharp snap, drawing attention from on deck, agitating for the gear to be released and the sheets pulled home.

"You're sure you don't want to come for the return trip? I'm confident we'll be home by Friday night, Saturday at the latest."

"No," William said. "I want to look around the foundries for engines and peek in at Bay City Saw on the way home. I'll take the train." With financing secured, William was itching to get a look at the new equipment and machinery he intended to purchase. Aflame with the initial enthusiasm of new enterprise, he knew the trip north in *Genevieve* would be intolerable to him, no matter how fast she went. And yet, and yet…there was also that one other thing. He would delay his trip north, and postpone by another day his long anticipated new mill; hold his eagerness in check just a little longer to know, know for certain, who lived in that house in the middle of town.

They were on board now, and Thomas took in Dennis Ringle's preparations for leaving harbor while William went below for his bag. Leaning into the companionway, the dog listened for William's movements in the salon, his yellow tail wagging uncertainly in slow short strokes. Thomas had reservations about leaving his brother to travel home on his own. Although he knew him to be entirely capable of looking after himself, or purchasing a saw fairly, he wasn't sure he could form an objective view of truth or trouble in any matter regarding the search for his wife. Left alone in this city, he might moon around for days; he could cause a commotion and be arrested, or he might just possibly meet her, reconcile, and bring her home to have children. Thomas smirked to himself in rueful amusement; his last idea he thought unlikely, perhaps even absurd. The woman they had seen yesterday could have been anyone. Thomas let his eyes travel the length of the warp reaching out to the next pier. He needed just such a mechanism, some invisible tow rope to pull gently upon William and dislodge him from this place. Looking at the dog's tail, he thought of a way to accomplish it.

To the dog's great delight, William returned to the deck, leather bag in hand.

"Will. You are going to leave the city, what, in a few days?" Thomas asked.

"Er, yes—I think so."

Thomas reached into his vest pocket and produced a billfold. "Would you be so good as to bring Mark home? The doctor said his arm would be fairly set in two days, and I'd like to see him out of this swamp or he'll get pneumonia. Here's ten dollars; I paid the hospital, so it will easily cover his expenses." Thomas handed over the bills without waiting for a response.

"Er, ah—I don't know." William made a sour face and held up a hand, refusing the money. He was not thoroughly pleased with the idea of being burdened by an injured man to look after on the way home. Mark was a nice lad, and incredibly lucky to have survived his scrape with nothing worse than a dislocated shoulder, but it would be a nuisance to have him along if anything should develop with Carmina. He tried to think of a delicate way around the matter.

Thomas didn't allow his hesitation to last very long; he pressed on. "Oh, I understand completely—I hadn't thought it through. It will be difficult helping a crippled man and managing your dog on the train." William was caught; he hadn't expected this turn.

"Surely, the dog can go home with the ship," he asserted.

"I don't have any time to watch him—he'll be in the way; he might even get sick."

William saw he'd been ambushed. "If I look after Mark, you'll take the dog home; is that it?"

"Do I have your pledge?" Thomas smiled.

"Oh, all right," William answered, red with pique, but then he relaxed. "I must say, quite honestly, Norman is a great man in a scrape, as you said. He certainly saved Mark's life getting the water out of him and warming him up."

Benjamin had gone into the river after Mark, having witnessed the splash when the longshoremen tossed him in. When Mark had come aboard, cold and waterlogged last night, Norman had hung him upside down in the galley, squeezed the water from his lungs, then got him breathing and warmed up in front of the galley stove. Mark had regained consciousness, but his pain and limp arm had convinced Thomas to get him over to the hospital on Randolph Street for professional attention. The boy truly owed his life to Norman, Benjamin, and the crew.

"I know. Well, he should be ready to move tomorrow according to the doc." He offered money again. "You'll manage okay with him?"

"Yes," William acquiesced and took the proffered bills.

Relieved, Thomas shook hands with his brother. "Thank you. Oh, say, by the way, do you have a name for the dog yet?"

"I thought Moses would be fitting, you know—the river, the basket."

"I think the basket in the Bible story was a little different, but I like it. Will you throw our lines on the way out?"

"Of course," William smiled. "Just have someone keep an eye on my bag. This is a rough neighborhood!"

"Don't I know," Thomas answered.

Twenty minutes later, the ship heeled at her berth. The southeast wind filled all of *Genevieve*'s sails, causing her to surge forward and back on the two lines that held her. Dennis Ringle directed the windlass crew cranking up on the warp running to the pier upriver. Thomas stood by Eric, who waited at the wheel for the moment when the ship would at last be set loose and he would control her. Pulling hard at the windlass, the warp had come up taut. The starboard side lines were now all cast off, except for the stern line, which was held to bring *Genevieve*'s bow into the current. She was already eighty feet off of the pier up forward, and the five-inch warp wrung water out of itself with the strain it bore, giving Dennis a moment of pause. He made a quick trip aft to see the captain.

"Do you think the warp can take much more?" he asked.

"It's holding now," Thomas answered, "and it won't see any increase in strain against it. We aren't pulling on something that won't go—the ship is sliding slowly up current. Keep her coming slowly."

And with that, Dennis noticed that the bow had eased a little farther up current and the warp had begun to sag wearily into the river.

"A little more, and as soon as there is a break in the shipping traffic, we'll slip the stern line. We'll keep the warp as a safety to prevent us from slipping back into this pier until we're moving. Once we're moving, let go at the amidships bitts and haul in up forward, quick as you can, understood?"

"Yes, sir," Dennis replied.

The wind gusted, heeling the stationary ship farther and forcing her forward, heaving against the impatient strength of the groaning stern line. When Thomas saw a gap in the shipping, he nodded to Dennis that he was about to let go. The crew cranked away at the windlass.

"Cast off the stern line," Thomas called out. Risto released the three wraps holding the line tight to the stern bitts. It shot through the fair-lead initially; he then quickly paid out slack as the ship surged once again. After William tossed it from its bollard and into the river, Risto heaved it back aboard.

Genevieve began to make her way now, very slowly at first, sliding more across the current than into it, with her bow pointing on a broad angle to the river and out of the slip. Seeing the gap increase between the stern and the pier, Thomas knew the ship was gaining against the current.

"Let go amidships!" he called, and Benjamin dropped the bitter end of the warp out of the amidships fairlead, as Morris and the crew up forward pulled ever faster, hand over hand now, to retrieve its weightless end. *Genevieve* gathered speed: two, three knots. The last of the warp was dragged aboard—four-and-a-half, five knots. Eric turned the wheel, and the yards were squared. *Genevieve* met the current head on making seven knots. Steadily downwind she ran, projecting herself into the distance, away from Detroit and her master's mottled troubles.

BOOK TWO

Endeavor

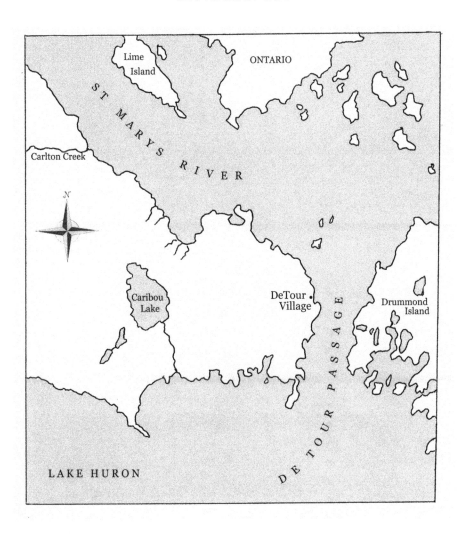

CHAPTER 1

November 26, 1891

I F ONLY THE *winter would hold off*, William thought uselessly, as he listened to the wind howl in accompaniment to the mill's rhythmic noises. Sitting, he leaned his chair back, propped on two legs against his old, maple desk, and gazed absently out of the window into early afternoon twilight. Heavy vibrations from the great water wheel climbed the rear legs of his chair and thrummed through the rolltop desk into his back. Outside, the wind lifted loose sawdust and spun it giddily in small funnels around the stockyard's graying obstacles.

"Perhaps it won't snow for another week or so," he repeated to himself as though it were a wholly new idea. But it wasn't a novel thought at all, for this wish had disturbed his peace for weeks now.

Each season was a footrace for a lumber company, but autumn brought on an urgency that infected the entire community; as farmers gathered the harvest, women jarred and jammed, putting by fruits and vegetables in earthen cellars for the hungry months ahead. Other men might worry over their woodpiles' breadth or a shed roof's ability to withstand the paired assailants of wind and snow.

Work had progressed well at the mill, however, and it wasn't for the work schedule that William wished to forestall the coming season: fickle during the early summer, the saws and machinery had reformed after August and run almost flawlessly since. The sawyers had been cutting steadily, and the last contracted shipment of planks had left with *Genevieve* the week before. In the meantime, almost all the lumber had been sawn for the new mill building, and today's work would complete William's requirements. He had broken away teams of men to prepare logging roads, burrowing deep into the new plats of forest where they would cut this winter, and there set up their camps.

A sharp knock on the door popped him out of both his reverie and his chair. Rearranging the chair, he called, "Come in!"

Boyle came through the door followed by a heavier haze of wind-borne sawdust.

"Nearly done, now, sir," he said while wiping his nose on his sleeve. "We have two more cants going in, and that will complete the list. Do you want to add anything else?"

"No, thank you, Boyle; that's all for the present. We're done for this season. We can start cleaning out tomorrow. I want to save the rest of the cants for boom material; we'll be making larger pens for the spring," William replied.

With new engines and saws, William expected to be milling at a much higher speed. To feed these saws consistently, he was planning to hire more lumberjacks and fell more trees. The trees would be cut into logs and hauled by horses to streams, and in the spring, they would be floated down to the mill and captured in the new larger pens. There they would wait until hauled from the river to be sawn into boards.

Boyle realized his boss was in one of his thinking moods and stepped quietly out of the door without waiting for dismissal. William commenced pacing the red pine boards of his office floor, partly to contemplate construction plans and also to push some blood flow into his feet in the chilly air. Eventually, the sawing was complete; the slash board was placed in the dam, blocking the chute that fed the water to the wheel. And the great undershot waterwheel, fainting from thirst, finally ceased its motion, possibly for the last time. As evening approached, colder air still rolled in with the force of a tantrum—enraged, grabbing, shaking, and throwing unimaginable weight.

William watched the men file out for the night and listened as the daily bustle dwindled to nothing, leaving only the wind's shrill whistles or low moans squeezing between timbers, searching for a weakness in the place. As he pictured men going to their homes, he felt pierced again by the quiet dread of winter that had been poking at him of late. Despite his felted wool coat, he was cold now and considered leaving as well, but with no one waiting, he hardly had reason to depart.

He poured a dram of whiskey from the corner cabinet to warm himself. Sitting again, looking out the window, he imagined his mill hands arriving home to home-baked bread, hot pots of stew, and the good women who had cooked for them. And therein, within that image of hearth and home, lay the core of his disquiet; he simply didn't want to face the long siege of winter again in a cold, empty house. It was at this hour, with the long evening ahead, that he most felt the magnitude of his loss. The weight of loneliness, pressed close by cold evening air, threatened to squeeze him flat. Even Moses was gone, having stowed away on *Genevieve*. Although he lived with William, the dog had a knack for being aboard the barkentine every time she slipped her lines.

In the deepening twilight, the pier's structures slowly lost their distinctiveness until only an impression of form remained. Swirling the tawny liquor in his glass, he suspected idly that *Genevieve* would not come alongside tonight. Thomas would not likely approach in the dark. Perhaps she would return tomorrow? That phrase—he smirked and nipped at his drink. How many times had he told himself that about Carmina?

The liquor warmed him slightly as his melancholy deepened. Perhaps a child would have changed her outlook? Perhaps not. He wouldn't find out without speaking to her, and he had tried—tried desperately hard to force a meeting and hear the truth of it from her own lips. Four times he had returned to the small, two-story house in Detroit, clothed in a forlorn hope of seeing Carmina, but each surveillance had left him unrewarded. At length, he had recognized the pattern—that he had trod this trail before and she wouldn't allow herself to be found. He penned a letter, left it at the house for her, and gave up. And now, now he ached to think he would probably never know why she left. Or would it hurt more to have a reason? Could he be blamed for some unacknowledged wrong he had committed? What part of his character couldn't be discussed or, in the end, forgiven?

He had reached the end of this stream of thought, stranded on the bank as always. He downed the last of his whiskey and determined not to have another. It was getting dark out, so he should get home. He pulled on an overcoat and returned to the thought that had started his morose introspection: It would be good to see *Genevieve* come in. He listened as the wind howled at a higher pitch and something in the mill shuddered. He hoped Thomas was faring well. Perhaps the ship would come alongside tomorrow morning. That would mean he would have Moses back; it nettled him slightly that even his dog was not always loyal. He wondered where they were—Moses, Thomas, and *Genevieve*.

Genevieve, heavily laden with new mill machinery, heeled even more sharply to a gust slightly more savage than the thirty-five knots already laying her over. The starboard rail, dipping briefly below the lake's gray surface, scooped aboard a swirling cold bath for the men suffering the misfortune of working the lee side. Recovering, she sat up to a moderate heel and freed herself from the burden of water in the waist, streaming it slowly from her freeing ports in steady waterfalls as she ascended another wave. Rising, and rising more, her deep coppered forefoot emerged from the crest, hung over a small amount of air for half a second, thrust forward and down into the trough ahead, then separated tons of water in the next wave with a purposeful ease.

Dennis Ringle watched this cold scenery in motion. As the overcast sky gave early afternoon the feel of a later hour, he wondered when he had last seen a shadow cast by any object or person on board. It was now November 26, less than a month until Christmas, and Dennis looked forward to the end of the shipping season far more than the holiday. With the wind increasing and light diminishing day by day, he felt uneasily that each passage was more perilous than the last. It was certainly more work during the long, tense night, navigating through darkness. A part of his mind dwelt on the possibility that he, the ship, and everyone were merely getting away with an act they shouldn't have dared. And more than that, he watched with dread for the evasion of consequence to end and an atonement to begin. This notion nibbled and gnawed, even when the ship sailed easily; perhaps especially then, he felt the illusory sense of safety and progress could be cracked open like an egg, and out would spill a messy reckoning for shipping late into the fall.

Eyes aloft, Dennis tried to gauge just how much longer it would be prudent to carry the upper topsail. *Genevieve* was making a steady eight knots into the head sea as the captain pushed her to be approaching DeTour before dark. Balanced against the desire for a speedy end to this passage was the unsettling knowledge that if any one item in the rig failed, a cascade of failures could result, and if that accretion grew large enough, it would amount to some greater or lesser calamity.

Still considering when to take in the upper topsail, Dennis scanned the sail and components that held it up, looking for one last sign of stress to propel him toward a decision. He eyed the chain that shackled to the yard, traveling through a sheave in the mast and ending at the wire block. From there, he followed the steel wire runner down to where it connected to the tackle. The tackle, taut but sturdy, brought the strain to the deck through rope and blocks. Next to the lead block on the port deck sat the bulky rope hauling part of the halyard, piled neatly in a beehived coil. And, lastly, between the coil and the bulwark lay Moses, curled and resting his lee side against the coil with his forepaws tucked under him.

Genevieve was rolled sharply into a trough by another powerful gust. The heel was extremely uncomfortable now. Tons of cold water swamped the starboard deck, licking at the hatch coamings and holding the lee side down, patient as a torturer, eventually allowing it to come slowly up. Once again, the water drained away, leaving a sloshed tangle of loosened coils to mark its passing.

It was definite now; the upper tops'l would have to come in, and right away. Dennis blew his whistle to alert the watch, and he ordered the helm to ease off of the wind. To his immediate relief, Dennis saw *Genevieve* stand up straighter as she fell off to a beam reach. The watch made ready at the halyard and braces, testing his patience as the ship lost precious ground to weather. A sailing ship went upwind on angles, much like a man climbing stairs; too much time spent with the wind abeam would be akin to walking back and forth on the same floor. It would not do to be off course for very long because they would not be able to point directly for DeTour when the ship was brought up to the wind again, and that would necessitate spending more time tacking, clawing to weather.

Eric groped his way aft with difficulty along the steeply sloped deck from his station at the topsail halyard.

"What is it?" Dennis asked sharply.

"I think the dog has eaten through the tops'l halyard!" Eric replied.

"You're bloody joking!" Dennis exclaimed.

"No. It's not all the way through, but one strand is gone, and the others are kind of chewed up!" Eric shouted over the wind.

Dennis would have to determine for himself the halyard's condition and whether the yard could be safely lowered into its lifts without parting. The lifts were tough, durable, steel wires that connected the ends of the yard to a spot on the mast above. When the topsail was set, the halyard hoisted the yard some twelve feet up the mast and the lifts hung slack. If the yard suddenly dropped into its lifts, they would be jerked tight, pulling up forcefully at both ends, and might crack the spar in half at its unsupported middle. It would be a terrible mess in this wind. Looking at the gnawed halyard, Dennis acknowledged it was as bad as Eric had described. Now what to do? He would like to beat the dog, but the mongrel had made himself scarce, and Dennis knew assuaging his anger would not help shorten sail. He had to come up with a solution quickly, as they continued to lose ground to leeward on this course, and in another five minutes, *Genevieve* would no longer be able to point toward DeTour when she was brought back up to the wind.

"Mr. Ringle," he heard faintly from aft. Turning, he saw the captain had come up; he immediately felt an extra jab of distress, being found in the middle of this predicament by the captain during his watch below.

"You're getting that tops'l off her, aren't you?" Thomas demanded.

Dennis tried to be concise. "Yes, sir. We have a big problem with the halyard, but I'm working on it. I—"

"Right. Clew up to the yard and we'll get back on course," Thomas broke in, shouting to be heard. "We can lower the yard later."

Of course, Dennis thought. *I should have seen the solution and might have had I borne the problem a moment longer.* Nonetheless, he berated himself for not having taken this action. The important thing to do was to relieve *Genevieve* of sail pressure in the upper topsail. The yard would swing a bit, deprived of either the steadying influence of the sail or the lifts, but the ship could return to her course. Everything could be put to rights aloft as they made progress toward home.

Thomas pulled on a long coat and some gloves while the sail was got in. He then remained on deck as Dennis oversaw the rigging of a heavy relieving line to the wire runner of the topsail halyard. Once the tackle had been effectively bypassed, the yard was safely lowered and Eric climbed the shrouds to furl the sail. Working his way along the foot-rope, Eric subdued the flogging canvas, tying gasket lines around it as he went. He was halfway through his task when he began waving and pointing to leeward. Clearly, something in the expanse of wild water over there remained unseen from the deck's altitude. Thomas scanned the leeward horizon and saw nothing at first, but scanning back, just as *Genevieve*'s stern stood tall on a crest, he thought he had seen something out of the corner of his eye. Concentrating on the area straight off from the starboard beam, he caught it briefly, definitely—perhaps a mast; he couldn't be sure. Eric completed the furl quickly, raced back to the deck, and reported: "It looks like a little schooner, but I only see one mast. She's not showing much sail, but she is laying over very far, almost on her beam ends. She might be in trouble."

Thomas sighed inwardly. He had hoped to be coming alongside the pier below the mill with the last light of day. DeTour was close. That schooner, or whatever it was, must be four miles to leeward. If he went to investigate, there would be no chance of seeing DeTour this day. The lake was becoming very lonely now. He had seen only two steamships on this passage. Most were laid up for the winter; if anything untoward happened, it would be unlikely that another ship would notice or assist him. The wind speed increased as he thought of this, and he reflected upon the idea that the schooner's master must be feeling this solitude acutely. As much as he wished to continue on home, he ordered the helm to bear away and had Dennis square the yards as *Genevieve* tore through the water downwind.

CHAPTER 2

K LARA'S STRONG FINGERS, reddened by cold, held back Bridget's equally red hair while the sick girl sent her meager lunch swimming from the schooner's lee rail. The spasms subsiding, Bridget stood up, looked into Klara's untroubled blue eyes, and asked, "How do ye manage? 'Tis the worst weather since we 'parted from Montreal."

Klara shrugged her shoulders as a gust fluttered her dry yellow hair over a subtle smile. Having left Poland not so long ago, she lacked the confidence in her spoken English to say anything meaningful. She rubbed her friend's back as an expression of sympathy.

"If we ever get in, to be sure, I'll never, ever set foot on another blessed ship," Bridget whimpered miserably. "I hate this boat; is it even going anywhere?"

Klara smiled fully this time, briefly amused at this burst of childishness from a young woman who was usually so self-assured. She, too, however, wished to see land, leave this rough lake, and get to Sault Ste. Marie, commonly known as the Soo.

The heavily laden schooner had put out from the Georgian Bay port of Midland five days earlier, carrying red brick and baled hay to the Soo. She had fought gamely against constant headwinds, but standing out into Lake Huron two days back, the little vessel began to labor in earnest, stalling near the crests as the building waves challenged her will to climb. Easing off of the wind, the ship would swing just far enough to make it up onto the back of a swell and then drop into the pit beyond. And so she slogged on, suffering her way westward.

The wind was getting stronger again, and Klara watched it make fine, furious ripples in the mounds of water; little claw marks, they seemed to her. She ventured a comforting thought. "We get in, have hot bath. Yes?" she said brightly in her limited English.

"That would be lovely," Bridget replied without much conviction. At this moment, she couldn't picture a bath soothing her raw stomach, and could anything else really matter? Klara, however, held on to the image of herself naked and melting into a steaming bathtub, her heated skin turning delightfully pink. Hopefully, there would be a good tub where she was going; she could think of no greater luxury. It had been primitive living on the schooner, making it hard to stay tidy. As the women considered the pros and cons of bathing, the mate approached from aft.

"Time to gybe again, ladies; it is change of watch and time to turn this old hay wagon around," he announced pleasantly. "You should really be below with your friends." The schooner couldn't tack through the big swells, so she was forced to turn downwind and gybe each time she went about.

"Uggh," Bridget groaned. "Can't we please stay up, sorr? We will stay out of t'way and not move at all." She couldn't bear the idea of returning to the dark, stuffy hold.

"Captain's orders, my dears," replied the mate patronizingly. "Go get tucked into that nice soft hay and rest up. We should be off the lake in the morning."

The five travelers had improvised bunks in the mate's marvelous hay, bringing some rustic comfort to the cargo hold; unused to passengers, the archaic schooner had almost no accommodations. Her afterdeck stepped up aft in the style of a former age, but it only provided some cabin space for the captain and mate, and access to the ladder leading into the hold. Klara took Bridget's arm, helping her up the inclined deck to the companionway hatch and inside the aft cabin, but here the young woman halted.

"Klara, I can't go down there again, so I can't. But I'm p-perishing cold; would you be a dear and fetch my coat up?" she asked through chattering teeth.

Klara descended from the inside cabin deck down the short ladder into the hold. Moving carefully over the uneven bricks, she wiggled her slim form between the loosely stacked bales of hay. As her eyes adjusted to the darkness, she noticed two of the other passengers, the little boys, nestled between bales and sleeping through the rough passage.

Coat in hand, Klara began to feel the different motion the schooner made paying off before the wind. The hay bales shifted ever so slightly, searching out new resting positions as their beds changed cant, coming from a sharp port heel toward upright. She disliked being among the resting cargo, in spite of its sweet smell, and made haste returning to Bridget and the aft cabin.

The maneuver continued; the sails gybed across with a sharp lurch to starboard, attended by a tremendous cracking noise, followed by a series of rippling snaps. And then, just as in any disaster, a variety of very bad things all seemed to happen concurrently: looking out of the companionway, the women watched, stunned, as the mainmast toppled overboard, strewing its rigging across the deck in front of them and into the angry lake alongside. A section of the foretopmast broke away and plunged through the cargo hatch, shattering several boards of the cover. Yelling and other chaotic noises ensued, prompting Klara to lean out of the companionway and see as much of the scene as she could. The captain and crew were all working to free the rigging from the hull. Iron shrouds and stays sunk below the schooner, but the sails and spars resisted the lake's pull and floated yet, hammering at the ship's side as waves beat them together. A shrill terrified scream echoed out of the hold, adding to the din of wind and wreckage. With spars and rigging dragging, the little vessel ceased forward motion and slumped sideways into the troughs between waves. Then, as bad as it was, elements of this evil circumstance forged together into something worse—the ship was flung sideways over the tangle of ruined rigging, the ends of which still clung to the deck. As wire rope and spars, now partially underneath the ship, began to drag heavily, they levered the hull over onto her side, allowing the broken mast to batter mercilessly at the vessel's submerged side with every other wave while water poured into the broken hatch cover at the low point in the roll.

A heavier wave hit and the schooner shook, sending Klara and Bridget reeling, landing them against the starboard cabin interior. A low rumble came through the fabric of the hull, and screaming from below began again, this time urgent and filled with agony. Recovering,

Klara pulled herself to the companionway with difficulty, desperate to see what had happened. But seeing was perhaps worse than not knowing, for the scene that confronted her appeared inconceivably horrific and hopeless. Her sense of direction was upset, proportion likewise. Familiar shapes were out of place, orientation, and context. The companionway hatch seemed to be a small island of relative safety surrounded by a chaos of dancing wires, broken lines, and the insistent greed of the icy lake. The entire lee rail was underwater, more rigging appeared to have gone over the side, and there was a figure—the captain it seemed—wrapped in some of it. Only the old cook and one deckhand remained, clinging to the mainmast stump, trying to pull some slack into the tangled mess of rope, canvas, and iron wire that had ensnared the captain, but they were having little success. The poor man flailed in his web, increasingly weighed down as saturating, hempen lines lost their buoyancy. He tried desperately both to free himself and pull his face above water for a good breath as the stricken hull dropped toward him. He was successful twice that she saw, but on his third attempt, his head didn't quite break the surface. Cursing and crying out above the wind's howl, the two men on deck seemed to redouble their efforts, heaving mightily against the wreckage. From her isolated position at the companionway, Klara saw veins bulging from their necks and foreheads as they pulled impotently against the inexorable, sodden drag of a ton of submerged rigging.

Suddenly, the shouting from below gained primacy in her awareness and she found Bridget jerking on her skirt hem from the ladder into the hold.

"Help us, Klara! Monique is caught under the bricks!"

Klara descended the steeply angled ladder and lowered herself into the hold's wet shambles. Water continued to funnel through the hatch with each descent into the trough. Some of the cargo had spilled down against the starboard side, sending the two boys into a panic as they tried to remove soaking bales of hay all tumbled up with bricks in an effort to free their aunt. Monique's upper body protruded from this mess, and the sloshing water washed across her unconscious face, toying with her graying hair in sinister rhythm with the motion of the crippled schooner.

The sight of Monique brought Klara back to the captain's last moments; suddenly, she knew hopelessness; they would all be buried under brick, hay, and the entire depth of the lake if they did not get out of the hold right away. Monique was gone.

Another large wave caught the ship deep in a trough and more cargo rumbled and slid. When two of the broken hatch boards washed completely away, the women lost their balance, tumbling into water against the starboard side.

"We get out. Out. Now, now, now!" Klara yelled. Abandoning Monique in guilt-ridden fright, Bridget and the boys obeyed and helped each other to hand holds, struggling up the small ladder aft. Once up, Klara looked out onto the deck. The situation had grown worse during her interval below. The schooner was now farther over on her side. The cargo hatch was underwater as often as it was above the surface, and there was no sign of the cook or the other deckhand. Possibly, they had been washed away in the last big roll.

They were alone. Would her story, her dreams of a new life, really end this way? Staring out of the companionway, Klara could see plainly the ship was going to sink. She contemplated numbly whether it would be better to drown or to freeze to death in this cold. Having witnessed the captain's death agony and Monique's terrible demise underwater, she thought it preferable to try to stay afloat. Freezing to death was supposed to be peaceful, or so she had always heard; you just fell asleep and didn't wake up. No thrashing, or gasping, or watching the sky blur away into the distance separated from you by an eternity of water.

The boys behind her were crying now, and the sound brought her attention back to practical matters. She was shivering in her soaked clothing; her skirts were heavy with the weight of absorbed liquid. As meaningless as it seemed, she wedged herself into the corner of the cabin to wriggle free of her skirt and petticoat, shamelessly baring her long muscular legs. She wrung the garments out to be as dry as possible. Dressing again with difficulty, she felt cold still, but lighter and a little better. She now decided to risk a climb out onto the madly canted deck to see whether there was any chance of floating free of this wreck. Timing her movements carefully, she gained the upside of the companionway hatch, and from there, she could almost see over the windward rail. A coil of rope dangled from a pinrail above her head. Reaching for the rope, she caught and pulled herself to the weather rail during the next short roll. The wind's cruel power could be seen and felt up here. She was struck anew by the majesty and violence of the forces clawing away at the ship. But then she saw something utterly beautiful—a lovely looking sailing ship was only a couple of miles off and racing toward her. Standing up straight and rolling only slowly, the ship was a symbol of dependable purpose in this gray turmoil of waves and terror. Overjoyed, Klara waved her hands over her head, whooping loudly with excitement until she was almost flung from her tenuous perch on the pinrail as a result of this dangerous indiscretion. Sobered by her near loss of balance, she caught the rope again and lowered herself to the companionway hatch. The ship was on its way to them! She had to tell the others.

Good God, it's cold, and soon we'll likely be wet as well, Dennis thought gloomily as he cleared away from *Genevieve*'s side in the ship's boat. It had taken some skillful handling to get the boat launched and manned in the big swell that was running. As *Genevieve* braced her yards around and filled away, a premature twilight settled over her, foreshadowing the long night to come. Dennis was in a state of agitated foreboding: to be cast loose, so to speak, from the known protection of *Genevieve*'s wooden body into this bitter, heaving lake with darkness approaching had shoved him closer to the spectral calamity he had been dreading. Suppressing his fear, he considered the task at hand. His best hope now was to perform every job perfectly, prepare for each maneuver, and leave nothing more to chance. He watched Benjamin and Risto each pulling an oar, rowing downwind toward the beaten schooner while Norman prepared the bow line for throwing. It was good to have Norman along; the old seaman was as tough as leg meat, and he had survived so many assaults of man and nature that it was impossible to believe he could ever be laid flat.

Dennis calmed down as he gained confidence in his boat handling. The swell was big, but they were managing. He steered to pass behind the schooner and into its lee. The scene of the tortured ship was the stuff of his worst fears; dragging her main rigging beneath her, she lay low in the water, just about on her beam ends, drinking in the lake through her shattered main hatch. A trained eye wasn't needed to see that the ship was clearly doomed; she might float for another half an hour, but one couldn't be sure. As the hull filled, it would permit more water through the hatch and the filling would continue to accelerate rapidly. At some point soon, down she would go. At least there wouldn't be a discussion of saving the vessel with the captain and crew. Hopefully, he could grab the crew and then be back aboard *Genevieve* before there was any chance of being separated or lost in the dark.

The schooner, waterlogged as she was, rose and fell sluggishly as the waves began to break over her.

"Easy now; stop pulling!" Dennis called to the oarsmen. The waterlogged hulk drifted toward him in slow, short rolls. Her movements looked predictable enough to take off the crew. Would he have to make two trips? Was there time? At present, he could see only one figure and two heads poking out of the aft companionway. They looked like a woman and children. He would come in close by the people and have them jump for it.

"Okay, boys, we're going in close. Pull together!" he shouted. "Be ready to get your oars in." If the oars became ensnared in loose rigging or caught on the ship's side, it could be disastrous.

Norman called to him, "There's only a woman and children. Should I throw the bow line, or do you want to put me aboard to hold us in?" Dennis studied the solitary woman on deck. She was tall and alert, having deftly accomplished the dangerous traverse from the companionway across the rail to the stump of the main mast where she had secured herself. Dennis judged her quickly.

"Throw her the line!" he called. "Oars in!"

Norman threw the line. The woman caught it and made a valiant attempt to hold the boat close, but she released the line when the hulls surged apart from fear of being torn from her position and swept away. Norman coiled in the line and threw again. The girl caught it close to its end, pulled in quickly, and wrapped it around the spider band on the mainmast stump. Dennis watched, surprised, as she used the extra friction to ease the line out slowly under heavy strain and hauled it in again as it became slack. Clever girl! Another big wave smashed at the upturned bottom of the schooner, drenching the girl with overwash. Water streamed through her yellow hair from above, even while it surged through her skirts from below.

"Come on!" Dennis shouted to the boys in the companionway as he came alongside, desperate to make the grab and get clear. But whether from fear, shock, or paralysis, they wouldn't move until the tall one holding the line shrieked at them, "Go! Go! We must go!" That seemed to be enough for the first one to come to a sudden decision; he took two rapid steps, barely touching the sloped deck, and landed in the boat between Risto and Benjamin. The second boy was gathering nerve when the helpless ship was hit by the next big wave. His fingers broke from their handhold and he tumbled gracelessly into the lake. Norman, as quick as a diving osprey, shot his hand into the water and pulled him into the boat.

Now a great change occurred—the distance to the companionway hatch became smaller, and a great sucking sound could be heard emanating from it, as water poured continuously through the main hatch. Settling lower quickly, the water slopped tentatively into the companionway as well, before confidently gurgling in nonstop. Bridget jumped and was caught by Norman, but then Dennis wanted to get away. The ship was going down and would willingly take them along.

"How many are left on board?" he demanded of Bridget. Numb with cold and shivering violently, she pointed to the deck.

"Just Klara, sorr."

"What of the crew?" Dennis asked, already sure of the answer.

"Gone," was all she managed to say.

He resolved to hold on a moment longer and bring away this brave young woman who had made it possible to save the other three. She had let the line go in order to move back to the companionway for a clean jump. The hulls began to separate as another big roller swamped the ship, treating the hulk more as a part of the lake than a rider upon it. Dennis ordered Risto and Benjamin to put the oars out once again and make ready to dash in.

Meanwhile, hampered by her skirts, Klara wiggled out of them for the second time that day. Free from encumbrance, she struggled through a series of handholds as quickly as she could to the companionway. Pulling her hair back from her face, she watched the rescue boat surging in and prepared for her jump. The dying schooner was not to let her go so easily, however; in a final act of treachery, the sinking ship righted itself for just a moment and put an impossible jumping distance between her and her would-be rescuers. She ran to the rail. It was ridiculously easy now, but it was too late; the stern was going down first, the wheel was just awash.

The boat surged in once again as the men strained at the oars and she jumped, certain there would be no other chance. She tumbled over the other bodies in the boat and landed hard against the gunnel on her forearm, audibly cracking it. Pain burned through the fractured limb, ending the creeping wet chill that threatened to own her as she slid down the boat's inside. She began shaking nonetheless, and Norman settled her in the bottom of the boat. Looking up from her pain-wracked, heart-shaped face, he witnessed the schooner's last moment; first her foremast, then her bow, and then her bowsprit slid below the marauding waves, already forgotten by the surface of the pitiless lake.

CHAPTER 3

BLACK RUM; IT passed from hand to hand tracing the long vee of the fo'c'sle, pausing to be poured, wetting the chipped enamel of tin cups before being ferried along again. The mood in the fo'c'sle was happy, in fact, even jubilant. Sometimes the rum bottle experienced a prolonged tilt, and voices down the line, fearing for the size of their ration, called, "Hey! That's enough! Send it along, ya skunk!" The bottle then carried on, making its way eventually to Norman, and he poured long. "Hey! Come on!" came the chorus of voices. Norman stopped and looked at the men sitting across the table from him, then scanned the faces of the men on his own bench, meeting each one's eye with an expression of innocent bewilderment. Everyone quieted down, anticipating what kind of justification the cook might offer, but when he had drawn the silence as far as four or five seconds, Norman quickly slopped a second serving of rum into his cup without looking down. "Hey, that's not fair! Come on, now!" the men shouted and laughed, in a mixture of mock and real annoyance at Norman's theatrics, as the bottle drifted on. Eventually, it had made the circuit of the fo'c'sle past twelve men and returned (empty) to Thomas from whence it had come. Thomas continued the comedy by shaking the empty bottle over his own cup and looking into the drained jug, to be certain the rum was gone. The crew roared with laughter at this uncommon display of levity from the old man.

Thomas made a quick toast: "Another good season, lads. Cheers."

"Cheers," erupted all around, and the crew swigged from their cups in great good spirits. The ship had come alongside before noon. The sails had been furled and a protective ice boom had been placed around *Genevieve* and then filled with straw to safeguard her from ice damage.

It was close to sunset now, and the workday had been curtailed early to allow for a celebratory drink. The pent-up strain of the past few weeks eased out of faces and limbs as rum and relaxation brought home the truth to the men, individually and as a group, that they had completed their work for this year—they had safely delivered their ship and cargo home. For many of the men, witnessing the old schooner founder had made them doubly thankful to be here now, relishing this moment of survival and success. Amid laughter and chatter, Thomas made his exit up the fo'c'sle ladder; he had to spend some time with William, and then he wanted to be off home.

Down in the fo'c'sle, Norman produced a second bottle to refill cups. When everyone had some more rum, Norman called for a second toast: "I think we should ask our newest deckhand to give the next toast—Morris."

Morris was surprised by the honor but, unimaginatively steady as always, felt equal to the task.

"Um—buh, it's nice to be back here, and I'm glad we didn't sink. *Genevieve* sure is a good bargentine."

"*Genevieve*," sang out the group on cue.

Whereas earlier there had been banter, conversation now became slower as the entire crew listened to one man or another recount his part of or perspective on the season's last passage. Liquor warmed cheeks by this time, and speakers tripped on the occasional word.

"What d'you think that old schooner was doing out in Lake Huron so late anyway?" asked Eric.

"Same thing as us: one more cargo," replied Dennis.

"I think she was doing something else," asserted Norman conspiratorially.

Morris took the bait. "What d'ya think she was doing?"

"I'm pretty sure she was sinking," he replied evenly.

A second of shocked silence clashed against this unsayable jest as each man asked himself whether this was funny. It was Dennis who responded:

"Really, Norman, you go a bit too far." But then a sneaking grin turned the corners of his mouth, betraying a small hypocrisy, provoking snickers and then open laughter around the fo'c'sle, until finally a wave of guffaws washed over any remaining pangs of conscience.

As if to atone for his laughter, Eric said, "It was too bad, all the same, to see the old schooner go down—and her crew."

Norman thwarted melancholic talk, countering, "Well, at least we saved the two young fellows and two pretty girls."

"Where are the girls? Where did they go?" Benjamin asked of the group. "I didn't see them go."

"The old man took them and the boys ashore a couple of hours ago. I think it was while you were stowing lines in the laz," Dennis replied.

"I thought they might at least have said good afternoon for the effort we made."

"Ha-ha. I see your problem. You missed out," Norman interjected. Now he pointed at Benjamin, lowering his voice in accusation. "You were hoping for a kiss!"

"Well, no. But, but, well, at least a little gratitude could be shown!" Benjamin flushed defensively.

"How much gratitude were you hoping for?" Norman pursued, delighting in squeezing Benjamin, now that, figuratively, he had him between his two hands. "From which one?"

The tipsy men all jumped in at this point, some pressing Benjamin for an admission of some kind, while others threw out lubricious suggestions as to which girl was fairer.

"Bridget has more meat on her bones! Klara has the lovely eyes! Redheads are fierier!"

Norman sat, quietly enjoying the way he had stirred the crew and put Benjamin on the spot. It fell to Dennis to settle the group.

"Easy, boys, easy. I'm sorry to tell you…those girls are both spoken for."

Thomas found William at his desk, attended by Moses, sleepily curled up next to his chair. A fire was burning down in the potbellied stove, radiating a small comfort that would never be found in the cold, silent mill outside the office door.

"Oh, good, you've come in," began William. "I wanted to see when you would have the new saws and machinery hoisted out."

"We'll have some out tomorrow, some out the day after," replied Thomas a little wearily.

"How about the log-hauling tractor, which day will that come up? If I could, I'd like to have it out early."

Fatigue hobbled the pace of thought in Thomas's mind. He tried to remember where the tractor had been placed in the stowage plan, but he simply couldn't think of its location.

"Listen; I can't quite remember where any one item is right now. We have a very full load of supplies, some of which have to be moved to get at the machinery, and then lifting the machinery out, even in parts, will take time; everything is enormously heavy." Thomas pulled out his chair and sat facing William.

"All right," William replied. "It's just that once we have them up, there'll be plenty to do: I'd like to get the tractor running and out to Camp A. We want to get the other engines housed; we have foundations in for them and plenty of planking for the building. At the same time, one of us needs to get out to our northern plats and check on Camp C up there. We have a lot of new men, but here's the bad news: We have Cedric Inch cutting in the plats immediately north of us along Carlton Creek."

This was unsettling. Inch ran a small mill, much like their own, and the McGrath brothers had had trouble with him and his lumberjacks many times over the years. Inch had been known to cut a "round forty," meaning he would harvest trees beyond the borders of the plats he had bought or leased. The McGraths also suspected him of outright log piracy since their log count was always off in any stream they shared, but they could never prove it with hard evidence.

As Thomas had been processing the news about Cedric Inch, William had been prattling along about expanding contracts for lumber in the coming year. Hearing the onslaught of words again for their substance, rather than as just plain noise, Thomas was now overwhelmed and exhausted.

"Will, Willie." He held up his hand to hold back the flow. "I need some time to settle back in. Tomorrow, we'll get supplies up—the next day, the engines. I'll hear about the other matters after *Genevieve* is taken care of; once she's emptied, I want to send down her yards and unbend sail. I also have to see how Annie is doing and help these unfortunate boys and girls move along, but in a couple of days, I'll be caught up and ready to help. This last trip has been long on hours and short on sleep between bad weather and the schooner business. I'm a bit too tired to give you my full attention at the moment."

William now ran an assessing eye over his brother, taking in his four-day growth of beard, puffy red-rimmed eyelids, and wind-tousled hair. He suddenly realized that the captain looked to be a weather-beaten remnant of his usual self: tattered, faded, and worn threadbare over the course of the last passage. Wishing to maintain the contact with Thomas for a little longer, William made a move to the corner cabinet and poured them each a small tumbler of whiskey.

"Sorry, Thomas. You do look dead on your feet. It will all keep, of course." William passed him a glass. "We'll have a quick one before you go home. Tell me about the schooner and the rescue."

Thomas recounted the story, interrupted periodically by William's thirst for details.

"Hmmph. That was mighty close. Imagine if you hadn't been shortening sail then and there—what might have happened?" William contemplated.

"Yes, the world would be less two nice little boys and deprived of two charming young ladies," Thomas said with a smile. His face turned grave slowly. "I wish I could have been in time to save the crew and the boys' aunt." He paused for a moment in reflection and then said, "To finish up the story, we slid down to leeward with *Genevieve* and picked up the boat. Norman set the girl's arm, and we made our way under easy sail through the night."

"Ah, but that isn't the end of the story," William disagreed. "Who are these girls, where are they going together, and why were they aboard the schooner?"

Thomas couldn't suppress a grin; it was conspicuous that his brother had not asked about the boys.

"All right, now we are at the meat of the meal, I see. Believe it or not, they're lonely hearts traveling westward to marry men they've been in correspondence with."

"You mean…?"

"Yes, they are betrothed. Their intended husbands have paid for the passage."

"They might have spent a little extra to get them on a steamer!" William spouted indignantly.

"Well, the story is that they missed the last passenger boat by a day, so the schooner seemed like the best option."

"What will they do now?" William asked.

"I guess they'll rest a while, and then we'll get everybody up to the Soo, where they were destined for. The boys have an uncle there—that will be a sad meeting—and the girls will connect with the train line."

"A sad meeting?"

"The boys lost their aunt on the schooner. She was trapped under the cargo when it shifted," Thomas answered.

"The poor children. They're staying with Boyle, I understand?"

"Yes, and I have the two ladies at my place."

"You'll be a bit crowded, won't you? They could have stayed at my house," William said.

Thomas threw back his head and looked at the ceiling in a feigned attitude of amazement.

"My God, haven't they been through enough?"

William's mood softened and he chuckled at this and at himself.

"No, but honestly, William, they could use a little mothering to get them on their feet again. The good Mrs. Boyle and Annie will set our foundlings right. And now I must get on my feet again as well," Thomas said, waving off a proffered refill of his glass and standing.

"I have to get home and see how Annie is managing with our guests."

"All right, good night, then. Sleep well," William said, letting him go reluctantly. He listened to Thomas's departing footsteps, slowly being swallowed into the cold silence of the empty mill, and wondered abstractedly, *Why had the tall woman been wearing trousers?* There was something disturbing about that.

Thomas climbed the frozen planked road, up the long rise to the top of the hill that hid his house from view. The sun had just gone, and over the crest, the landscape glowed blue beneath a thin blanket of recent snow. He was cheered by the sight of rising smoke emanating from both chimneys of his ample two-story home. A huge silver birch, stripped of its leaves, blocked his view of the kitchen window, but the front room beckoned softly with the languid effusion of curtained lamplight. *Comfort,* he thought. Tonight, he would be truly warm for the first time in over a week. A good hot wash, followed by dinner, and then a few hours spent with the children stoking up a blazing fire in the hearth, until he could feel heat pulsing from the ends of his toes. He planned on heating some extra bricks to warm the bed right through. And then he would curl up next to Anne, snug under a weight of blankets, and sink into an oblivious slumber until dawn.

These thoughts carried him down the lane. Passing through the front gate, he mounted the porch, lifted the bronze door handle, and stepped inside. No one was to be seen in the front room, so he took a moment to savor the familiar domestic scents of his abode. Arriving from the cold keen air, the inside warmth carried subtleties of cinnamon, cloves, wood smoke, lamp oil, and the ever-present pine; stronger were aromas of venison stew and baking bread; and then, faintest of all, but distinct and most dear to him, were blended traces of cardamom and ginger—the exotic fragrance of Anne's hair. A thrill ran through him, vaulting over mere comfort; he would see her any second now. He hurried through the dining room and into the kitchen.

But in the kitchen, the room's mood did not match his own. Thomas's sense of wellbeing staggered at the sight of his two houseguests sitting, staring into teacups at the kitchen table. They looked fresher than when he had seen them last, but still tired. Somehow, he was surprised to find them there. Klara noticed his entrance first, lifting her heart-shaped face from contemplations of her teacup, just as he shifted his gaze to Anne, who was silently, vigorously stirring the stew.

"Good evening there," he said awkwardly. It was not the greeting he had planned.

"Hullo." "Allo." The girls were the first to respond in their varied accents.

"You've come home," Anne answered flatly, briefly looking up from the stewpot. *A chilly reception,* Thomas thought. *Something's amiss, or maybe it's the presence of the houseguests.*

"Yes," he replied, "in for the winter at last." He moved toward her and the stove, hoping he might thaw both his body and his welcome by physical proximity. He removed his gloves, unbuttoned his coat, and bathed his spread fingers in the radiance of hot iron. Anne was unyielding, however, displaying an extraordinary concern for the delicate morsels at the bottom of the pot.

"Pardon me," she said, wanting him to move aside as she briskly opened the oven door and inspected the bread. *Definitely upset,* Thomas realized. He decided to be equally unyielding to her oblique message; as the oven door closed, he resumed his position by the stove, warming his hands. After a moment, he edged closer to Anne, crowding her slightly, provoking her to confront him.

"Dinner will be a little while yet," she said in an attempt to move him along.

"I think I'll wait for it right here by the stove," he replied with an expansive smile, seemingly unmindful of Anne's implication that he was in the way.

"It's wonderful to be in a warm house, am I right, ladies?" he asked the girls at the table, shamelessly strengthening his position with assured and unavoidable agreement.

"'Tis indeed, Captain," Bridget answered for them, and she was about to add to her answer when she felt Klara's foot touch her leg under the table. When Bridget turned slightly to meet her eye, Klara hinted, with a subtle tilt of her head toward the doorway, that they should leave the room.

"'Tis lovely to be warm and dry," Bridget continued. "Perhaps you'll excuse us. We'll leave you and sit by the hearth," she said as the two girls stood.

"But of course," Thomas answered pleasantly.

Finally alone in the room, Thomas made a second effort at a greeting. He stepped behind Anne and put his hands lightly upon her shoulders, but before he could utter a word, she shrugged him off. Opening the oven door once again, she fussily shifted loaves of bread around for even baking. At last, she began to speak in a low voice.

"The children are sick," she began matter-of-factly. "George is almost over it, but Molly and Curt are still running a fever." Thomas sensed that the slash board had been pulled and the floodgate was now open.

"Molly was sick in the bed—pretty hard to clean up because, earlier today, the pump stopped working."

"Oh, it probably wants a new flapper," Thomas interjected helpfully.

"Whatever might be the cause," said Anne, her blue eyes flashing the cold blink of distant sea ice, "I have been hauling water from William's pump; seven trips, just to manage laundry, bathing the children, and cooking. Then, without warning or even a note from you, I am given two houseguests who certainly need baths—an additional four trips. Now you're here, but we are out of water."

Fleeting, disparate thoughts raced through Thomas's mind as he tried to process the news. He should look in on the children; he would see to the pump tomorrow; it would be more difficult to obtain a bath now; with two five-gallon pails, Anne would have carried over eighty pounds per trip, multiplied by eleven trips from the other side of the hill. That was…that was—his weary mind slid to a stop. It was a great deal of work even for a strong woman, his train of thoughts concluded.

"Meanwhile, you have been at the mill enjoying a drink, no doubt, with your brother while the pretty one has shown up here in your pants!" she concluded. The sight of Klara wearing an article of his clothing had imbued Anne with an unaccountable, primal jealousy.

"Maybe I should have let everyone drown." Thomas felt wronged; he certainly hadn't tarried with the crew or with William, only observed a brief civility with both. And the only reason Klara wore his old pants was that he was the only one on board with a spare set, clean and dry. Norman had borrowed them on her behalf, saying it was only decent she should have something to cover her legs. How humorous to think that had he neglected his duty to the distressed schooner, he would be better off at this moment.

"That's not what I meant and you know it," Anne said, but more softly.

The little rage ran out of him, and then he saw his wife as she stood— she was tired. Could she be as tired as he was? She was worried about the children, and perhaps cheated of the homecoming she wished to provide him by unforeseen difficulty and frail houseguests. He decided he must let her last remark pass unrefuted and do his best to shore her up.

"Annie, come to me, dear," he began while gently taking her arm and drawing her close. She resisted only slightly, abandoning the spoon in the stewpot, and once he had his arms around her, he said, "I'm home now, and I'm sorry for these circumstances. I'll check on the children now, and tomorrow, I'll fix the pump. Everything will come easier tomorrow."

She began to relax into his arms, surrounding him with her own. And so he kissed her forehead, and then her ear, and then her cheek. Fully relaxed now, he slid his hands slowly down her back and impishly squeezed her left buttock. She pulled back and swatted him, but her eyes gave him the smile he had waited for.

"You are a bad man."

"I suppose I am," he replied and hugged her again.

CHAPTER 4

December 15, 1891

"MICHIGAMME, NEXT STOP," called the train conductor as he passed through the car. "Michigamme; transfers to points west; this train continues on to L'Anse, Houghton, Hancock, and Copperrr Countreeee." The last line was delivered with a ringmaster's flair and seemed to follow him into the next car.

Klara sat across from Bridget, looking out of the window intermittently. They had chosen to travel together this far, but the moment of parting was at hand: Bridget was transferring to another line and on to Minnesota, while Klara was bound for Lake Junction on the Keweenaw Peninsula via this train.

"Well, Klara, you'll be sure to send some word to me of how you're faring, won't you?"

Klara nodded and pointed back to her. "You write?"

"To be sure I will," she answered, her eyes welling dangerously close to tears.

"We've been through so much together and come very far."

The train slowed and the girls stood up as it rolled to a stop in the station. Bridget took up a small sack that held the few possessions she had accumulated in DeTour Village. They embraced for a moment; then, with a kiss on the cheek and a soft "goodbye," Bridget took her leave and stepped down off the train and into the gray afternoon.

Klara took her seat again and watched the Irish girl disappear into the depot where she would wait for her connection. There was a small thump under her feet, and then the train began to roll ponderously forward once more. She leaned her head against the window and closed her eyes, hoping she could fall asleep. She had not felt this alone in a very long time, except perhaps for the moments when the schooner was sinking, but this was entirely different; at this moment, she had no company and didn't know a soul in this wide, wild land to which she had committed herself.

As the train arced slowly north, she marveled at the endlessness of the forested terrain, and wondered who had decided to come out here, so incredibly far from other people, other towns. She hoped she wouldn't continue to be lonely. Ah, but then there was Anton. She wondered what her intended husband would be like. Hopefully, he would be kind and good company, like her father, or the captain. She had enjoyed staying with the McGrath family in the end. Although the first night had been awkward, Anne had warmed to her, and she could see that Anne and the captain had a good life together. One night, she had stumbled upon them while the captain was stealing a kiss in the kitchen. Anne had been embarrassed, but the captain had just smiled.

Klara hoped she would have that sort of warmth between her and Anton. His letters had been very nice, and he looked very handsome in the photograph he had sent her. Although she knew he had dark hair and a bushy moustache, that he was tall, and that he was a pump man in the copper mines, so much was left to be discovered: Was he a tidy person? Did he like music and dancing? Was he ever moody? Did he have the makings of a good father? The thoughts swirled around in her head until, suddenly, she realized that thinking about him, even though she didn't really know him, had made her less lonely. She wished she still had his photograph to look at, but it had been lost with the schooner. As the gray afternoon turned into early night, she felt a building excitement, knowing she would be meeting this complete stranger with whom she was barely acquainted in the morning.

The train rumbled north through the wooded land, pausing briefly at L'Anse. Onward it ran into the night at a reduced speed of twenty-five miles per hour, and when it arrived in Houghton, it stopped. Well-off passengers staying aboard reclined in the Pullman car, whereas Klara and others in all classes assumed various sleeping positions on their seats. After a fitful night, trying not to lie on her splinted arm, Klara awoke with a stiff neck to the pulse of a slow roll on the train. Following a brief stop in Hancock, hers would be the next stop. Making her way to the water closet at the end of the car, she took some extra time to tidy herself in preparation for meeting Anton. Her toilet complete, she returned to her seat and tried to keep her mind from racing through all the possibilities of this first meeting with her future husband. Oh, how she hoped he would like her!

The train slowed and began braking, rolling very slowly into the station. She took her small sack, gathered her coat around her, and looked at the crowd of people waiting under a light snowfall at the depot. She saw several men who could be Anton, but she was unsure.

The train stopped. This was the end of her long journey, the moment she had been preparing for. Her stomach fluttered and the blood pumped more swiftly through her limbs. When the doors opened, the conductor helped her down onto the trampled, snowy ground outside the depot. Reunions were being made around her; men hurried to and fro, boots squeaking in the snow, helping women with their bags. The various young, dark-haired, mustached men she had suspected of being Anton had met other passengers by now, so a tremor of worry rippled through her mind. *What if no one is coming to meet me?* The captain had telegraphed her arrival to Anton ahead of time. She hoped neither of them had mistaken the date. As the depot cleared, she was approached by a young blonde man of medium stature, thickly built, wearing a brown overcoat and carrying a photograph in his large gloved hand.

"Klara?" he asked as he got close.

"Yes," she replied in English, not knowing what to expect.

"It is me, Anton," he said in Polish.

She was crestfallen. The man before her didn't look at all like the photograph she had had. She had spent so much time looking at the photograph, imagining him, speculating on such subjects as how he would walk, how his voice would sound, and how he might gesture that she had animated the picture of him in her head almost to the point of becoming a real being. Could she have imagined too much? No, this was definitely a different man. Her expression gave away her turmoil for suddenly his face hardened before he quickly forced a smile and spoke again.

"Come." He reached for her hand. "We have some distance to go before we can get out of the weather."

She pulled back her hand, asking, "Who are you? You are not Anton."

"I am; don't be silly."

"Anton has dark hair. I have seen his photograph."

"The photo I sent you was not the best for light or shading. I'm sorry."

"What about the mustache?"

"I shaved. I thought you might prefer this."

She was unconvinced, but she had to ask herself whether it could be true. Who else knew she would be here? No one, and yet.... He was becoming impatient, shifting his weight from one foot to the other. A faint scowl molded his features with an omen of harshness, as he looked at her broken arm poking out of the sling under her coat. She knew she must save this beginning. He wasn't unpleasant, just not as she imagined or remembered. Where else would she go anyway, now that she had reached the end of her journey? What could she do but believe him and go along? With an uncertain smile, she took his hand.

"I'm sorry. I lost the photograph. Perhaps I forgot—"

"Never mind," he said, waving his free hand dismissively and then changing his tone. "We'll travel home now. I have a carriage for the day waiting outside the depot," he finished softly.

Chapter 5

January 11, 1892

THE JANUARY NIGHT is long in the Upper Peninsula of Michigan. The sun dips behind the treetops at about 5:30 in the afternoon and won't be seen again until 8:30 in the morning, but aside from this measurement of passing hours of darkness, there exists a timelessness that is folded into the quiet of the northern woods between dusk and dawn. Down through the centuries, sounds of the forest have repeated themselves; faint footfalls of red fox, lynx, gray wolf and deer; the whoosh of a great horned owl's wings diving between branches in pursuit of pine squirrels. And then there is the easy whispering of pine needles, slowing the restless breeze high above, sounding softly and alone at times or blended with the velvet chase of predators and prey into the snowed, murmured notes of a music that has played since before the tallest pines had been mere saplings among other ancients.

Dawn introduces new sounds. Sounds from men—men who have little reason to be quiet, who have no fear of announcing their whereabouts, who hide not, but create openings where they can see and be seen.

The men of the lumbercamp were not all up at once. The early ones rose in darkness, chore boys who stirred coals in the stoves and built up the faded fires. Next came the cooks and their helpers, clanking metal implements in pots and pans, popping bread loaves in and out of the ovens, hot and aromatic. Teamsters began to put their horses into their tack, feeling and patting the big brutes as they prepared them for their day. And at about the same time, the lumberjacks, or shanty boys as they were sometimes called, crawled sleepily out of their snug bunks and pulled on heavy socks, long underwear, and felted woolen clothes, all of which had dried overnight by the stove. In twilight, the loud banging of a heavy wooden stick on a large battered iron pot would announce breakfast and a mass shuffle would begin toward the cook hut.

Breakfast being complete, the sun rose behind the trees and the real noise began; the teamsters pulled out with their horses and sledges, the lumberjacks made their way to the cutting, and soon the air was filled with the song of the saw on tree trunk, accompanied by the dissonant axes of limbers and sawyers dividing the giants of the forest into manageable logs. Every so often, the din of axes and saws would halt, punctuated by a warning cry of "Timberrr!" and the jarring crash of another leviathan brought to earth.

Thomas rode into Camp D amid the noise and activity of an average January day. The weather was cold, the snow was deep, and the men were trying to make the most of the short hours of daylight. Arthur, his handsome appaloosa horse, had no trouble clip-clopping along the ice road in his spiked shoes, pulling the light load of provisions for the cookhouse. Leaving Arthur in the charge of some teamsters, Thomas walked out to the cuttings to find Svensson because they were due shortly to be at the northern boundary of this plat to meet with the land surveyor and Cedric Inch. Svensson was the boss for Camp D, and he had sent a message that trees had been cut and removed from the northern part of their plat when he had been out to walk through the area. On the next day, he had returned to the same place and found men from Inch's crew sawing into another tree. He had tried to intervene, but was told he was mistaken about the boundary line, even though it had been well marked. The boundary had been close to the bottom of a short hill, a ripple in the rocky land. Adjacent to the north were acres that Inch had contracted for, and these had been well harvested nearby. What Svensson saw next was that twenty-five or more prime trees had been removed from the land the McGrath brothers had bought in, down to the bottom of the hill.

Having met the land surveyor and Svensson, Thomas walked in their company to the disputed area, only to find that Inch himself was supervising a crew of three sawing away at another tree. Thomas rankled at the pure gall of the man, to think he would show up to discuss an item he was in the process of stealing. Inch looked up to greet the newcomers.

Inch was a man of average height, but he looked rather taller as he carried his great bulk in front of him, suspended and stayed by the straightness of his back. All of his features were round and thick but not soft. He did not appear corpulent, for his had been a hard-working body, but the impression of size was left. His puffy face was clean-shaven, displaying clearly that the individual orbs of his cheeks as well as his broad nose were infiltrated by a network of red and blue veins, a legacy of his years spent out of doors and a warm romance with the bottle. Above the field of broken blood vessels, he presented a pair of blue eyes, trained to convey an attitude of innocent amazement that often served him well in disarming the aggrieved.

Thomas would not exchange pleasantries with a man who was robbing him. He had known Inch would rely on civility to dampen the heat of the upcoming discussion.

"Inch, what are you doing here?" he asked.

"Why, I'm cutting timber, just like you," Inch replied with a very slight upward push of his guiltless eyebrows. As the men behind him continued to saw, Thomas vowed that though they might fell this tree, they would not have it.

"You are cutting on my plat," Thomas said. "You've already taken a good many trees, and I'll want them back."

"Your plat? I'm sure the boundary is along the low land here. I think you're mistaken," Inch replied and set his mouth in the faintest of smiles. Together with his eyes, his mouth hinted that Thomas had made a fantastic suggestion and that he, Inch, was tolerating it as though it had come from a small child.

The land surveyor stepped forward at this point with some pages traced from the plat book. "Mr. Inch, we clearly blazed out the boundary in the fall," he said, indicating with his finger some remaining places where boundary trees had been marked. "Surely you didn't miss these marks."

Confronted with proof, Inch admitted, "Perhaps I did see something, now that you point it out, but these surveys are sometimes old and open to interpretation. How well do your maps show this rise? It seemed to me that the line was meant to run along the bottom of the hill."

The surveyor spread his pages against the side of a tall, recently made stump. As he began the process of arguing the line with Inch, Thomas sent Svensson to round up some men to occupy the boundary and begin cutting.

In a little while, after a certain amount of chaffering and prevarication, Inch was cornered as perhaps he always knew he would be. With the facility of a stage player, he began a new act.

"Well, good gracious, I don't know how we could have missed the marks," he said, ignoring the fact that he had earlier admitted to seeing them. Next, he moved on to contrition. "Thomas, I'm terribly sorry; we had no idea we were across the line." His face was suitably open and guileless as only he could mold it.

The expectation in polite society is that, once an apology is tendered, the wronged party accepts the apology and the matter is ended, but Thomas had known Inch and many characters like him, working in corners of the world where law might exist but was rarely enforced. Inch's apology didn't move him whatsoever.

"Inch, I'm going to want every log that has been hauled from this plat."

Now Inch was wounded. "But, Thomas, how can that be fair? My men cut those trees and did all the labor to make them ready. Besides, I don't know which ones came from here precisely. Surely we can just bring over a few loads to your road and be square."

"It was your mistake; it will be your loss. I want everything back or I'm taking this to the marshal. It will be more than a few loads. I count twenty-eight trees, including the one your men are still sawing. That will be twenty loads."

Inch had one additional gambit—calculated more to infuriate than to be a suggestion of restitution, for to Inch, this was merely a game—he already had the logs.

"Thomas, I wonder whether we could come to some sort of deal over this."

"What kind of deal? All I really want is my timber. Any other deal would have to involve a lot of money."

"Precisely," Inch agreed. "I've been thinking of paying a visit to you and William recently. I know you're going through a big expansion, so you could probably use a partner in your new endeavor. I can be a big help to you. We can share our supplies and stocks for mutual benefit. Why, if we come to an agreement, these logs won't matter that much. I could throw them in as a show of good faith."

Thomas was momentarily astonished at the man's temerity to offer to return stolen property as payment for a share in his company. He quickly determined he must stick with retrieving his logs and ignore Inch's impertinence.

"Listen, Cedric," he said with a short laugh, "the only deal is that I get my logs back or I go to the marshal. If that happens, it won't go well for you. So, try giving that some thought. Svensson will be expecting the loads equivalent to twenty-eight trees, assuming your men finish cutting this one. You have until the end of the week."

Inch shook his head sadly and silently, all the while holding on to his slight, tight-lipped, amused grin.

Riding back to the mill, Thomas was still reeling from the thought of his interview with Inch. The man had no belief he would be part of the McGrath Brothers Lumber Company. He had simply shot that bolt to annoy him. Inch had worked for his father two decades previously until he had been dismissed for pilfering planks and selling them on. He was faithless, so there was no way they could possibly work together. Thomas wondered how many of his logs would get returned. He knew the marshal would not be anxious to get involved in this—the man was a bit hopeless in his opinion—it would be up to him to retrieve his own goods. In matters of this sort, there was no one better to talk to than Norman. Arriving back at the mill, Thomas unhitched Arthur and led him to the stable; then he turned toward *Genevieve* to seek out his cook.

"Blockade," responded the cook at the end of Thomas's story.

"Blockade? Norman, this isn't the Napoleonic wars. We're not the British Navy. We can't beat about day after day hoping to snap up a sluggish merchantman. What do you mean?"

"No, no, we're not the navy, but you can dam up his road with men and horse teams and simply demand the logs as agreed if they aren't handed over."

"That could be costly. I'll be keeping ten or twelve men idle waiting to take back the logs."

"It will cost something, maybe as much as the timber, but probably not. The important thing is it'll cost Inch much more. He'll get nothing for his effort. As it is now, you'll be the only one to suffer the loss."

"Hmmph. You're right," Thomas replied.

Norman delighted in trouble. It didn't bother him to tread the crumbling edge of a dangerous precipice. He always had a plan and an abiding, ruthless self-confidence that had seen him through many a rough misadventure. With a savage twinkle in his eye, he said, "I'll come out and set it up. We'll have everything back in a couple of days."

Thomas mulled it over; Norman would certainly get the logs back, but he could start a war in the process; it really wouldn't worry him. In the end, Thomas agreed in principle. "I'll give him a chance this week, but after that, I'll set up the blockade. I want to be sure it doesn't come to blows."

Norman gave a snorting laugh. "Best of luck."

Later, Thomas met William in the office. When William became excited, he became garrulous. Thomas had trouble remembering the last time his brother had spoken in such a long unbroken streak, but William was understandably animated these days since he was engaged in building his long-dreamt-of mill. His ebullience made it difficult for Thomas to be sure his brother had heard him at all. When he finished his account of Inch's doings, William had replied with another round of beams and rooflines, sheathings and shingles, joists and subfloors. After a long description of how he intended to assemble the trellis for the railcar to the third floor of the mill, he surprised Thomas by asking whether he would bring in the marshal to deal with Inch.

"I'll talk to him," Thomas replied, "but he hasn't been very effective against anything other than drunken behavior."

William returned to his soliloquy. "The roof should be completed over the engine room by Friday. After that, we can move the engines in from the shed. Boyle won't be able to assemble them yet, but it won't be long. I hope we can keep up the pace. April isn't so far away." He continued in this line while his brother sat back to brood on Inch alone.

Thursday followed Wednesday and ushered in a spell of snowy weather. The wind piped up and the treetops bowed as they shook loose the dry, fluffy flakes from their upper branches. Svensson had sent word to Thomas that he had received seven loads of logs by noon on Thursday, and then they had stopped coming. Inquiring more closely, Svensson was told the weather was hindering loading and not to expect anything more until Monday. Thomas took the news evenly and laid his plans.

Thomas rode out behind Arthur on Monday. *A day of reckoning*, he thought, on his way to Camp D. By his count, he was still about thirteen loads short on the twenty-eight trees that had been cut. Svensson had two horse teams ready with ten men to transfer loads stationed at the end of Inch's road. They didn't have long to wait before a horse team came along pulling a loaded sledge down the trail toward the riverbank. Svensson recognized Inch's teamsters from the previous week, and as they pulled up at the blockage in the road, he greeted them.

"Good morning, fellas; are you on your way to my rollway? We thought we could save you some of the work. We can run these logs over, and you can bring out some more with one of your teams."

Inch's teamsters looked at each other and then at the group of men and horses barring their way. Another loaded sledge was coming up the road behind them. The driver from the first sledge replied to Svensson. "Mister, we been sent to the riverbank with this load, and I'm not unloading 'em anywhere else, and nobody drives these horses but me. If you want these logs—you unload 'em."

Svensson was surprised at the answer, but Thomas felt that permission had been given and moved his men into place. One of Inch's men went back to camp on foot while the transfer of logs began. It was delicate work to perform safely, but at the end of an hour, both of his sledges were on their way to Camp D's rollway at the creek. Inch's empty sledges had returned to their camp, and the next sledge to come up the road was driven by Cedric Inch himself. He looked at the troop of men from Camp D and feigned surprise.

"What's this?" he asked as though his drivers hadn't told him of the day's events. "Move aside now; I want to get through."

"We're here for the logs you promised, Cedric," Thomas replied. "I count that we're still short eleven loads."

"I brought everything back last week," Inch said.

"Come, come, Cedric; we both know the seven loads that were returned don't represent twenty-eight prime trees."

"That's all there was from those trees, I swear."

At this moment, Griffiths, the marshal, finally showed up. After cordially greeting everyone, he asked what was going on. Thomas spoke first.

"Marshal Griffiths, we're here to collect some logs from trees that Mr. Inch here, and his crew, cut off of our plat."

"I see," replied the marshal. "Well, what about it Mr. Inch? Do you have his logs?"

It was impossible to tell whether Inch had prepared for this moment or he was simply relying on natural talent. His blue eyes expanded in bewilderment, and his story came forth without delay or a stutter. "I mistakenly harvested some trees, Marshal Griffiths, along a line that had no marking but which Mr. McGrath says, or rather insists, is the boundary between our plats. To be neighborly and assure no hard feelings, I sent the timber from those trunks to his camp last week. Now he's demanding more. His road gang here took the logs right off my sledges today!"

Griffiths turned to Thomas. "Well, Captain McGrath? Did he return the logs to you? And did your men take logs from his sledges?"

Thomas didn't like the direction this inquiry was taking. "The answer is yes to both questions, but he cut down twenty-eight trees and returned only a third of the timber."

"And your men took logs from his sledges?"

"They—we were told by Inch's driver that we could unload the sledge. He stepped aside for us to do it. We were retrieving what has been taken from our plats illegally."

"Mr. Inch?"

Inch deftly sidestepped the allegation of theft and counter-punched by emphasizing a fictitious victimhood: "Marshal Griffiths, my men are worried about being hurt. We don't want trouble." At this point, his face changed subtly from a look of concern to a picture of dutiful resolution; he lifted his chin and went on. "I'm now driving this sledge myself; it's unfair my men should be exposed to threats!"

Thomas couldn't contain his indignation at these slurs: "What threat?" he asked. "No one has been threatened or hurt here. This is all nonsense!"

Marshal Griffiths clasped his hands behind his back and looked from Inch to Thomas to the logs to the men. He was clearly trying to evaluate the truth but having a hard time of it. He was an unimaginative man who did not have the gifts necessary for his job. A lawman should be, above other things, a shrewd judge of character, but the marshal was not. Without that guiding influence, he tended to be swayed when resolving conflicts by appeals to his emotional side. Consequently, when Inch brought up the idea of fear, he had handily garnered the marshal's sympathy; Inch knew his man. Still there was the question of whose logs these were. Sensing that the marshal was teetering on a fulcrum, Inch fired a final shot: "Marshal Griffiths, my men want to earn their pay; if you would ask these fellows to clear the way, we'll let bygones be bygones, and there won't be any more trouble."

Thomas was seething by now, but he made an effort to remain calm. "Marshal Griffiths, I hope you're not putting any stock in Mr. Inch's tale here; there has been no rough play between my men and his teams. His teamster told us we could transfer the logs, and I must say that if we simply walk away, it will leave his theft unaddressed. May I suggest you come take a look at where these trees were taken from? The land surveyor marked the line again last week."

The last suggestion was a miscalculation on Thomas's part. Marshal Griffiths was not the sort of man to track trouble to its nest and wipe it out. He had come at Thomas's request to see about some stolen wood, but now confronted with Inch's plausible alternative story, he saw the matter as troublesome and hard to prove either way. He wanted someone else to decide the right and wrong so he could be free of this and return to the Soo.

"Captain McGrath, I won't be coming to see some sawed-off stumps. How am I to tell whose land they are on or who cut the trees? What I see here is that your men are blocking Mr. Inch's road and that could start a fight. I want you to take them back to your camp, and if you want to take this business further, write to the State about it. If you don't move on, I will have to take further action."

Silence hung over the group as the marshal concluded. As one of Inch's horses snorted over the background sigh of the pines, Thomas knew bitterly that he had been trumped by a pretender.

Chapter 6

January 6, 1892

KLARA STARTED AWAKE and listened: It was him again, standing outside the bedroom door. She could hear his breathing. He had tried to come in with her on her second night, but she wouldn't share the bedroom until they were properly married. And so he spent his nights on a makeshift cot of his own construction, close by the stove. She had supposed this circumstance would have hastened the procession to the altar, but somehow it had not. And as time went by, she began to feel an underlying reason existed for delay—it had been three weeks since her arrival. Perhaps he wasn't sure about her or didn't like her after all, but if so, why did he moon about outside of her door at night? It was unsettling behavior.

The few times she had broached the subject of a wedding day, he had been evasive, promising he was getting something organized. Further questions then made him moody and irritable, leaving her feeling confused and alone. Up to this point, she had told herself to be patient, but now she resolved to press the matter.

In the morning, Klara got Anton's breakfast and lunch, readying him for his workday at the mine. She had a list of chores planned for the day, among them some grocery shopping.

"May I have some money today? We need some things for the kitchen."

"What do you need?"

"Eggs, milk, butter, more potatoes…. We are low on almost everything," she answered.

With a small grimace of discomfort, he drew out his billfold and handed over some cash. He then put on his coat, pecked her on the cheek, and left for work.

After the morning routine of dishwashing and cleaning had been completed, Klara made her way to the general store with a small sled in tow. Parking the sled outside, she went in and began collecting the items on her list. In the second aisle, she saw a young mother with two toddlers picking up a sack of flour. Klara recognized something familiar in the woman's features and carriage. *She—she looks Polish!* she thought suddenly.

"Allo. It is very cold out today," Klara greeted the lady in her own native tongue.

"Yes, it is," the woman agreed in Polish. "I am Felka." She held out her hand. "What happened to your arm?"

"It's a long story, but I broke it jumping into a boat. I am Klara, Anton's fiancée," Klara replied warmly, delighted that she had guessed Felka's nationality correctly.

"You mean Mateusz's fiancée, no?" Felka asked, puzzled.

"Anton," Klara said. "I don't know a Mateusz."

"You live down the road on the west side, don't you?"

"Yes." Klara began to have a bad feeling about what Felka might say next.

"My dear," she said sympathetically, "that is Mateusz, Anton's cousin. Anton was killed in the mine last August."

Although Klara had sensed that something like this was coming, she felt as though she were losing her balance once the news had been delivered. As her mind spun through all the events since her arrival, she realized this was the unsavory truth. Her heart beat faster and she shook ever so slightly.

"My dear Klara," Felka called her softly, "you don't look like you knew this. I am sorry."

"It's…it's…. I must get the eggs and return home." With the dual difficulties of a debilitated arm and a mind reeling in shock, Klara hastily completed her shopping. After the grocer carried her packages to the sled, she made her way home in long rapid strides.

She was living with a man she knew nothing about. It had been a leap of faith to have come to marry Anton, but at least through his letters, she had developed some idea of his character. She had nurtured a tenderness for him that she had believed would blossom into love. Mateusz, on the other hand, was a complete stranger. Why had he not told her? How should she interpret his actions in light of this enormous deception? Was he really considering marriage? She also wondered whether she could feel grief for Anton. All that remained of their relationship—the picture and his letters—had sunk with the schooner. Should she mourn for someone she had never truly seen? Sifting through her thoughts, she filtered out one idea: She would get the truth out of Mateusz—whoever he was—tonight.

Klara had dinner ready when Mateusz arrived home from work. A big iron kettle steamed over a well-stoked stove as she made a small fuss over him, taking his coat and getting his tea as he sat down to the small table. He leaned forward on his elbows, weary from the day. Bringing two plates of hot pierogies, Klara sat across from him and watched as he started on the meal.

"I met a woman at the store today," she said and noticed that he had stopped chewing. "She knew your cousin."

When Mateusz looked up from his plate, Klara saw a flash of irritation sizzle in his eyes, but he remained silent. She continued, unintimidated. "I picked up flour, eggs, onions, and potatoes."

He had returned to his dinner, picking moodily at his plate.

"And with some new ingredients, plus a little cheese, I made these pierogies. Do you like them, Mateusz?"

She watched as his head snapped up at the sound of his real name.

"Anton once wrote to me that he liked pierogies with cheese," Klara continued, "but I must see if you like them."

"So now you know. I like them well enough," he admitted unapologetically.

"Did you think I would never find out? Is this why there has been no wedding? Why have you not told me that Anton was dead?" she peppered him.

Seemingly inclined to be belligerent at first, Mateusz wilted before the hot gust of her ire.

"How could you have allowed me to come here...and for what? Would you try to pretend forever? When would you have told me?"

"I wanted to tell you. I—I was going to tell you after the wedding."

"How gentlemanly, how truly romantic," Klara responded. "And who would I have been marrying? Did you even think of how that could work?"

"I wanted to tell you, I did. I am sorry. I will make it up to you. Please settle down. Please believe me."

"Believe you? How can I believe anything from you now?" she raged. "How did you expect me to take this news? I have come all the way here to be met by an imposter, not the man I had come to know by his letters."

"Klara," Mateusz said desperately, "please listen; I wrote those letters." She cocked her head to one side and gave him an unbelieving look. "Not all of them exactly," he corrected himself. "Anton couldn't read well or write, and so I wrote his words for him, but after the accident...those were my letters," he choked.

He was visibly upset now, whether from remembrance of his departed cousin or from the impending ruin of his deceitful scheme, she couldn't tell. He avoided her eyes as he withstood her withering silence.

Klara calmed down, and when she spoke again, her tone had softened. "Tell me why you did this," she requested.

He exhaled and gathered himself, rubbed his eyes conspicuously, and then began his tale. "It all started with Anton; he wanted a wife and had saved enough money. He advertised in the circular and found you. I wrote the letters for him because he could only write a little. When he got letters back, I would read them to him at first; then he would keep them to himself.

"On your third letter, you sent your photograph. After seeing your picture, I thought...somehow I began to tell myself that you were writing to me. And then...well, naturally, I began to write back. So you see, those words were mine."

"What about Anton?" Klara asked, incredulous at this revelation.

Mateusz's eyes flicked in desperation down to his cooling pierogies and then back to her demanding countenance. Her anger had enhanced her beauty, he thought, but at the same time, he was resentful that he had been forced to explain himself to this degree. But it couldn't be helped now. He answered, "Anton couldn't tell exactly what I had written, but in any case, it wasn't more than a couple of letters, and then he had his accident in the mine. He had sent your passage money by that time, and after that, I wrote those letters freely, by myself, you see."

She did see, but she was uncertain what this really meant to her—Mateusz had deceived not only her, but also quite recklessly his own cousin. What would have happened if she had met Anton alive and well, and he had found out that Mateusz had not faithfully taken down his words? On the other hand, it really was Mateusz who had written the letters, setting down his dreams and hopes and penning the tender endearments that had warmed her heart and accompanied her on her long voyage. She now wished she had the letters to compare with the man before her to try to find common substance.

"Let's finish eating," she said and returned her attention to her pierogies.

CHAPTER 7

March 21, 1892

ONEY. MONEY UPON money. Money thrown after more money. Money all rushing uniformly out. Money for engines, drive belts, lubricating oil. Money for blades, spares, some new age planer blade sharpener. Money for labor and money for bolts. Thomas bit his lip as he looked at the number of times bolts listed in the expense column. Bolts were expensive and largely forgotten in William's budget. Every machine sought the security of robust bolts to steady them during their mechanical quakings, and the mill currently employed two men just making specialty bolts. Thomas cringed at the outflow of borrowed capital; it was a fright to be burning through such quantities of loaned cash when there was nothing in the credit column to bring future balance to the books.

He had the office to himself and had taken the opportunity to look over the mill's finances without being under the overhang of William's outcropping chin. His brother tended to usher him through the pages, stopping where it suited him and hurrying past any items that might foment discord. What Thomas saw now alarmed him—the present rate of spending would see them insolvent before they could begin to sell lumber again next summer. Although the mill expansion may have been necessary, it was running over-budget in the jolly company of William's enthusiasm. He ran his eye down the columns again, completed his notes, and bundled up to search out his brother.

Scrunching through a shallow layer of fresh snow, Thomas approached the new mill. It was still strange to him that it didn't have to be situated directly above the creek, owing to the steam plant. It was a big three-story facility, modest by comparison to the mills further west, but large for them and with lots of capability. William had put great forethought into the layout of the new operation, concentrating on good traffic flow so that logs might become lumber in as few steps as possible. Built against a rise in the land, the second floor had ground access at the back of the building and a rail trellis reached the third floor. The roof was fitted with a series of water barrels that would be filled and standing by if needed to extinguish flames in the dry summer months. Off to one side of the building was the engine plant, separated from the rails, saws, and tools of the mill proper by a thick timber wall. It was there that he found William.

With a small amount of amusement, Thomas saw Boyle chafing; his internal, assertive self rubbing hard against his exterior, which he commanded to be still and tolerant under William's tuition on the assembly of the main flywheel and crankshaft.

"You need to lower it more to push it on," William instructed.

The great iron flywheel hung suspended by a chain hoist from an overhead beam as Boyle and his men struggled with the final alignment to slide the hub onto the shaft.

"Begging your pardon, Mr. McGrath, but I don't think so; the height is correct, but there's a small burr getting in the way."

Thomas smiled unseen, thinking Boyle perhaps had a double meaning, describing William as the current problem. He wondered whether Boyle was capable of such cloaked jibes. In any case, he would relieve the millwright of this torrent of unsolicited advice for there was nothing in Boyle's past that suggested he couldn't do the job.

"William," Thomas called, "can you come have a look at some things at the office with me?"

"Thomas, I didn't see you there. Certainly," said William, secretly relieved to be free of even minor conflict with Boyle.

"Do you have it, Boyle?" he asked.

"Yes, sir, I believe so," Boyle replied, also relieved but concealing it well from all but Thomas.

Thomas's desk was nearly covered by lists and diagrams he had made to help visualize their projected spending. As he subtracted upcoming expenses, he wrote down the amounts of their future bank balances on a calendar.

"So, here we are then; we will run out of cash in late May if we continue to spend at our present rate," he said. "Since it's almost April, we must think of cutting back somewhere."

"Humpph," William replied. "I don't think it'll be that tight; we almost have all of the saws ready in the main mill; with a little luck, the main engine setup will go quickly. Once we have everything going, we'll be back to making lumber and getting paid for it."

Thomas couldn't believe what he was hearing: William was usually the scrupulous economist and he himself more approximate in his figuring.

"True, but we won't be paid right away; we may have to wait for our money. And you say with a little luck—but we can't count on luck—except maybe bad luck. There are always unforeseen problems. What if one of the saws won't operate properly? It took two weeks to get the new bandsaw to cut a straight board over in Manistique. Something like that could easily happen, and it's better to account for a delay now than be surprised when it happens."

"Thomas, sometimes I don't understand you. First of all, we don't have a bandsaw; you particularly didn't want it. Second, there's no reason to believe we'll get stuck on reassembly; these machines were tested before they shipped."

"I know that sounds right, William," Thomas rebutted patiently, "and hopefully, the rest will go as you planned; however, I do worry there'll be a surprise that could hold up the whole process."

"What's that?" William demanded.

"We don't know yet; can't know. It could be more bolts or perhaps a completely different problem."

"Now I don't know what we're talking about."

"Simply this: We should save back some cash for emergencies—just in case. That means cutting back somewhere. To start with, we can both skip on drawing pay."

"Machines require bolts," William shot back, overly defensively, and then he took a moment to consider things. "I agree we can get by without pay, but I don't know what else we can do without; it's all part of a production plan."

Thomas exulted inwardly at this tiny admission from his brother, but he decided not to squeeze him toward a compromise right away. "Let's see it fresh in the morning. If we have to make a change, I'd like to come to a decision before I go on the trail tomorrow."

As the two men dressed for the cold, someone knocked at the door. Thomas opened up to admit a grave, weathered Chippewa man dressed in buckskin pants and a woolen coat topped by a fur hood. He pulled a packet from a buckskin bag and handed it over, uttering the single word: "Mail."

"Mail," William repeated incredulously. "We haven't had mail in months."

Thomas took two dollars from his billfold and passed them to the Chippewa who silently accepted them. "Where did you come from?" he asked.

"Crossed the ice to St. Ignace."

"It's a bit late in March to cross the ice. What brought you up here?"

The Indian stood, quietly meeting Thomas's eye, and as the silence stretched out between them, Thomas realized the man had no wish to discuss his business. But surely he hadn't crossed the ice in late March just to deliver them mail; he might be caught on the Upper Peninsula until after the spring thaw. In some years, winter grudgingly released its grip upon land and lake in late April. In other years, lake ice was broken up by a gale-driven rain in March. Even in January and February, when ice conditions were at their most certain, crossing the frozen lake had its hazards: the surface was not simply one flat sheet; it buckled as it expanded, trying to find room for its increase. Pressure ridges formed, sometimes nine or ten feet high, each edge of the fractured ice trying to surmount the other. One inevitably ascended to dominance while the submissive edge sank below its victor in cold shame. New thin ice would then form in the wet rift, waiting in silent treachery for the unsuspecting. Another hazard was the utter sameness of the icescape once one had lost sight of any landmarks; if clouds covered the sun and the wind shifted, a traveler might walk in circles or veer far from any shore finding nothing but frozen confusion and perhaps his own footprints.

Thomas considered the Chippewa. His age would be difficult to guess, but certainly, the man was weathered enough to know the ways of the lake and ice travel. He ventured a final question: "Will you be returning south, or will you remain until the thaw?"

The man put his hands together and made a slight bow. "Soon I will know," he replied and turned to leave.

William spoke up. "If you're going south, would you call in again? We'll have mail going out." The Indian bowed again and left.

"Do you think he meant yes?" William asked.

"I'm sure," Thomas replied. "Some of these fellows don't like to talk."

Chapter 8

March 22, 1892

THE DAY WAS bright and breathless; silently, the snow glistened, reflecting the sapphire brilliance of the empty sky above. Arthur's muffled hoof falls produced the only sound as he pulled his loaded sledge beneath snow-laden, verdant pines along the powdery white trail. Thomas admired Arthur at his work, his dappled coat gleaming; an appaloosa was a rare horse in these parts. He also relished the clean cold of the day, tempered as it was by the morning sun; and the quiet of this lonely ride, where he could think without feeling he should be spending his time in some other fashion. It was a seven-mile ride to Camp B.

With the weather so pleasant and an agreeable day's work ahead, Thomas asked himself why he wasn't in a more cheerful mood. He usually enjoyed these runs out to the logging camps; life at home was as good as ever, the winter's work on *Genevieve* was progressing well, and despite costs, the new mill was beginning to shape up; in fact, he had even had some success with William, discussing expenses, and they had agreed to postpone the purchase of a small locomotive and portable track for hauling logs out from the camps to the river. They were already using the new log-hauling tractor, and until they could afford it, the horses could do the hauling. Thomas had expected more resistance, but William had given in surprisingly easily. Somehow, he had even seemed detached, as if the portable railway had been optional in spite of his earlier position. And perhaps that was what was chafing him: that William had given way so easily; he had definitely seemed a little out of trim this morning. He shook himself and resolved to cast aside these damp, dirty rags of someone else's spoiled humor and see the day afresh. Arthur was clump-clomping along in the snow, and before long they would be at Camp B.

By three o'clock in the afternoon, the air was losing what feeble warmth the sun had granted it in the morning. Thomas, once more in train behind Arthur, thought it would be very cold in the night if the sky remained clear. Halfway back to the mill, he realized that although he had tried to enjoy his day, he had swayed back toward irritability. He was bothered by his visit to Camp B; after several months of steady cutting, scattered bits of timber lay horizontal across the landscape, interspersed by forgotten, severed stumps. The scene he had left behind was one of desolation; it was in some ways a terrible thing they were doing to the land. Perhaps the trees would grow back some day, but they had made it a wasteland in a very short time. Next, he fell to thinking about Inch, which dragged him down into pointless undertows of thought—he revisited old conflicts with the man and despised all over again his words, his actions, his mannerisms, and most of all, his look of wounded innocence when confronted with his own deceit.

Pulling up to the mill at last, Thomas thought he would shake off his funk over a glass of whiskey with William and give him the news of the day. He pulled the sledge under a shed roof, unhitched Arthur, wiped him down, and led him into the stable. Once the horse was settled and fed, Thomas walked up toward the old mill and their office. It was late in the day, so all was quiet at the new mill and its surrounding works. The men had gone home, leaving behind partially constructed cribs, stacks of rail ties placed ready for laying track, and a skeletal shed that would get its skin tomorrow. Arriving at the office, Thomas was surprised to find that William was not there, but he was greeted by Moses, whirling his tail in rapid circles. Odd. William usually worked in the office until five o'clock or later; perhaps he had gone to the new building for something. Thomas went to the corner cupboard and poured himself a small glass of whiskey. He was about to settle in and wait for William when he noticed a folded paper left prominently on his desk. Perhaps the earlier events in his day caused him to view this note through a bleak gray lens, but he sensed that what awaited him would not be welcome news. Unfolding the note, he read:

Dear Thomas,

I have left for Detroit. I am sorry not to have given you any warning, but something has come up that meant I had to leave today. I hope all is well at Camp B. Boyle and his crew will be working on the main engine assembly for the rest of the week; after that, they can start on the planers. Boyle can keep an eye on the tap and die men making bolts—he knows what he will need next. We have the six men working on cribs for the log pens; they are a little behind, so you should keep them moving because we want to have the cribs positioned before the ice melts. In my desk, you will find a list of people who need to be paid. In all other matters, I'm sure you will know what to do. If all goes well, I will be back in a week.

William

With the note read, Thomas experienced the final collapse of his earlier resolve to enjoy the day. He vigorously ruffled his sandy hair, rubbed his eyes, and pulled one hand down his face, ending at his chin. His mood now turned to resentment. How could William leave him here to cope with his enterprise when parts of it were so needful of his supervision? Other questions came to mind: Why was he going to Detroit? What was so urgent? Was it the money? If it had something to do with the mill, why had his brother not told him about the nature of the trip? And lastly—how was he going to get there? Neither trains nor lake boats would be running for at least another month, and it would be a long, uncomfortable trip by horse. He drank down his whiskey, locked the office, and brought Moses along for the walk home.

As twilight deepened to dusk, Thomas noticed Sirius, the Dog Star, rising in the east. He then turned around to look for Capella. Finding it, he patiently waited for the darkness to reveal the Charioteer. Moses sniffed for mice nearby and eventually sat on his foot. Thomas squatted to pet the dog and thought about sailing south—far south, below Capella, below the cold, and out of these woods that he had loved before he saw them ruined by his own hand, once the siege of lake ice was broken. It came to him then how William would travel to Detroit: the Chippewa must be going back. After a long while, he could see the stars of the Charioteer glimmering toward him out of the blue-black sky. He stood, cold and soothed, ready to take up the path toward home.

CHAPTER 9

BY CREEPING AND crawling, some things spread, gain their ascendancy by stealth, and once established, become very difficult—sometimes impossible—to eradicate. A bad rash from being constantly clad in wet clothing is such a thing; what starts as mild discomfort at a fold in the skin gradually blossoms into a garden of chafed, red patches that cannot be left alone at any hour of the day or night. Wildfires are an example on a larger scale; in hot dry weather, the woods and underbrush dehydrate slowly, day by day, becoming more parched, sometimes showing very little evidence of their want of water. They wait stoically for it, but having it not, sit helpless when flint strikes tinder and produces the small, smoldering blush of ignition. Faint wisps of smoke appear, and the lightest of breezes feeds the fledgling fire, driving it slowly along the ground until it runs up, hard and hungry, against dry brush, then comes fully to life. Growing now, it begins to draw its own breath, inhaling deeply, swelling its chest and growing again in height and breadth until strong enough to climb a tree. Once in the treetops, it will rage, sometimes consuming everything left before it, no matter how man might attempt to sway or cease its fury.

Rumors start as a small remark, become hushed talk, graduate to open discussion, and in the worst scenarios, finally end up as the truth. Thomas was only too aware of how William's sudden departure could stoke a brushfire of speculation among the lumberjacks and mill hands in an insular society thirsty for human drama. His apprehension was that the command structure for their business might suffer in some way if the men believed the mill could become insolvent. Some of their best men might begin to look for other work, and to lose them at this point would hurt.

Thomas began his day at the engine room of the new mill with Boyle. With the great flywheel on the engine keyed in and securely bolted, the men were now assembling the connecting rod and piston slide. The air was filled with activity and cold oil as Boyle judiciously parceled out tasks. William had hired Boyle two years ago, most likely with an eye toward conversion of the mill to steam. Although always competent, Thomas was surprised at Boyle's depth of skill and experience with modern machinery. He was at home among the dull gray surfaces of oiled iron.

Boyle usually reported to William, but Thomas wanted to find out for himself how the work was progressing; he also wished to probe, gently, to find out if any event yesterday had precipitated William's trip, without giving away the fact that he had not expected it.

"Good morning, Boyle. It's impressive to see the flywheel on," he said.

"Good morning, Captain; thank you, sir," said Boyle as he laid down his wrenches on his bench.

"I wished to check in with you on progress and see if there was anything you had asked of William, before he left, that I should be taking care of."

"Nothing to speak of," Boyle replied, addressing the last part first. "We have the connecting rod coming together; I'm working on the flyweights for the governor. I think we'll have most of it together by the end of the week. Perhaps it'll be ready to run when Mr. William gets back," he said with a mildly inquisitive raise of the eyebrows. Thomas gave him a curt, non-committal nod and admired how Boyle had neatly, subtly posed the question about William's movements. As he had thought, Boyle and the rest of the company would be nattering away about this news, and anyone who could glean new information would enjoy some brief elevation of status. Well, it couldn't be helped. The men would talk, and why not? All of their fortunes were tied together. It would be best if he could hand back some bland explanation for his brother's erratic behavior, control the discussion, and find out what he could for himself.

"Hopefully, the roads will be good enough and he won't take long," he countered. "I was at Camp B all day yesterday; what time did he get away?"

"I can't say for certain, sir, but I last saw him at 11:30, so perhaps about noon?"

"Ah, good, he will have made a good start."

Boyle, still feeling unenlightened, continued to look at him expectantly. Thomas dithered between ending the interview and trying once more for information; he decided on the latter.

"Oh, by the way, Boyle, have you seen that Chippewa Indian fellow around here?" he asked.

Boyle looked up from his bench. "Yes, sir. He was here yesterday in the morning. I haven't seen him since."

Ah, Thomas thought. A piece of the puzzle falls into place.

"If you see him again, try and send him to me—he carries the mail. And if you have anything holding you up, see me; I'll be looking after construction details until William's return."

Thomas stopped next outside, where the cribs were being constructed. The cribs were big square pens, about sixteen feet per side, built from cedar logs interlaced at the corners and bolted together in the same fashion as a log cabin, but not as precisely. They had a base of logs across the bottom that would hold enough rocks to sink the crib. Once submerged in position directly before the mill, they would be filled with stones and make a solid anchor for the great wooden booms that corralled and contained all of the logs to be driven downriver.

As Thomas approached, he sensed the work was in disarray; one man was trimming the end of a cedar log for fitting, two appeared to be watching him (one advising), and the other three were trying to look busy with bolts and an auger.

"Good morning," he preambled. "How are we coming along here?" he asked of no one in particular.

Edwards, who, in theory, was in charge, began to respond, but he was quickly drowned out as four of the other men began to speak at once.

"We're low on bolts." "Most bolts aren't long enough, sir." "These augers aren't quite sharp."

Suddenly tired, Thomas drifted briefly, wondering what on earth William had left for. He appeared to be listening, letting the barrage of difficulties flow past him for a moment before holding up his hand for silence.

"Edwards, tell me, how are we coming along?"

Francis Edwards had an alto voice that reminded Thomas of wind whining through a small boat's rigging at twenty knots.

"It's a little slow, sir. We are short of bolts, or more like the bolts we have are short, and we need to have sharper augers; they aren't cutting through the cedar very quickly."

An auger that wouldn't cut cedar was dull indeed. "When did you have them sharpened last?"

Edwards looked at the other men for help with the answer, but they wouldn't make eye contact. "They were sharp when we started," Edwards offered.

Thomas moved on. "Let's see your bolt supply." Looking at the bolts, he could see the difficulty: the bolts were the exact length as the logs' width. In most cases, no room had been left for the nut and washer. They would either need longer bolts, which were not at hand today, or a plan to make these work, which Edwards didn't seem able to come up with.

"Okay, lads," Thomas said. "Start by sorting the logs. Who's got a measuring stick? You? Good. Get all the smallest ones, everything under ten inches; those can be bolted together with what we have. Let's concentrate on finishing your second set of cribs. I'll see about the other bolts. Edwards, bring those augers and come with me." *More bolts*, Thomas groaned to himself.

Once alone, Thomas said to Edwards, "These augers should be getting sharpened constantly. Drop two of them in to Boyle after lunch each day; that way you'll have them the next morning. We'll talk to him about it now."

"Mr. McGrath never mentioned them, sir, and they seemed sharp," droned the hapless Edwards.

Thomas was busy working on two problems: Where had his brother gone? And how would he get this work in hand on his own? Dealing with Edwards and his bolts seemed like a distraction right now—necessary but annoying—and he had no patience for wasted words when he felt too busy. One of the worst things a mill hand could do was give him cause to repeat himself.

"They always seem sharp until they're dull, so dull that they won't cut cedar, and so they don't cut, and then the men can't produce." Thomas rounded on him sharply. "See that the augers are sharpened daily," he reiterated with finality.

It was just before lunch, and once clear of construction projects, Thomas had time to go aboard *Genevieve*, the old familiar strength of her form a great comfort after the mill's newness and turbulence. The main hatch was opened for light and air as the day was nice, and Norman, Dennis, and Benjamin were in the hold, busily refurbishing the main topmast rigging. Norman was tarring and parceling a wire backstay, a process to coat and wrap the wire before it was served. Serving was the final layer, a wrapping of twine that was applied with a special mallet to lay the twine on under tension. As is usual with rigging work, the cook had Stockholm tar, black and sticky, all over his bare fingers.

Thomas made a joke: "Hey, what have you been cooking?"

Norman grinned, wrinkles deepening in his cheeks and around his eyes, as he finished parceling the wire he was working on. Although he wiped his thick hands on a rag, his index finger remained sufficiently sticky that when he touched it to the cigarette above his ear, the cigarette came away and was neatly transferred to his lips. Benjamin and Dennis were completing a wire seizing that formed an eye in the lower end of the topmast backstay.

"I have some soup on," Norman said. "If you're staying for lunch, I'll add a bucket of water." It was a well-worn joke of his. Thomas decided he would stay as he often did and followed Norman up to the galley.

"Where has Mr. William gone to? Is he chasing that skirt again?" Norman asked. He and Thomas had a long history together, so Norman felt no need to pussyfoot around questions.

"Detroit; no, Carmina is long gone. I'm sure that's finished," Thomas answered. He thought it interesting that his crew, who were largely separate from mill work and activity, should already be wondering about William. "He said he would be back in two weeks."

"I saw him go out with that Indian yesterday."

"I heard as much. I hope he'll be all right on the lake."

"It's still cold; he should be fine as long as he keeps moving."

After lunch, Thomas checked on Edwards and his crew. The tap and die men were working up some longer bolts for the cribs, and the men had freshly sharpened augers; by tomorrow, they would be able to move more rapidly on assembly. He left them for the office. Outside his door, he found Moses, asleep and curled up with his tail covering his nose. The dog got up and stretched out his front legs, then his back, before following Thomas inside. Thomas lit a small fire in the stove, hung up his overcoat, and opened William's desk to look for the list of vendors to be paid. A letter that had been crumpled and then smoothed out again caught his eye, sitting in the far right corner. It was postmarked from Detroit. His curiosity piqued, he opened it:

Sunday, November 20, 1891
My Dear William,

It is after considerable time and reflection that I finally feel courageous enough to write to you. What is there that one can say when one has acted rashly? What explanation can be offered to a person who has knowingly been given short commons and still hopes for understanding? And yet, William, this is what I ask.

I was foolish to have left you. It was indecent to have disappeared without a word of explanation; I am sure it has caused you distress, as has been evident from your attempts to find me.

In September—when you saw me by accident or perhaps grand design—I was as yet unprepared to meet. It was indeed me that you pursued to this house that I share with my auntie. I do now wish to meet again; I have much to say and apologize for. Perhaps you can write to me to arrange a proper time and place, if you are agreeable.

My auntie is moving to San Francisco in the spring; if I have not had some word from you by then, then perhaps I will travel with her.

Ti amo,
Carmina

And so there it is, Thomas thought. Anne had hinted at this and Norman had known it, but he himself had thought William to be finished pining for the lost Carmina. He felt his resentment over William's absence melt like April ice, breaking into small pieces, soft-edged and slushy, each diminishing in size. The letter was over four months old; by the time William sent a reply, it would in all likelihood miss its recipient. The only way to make sure was to go.

Thomas smoothed out the letter and replaced it in the far right corner of the desk drawer. With this mystery solved, he could occupy his mind with the business of the mill and the wonders of Edwards's management skills.

Chapter 10

MORNING LIGHT BLEACHED bright an expanse of whiteness that hurt William's eyes. Looking south, the white took on a set of textures within itself, for there were lighter whites and bluish whites and unseeable, brilliant silver whites that gave the possibility of shape to the emptiness before him. In the farthest reaches of eyesight, the icescape was edged and irregular, radiant and yet silhouetted against the background blue of the endless sky beyond.

He had been preparing himself for this journey since leaving DeTour, and now that the moment had come, he hesitated in the doorway, peering into the room beyond. The Chippewa who was guiding him had already left the shore and was moving briskly over knee-deep snow in a pair of snowshoes. William had put on the pair the Indian had acquired for him, but they had no motive power of their own to propel his feet forward. It would require of him a leap of faith to set out over the ice, a trust in his guide, and a belief in his own ability to endure and overcome. All were required to get the feet to move. He had read, somewhere, the old Chinese proverb that "A journey of one thousand miles begins with the first step." Nothing was ever mentioned about some critical step in the middle. He felt it would have been easier to have taken this step directly upon leaving home. Perhaps he was just making an excuse for timidity. Optimists couldn't give in to their fears, not outwardly anyway. Marco Polo must have had some instant of doubt, as did David Livingstone and perhaps even William Clark. But there were the unhappy examples of optimists as well: Henry Hudson, Sir John Franklin—swallowed by the arctic—and long ago Vercingatorix when he rode out to face down the Romans.

The Chippewa was now a shrinking figure as he receded into the near distance. He had made it plain that it would be William's job to keep up; that he would lead the way, but each man would be responsible for himself once they were out over the lake. William gathered, commanded his feet forward, and hurried to catch up.

The first couple of hours were an education. William had walked on ice many times as part of his work; he had even tried using snowshoes before, but he was finding ice travel a greater physical challenge than he had imagined. The Indian chose the best course he could, but the direct route they wished to travel, between closest points of land—the Mackinac Strait—was constantly being squeezed from west and east. Ice buckled and heaved into humps and ridges that had to be climbed and slid down or circumvented. Even with a very small pack on his back, William was damp with exertion. Whether the Indian sometimes waited for him or whether he too was fatigued, William couldn't know, but even with his clumsiness in the snowshoes, William was pleased he was keeping up.

The sunny day became tainted by high wispy streaks, and then it gave way to a long bank of flat solid cloud setting in with a freshening breeze from the southwest. They had made enough progress that they could no longer see anything of St. Ignace behind them, and as yet, the far shore was not distinctly in sight. As the wind increased, the Indian began to pick up his pace and halted less often; he appeared to be drawing on unseen reserves, and William began to worry about his ability to stay with him. Climbing over an ice hummock, William snagged the front edge of his snowshoe on a lump he hadn't noticed; caught on the uneven surface, he was thrown off balance and went down flailing into a thin layer of snow. The fall had hurt only a little, but as he began to walk again, he found that he had torn the deer-hide thong that held his left snowshoe around his ankle. The shoe dangled each time he lifted his foot and threatened to topple him repeatedly. There was nothing else for it; it demanded repair or he would never make progress. He looked anxiously ahead and was reassured that he could see the Chippewa cresting another hummock. He sat down in the snow, removed his gloves, and began working on the hide binding that would immobilize his foot. The frozen hide had to be softened to retie, but in about ten minutes, he had it securely back together on his foot. Standing up again, a flash of panic touched him because he could no longer see the Indian—anywhere. *It's all right,* he told himself. *Start walking; follow his tracks—you'll find the way.*

It was afternoon now and the cloud cover had dimmed the vast corrugated plain of ice. Instead of the earlier whites, the snow and ice reflected the grays of the clouds overhead, once again in differing shades, aiding William in discerning the shapes and structure of this frozen, accidental terrain. When the southwest wind brought an appreciable rise in temperature, William could smell something different, something familiar and forgotten; he could almost place it...and then he knew—he could smell rain. Straining to see, he still could not make out anything of the southern shore, and as the cloud became heavier and advanced, his concern grew. He continued to follow the tracks since it was the only sensible option open to him. For another hour and a half, he exerted himself fully, hoping he would spot his Indian guide as he crested each ice hummock. His snowshoe was holding up with the repair he had made, the tracks ahead were clear, and even though he was alone, he began to feel he could complete this trek to the other shore unaided. He crossed over the top of another ridge, this one quite tall, seven feet or more, and as he looked ahead, his heart sank: there crossing the path before him, stretching as far as he could see in both directions, was a long rippled stream of bluish-gray water and the Indian's tracks on the opposite side of it. It could only be twelve feet across, but it was certainly too far to jump. The cold water, newly born, crawled lazily along it, but even as he stood there, William fancied the gap had grown larger.

William knew he had three options: follow the edge of the stream right or follow it left and hope it would become narrow enough to jump, or go back the way he had come and give up on this quest. To a man of William's temperament, the thought of turning back was insufferable; he would have to experience the hardest press of circumstance before allowing himself to return; not only would he have wasted his time, but in all likelihood he would be relinquishing the last hope he had of resolving his past with Carmina. He had not jumped ahead to any idea of reconciliation with her; it was just that after reading her letter, he knew there would forever be an unanswerable question haunting him if he didn't make this last effort to see her.

So—left or right? Left appeared to head in a northeasterly direction or what he thought was away from shore; right appeared to go southwest, possibly toward shore. He went right, realizing with alarm as he did so that the stream had widened to almost twenty feet. He kept back from the stream because he could see the ice edge was becoming undercut and thinner, diminished by the current flowing along it. He hoped the ice he had presently underfoot was not being quietly eaten away.

The warmer air made the snow clingy; it stuck to his snowshoes now, giving them weight and resistance. He had been walking at his best pace southwest for about an hour, so he began to sense the grim tug of fatigue dragging at his legs as he climbed a softened ice hummock. Descending the small hill, he reached its base and put his snowshoe down into a patch of very wet snow. He could feel water begin to swirl around his foot. He was sinking. Horrified, he turned as best he could and sloshed and scurried back to the top of the ice ridge he had just crossed. Where he had just been standing was now all wet, and he realized he had stepped onto young or new ice: there was a recent pressure crack beneath the ridge. Looking farther out, he could see the open water stream had grown to a fifty-foot width, and in the distance to the southwest, there was a larger body of open water still. Certain that hesitation could bring about his demise, he turned around and struggled back northeast.

Keeping panic at bay was quite difficult. His mind was scrambling from thought to thought in the same way as his tired body rose and fell over softened humps of snow and broken ice chunks. Calculating how far he might get before it was truly dark, he watched warily to see whether the stream appeared to be widening toward him. Mingled into these practical considerations were needles of self-castigation; he called himself ridiculous; he told himself he should have burned her letter unopened; he hated that he had allowed himself to be put in this dire situation. In a little time, his feet were slogging out a heavy rhythm and his improved fortune with the firmness of the ice helped to settle his mind again. He noticed the stream of open water was becoming narrower, and he realized the smell he had earlier thought of as rain was, in fact, the open water. At last, he passed the spot where he had first found the stream; it was now about forty feet wide. The late afternoon was slate gray, blotting out all but the most pronounced forms on the ice. He continued on.

Meanwhile, the Chippewa Indian had made it to the shore. He had smelled the water and had crossed the rift when it was little more than a crack. Looking southwest, he sensed that a broad current was being stuffed into this narrow section of lake from a large body of open water in Lake Michigan. How long the ice might last after that could be a matter of hours or days. He had hoped the cold of two nights ago would hold the ice for his return trip, but now he was sure he had made a mistake; it was certainly a mistake to have brought along the white lumberman. There was that about the lumberman that made it hard to turn him away. He felt that the boy (for he thought of him as a boy) would follow him anyway, no matter what he said, and why not have the offered money? Reluctantly, he had set some conditions and allowed himself to be followed. The boy had turned out to be clumsy, terribly slow, and not used to snow travel. He had waited for the boy when he could. When he saw that the ice was breaking, he had to make speed for the far shore or they would both be caught on broken floes. Safely over land once again, he thought of the lumberman, alone on the ice, and felt sadness for him. Even though each man took his own risk out there, his unnamed conscience had prodded and poked at him as he had hurried ashore.

William was thoroughly miserable. He had gotten wet below the knees, and his outer clothing was soaking through. The sun was about to set somewhere behind the thick veil of clouds, and the wind's earlier warmth was offset by a sublimation of snow and ice into vapor. Nothing appeared to be melting; it just seemed to disappear slowly, gradually transforming into raw, searching air.

Trekking northeast along the rift, William was forced to consider retracing his steps to St. Ignace. The difficulty now was that night was coming on; there would be no moon to see by under such an overcast sky, and what if he walked into water again? He had no way of knowing whether the ice was deteriorating along the trail he had walked in the morning. If he made it to an end in the current opening, he could get across, and surely, he would see some light from Mackinaw City.

Then he would just have to hope there was enough ice to finish the trip. Hope—it wasn't much of a business plan. He mocked himself—the planner. He wondered whether if he made it safely to Detroit, there was anything Carmina could say that would make his current jeopardy worthwhile. Her letter hadn't really said anything other than that she wished to talk. *And now, of course, it's up to me to make this possible*, he thought with mild resentment. Perhaps she could have caught a steamboat to DeTour when the idea had first entered her pretty head.

No, he mustn't think about this; the important thing now was to get off of the ice. Looking ahead, he found that a large area of ice was very wet. The snow was entirely gone to slush, and he imagined the little creek he had been following had hit a dam and was spreading out into a snow marsh. It was deep into twilight, almost dark, and now he had to choose: walk across the wet, suspect ice, or return home. It would be suicidal to go any farther.

With a heavy heart, he turned around, frustrated, and hoped he would be able to find his own trail. The light was fading fast, and the mist was thickening around him, tightening in his horizon oppressively. With aching legs and a painful compression in his lower back, he slogged out a return, almost to his old trail until he decided it was too dark and he would have to give it up for the night. Finding a solid-looking ridge, he decided to wait in its lee until dawn. He knew the cold would be penetrating, and he had not come dressed to bivouac on the ice, but he was completely out of other choices. Sadly, he considered that only the Indian could say where he had gone, and that no one he knew had any idea where to look for him. Once again, he fell back heavily on hope—he hoped his destiny was to be different from that of the enigmatic Franklin.

Chapter 11

WILLIAM HAD SPENT a miserable night on the ice. At first, he had made a bed using his snowshoes and knapsack. The snowshoes he positioned below his hips and back—the knapsack under his head. Successful in falling asleep this way, his slumber was broken when the snow beneath his makeshift cot compacted, melted, and inevitably seeped into his clothing. Awake again and a degree or two more unhappy, he set the snowshoes up as a chair, planting one in the softening snow as a backrest and placing the other over the knapsack for a seat. Hugging his sides for warmth, he slept fitfully, having to balance himself on the awkward chair, and occasionally waking with a start as he tipped over. The night became a series of naps then, light to ponderous and haunting. He slipped between planes of partial consciousness and dream, carrying his anxiety to and fro. When he dreamed, he saw images of ice melting, melting into smaller pieces, melting into wet mush, swallowing him into an immersion of cold panic. Once again, he would awake, fully alarmed, only to find that his frightening dreams were mostly true. The pervasive damp of the misty night burrowed toward his bones, and at a point, he could no longer stay warm enough. His teeth chattered and his ribs fairly rattled as wave after wave of cold rippled through him. Giving up on sleep, he passed the hours instead by walking in small circles and performing other exercises to keep blood moving through his limbs.

Since Prometheus took fire from Olympus, man has feared that which lies beyond the farthest reach of his beaming flame. Darkness acts upon the mind, swelling the unknown, or partially known, into bestial immensities, dismissed only by the return of light. William could hear the open water lapping against the ice edge, and the timpani of decaying ice chunks colliding as they rotated downcurrent. He pictured the gap in the ice widening by the hour. Possibly by now, it had split and surrounded him, leaving him afloat on an island. He had given up on the idea of reaching Mackinaw City, and at this point, he could only hope that the ice to his north would be sound enough to allow him to return to St. Ignace. Dawn alone would show how desperate the situation was. Longing for the sun's warmth, he simultaneously dreaded what it might reveal, as well as its potential deleterious effect on the ice. Desperately tired, he sat once again in his makeshift chair, leaned back, and slept hard for the remaining hour until dawn.

The sun gave a brief burst of light, shining on William's face before ascending into a flat cloud above. William awoke stiff and cold. With difficulty, he stood up and shook some life into his sleeping limbs. Grateful to have survived the night, he began to survey his environs, looking for his old tracks. Rummaging around in his knapsack, he pulled out the other half of a crushed beef sandwich he had saved from the previous day. It was a little soggy and misshapen, but it brought new strength and hope as he ate it. The sandwich gone, he scooped a little snow into his mouth, laced on his snowshoes, and set out to find a way home.

The open water had indeed widened during the night to more than two hundred yards. Happily leaving it behind, William was pushed by the persistent west wind as he followed mist-eaten remnants of his old tracks toward St. Ignace. By the end of an hour, the wind had increased considerably in speed, but the ice beneath his feet had given him no cause for mistrust. A short distance farther, however, he began to have misgivings over what he saw ahead. The ice surface was flatter than the jumbled road he had been traveling, and as he made his approach, he could see plainly that it was wet. He had no idea whether to trust it or not, and yet what choice did he have now? He couldn't see a way around it. It would be possible to walk all day, just as he had yesterday, only to find suspect wet ice, or even worse—open water. He began a slow lament: Why had his guide deserted him? Why had he done this to himself? He was on a fool's errand at the risk of his own skin. A new worry asserted itself—he thought he could feel motion;

could this really be? No, he was imagining it, but there it was again—a slight sensation of motion, not laterally—vertically. It was just possible that waves somewhere in the open lake were pushing their way under the ice. If he didn't keep moving, there would be no chance of surviving this. Surviving. That's what the situation had become, a struggle for survival. He was suddenly overwhelmed by a sense of despair. Standing, scanning the horizon, he knew he must pick a direction, but he felt powerless to do so.

He was fighting off an urge to weep when he heard a sound far out behind him. It was not readily identifiable, just barely distinct from the noise of cold air rushing over ice and past his ears. There it was again: a voice! A deep voice carried and distorted by the wind, shouting two unintelligible words. *Some other human is out here on this ice,* he thought. When the voice came a third time, he shouted a long hello for reply. It was unlikely his own voice would carry far upwind, so he decided to set off in the deep voice's direction. His most immediate problem had been solved at the very least—he now had a direction. It passed through his mind briefly that the voice might be a trick of the imagination, a sonic mirage that would disappear upon his approach, but he had to take that chance. It was better to believe in the voice and move on than to stare in forlorn helplessness at the vast perishing field of ice.

The voice came again, garbled but a little louder this time. William bellowed "Helloooh!" at the top of his lungs and quickened his pace, slogging down the soft tracks he had just made. Soon he came to a small ice hump, the remnant of one of yesterday's larger hummocks. Cresting the rise, he saw two figures, more than half a mile away, moving steadily in his direction. Moments earlier, he had been ready to weep out of frustration; now he shed a few tears in profound relief that he was no longer alone. He had no idea whether the others would have a way out of this predicament, but their mere presence offered that possibility.

Hurrying on, as the distance closed between him and the newcomers, William recognized the confident gait of his guide and saw that the other man was also Chippewa. Between them, they towed a small wide canoe, each man connected to the little craft by a short length of braided deer hide. For a moment, William's joy at seeing the two men eclipsed the canoe's significance, but shortly, he realized this was his rescue—he was going to escape this field of rotting ice!

Although he had composed himself by the time he met the men, words failed him. Somehow, he could not decide whether to ask questions or offer thanks to his guide for returning for him. The Chippewa guide, if he experienced any similar quandary as to how to start conversation, gave no sign of it but just offered William a deer-hide tether and said, "Come." Turning the canoe, the three men started together for the southern shore.

CHAPTER 12

Late March, 1892

B Y MY COUNT, we are eleven logs short at the riverbank."
Svensson delivered this bit of bad news with his usual equanimity. Had he been reporting the loss of his left foot or the discovery of a keg of aquavit, it would have sounded the same. He had come to the office himself because he didn't want the message to be garbled in any way and it was his news to give.

"Eleven!" Thomas replied. "There's no chance that it's a miscount, or perhaps the logs were sent to the wrong riverbank?"

"No, sir; I've checked."

Thomas sat silently. Of course Svensson would have checked. It was not entirely surprising either; logs had gone missing in every season he had been forced to share a stream or ice road with Cedric Inch.

"I think we know where they've gone. I'll look into it," Thomas said and stifled a sigh. "But judging by our earlier experiences, I'm not sure we'll be able to recover them."

"A shame," replied Svensson. "We had some premium pine there."

Inch. The mere thought of the man brought Thomas's blood up to a boil. If Inch would put some effort into sawing his own timber instead of poaching, he would be further ahead. But honest endeavor wasn't what drove Inch—Thomas knew that; no, Inch enjoyed the game—the knowledge that his advance was costing someone else his own. Thomas moved on to another subject.

"Listen; I'm going to be tied up here for a week or more; I might not make it to camp next week."

"I see, sir," Svensson said evenly.

"Keep an eye on the ice roads; they may be hard to keep up if we get a warm spell. I'm going to leave it up to you to decide when to stop cutting."

"Yes, sir."

"And do you have a man we can post at the riverbank—someone to keep an eye on things?"

"Yes, sir. It'll be slowing down soon. I can put someone out there. In fact, I have someone in mind for that."

"All right; thank you, Svensson. You're a big help." Thomas shook hands with his camp boss and saw him out the door.

Alone again, Thomas took a moment to consider the weather. There had been a brief warm spell in the morning, brought in by an errant southwest breeze, but after lunch, the prevailing northwest wind asserted itself and the weather grew colder. For the moment, it appeared that the ice roads would remain sound. Still, that brief warm shift to the southwest was a worry; it was the beginning of the seasonal trend as winter slowly lost its hold. There was still plenty of timber to be moved, the cribs to be shifted into place, and somewhere out there, William might be traversing the lake ice. Well, Thomas knew he couldn't help William, but he could see the cribs brought into position. He set out for the new mill, trailed by Moses, to see how the cribs were coming along.

Once outside, Moses wagged happily, nose to the ground until he caught a scent and scampered away to the far side of the old mill race. The wind had died completely, and the low light of early evening revealed a previously unseen haze—slight but definite. Thomas also caught a scent; he smelled water—vapor—not the sharper ozone smell of coming snow. An unacknowledged disquiet preyed upon him, coloring his view of Edwards and his crew's effort to finish and place the cribs. The task had taken far too long already, and it seemed as if the men down there were once again moving about lifelessly without any great sense of purpose.

"Hoh—the cat is among the pigeons now," Norman crowed in delight. Dennis looked up from his work where he had been replacing

Genevieve's forward hatch boards for the night. "What do you mean?" he asked.

"Have a look. The old man is on the march toward Edwards and that gang of circus performers working on the cribs."

"Oh, yeah…. Even from here I can see he's got that look."

"That look?" Norman asked.

"You probably never see it, but if he's not happy with your work, his face goes all blank like he's not thinking about anything at all, and that's just what fools you because in the next moment, he'll have a few hard words for you to think about."

"You're right; I haven't seen it," said Norman.

"Let's not be caught gawking or he'll be here next."

"I'm not worried," Norman scoffed. "But we'll finish packing up and have a smoke. I want to see how Edwards weathers this little squall."

In twenty minutes, *Genevieve*'s small crew had completed its day's work and cook and mate sat back on the stern rail to enjoy a smoke together as had become their custom.

"The old man is still over there." Dennis grinned as he filled his pipe. "I think he's going to work them late tonight."

"It does serve them right; they've been messing around on those cribs for quite a while, soaking up free pay. I see some of that crew carrying cedar logs one way, and later, someone else drags them back to where they came from untouched. How long has it been?" Norman asked.

"I think over two weeks. It's a lousy job when it snows, but it should be simple enough now. They must be almost done."

Norman counted the cribs, jabbing a thick index finger toward each one as he did so. "…sixteen, seventeen, eighteen…nineteen. Yup, they're just finishing the last one."

"Nineteen. That's going to be a huge log pen."

"Well, you know how many crews they've had cutting this year."

Dennis nodded silently since his mouth was occupied with the lighting of his pipe. After a few puffs, he had a healthy glow in the bowl and blew a short jet of blue smoke up into the cold evening sky.

"I guess that's the big pressure now; as soon as the ice breaks, the logs will be sent downriver. And they sure won't fit in the old pens," he said at last.

"Yeah," Norman pulled on his cigarette contemplatively. "The old man has got a lot to contend with now that 'the pup' has left it all to him." Norman never took pains to hide his dislike for William from Dennis. "And if those maroons don't have these cribs out on the ice before it breaks, there won't be any place for the timber to go."

"The ice is still pretty solid; we should have it for a couple more weeks. They should manage it, don't you think?" Dennis asked.

"Not at the rate they're going," Norman said pessimistically. "Anyhow, cribs or no, I can't wait to see this ice break up."

"Me, too. But as for the cribs, my bet is that the old man will ride that crew and push the job ahead."

"That will be some fun in the next few steps."

"What do you mean?" Dennis asked.

"It's just that the work will keep getting heavier, and I can picture the flogging he'll have to give those sluggards to line up the cribs, haul heavy line to them, and load 'em with rocks. Those slobs are barely moving now; can you even imagine them on the hustle? They don't show the pepper they need to saw ice around a crib, never mind filling one full of rocks once it's properly sunk. The whole thing will be a long haul to windward—all with the old man watching." Dennis nodded sagely. "Well, he's not so bad, but all the same, I guess it's better them than us."

Night had fallen some time ago, and the fire in the office stove was reduced to a handful of glowing embers. The earlier warmth had escaped the office air, so Moses came periodically to present himself at Thomas's knee, anxious to get to his evening meal. Thomas patted his head absentmindedly, finished a few more notes for the morning, and to the dog's sudden delight, stood up to go home.

It was eight-thirty by the time he entered his own front door. The children had gone to bed, but Anne was waiting with a book in the parlor, and a pleasant smell of potatoes and pastry drifted in from the kitchen. Anne got up.

"You worked very late tonight," she said.

"I know," he answered as he hung up his coat. "There's so much to do with William gone." He gave her a quick smooch.

"Dinner is ready. Hopefully not—oooh!" she exclaimed. Moses had nosed her from behind at the word "dinner."

"I never get used to that. I was saying I hope it's not overdone," she said.

Thomas gave a mock growl to the dog. "Moses—that's no way to treat a lady."

They went into the kitchen where the table was set for two. A basket of fresh bread sat to one side of a bare cutting board, and a bowl of pickled cabbage balanced the table on its other side.

"You haven't eaten, Anne?"

"I had a small bite with the children, but I'm hungry again now."

She gave the dog a bowl of scraps and old porridge. Then she pulled a covered pan with a venison pie and some roasted potatoes from the oven and set it in the center of the cutting board. Removing the lid, she served, and although they were both hungry, they talked as they ate.

"So, how did it go today?" Anne asked.

"Well, it seems as though Cedric Inch has made off with more of our logs."

"Again? How do you know?"

"It's my best guess. Svensson is eleven logs short on his count."

"That's a lot. It doesn't sound like a miscount."

"No. Svensson is precise. It's more than ever; add it to the logs he poached earlier this year…it amounts to almost sixty or thereabouts. I wish I could get proof of it and make Marshal Griffiths confront him."

Thomas fantasized about more than mere confrontation; he envisioned arrest, trial, and a cold dingy jail cell with Inch in it, but he knew such things didn't come to be in an unjust world. He ate quietly for a few bites, leaning toward a brooding silence until Anne quickly changed the subject.

"Did the boys finish the cribs today?"

Thomas humpphed. "They're close. They're almost done with construction. Edwards needs a lot of guidance. Tomorrow, we'll start positioning them on the ice; I'm beginning to think we'll have an early thaw."

Anne chided herself; she had picked badly again, but now she had to follow the topic through.

"Why?"

"It just feels like it—hard to put a finger on—and if the ice breaks before we have the cribs set up, we'll be in some trouble. We've already spent more on them than we planned. It's funny; when I pictured complications building the new mill, I expected trouble with the mill itself—all this new machinery—but Boyle has that coming together right on time; instead, we're getting hung up on something as simple as cribs."

"Can you put more men on the cribs?" she asked.

"I don't have anyone to spare right now, not until we close down one of the lumber camps. Boyle has most of the best men. No, I have to make do with Edwards and company for now...well, except...."

"Except?"

"Except for *Genevieve's* crew; we started Morris and Risto back aboard last week, so with Benjamin, Dennis, and maybe Norman.... But I don't want to interfere with getting the ship ready to sail. *Genevieve* has got to be fully prepared at the same time as everything else. We're going to have a lot of lumber to move." Thomas lapsed into silence for a time, so Anne let him enjoy his food quietly. But when he finished his plate, she asked, "Are you worried about something else?"

He looked up at her and smiled. She was good.

"I am," he replied. "I'm worried I might get cold over here all by myself; maybe you should come over and sit on my knee."

The next day, Thomas had made his rounds by mid-morning and forced himself to his desk in an effort to keep up with administering the variety of enterprises that had fallen under his supervision. He was writing a response letter to a company looking for a supply of "B" grade white pine for railroad station construction. A draft tickled his neck and took his mind to the work outside, but he knew he must keep up with new customers or there would be no one to purchase this coming glut of timber that soon would be driven downriver. As Thomas continued to write, the draft strengthened its assault on the bare back of his neck, causing him to hunch his shoulders and sink his head forward in an unconscious mime of a threatened turtle. After completing the letter, he signed his name. It was only then that the draft registered on his mind. The office and the old mill seemed to be getting draftier with disuse, but he had felt this draft before, and it came to him that he only felt it—through some specific flaw in the structure—when the wind blew in from the southwest.

He pushed aside his correspondence and walked over to the window. Sure enough, the wind was picking up from the southwest. Grabbing his coat, he abandoned clerical work and strode outside to get a better look at the weather. The smell of vapor was in the air again, an alien damp breeze, thick and rich when drawn into the lungs. Quite suddenly, he felt a shiver of panic over the fate of the still struggling crib project. A rainfall would honeycomb the ice, leaving it deceptively solid looking, but totally unsafe for moving heavy weights over. Casting an eye toward the cribs, he saw once again that Edwards and company were limping along, but the progress was no more than halting. Somehow, they were stalled on the completion of the final crib; it was almost done yesterday, but it was still almost done now. It was time to shake up this operation or these cribs would wind up being stranded uselessly ashore.

Afternoon brought with it a thorough, featureless cloud cover and a greater sensation of coming dampness carried on the warming southwest wind. Thomas, ignoring all other tasks, put himself fully into the job of seeing these cribs in place by the end of the day. When a second team of horses arrived, he assigned some of *Genevieve*'s crew to readying the hauling lines on the cribs so the teamsters could simply hitch up and pull. Within an hour, he had each team of horses working in an opposite rotation, so that one was placing a crib while the other was being hitched to its load.

As the afternoon progressed, it became apparent that one horse team could complete the hauling of cribs, so Thomas broke the other one away to pull down a sledge loaded with ballast rock. Next came the back-breaking work of filling the cribs enough to sink. Each crib had been built to a different height to accommodate the water depth it would be submerged into. Consequently, the tallest cribs stood nine feet off the ice. Thomas himself fetched Arthur and the little sledge he used to bring supplies to the camps. On the back of the sledge were some crates he had got from Boyle. After pulling the sledge alongside a tall crib, the men formed a human chain, handing rocks up the escalating crates to Morris, who stood at the top, flinging rocks to all corners of the crib. For the shorter cribs, he had Dennis and Risto fetch some long planks to convert into a makeshift gangway, which they nailed up to the rim. Two more planks led across the great box, and a single one declined from the opposite rim, allowing the men to carry rocks up, drop them into the crib, and walk down the other side, keeping a smooth single direction of flow to the work. As Thomas watched this plan in action, he smiled to himself, wishing William could see this; his brother had spent many an hour talking to him about good flow.

It began to rain lightly—so lightly that it seemed not to penetrate clothing. The late afternoon light became a dismal gray dishwater glow, but Thomas continued the work, encouraging the men, passing rocks if a gap appeared in a chain, all with the goal of securing these cribs by nightfall. Gloves that had been wet from the beginning were sopping, wicking moisture up men's sleeves, and turning rough, calloused hands to bleached, wrinkled, spongy flesh. Even so, the leaders among the group felt the momentum and carried the less enthusiastic along with them.

The work continued under an onslaught of heavier rain, and even the stalwarts in the group admitted to themselves that they were getting wet through and becoming uncomfortable. Still, Thomas carried the project forward, becoming visibly wet himself so that even though some grumbled, no one wished to be the first man to give up. The cribs continued to fill, each one starting as a vacant box and finishing with a solid floor of broken rock. The gray light weakened and lost its ability to illuminate clearly, blending individual shapes into clumpy masses. Thomas broke away *Genevieve*'s crew to secure the cribs with heavy ropes to each other and to rods spiked into the ice and shore. Finally, it was dark, not black, but dark enough that a couple of men had tripped over the lines that now crisscrossed the work area. Each man was, at this point, dragging around with him an additional twenty pounds of entrapped water, held in the layers of his clothes. Rain that had seemed warm earlier became distinctly chilly when seeping down one's back. Islands of misery, the men scarcely spoke as they shuffled about shifting rocks and ropes until at last, to the enormous relief of all, Thomas called a halt to the work.

Two-and-a-half days later, Thomas awoke early, having gone to bed early. He lay quietly in the dark, listening to the rain pattering on the roof, enjoying the sound since it meant spring's dissolution of snow and ice, and he relished his present comfort, especially after the last two days' wet misery. Yesterday, even though it was Sunday, he had been out on the ice once again with *Genevieve*'s crew, checking and tightening the lines that held the cribs. He had dismissed the idea of sawing through the ice to sink them because the driving rain was rapidly making the ice more unstable. He congratulated himself for having pushed the crib project along as far as it had come. A squall rattled the sashes as the rain belted down; he had only beaten the season by a day. The broad-based cribs themselves might fall through at any time, but it was hard to predict.

The multitude of tasks left undone and awaiting him slowly purloined the comfort of his bed. Gently pulling his arm away from Anne, he slipped out from under the quilts.

It was still raining lightly when he arrived at the mill. The visibility was just enough that his eye was drawn to a ribbon of darkness out in the gray ice field. Concentrating, he could follow it—open water, stretching from some distant spring, far upriver, to a wider band banked by irregular ice shores leading out to the lake. A small thrill of release swept through him; the long siege of winter was being broken. His eye had hungered for the sight of water, and even this strained glimpse was rich sustenance. Soon, he would see water every day, his ship would no longer be captive, icebound, and he would regain a freedom that, whether he availed himself of it or not, meant so much to him. Looking at the cribs, he was brought back to more immediate concerns: eight of the largest cribs had broken through the ice and appeared to be in position. The water had engulfed four or five of the others; they had not sunk in position, but they were not far off. What was a worry was that the remaining structures sat along the edge of a new rift and were sagging to one side as though they might tip ninety degrees before sinking. There was nothing more he could do about it now. Seeing the decay of the ice, the only sensible thing to do was wait. He hoped William had made his passage across the lake.

Once inside his office, Thomas lit a fire in the stove. Moses came in shortly after him; the dog shook off violently, sprinkling Thomas's desk with shed raindrops. Although he had a full day of deferred paperwork ahead of him, he couldn't help but walk over to the window every so often to observe the slow changes taking place in the ice and the increasing tilt of the remaining cribs. At one such viewing, he fancied that he could see movement on one of the cribs. Farther over by the new mill, he saw a small group of men also watching. The crib was moving. What had started almost imperceptibly began to be a noticeable slide as the angle increased and the wooden box slowly lost its grip on the ice. There was a soft crack, almost a sharp groan, and the ice broke behind the cedar structure, tipping it into the water on a sharper angle still and shooting the thick fragment of ice that held it buoyant skyward. The crib rolled onto its side in its final descent, pushing out a disappointingly small ripple.

Thomas returned to his desk, intermittently disturbed by half-formed strategies for righting the capsized crib. Later, he was more forcibly interrupted by the sound of excited men talking, chattering outside. Returning once again to the window, he was barely in time to see the remaining cribs tip, one following another, into the ice rift—gracefully approximating the performance of the first one. Ice chunks popped, water rippled, and cribs settled, some by chance upright and others on their sides. Over by the mill, men cheered, but Thomas shook his head ruefully and consigned the overturned cribs to tomorrow; for now, he had letters to write.

Chapter 13

Surrounded by still, impassive men, Fitzpatrick sat at a dimly lit, felt-covered table, looking deep into the cavity of another losing hand and reminding himself not to stare. If he were to have any chance at all, he knew he must not stare. Bereft of luck, his hands had worsened to the point where skills such as he had no longer helped, and after playing for only a couple of hours, he was already on house credit. The best play right now would be to fold early, leaving another twenty-five dollars stranded to be claimed by an opponent, but he couldn't do it. The grinding reality was that he couldn't afford to lose any more, so he caught at the reins of his runaway horse, dug his heels into soft sand, and bluffed. Could anyone expect that this losing streak would continue? With one good winning round, he could still break even on the night and then go home.

"What will ya have then, Fitzpatrick?" Sullivan the dealer demanded.

"Give me two, please," Fitzpatrick replied, darting furtive looks around the table at his opponents.

He trudged home through lumpy, trodden slush that verged on freezing, whiskey blunting the familiar trauma of loss; he always saved back a little money for that. Sadly, this was a pattern—becoming a tradition. If he believed he could win, saving the cost of a few drinks would be unnecessary, but deep down, he knew he would be fortune's fool right down to the end, retreating from the tables worse off, and so it came to be. Tonight, he had fallen further than before; previously, he had won and lost in medium stakes games, and if he came up short, a small loan from the house could be covered by a small loan from the bank. With a few deft changes to Paul's work before it was entered into the ledger, cash discrepancies could be hidden temporarily and give him enough time to win again. Money in hand, he would slip it into the vault and clean up the whole business before anyone noticed or the books had to be cooked. If anyone did notice, the discrepancy would be blamed on the hapless Paul. Perfect. Tonight, though, he had played for huge stakes in a desperate bid to right his listing ship, and he had finally lost such a sum of money that there was no hope of winning it back in short order. Worse yet, it was too great an amount to pull from the vault and have the deficit remain unnoticed, even for a short time. He was in arrears to the figure of $2,500 this time, and as his negative total climbed, Sullivan's manner toward him descended; the dealer's words were hard-edged when he discussed repayment of funds. He had even addressed him several times as "Fitzpatrick," omitting the "Mr.," a message of loss of status. Fitzpatrick knew Sullivan's tables were owned by a Mr. O'Shea, an individual who would operate outside the rule of law when patience ran short and the money ran long. To obtain house credit, he had divulged his address and place of employment—it was not comforting to be known by these people.

He stumbled in hardening slush, caught himself, and smartened up his gait for the final few blocks to his home. He had to present an untroubled face to his wife or she would ask a wide variety of bothersome questions. Beatrice was shrewd, and although aware of his card playing, she thought he was a member at some club. Beyond these two ideas, he had left her in a benign and comforting ignorance.

Arriving at his front door, Fitzpatrick reached for the door handle, only to have it magically swing away from his hand. Beatrice stood in the doorway, impatient and distraught, and for a moment, he thought he was in for a serving of the quiet disapproval she ladled out when he had been drinking.

"Have you been waiting up?" he asked, the pleasing timbre of his baritone calculated to convey warm concern, as he stepped into the front hall.

"Oh, John, I'm glad you've finally come home. Paul has just left: Papa has had a bad fall and isn't well. The doctor thinks it's a palsy of some kind. I want to go over to be with Maman and help," Beatrice rattled out.

Wrinkles formed up vertically, pinching between Fitzpatrick's eyebrows, ending at the shiny plain of his bare scalp; he felt considerably put out. What he desired most was to go to bed and sleep away his troubles, but now.... *Damn old, Edgar,* he thought, *the man is a constant inconvenience.*

"Bea, Bea, what can we really do tonight? Is the doctor there?" he asked.

She drew her lips into a thin taut line, and then Fitzpatrick stumbled over a second notion: If Edgar were not well enough to appear at the bank for a few days, he might best use the time to find a solution to his debt crisis. He decided on a quick change of course.

"Let's look in on your father anyway. Your poor mother will be beside herself."

Beatrice pulled on her coat and they set off.

Arriving at Edgar's house, they found Paul standing on the front porch.

"Paul, what are you doing out here?" his sister asked.

"The doctor has just left; I was seeing him out when I spotted you coming up the street," he replied with a subdued smile.

"Anything new?" Beatrice asked.

"The doctor says Papa needs to rest undisturbed for at least three days," Paul answered while showing them inside and taking their coats. "Maman is upstairs," he continued, leaving them to make their own way up. Fitzpatrick accompanied Beatrice to Edgar's room, where he remained in the hallway, just outside the open doorway. It had been his objective to see his father-in-law with his own eyes to determine how unwell he might be. The scene before him now was encouraging: Edgar was in nightdress, in bed, propped into a reclined sitting position by a small mound of pillows and quilts. He was covered to the waist by a bedsheet and a weight of fine woolen blankets. Lying there, slack-jawed and ruddy, he looked much older, worn and tired; his wrinkles etched deeper, and his gray hair strayed out in various uncharacteristic patterns of disarray. It was hard to equate the sleeping man with the domineering manager of the Industrial Bank of Detroit. Fitzpatrick gloated over his own wellness and wondered whether this might be the tipping point for the old man. His mind leapt to an obscene hope that perhaps Edgar would not recover from his fall. *Maybe he might even die!* he thought gleefully. That would be a wildly exciting outcome.

While Fitzpatrick had been evaluating Edgar's state, the patient awoke and cast one eye about the room, leaving the other eye closed. Spotting Fitzpatrick in the hall, Edgar rasped quietly to his wife, "What is he doing out there?"

Misconstruing his question, Louise asked, "Shall I bring him in?" But Edgar winked twice and closed his eye again wearily.

"Dear God, no!" he slurred, but then he said more strongly, "Give him to Paul; get him a drink, but just get rid of him."

Louise had obediently escorted Fitzpatrick down to the parlor and left him in Paul's company with a rye whiskey and soda. With nothing to do, Fitzpatrick sat in a Georgian rocker, sipping constantly from his drink, and evaded being drawn into what he thought of as vapid conversation with Paul. As his mind spun with the turn of the evening's events, he considered how much to dare as he exploited this opportunity. His initial euphoria having waned, he recognized that Edgar was a tough old goat who might bounce back from his ailment in short order. He now owed $2,500 to Sullivan and company. If he pulled a thousand dollars out of the vault—which would be easy in Edgar's absence—he could pay down five hundred and play with the other five to make back the rest of his debt. Playing for lower stakes, he could trounce lesser opponents; if he started tomorrow night, he might pull enough winnings to clean his slate at the bank before Edgar was up and around. Wildly optimistic, he fantasized about making some money, for surely this was a significant turn in his luck. The key to everything now would be to secure the money from the vault before any other change might occur; with this in mind, he finally decided to engage with Paul.

"Your father will be on his feet in a few days, but for now, we must carry on as best we can in his absence," he began reassuringly.

"Yes…yes, I suppose so," Paul answered, his mind awhirl with the complexities of picking up his father's work.

"I will, of course, help out in any way I can, Paul," Fitzpatrick assured.

"Thank you, John. I'm sure there will be a lot to do."

"You've had a long night and a shock; perhaps I can open the bank for you tomorrow," Fitzpatrick offered.

Mistrust flickered through Paul's mind; Edgar had warned him repeatedly that he and he alone must open the bank—that he must never delegate this duty to another, but he smiled and answered simply, "Thank you, John. I'll open as usual; Papa hates changes, and I don't want him to be upset."

Fitzpatrick was astonished that Paul had not only refused his offer, but even more, that he had a reasoned response. He would have to employ his usual tactics of diversion to get some time alone in the vault.

Four nights later, he was clearing a table of poker chips. It had been child's play to get around Paul and take the money out of the bank, and whether it had been a greater sense of self-assurance or that his luck had truly changed, he was suddenly winning once again. Having turned in later than three in the morning on the previous three nights, he was quite short of sleep. Thankfully, Beatrice was staying with her mother and Edgar, so at least his movements could be left unexplained. Nonetheless, it was time to cash in for the night. Counting his chips, he had gained by three hundred tonight and could put that down against his "account." Altogether, he would have erased $1,300 of his debt, leaving him with $1,200 to go. Having returned $500 to the bank vault, his working stake was still $500; he hoped to come out of this situation with that amount intact. He had had word from Beatrice and Paul that Edgar was showing signs of improvement, so he was toying with the idea of rejoining the higher stakes table, in order to close the gap more swiftly, when Sullivan appeared at his elbow.

"Mr. Fitzpatrick," he said amiably, "you've been making progress."

Fitzpatrick guessed correctly that Sullivan was there to make sure he was paying up with his winnings. At least he was back to being "Mr. Fitzpatrick."

"I have. Luck has been with me tonight."

"I hope you will join our table again soon?" Sullivan asked.

This was the little bump Fitzpatrick needed.

"Yes, perhaps tomorrow."

After he had turned in his chips, Sullivan extended his hand toward him.

"Until tomorrow, then."

Fitzpatrick shook, bidding him good night, and began to contemplate his path toward a big win.

Hunched over his desk in the bank the next morning, Fitzpatrick was having difficulty keeping his eyes open; the hours of lost sleep were catching up with him. As he worked through the reams of paperwork that the bank had generated, he repeatedly found his eyes crossing and would catch himself falling into his work. Pulling up, he would look around to see whether he had been noticed, rub his eyes, straighten his spectacles, and try again. *I must get some sleep*, he thought. He had to be sharp when he played again tonight. If only he had a place to hide for a short nap....

"Mr. Fitzpatrick."

Fitzpatrick smothered a flinch at being summoned by Paul. It was almost as bad as having to grovel to old Edgar; the father could be short, but he knew his business. Paul, however, was trying on his father's shoes without a knack for tying them, in his opinion. Oh, well, a short walk might clear his head.

"Yes, Mr. Standish," he answered from the reluctant post of Edgar's office doorframe.

"I've just had a telephone call," said Paul, beaming. "Papa is coming in this afternoon."

Fitzpatrick's stomach flip-flopped. He didn't share Paul's excitement, but the news had woken him up.

"Wonderful," he replied, "but is he really ready for that? You mustn't let him tire himself."

Paul's ready smile had slipped away. "Oh, and here are some papers for you," he said with a peremptory nod of his head.

Fitzpatrick swallowed his annoyance, entered the office, took the proffered folder, and escaped to his desk. The thought of having Edgar return to the bank marred his sunny projections for a big win at cards—he needed more time without any awkward nosing around in either the vault or the affected files. If he simply replaced the money now, he ran the risk of harassment from Sullivan and company. No, there had to be some way of stalling Edgar for a couple of more days. In a stray thought, he realized Beatrice would likely be home tonight. More inconvenience. Try as he might, he couldn't think of a way to prevent Edgar coming in; he decided instead on the desperate tactic of arranging for him to slip and fall. Down the rear hallway past the water closet was the janitor's room. Making his way there when everyone seemed occupied, he looked in briefly and found what he wanted: several tins of wax floor polish. He took one, as well as some rags, then returned to his desk. It only remained now to create a nice slick on the floor of Edgar's office while Paul was out at lunch. Paul would lock the office, but he had copied a key months ago. With his plan formed, he felt better, returned to his work, and waited for noon to come.

At twelve exactly, Paul locked the office door and departed for lunch. Allowing enough time to elapse to be sure Paul was gone and hadn't forgotten anything, Fitzpatrick quietly unlocked Edgar's office and slipped inside, closing the door behind him. Kneeling, he pulled the rags from his pocket, opened the tin of wax, and began smearing it on the floor behind Edgar's desk. In short vigorous strokes, he smoothed the globs of polish until he was satisfied that the surface appeared innocuous. He had chosen this area as the most likely place where Edgar would turn and possibly be on one foot while taking his seat. Standing back, Fitzpatrick admired his work briefly before gathering his accessories and returning them surreptitiously to the janitor's closet.

Promptly at one o'clock, Paul returned from lunch and unlocked the office. Fitzpatrick knew he had to keep him occupied until Edgar's arrival or risk an accidental discovery of the wax before it had done its dirty work. He cobbled a patchwork of questions, and drew tortuous answers from Paul, often feigning a misunderstanding until Paul became surprisingly frustrated with his obtuseness. It was then a relief to both of them when Edgar's hansom pulled up in front of the bank. His driver helped Edgar down from the hansom, lending more support than usual, but once down, Edgar walked with the aid of a cane in a firm steady stride. It maddened Fitzpatrick to see this display of his father-in-law's strength. A clear message was being sent as Edgar mounted the stairs, entered the bank, and then proceeded toward his office, acknowledging various employees as he went. Paul hovered, offering to take his father's arm, but he was quietly shrugged off. Paul then opened the office door and the father and son stepped inside.

Fitzpatrick waited at his desk with bated breath; any moment now, he might hear the slip and fall, perhaps with a good delectable shriek on the way down. If he was really lucky, Edgar might hit his head—it might be too much to hope for. For more than two minutes, he was on pins and needles, listening to Edgar put questions to Paul, and he began to wonder whether the man was ever going to sit down, when suddenly he was summoned.

"Fitzpatrick."

He had developed a distaste for the sound of his own name when called out this way, but this time, he thought it wonderful; perhaps he would get to watch the whole business. Upon walking into the office, to his chagrin, he found Edgar and Paul sitting like old friends in the armchairs before the desk. Edgar had tired himself on the way in and had taken the first available seat. Masking his disappointment beneath his best poker face, Fitzpatrick consoled himself that there still existed the promise of a fine mishap.

"Get us the Abernathy loan file—Howard and Dora Abernathy."

"Yes, Mr. Standish," Fitzpatrick replied in a guardedly neutral baritone. When he had returned with the expected file, Edgar had another task for him: "Would you fetch the cleaning man? Something has been spilled behind my desk."

He had been so certain that the wax was invisible that Fitzpatrick felt compelled to step in and look. Sure enough, from the angle of Edgar's chair, the floor appeared hazy around the desk, compared to the encircling shine of polished boards. Paul was about to protest, feeling that fault was being found with this small aspect of his short tenure as guardian of the bank, but Edgar raised a hand effectively, halting the words before they were spoken.

"And also," Edgar continued, "I will need you to stay late tonight. I have some catching up to do."

Fitzpatrick swallowed. "Yes, Mr. Sta—"

"What have you got on your trousers? I shouldn't have to remind you that proper dress is expected at all times; keeps up the bank's image."

Fitzpatrick looked down to see that he had got some floor wax on his knees.

"Wear something clean tomorrow," Edgar finished, dismissing him.

Leaving the room, Fitzpatrick ground his teeth. This was getting worse and worse; not only had his plan failed, but he now had to worry about the old goat nosing around after hours. His fatigue was returning, but fetching the janitor would give him the chance to breathe a little cold air and clear his head. Outside, he reviewed his options: if he put the money back, he had little chance of getting free of Sullivan; if he played tonight, he ran the risk of discovery by Edgar; if he could get Edgar out of the way for only a little more time, he would likely satisfy all of his needs. He set his mind to the task of sidetracking his boss.

Edgar put in a surprisingly full afternoon: he had negotiated a refinancing of the Abernathy loan, met with the chairman of Crosstown Streetcar Company, started a new loan to an expanding paint manufacturer, and had even had time to organize the sale of fifty of his safes to a San Francisco company in a deal conducted over the telephone. His sales pitch for the safes had come booming out of his office door in compensation for a deficient connection.

"…It has triple deadbolts, solid wrought iron casing; it's fireproof—practically airtight, and is fitted with the most sophisticated lock mechanism in the industry. It will foil any thief!"

As Edgar finished triumphantly, no one within earshot could doubt that he was bouncing back. He had involved Paul in all of his dealings, and to Fitzpatrick's relief, they were kept busy enough that no movement had been made toward verifications in the vault. The clerk realized that very soon the overdue reckoning must occur. He had to replace the money tomorrow or permanently cook the books and hope the changes would go unnoticed.

Finally, at 8:25 p.m., Edgar announced he was going home. His hansom pulled up and he departed, leaving Paul and Fitzpatrick to close up. Fitzpatrick looked ruefully at his pocket watch. He had run through his day fueled by nervous energy. He should go to play poker tonight, but as Edgar left, his stamina ebbed away and he knew he probably would not do well—it was also too late to get in on a preferred table.

Although it would prolong his dilemma, he decided to go home for some rest.

The next afternoon found Fitzpatrick better rested and buried in newly assigned tasks. Deep in his work, he looked up from his ledger to discover two unannounced visitors looming over his desk. Sullivan was one, and the other was a fairly solid-looking man in his early thirties with a badly bent nose that gave accent to a habitually nasty expression.

"Good afternoon," Sullivan led.

"Er, good afternoon," Fitzpatrick replied. "To what do I owe the pleasure?" he asked in an effort to appear unperturbed.

"Just happened to be in the neighborhood," Sullivan lied. "This is an associate of ours, Mr. Thompson."

"Well, this is a surprise," Fitzpatrick said while extending his hand toward Thompson, his eyes darting left and right to see whether anyone was watching this interchange. Thompson remained stiff, hands clasped behind his back, and stared for a moment, but then finally spoke:

"We had been hoping you would be back to join us last night. At the very least, you need to continue to show up to take care of what you owe."

"You…I…the problem was…well," Fitzpatrick stumbled. "I was kept here late yesterday, but I will be in tonight," he finished.

"That will be grand," Sullivan said, dressing his reply with a mirthless smile. Thompson simply kept up the menacing stare he had displayed from the beginning. The two men stood as though waiting for something more of a dismissal, so Fitzpatrick reached about for an idea of how to be rid of them politely when Edgar saved the situation: "Fitzpatrick," he bellowed from the depth of his office.

"Gentlemen, I must go," Fitzpatrick said, relieved to have a diversion and concurrently ashamed to be so brusquely summoned in front of Sullivan.

"Yes, sir," he called to Edgar and took his leave of the men.

"Until tonight, Fitzpatrick," Sullivan said.

"Until tonight," he responded woodenly over his shoulder.

In the office, Fitzpatrick made notes as Edgar requested a series of files and ledgers. With a sick, sinking feeling, he knew that among the list he had been making were accounts with which he had doctored the numbers to hide the amount of money he had borrowed. The changes he had made were all large enough that he had little confidence they might escape Edgar's keen scrutiny. If he managed to return the money to the vault now, the changes would be thought of as mistakes. If the discrepancies were discovered and the money were missing, he would be found out. *I mustn't panic yet*, he told himself. He massaged his self-image, telling himself to be the man of iron nerve he knew himself to be. The accounts had not been reviewed yet, and even if Standish saw through the paperwork by closing, it was unlikely the vault's contents would be tallied until tomorrow. All of the same options applied; he would hold on, win tonight, and clean up this mess for good in the morning.

The last hour of the working day was oppressively quiet for Fitzpatrick as Edgar pored over files—tallying, checking, verifying. Closing time approached at last with the usual bustle of tellers and clerks: counting tills, closing windows and wickets, chairs scraping floors as they were pushed under desks. Paul locked the vault before departing, and soon there were no more good nights being called, the bank being emptied but for the manager and his clerk. Fitzpatrick knew he would not be dismissed until Standish was done for the day, so he began to fret about his card game. At last, he could hear Edgar hobbling toward his door, but his hopes of ending the day fermented swiftly to an all-consuming dread. Edgar carried numerous files toward the vault, spun the locking dials in sequence, and opened the door wide for light before going inside. Fitzpatrick could see his father-in-law doing a rough tally of the vault's contents, making his way from one drawer to the next, looking methodically. The discovery he had feared was at hand, he realized; he had to do something quickly or all would be lost.

"Fitzpatrick!" Edgar bellowed.

God, how he hated being summoned that way. His mind slipped backwards to his hopes last week when the old man had been bedridden and there had been a slim but pleasant prospect that he would not recover. And then—no more being summoned this way. He began to act without forethought.

"Yes, Mr. Standish."

"Fitzpatrick, I need—"

KLAANNNNGGG—the vault door slammed shut, interrupting Edgar for once. Fitzpatrick spun the dials that tumbled the deadbolts into place with a sweet and sour mixture of delight and horror. He was committed now; there could be no way to explain this.

Edgar pounded furiously on the inside of the vault door, shouting for Fitzpatrick to call Paul. Fitzpatrick, meanwhile, reflected on the nature of fortune. The Fieldgate safe had made Edgar Fieldgate Standish, and now it would be his undoing. If Edgar were lucky, he might have another attack of palsy; if not, he might spend a few hours thinking about how airtight he had made his vaults. The clerk pulled up a chair to listen to the old man struggle. There would still be time for poker later on.

CHAPTER 14

IT WAS AN irony that the rarely experienced rumble of iron wheels rolling along parallel rails could bring about a sense of ease in William. He found the muffled "shush-shush" of the distant engine agreeable and subconsciously anticipated the "clunk-clunk" sound as the car passed over evenly spaced joints in the track. Lulled by motion, he could relax almost completely since there was nothing much to be done beyond the immediate passive task of traveling. Following his escape from the ice, he had spent just one night in a Mackinaw City inn before embarking for Detroit. Consequently, he was still tired from his ordeal, so a spell of inactivity, where he could watch the scenery blur past the window, was comforting.

The irony of his pacific humor was that his most traumatic experience as a young boy had taken place on a train: when he was six years old, his father had set out from Massachusetts by rail with him, Thomas, and their mother. Moving west toward Michigan held the bright promise of a new home in rich timberlands, but his father's vision of that happy future was never to be realized.

Early trains had rolled over flat rails that distorted and curved upward with repeated use. As they strained up, they loosened from the track bed, sometimes rocking when the train passed over them. One of these snakeheads (as they were known to railway men) had burst through the wooden floor of their railcar, impaling and mortally wounding his mother as she sat next to him. His father had made an effort to comfort her, but there was really nothing to be done against so massive an insult to her poor body, and in a moment or two, it had been over. Shrieks and shouting coursed forward from farther back in the car, denoting more killed and injured passengers, and there, surrounded by screaming and pandemonium amid the blood and wreckage of furnishings and lives, sat William mute and horrified.

The sight of his mother's inanimate face had faded down through the decades to the point where now, when he did think of that terrible day on the train, it was as if it were a story that had happened to someone else. On this train trip, however, he was thinking of another woman: Carmina. With her, too, his thoughts had become vague, indistinct. He had thought about her with such passion and force over the period of their separation that, surprisingly, as he drew nearer to seeing her, images of her had begun to diminish, as had the poignancy of his mother's demise.

Across the aisle from William, a man folded up the newspaper he had been reading and, having made eye contact with William, extended the rumpled publication toward him.

"Do you want an old paper? It helps the miles pass by."

"Thank you," William accepted. It was the morning edition of yesterday's *Detroit Free Press*; it had probably ridden the train from Detroit on the previous day. William thumbed through the paper; it was all out of order, but he found the national news first, and when he had finished with that, he was confronted by a headline that grabbed his attention in the financial section:

CAPTAIN OF INDUSTRY FOUND DEAD IN BANK VAULT

His eyes flittered about the page, bringing key words into focus before settling down to read the article:

DETROIT, MI. Edgar Fieldgate Standish, Founder and Managing Director of the Industrial Bank of Detroit, was found dead at his bank shortly after 1 a.m. this morning. His body was discovered by his son, Paul, and his driver. Mr. Standish appeared to have collapsed in the bank's vault where he expired. Mr. Standish had suffered an attack of palsy in the previous week and the coroner is looking into the cause of death.

William was shocked. *Poor Standish*, he thought. He had liked the man, even though Thomas had found him overbearing. Standish had embodied an ideal of the self-made industrialist: with hard work and vision, he had built a successful business that produced an excellent product, and he had gone on to run a thriving bank. He would be missed. What a blow to his family. William wondered how the son would manage in his father's absence; he decided he would visit the bank to offer his condolences to the young man. He didn't want to read any more of the paper. The article about Edgar Standish's passing had hit close to home. People mentioned in the newspaper could usually be comfortably read about, distanced across an insulating moat of unfamiliarity. The article, however, as well as his harrowing passage over the ice, reminded William that life could be short. Contemplations of mortality and his hopes for the future alternated in his mind, occupying him for the remainder of the train ride while he gazed out the window.

From the moment he stepped off the train in Detroit, William's glum patterns of thought fell away. The race of the city never failed to charm him; each visit held something new and novel, even while he enjoyed a comfortable familiarity with its streets and establishments. But, like any city, Detroit had its seedier inhabitants, particularly near the train station—people who lay in wait, watching for a fresh face, an innocent—a target who had wandered into the urban wilderness naïve enough to believe in his fellow man. However, for all the efforts or desires of the hustlers and hucksters, the pickpockets and purveyors, sad story confidence men and sharks, William was not their mark. Every man will exhibit a weakness at some moment, though, so despite escaping the gauntlet surrounding the station, William later fell into the hands of a loquacious tailor.

It seemed to happen by accident; on his way to a favorite barbershop, he had been walking slowly along Shelby Street, eyes skyward, admiring the marvelous Romanesque revival architecture of the federal building where the post office was located. He was in awe of the beautiful towering columns holding aloft the great clock. Everything about the building struck him as elegantly proportioned, from the sizes of the grand arched doorways and the soaring windows to the pyramidal roof cap sheltering the enormous timepiece. Looking up as he was, it wasn't hard for him to blunder over a small man who had been crouched down tying his shoe.

Three days later, a freshly scrubbed William preened before a mirror in his hotel room, twitching the collar and cuffs of his new morning-blue jacket into place. The tailor he had literally stumbled over had sold him the unusual color on the premise that a change would be refreshing. He was then promoted toward a new tie and talked into purchasing boots that would better complement the new suit. His fresh haircut and whisker trim completed the job. Thankfully, his hat matched his new ensemble, for the rest of it had cost him forty-six dollars, but now he could admire the effect. The suit fit better than any he had worn before, and so, despite mildly resenting the tailor's slick sales methods and the resultant expenditure, he had to admire the man's skill. He looked good. After a final comb of his hair, he felt ready. Picking up his wallet, watch, and keys, he headed off to meet Carmina.

To his great relief, Carmina had replied immediately to a note he had sent her, confirming that she had not yet departed for San Francisco. He had waited years for this opportunity, and after his difficult journey, he would hate to think he might have missed her by a day.

The morning was bright and chilly; high cumulous clouds hinted at the promise of spring but remained coy as to what afternoon might bring. On his way to Carmina's house, William stopped at a German delicatessen and bought some marzipan candies he knew she liked. Armored in his new clothes and armed with marzipan, he strode at a measured pace across town so as not to break a sweat. Grounded lectures he had given himself on reality and expectations could not hold down an inflating balloon of excitement; he was too excited by far simply to ride the streetcar. And so his balloon filled and filled, its heated gas exerting a pull up on him until his toes merely tickled the path he had given himself to follow. He couldn't help but think about the slim possibility of reunion, even though by now he knew it made little sense. He floated and tumbled, floated and tumbled with these thoughts, over and over, until at last he was at her door.

He knocked and retreated to the top step of the porch so he could be seen from the upstairs window, and have a chance of escape should an old chamberpot suddenly plummet from the second floor. Standing in a stately pose that he thought would show his suit to good advantage, he smiled expectantly. A minute passed. And then another. He knocked again and resumed his position on the top step. After a few more minutes and some more knocking, he realized either Carmina wasn't home or was hiding from him. As a cloud blocked the sun, he began to shiver, clad only in his lightweight new suit and standing motionless as he was. Surely she wouldn't hide from him after having written to him in the first place and then responding to his most recent letter. He began to have a sinking feeling this meeting would not take place after all. He was considering leaving when he saw her down the street, carrying a basket and another parcel, making her way home. As she approached the house, he came down the steps and gave her a reassuring smile.

"Carmina!" he greeted her as he drank in her appearance.

"William, hello," she answered anxiously.

He had hoped for some sign of pleasure from her, but he understood how she might feel anxious at this meeting.

"I forgot you were coming today," she said.

This he had difficulty believing since he had thought of little else for the past two days. He pulled out his note from her and checked.

"Yes, here it is. Ten o'clock on Thursday. It is Thursday, isn't it?" he smiled.

"Er—yes, yes it is. I'm sorry," she replied, her face tense. She fumbled past him with her parcel, found her keys, and opened the door.

"I meant to tidy, but uh—come in."

She led the way inside, leaving him to close the door while she carried her parcel and basket to the kitchen. He stepped into the living room and surveyed his surroundings. The room was not overly furnished, but it had an overlay of clutter that made it feel tight and uncomfortable. Set against one wall was a Georgian sofa, and across a heavily laden coffee table, a loveseat and armchair stood opposite. In the corner, a platform rocker completed the set, all made in a dark rubbed wood and upholstered in burgundy velvet cloth. Interspersed between chairs and sofas were small end tables perched on spindly legs, draped in linen cloths but covered in books, periodicals, papers of all kinds, and various household items. The room had a faint smell of something sweet and rich; it took William a moment to place it…

"Would you like some tea or coffee?" Carmina called from the kitchen.

…pipe tobacco, or maybe foreign cigars.

"Yes, some of your coffee would be nice," William said.

Feeling out of place and still clutching the marzipan, he slowly roamed the room, idly looking at old issues of newspapers left open on random pages. Stacked haphazardly among the letters and envelopes on one table were a cup and saucer, the cup still half-full of a milky tea. As he heard Carmina unpack her parcels in the kitchen, he decided to sit down on the sofa. He nestled the marzipan into a thinly occupied spot on the coffee table and fidgeted, pulling at his fingers as he tried to think of something to say. He had not fully prepared himself for a lukewarm reception. Clumsily, he called out: "How has your winter been?" as though Carmina were a fellow lumberman with whom he could trade tales of felled trees and ice roads—even as the words were absorbed by the room, he realized it was a poor start, but he knew nothing of what his wife had done in the last three years.

"Oh… fine," she called back.

Perhaps he would wait for her to initiate talk. It was she who had finally wanted to see him. He sat uneasily and picked up the box of marzipan again, but in so doing, he capsized a stack of old correspondence. In the strewn pile, he could see his letter to her from three days ago. He quickly began gathering up envelopes and letters, trying to reassemble the loose disorder of the erstwhile stack. His eyes fell on individual papers as he performed his task, letters addressed to Carmina… Dear Carmina… Carmina… Jasper? Here was another one—Mr. Jasper Tate. The sound of cups and saucers was a harbinger of Carmina's approach, so he hastily placed the last few items atop the stack, sitting back just as she entered the room carrying a tray.

She looked more composed; there might have been a hint of excitement in her eyes that reminded him of their early times.

"William, how good to see you!"

He stood up and smiled, but inwardly, the uneasiness he had felt since entering the apartment clamped onto him more securely. It was certainly false to greet him so when she had run and hidden to be away from him. It hit him that her facial expression was contrived in a way he had long ago seen her employ socially.

"Carmina," he said warmly as he stood. Her dark hair hung in loose curls that tumbled to her shoulders. She still had a prettiness to her that appealed to him, but in some way, it was unfamiliar and distant, a faraway hillside of uniform color.

Realizing she had nowhere to put the tray, she set it carefully on the armchair so she could clear a space on the table.

"I'm sorry; I should have prepared better. Everything has been… well, a little mad lately."

He picked up the marzipan while she tidied, and once she had set down the coffee tray, he presented the little box to her.

"I brought you something."

"What is it?" she asked with a knit brow as she accepted it.

"Marzipan."

"Oh, thank you," she said briefly, and then she seemed at a loss for a place to put it. She perched the box on a stack of newspapers she had moved to the loveseat. Then she poured coffee as William sat once again, and they fell into a strained silence while each sipped at his or her cup, wondering where to begin. For William, there was an unreality about this situation: to be in such close proximity to this woman whom he had loved and seemingly lost, pursued futilely, dreamt of, pined for, and pondered until he was hopelessly confused. He had rehearsed this meeting in his head numerous times, but now he couldn't think of the first thing to say. Finally, he decided that was what he should tell her.

"Carmina, after all this time, I find myself at a loss for words."

"I feel the same, William. So much has happened over these years…. I…I…. What can I tell you?" she finished helplessly.

He decided to be dispassionate and appear to have evaded the thralldom of a past that promised no future.

"Well, tell me about your plans. You mentioned moving to San Francisco. When are you going?"

"Oh, pretty soon," she said vaguely. "We have a few more things to organize before we can go."

William nodded. It looked like getting clear of this house would take some time.

"And your auntie, did I ever meet her? Why did she decide to move?" he asked.

"My auntie? Oh, she thought she would move for…the climate," Carmina replied as though she had just learned the answer herself.

Again, William felt a visceral uneasiness about her reply; she had avoided his first question and there was something…something invented in her answer.

"And you? What made you decide to move west?"

Suddenly, she seemed to be her old self again as her face lit up with excitement.

"Oh, William, I need a fresh start, and San Francisco is so wonderful; it has steep hills and the sea, and in the countryside, there are enormous trees—redwoods."

A fresh start, he thought. The words, hot and pointy, pricked between seams in his armor. What had been so wrong with their life together? What had she been asking for in her letter? He began pulling on his ring finger, but then he stopped himself.

"Have you been there?" he asked instead.

"I went last year; just for a visit."

"I've read about the redwoods; there's a fortune in lumber in each tree."

Her face fell. "Yes, but they are so majestic standing," she said quietly.

He had blundered. She loved the trees, but he couldn't help but see them as timber. As a silence ensued, William tried to think of a new line of pleasant conversation, but in the end, he decided it was time to grapple with what sat dense and immovable between them.

"Why did you want to see me now, after all of my attempts to reach you?"

She hesitated, caught off guard by his sudden directness, and poured more coffee. Keeping her eyes down, she fiddled with the sugar bowl, before adding a spoon to her cup and stirring, stirring, stirring. Finally, she looked up, having steeled herself for what she would say next: "William, we have led separate lives for over three years. I think it's time to divorce so we may each start again."

Now he did feel like a fool. Why else would she have wanted to see him after all this time? He considered his appearance; sitting here in his new finery, hair freshly cut…. He had brought her a gift! What a fool he was—how he must look. Resentment crept into his heart. He had risked his life out on the frozen—or almost frozen—lake. How he had suffered just to hear—this! And then he was trampled by the comprehension that he mattered to her not at all beyond her sudden need to be legally severed from him. He saw she had someone else—that her "auntie" was likely Mr. Jasper Tate, and that whether they were moving or not, it would be better if Carmina could obtain a divorce. He had become angry—angry about her message, angry over her lousy reception of him today, and angry for all the time he had wasted on her. He had stared into his cup for a little too long and decided he must answer, but he wouldn't let his anger show. He pictured the high pressure release valve on his new steam engine, bleeding off the steam, allowing the internal forces to remain workable and safe. He exhaled covertly and looked her in the eye.

"Who is Jasper Tate?"

Her stricken look told him what he already suspected.

"Jasper is a friend, a—a dear friend. He's an artist I met."

He continued to look at her until she broke contact and gazed into the murky depths of her cup. It was obvious he would never get the full truth from her on this or any of the other questions he had tormented himself with, and now it didn't seem worthwhile to pursue the answers any longer. It was all irrelevant; they would each go their own way. A new, more promising future would open out before him. He thought of his tailor, who had persuaded him that change was good. He now had this new suit, and it would be only his first change. He would enjoy himself. He would leave in this room the misery she had made for him.

"I think I shall get going." He set down his unfinished coffee and stood. She stood as well, mystified by his action. She was about to ask him more pointedly about the divorce when he stepped forward and took her hands into his own. He leaned forward, kissed her on the forehead as he contained a weary rage, and said, "I'll get the divorce arranged." Then he let go of her hands, picked up his hat, turned, and left the house.

CHAPTER 15

FITZPATRICK FIDDLED WITH the papers on his desk, feigning busyness but morbidly curious, pondering what conclusion might come from the coroner's report. He himself couldn't be sure which way Edgar had died; he had waited until the noise in the vault had died away and then waited three more hours before opening the great metal door. All he could be certain of was that the old man had gone to his great reward, but whether he had expired from a second attack of palsy or had suffocated, he couldn't tell. If Edgar had succumbed to palsy, he would have nothing more to worry about; everyone seemed to have accepted his story that Edgar had dismissed him for the night and was about to call his driver. And then the call never came—so sad. But if, on the other hand, the police coroner found that Edgar had suffocated, some uncomfortable questions might be asked.

And Edgar—tough old goat that he was—hadn't given in, had he? Even when he knew he had been locked in purposely. He had taken the fancy ballpoint pen he always carried and had written 'FITZP' in bold letters on the tile near the inside of the vault door—admirable in a futile sort of way. It had been a simple matter of a trip to the janitor's closet and three minutes' work to wipe away the ink and polish up the floor. Then he had collected the files Edgar had dropped and refiled them. Finally, while fighting back a strange nausea at touching a dead body, Fitzpatrick replaced Edgar's pen in his jacket pocket and rearranged him to look as though he had fallen while examining the contents of a vault drawer. Looking at his father-in-law, Fitzpatrick had the mingled sentiments of disbelief that the man would not wake again, a certain sickness over his deed, and grim satisfaction with his night's work. He had departed to play cards, but knew he wouldn't be able to concentrate, so he went home and rehearsed excuses for Sullivan instead. He had left the front door of the bank unlocked, thinking that if someone else should come into the bank, so much the better.

It had been five days now since the…the murder. Surely that word didn't exactly apply; he couldn't think of himself as a murderer. Edgar had been sick and might have popped off at any time; he had probably only helped him along. This was the underlying issue—a strange question of morality and status feeding his apprehension of the medical examiner's findings; not only did he want to be unsuspected of wrongdoing, but he hoped to convince himself that Edgar had died of disease and that he—John Fitzpatrick—was not a murderer. But…even if he was, the future suddenly looked much brighter; the Board of Directors had met, and with Louise Standish's influence (and financial holdings) in the bank, it seemed that Paul would step into his father's position. Following Paul's promotion, it came naturally that he would move into Paul's office; he certainly understood the work. It only remained to be confirmed by a vote at the next directors' meeting. *How pleasant life will become without Edgar around here*, he thought. *No more harsh summons, easy access to the vault, and it will be so simple to run my stratagems around Paul.* It now all depended on a nice, clean cause of death.

The front door to the bank opened and in walked a sharply dressed man with a red handlebar mustache. As the man approached his desk, Fitzpatrick had to snap himself out of his brooding and put a name to this face. He was a past client of the bank…. He had seen him, when? He was almost to the desk….

"Hello, Mr. Fitzpatrick," William said, extending his hand.

"Hello, Mr. McGrath," he answered, remembering in the nick of time. "We haven't seen you in some time; how is business?" Fitzpatrick asked, hoping for a clue to the man's identity beyond his name.

"Very good; the new mill is coming along well," William answered.

The mill! He had it all in place now; this was one of the two brothers from that sawmill loan on the Upper Peninsula.

"I'm glad to hear it," Fitzpatrick intoned pleasantly and was about to ask another question when he saw Thompson, Sullivan's attack dog, enter the bank. The clerk's eyes darted right and left, looking for a place to escape to, but it was no good; Thompson's baleful stare had found him. Fitzpatrick blanched.

"Are you all right? Is something wrong?" William asked, having noted the sudden change in the clerk's pallor.

"No, I...I'm sorry; we've had an upset here recently." Fitzpatrick fumbled toward a play for sympathy.

"Yes, that's why I'm here. If Mr. Standish isn't currently engaged, I wanted to look in and offer my condolences," William said.

"Of course." Fitzpatrick had recovered and was glad to have something to do. "Let me see if he's busy." He went to Paul's office and momentarily showed William in.

Thompson intercepted him as he was returning to his desk. The thug's upper lip curled very subtly upwards, enhancing the ugliness of his disfigured nose. He stared down that nose for a full minute while Fitzpatrick's quivering mind loped through different versions of what to tell him. Finally, Thompson spoke in his low rasping voice.

"I was reading the obituaries regarding another matter and saw your late bank manager in there—most unfortunate."

"Er, yes. He was actually my father-in-law; we had the funeral yesterday," Fitzpatrick mumbled, feeling off balance making conversation with this enforcer.

"And how was that?" Thompson asked, unusually loquacious, almost with the hint of a smile.

Fitzpatrick recalled yesterday's ceremony; the incense in the church, the sniveling of Beatrice and her mother, the annoyance he had felt at this outpouring of grief for that domineering old goat....

"It was dignified," he managed to tell Thompson.

Thompson's face lost any pretended trace of bonhomie as he said, "I love a good funeral. Did you enjoy it?"

Alarm bells rang in Fitzpatrick's head. What kind of question was this? "Did you enjoy it?" What did Thompson know? Most likely nothing. How could he know anything? It was bound to be a cheap taunt, nasty and low. Despite having killed Edgar and going on to fake sadness through the funeral, Fitzpatrick was offended.

"It was dignified," he repeated, looking around the bank to see who was watching.

"All right, enough tomfoolery. What is not dignified is a welcher, a man who doesn't show up to take care of his debts. We had expected to see you by now."

"As I said, I've had a death in the family," Fitzpatrick responded in a wounded baritone. "I've been home with my wife."

"How cozy; I have made an allowance for that, but you still owe us a pile of money, so we better see you tonight."

"Tonight is difficult. I—"

"Like I said, I love a good funeral," said Thompson, cutting him off, his dispassionate eyes devoid of any hint of humanity.

Fitzpatrick's sense of umbrage swelled. Who was Thompson to threaten him? Such was the fluidity of Fitzpatrick's self-image that although moments ago he had been contemplating a loss of innocence, now he flattered himself that he had become a dangerous person on the merits of having locked Edgar in the safe.

"What is that supposed to mean?" he asked indignantly.

Thompson stepped closer to him, forcing him to take a step back.

"Use your head," he rasped out coldly.

Fitzpatrick's pulse had started to race and he was breaking into a sweat. Just then, Paul emerged from his office as he escorted William to the door. On his way out, William gave Fitzpatrick a cheery wave goodbye, and in spite of his physical distress, Fitzpatrick beamed back a fake smile accompanied by a subdued wave. Thompson turned to see who had taken Fitzpatrick's attention and recognized William from somewhere.

"I'm leaving now. Let's see you tonight at the tables, Fitzpatrick," he said.

"Okay." Fitzpatrick gulped down his fear and resentment.

"And one more thing; who is that man with the red hair you just waved to?"

"That's William McGrath—a lumberman from the Upper Peninsula."

Memory flooded through Thompson's mind. Suddenly, he was back on the docks, chasing a brat over lumber piles and clutching at his windpipe. He hadn't forgotten the red-headed man; he had been there, too. And now he had a name.

"A shareholder?"

"No, we're financing his mill," Fitzpatrick blurted out.

"Thank you, Fitzpatrick. Until tonight."

CHAPTER 16

YOU DID THIS to us; you're the one who offended the gods," Norman accused, not for the first time. Dennis had been unsure how to respond the first few times, unable to tell whether the mercurial cook was angry or joking, but being tired of the assertion either way, he remained silent now. Misty air had plastered Norman's sparse white hair to his forehead, and he rubbed the thin wisps back with the improbable comb of his thick paw as he continued: "You brought down the lightning. You said, 'Better them than us,' and now it's us." He was referring to the disagreeable task of filling cribs. He and Dennis were now in charge of the operation; Thomas had no faith in Edwards to get the job finished, so while the men were loading rock onto a wide, crude raft of lashed pine beams, he had taken this opportunity to poke at the mate. This time, Dennis had poked back: "Don't be silly, Norman; I'm small fry in this great cruel world. Why would the gods waste an afternoon eavesdropping on me? I'm fairly sure we're moving rocks to make up for some unpunished crime in your past."

"Not so. No, the gods have had their time with me already. That's how I come to be here in the first place," he said slowly with unmistakable sincerity.

Dennis realized the teasing had somehow ended. "Anyhow," he replied, "we're close to the finish line, and then we can get back to the ship."

"Thank goodness. Moving rocks is work for *prisoners*, not seamen," Norman said loud enough for Edwards to hear, but Edwards was at least shrewd enough not to take the bait.

As Thomas watched, a small wagon rolled up to the stable pulled by a single horse driven by Dalton, Camp B's young boss. Dalton hopped nimbly down from his trap, hitched his horse to a post, and walked over to join Thomas.

"Good morning, Captain," Dalton hailed and crouched down to pat Moses.

"Good morning, Dalton." Thomas liked Dalton's self-assuredness and warmth; he was a good camp boss, and with a few more years, would be a great one.

"It looks like the log pens are almost ready," Dalton said conversationally.

"Yes, and it's about time too; I need to get *Genevieve*'s crew back to work on the ship."

"I hadn't thought of that, sir. I was just thinking that the pens will be ready in time for the first batch of logs to arrive."

"This is true," Thomas replied. "It seems, Dalton, that everything must be ready at nearly the same moment. We're behind on *Genevieve*; I need to get her crew on board to sway up the main topmast, set up the rigging, bend sail...the list is long. Anyhow, I'm glad to see the pens coming to completion," he concluded brightly, and then his thoughts roamed over unfinished details as he watched the men hurl stones into the cribs.

Dalton remained silent as his boss appeared to be considering something until at last Thomas spoke: "Well, what do you have for me?"

"I've brought in the ledgers as you asked, and I have something less than pleasant in the back of my trap." The two men walked over to the little wagon. Dalton hopped up in the back and lifted a three-foot-diameter disk of wood, approximately two inches thick; each company identified its logs with a distinctive stamp, and this disk was imprinted with a large MG in capital letters—the McGrath Lumber Company's mark.

"One of the boys found this washed up on the riverbank I'm afraid, sir."

Thomas nodded, aware that Dalton was bracing for an ugly response. "I see, Dalton. I know we've lost some logs this winter; this finally proves what happened to them." *Blast Inch*, he thought. *The man is nothing more than a common thief.* He decided there was nothing more to be said and abruptly changed the subject: "Is Camp B just about packed up?"

"Yes, sir."

"Ready for the river drive?"

Dalton smiled his warm smile. "Yes, sir. I think Svensson wants to pull the pegs on Monday; I've been looking forward to it."

Dalton was still young and agile enough to enjoy being a river hog: one of the men who rode rolling logs down streams, rapids, and rivers, poking and prodding with peaveys, working loose jams, keeping unwieldy timber from grounding on sandbars or snagging in bends and, thereby, damming the river. It was exciting, skilled, and sometimes dangerous work, and it paid well.

"Good," Thomas said. "Come into the office and we'll have a look at the books. Oh, and bring that cutting with our stamp on it."

Inside, Thomas scanned the totals for Camp B's pay and reflected that the upcoming spring payout would tap the mill's finances quite severely. It was nerve-racking assessing the weight of the delicate and diminishing bank balance against its ability to complete the intended work. He brought himself back to the business at hand.

"Your totals look about right; I see the men's days…as well as deductions from the camp store…." He looked up from the ledger. "I'll do a final check before payday; if I find any correction, I'll see you."

"Thank you, sir," Dalton replied.

"Seney should be lively this Saturday night," Thomas remarked with a smile.

"That it will, sir," Dalton grinned. "It's a long way, but some say it's worth the trip." A number of establishments in the town of Seney were set up to fleece as much of a lumberjack's winter pay from him as they could. Taverns, soft beds, and easy company would divide many a shanty boy from the small fortune of his season's earnings and return him to the mill with a sore head and empty pockets.

"You aren't going to blow your pay, are you?" Thomas asked.

"No, sir," Dalton responded seriously. "I have some obligations."

"That's good. Money comes hard and goes easy; I hate to see the boys lose six months of labor in a short week. Okay then, I'll see you on Thursday for the payout. There should be some happy faces."

After Dalton departed, Thomas was left alone for the first time that day. In this late stage of mill construction it was typical for him to have to hop from one task to another, often finding himself occupied by minute, urgent matters that had not been on his work list. In any year, March and April were restless months for him. With the additional burden of building the new mill in William's absence, the time was passing all too quickly toward a coincident set of deadlines, and though he was busier than ever before, his restlessness was perversely greater. To cope, he had disciplined himself; starting work before the men, he roamed the various operations all day, grappled with technicalities that were new to him, and kept pace with paperwork until well after dark. But in some of his moments alone, his suppressed agitation broke over his routines, parting thin moorings that kept him on task, and sent him drifting between the pressing needs of mill operations and themes of greater enthusiasm. He would give way to this part of himself that he considered inherited—bequeathed into his build by elemental, Celtic ancestors who had felt such urgings toward action as their great wheel of seasons turned.

He decided he needed a walk; Dalton's ledgers and the pile of paper on his desk could wait a little longer. Grabbing his coat, he left the office with Moses in pursuit. Even better, he thought he would take a short row in the work skiff; a few good pulls at the oars would loosen him up. It would never do to be seen rowing for mere exercise; he would have to make a show of looking over the new log pens. Ever alert to the possibility of a trip somewhere, Moses was in the skiff before Thomas had it untied. A quick push from shore, and in a moment, Thomas was leaning back against the oars, enjoying the rhythm of movement as his muscles awoke to the demand of sending the boat forward. He made a short tour of the outer perimeter of the pens, pausing appropriately to examine individual cribs and the hinge chains and staples that would hold the floating gates. He was about to turn back when he caught Norman's eye and suddenly thought about provisioning the ship for sailing. Immersed in all the other work, he had forgotten this vital detail; if Norman had organized anything for food stores as yet, he hadn't mentioned it. Rowing alongside the raft, he beckoned Norman to come over. "Norman, hop in."

"If you wanted to see me, you could have hollered and I'd have come up," Norman grumbled as he shooed Moses away, clambered in, and settled on the stern thwart.

"I like to see the progress," Thomas replied as he pulled away from the raft. "Besides, there are days when I need diversion from the office," he admitted quietly.

"Throwing rocks is a dandy diversion if you need one; maybe you want to stay," Norman retorted.

"No," Thomas laughed good-naturedly. "I have plenty to do; besides you fellows are so good at it. I'll be glad when this bit of business is behind us."

"So will we," Norman answered pointedly.

"Okay, I came to see if you have a supply list ready for the galley. We're sailing in a couple of weeks, going north," Thomas came to the point.

"I haven't put anything together while I've had this busy rock-throwing schedule," Norman jibed.

Thomas gave a taut smile: "All right, I promise—no more mill jobs, but you and the crew have saved our bacon on this crib fiasco. Can you get the food list together shortly?"

Norman nodded, somewhat mollified. "Can we load up food stuffs in the Soo? Supply is better up there."

"Sure; we'll leave some time for that on our trip through. We'll just get what we need here for the trip upriver. And," he said, changing the subject, "I'll bet you could use a little diversion, too. Come with me on Monday; we'll watch the beginning of the river drive."

"Oh, that does sound good; maybe someone will get maimed," Norman said, rubbing his big hands together.

"You're so bloody-minded."

Later that night in the office, Thomas's ears rang as a result of too much time spent near the men riveting the great water tank for the boiler together; it had been purchased unassembled for ease of shipping aboard *Genevieve*. At first curious, Thomas became spellbound by the glowing orange rivets, plucked from the blacksmith's furnace, flung through the air, stuffed into their holes, and battered flat.

Suddenly, Moses stood up, ears erect and tail wagging in short uncertain lashes as he stared at the door. The door opened and in walked William. The dog's yellow tail became a windmill as he danced and rubbed against the legs of his long absent master.

"William!" Thomas said with pleasure as his brother rubbed the black diamond on the dog's forehead.

"I saw the light in the window as I was passing. You're working late."

"Yes, well—you can imagine. I was just about to pack it in. Have you eaten?" Thomas asked.

"No, I pressed on from St. Ignace; I wanted to get back tonight."

"Good. It's late, but Anne will have some dinner ready. Let's go—maybe you want to stay the night and you can warm up your place tomorrow? We can have a little whiskey later."

William considered it for a second and agreed. He had thought about his own bed for the last few nights but food, warmth, and company now had greater appeal.

At Thomas's house, Anne stretched dinner between three, serving it with beer, extra bread, and cheddar. William recounted the desperate tale of his passage across the ice and was touched to see the obvious relief exhibited by Thomas and Anne at his safe return. Talk of ice led to discussion of the cribs and all other projects and endeavors at the mill. After the food had been consumed, they were picking over cold scraps of mill business to the point where everyone could feel they were tiptoeing around the question of why William had gone to Detroit.

"I think I'll clear the table," Anne announced. "Perhaps you'd like to have a little whiskey in the parlor."

William thanked Anne for dinner and the men adjourned to the other room. Thomas built up the fire in the hearth, went to the sideboard, and poured two fingers of whiskey into a pair of etched glass tumblers. They each took an armchair and sipped meditatively. After a while, William began to talk. "I suppose you know I went to Detroit to see Carmina."

"I guessed."

"I'm sorry I left you holding the bag once again."

Thomas dismissed this with a wave of his hand. "Did you see her?"

"Yes."

"And?"

William and Thomas both noticed a sudden cessation of dish clatter coming from the next room. With a wink and a smile, Thomas caught his brother's eye and wagged his head toward the kitchen.

"We're going to be divorced."

Thomas nodded soberly. "It's too bad to see something that was wonderful come to an end, but your marriage let you down a long time ago. I think this is good news."

"Yes, I know it's the right thing," William said with weary resignation. He went on to tell about Carmina's enigmatic request to meet, his subsequent visit with her, and his suspicions of her having another man. As he continued, he built to some emotional heat, revisiting the implied promise of her letter and what a fool he had been.

Thomas listened attentively through it all, and Anne quietly joined the men while William finished. Thomas refilled glasses and poured Anne a small sherry. He decided to refrain from further comment or advice to William on his decision to divorce since he knew it might be taken as patronizing and he didn't want to spoil the evening's warm intimacy. It was Anne who made the next comment. "There are worse things than being a fool for love; it means you have a big heart. You'll meet someone with as big a heart one day," she predicted.

"Thank you, Anne," William said earnestly, but privately, he felt quite awkward discussing how big his heart was. He turned the conversation to other matters: Edgar Standish's death; news of the city; the market price of lumber—until Thomas stood up, yawned, and said good night. More work waited for them tomorrow.

To Thomas's great relief, William fell into step with the work immediately, quickly assuming all of his customary roles—from correspondence with customers to harrying Boyle. Boyle, for his part, had the water tank for the boiler standing erect and was plumbing it into the valve header that would direct the flow of steam to numerous locations. Thomas now had a moment to stand in the middle of the empty stockyard and look around objectively; it seemed that with the completion of the log pens, a tipping point had been reached where more items were being completed every hour than new problems arising. And the problems that did come up were smaller and more easily dispatched. In a few more days, the boiler could be fired and all the engines and machinery tested. Turning his gaze to *Genevieve*, the crew were at work sending the main topmast aloft, its newly served and freshly tarred rigging stark and black against the sky's pale blue brightness. Finally, he was free to spend some time on her, preparing for the sailing season.

Thursday evening saw the largest payout in the history of the McGrath Lumber Company. With the exception of a few cleanup crews, the lumber camps were now shut down, and as expected, the idle, flush lumberjacks made their way to Seney to slake a long-building thirst. Some would return refreshed, others in spiritual or physical pain, as they assumed their summer roles in the mill or on the river on Monday. In the past, the beginning of work at the mill sawing logs almost always coincided with the start of the river drive, bringing timber downstream; the same vital high water that spun the old water wheel was also needed to float logs through swamps and down shallow streams. In its first season, the new mill would not flounce against tradition; not requiring a swollen stream to power it, the boiler was nevertheless scheduled to be fired on the same Monday the river hogs would start rolling this season's cuttings into the creeks.

Thomas picked up Norman as agreed and drove out to the rollway below Camp C where the drive would begin. Good weather prevailed, Arthur clip-clopped easily along, and the two men chatted about the upcoming sailing season, ports, and reminiscences of ships in their past until they arrived at the creek. There, a large group of men lollygagged around the rollway, enjoying a festival atmosphere as river hogs held peaveys and spectators boiled with anticipation for the upcoming show. Logs neatly stacked twelve high were strategically placed at a tall but gently sloping bend in the riverbank. They were unmistakably poised for a dive into the lazy, rippling stream, and from a small distance, one could not discern what prevented their immediate launch.

But from the choice vantage point where Thomas and Norman awaited the spectacle, it could be seen that the weighty timber mass was held back by nothing more than two diminutive wooden pegs bracing the lowest log near its ends. To start the river drive, by tradition, it fell to the two youngest river hogs to knock out the pegs and clear out of the way before the logs mashed them into two dimensions, like gingerbread men beneath the baker's rolling pin.

Svensson was the walking boss—the man in charge of the drive—so he presided over affairs. He was giving the two peg pullers some last bits of advice, and then stillness settled upon the gathering as they sensed the moment was close. The two young hogs took up their perilous positions before the stack, sledgehammers in hand, watching each other as they prepared to swing simultaneously.

Svensson called out, "Ready? On my count—three, two, one, strike!"

The men swung in unison—knock, knock. The pegs were loosed and being pushed over by the mass of timber behind them. The man upriver dropped his hammer and ran clear of the pile, which was shifting, beginning a slow tumble, starting to roll. The other man had forgotten himself briefly, hampering his escape by trying to run with his sledgehammer. It was no more than a second of delay, but the logs had begun to roll and were almost upon him when he finally dropped the hammer and dove for safety. He was then obscured from view by the welter of logs tumbling, splashing into the stream, colliding, and sending up spray. Concern rippled in quiet murmurs through the men as they looked for the second peg puller, until at last, the tumbling stack had rolled out, drifting in docile chaos downstream. Unaware of the crowd's consternation, the young man stood up from where he had landed in shallow water, partially wet but entirely whole. Roars of relieved laughter and cheering echoed across the stream. The river drive was on.

Later on, back at the mill, a similar sense of festival was building as men stoked wood into the furnace that would fire the boiler. Boyle had worked right through Sunday to have the steam plant ready, but he appeared quite fresh as he methodically triple-checked all systems. Townspeople, men and women, had come to see the new mill start up;

some with a sense of history wanted to say they had been there at the beginning; others came because they had family working at the mill; and then there were still others, the small number in any community, who nursed sour sentiment—the doomsayers, whose fervent hope was that the new boiler might explode, or they might witness some other monstrous failure, and later remind everyone it was they who had predicted it. On their return to the mill earlier, Norman had even pointed out Inch to Thomas, skulking about outside of the property. Thomas had ignored the man, giving him a wide berth, determined not to let anything spoil his day.

Smoke plumed up from the tall chimney, rich and opaque. Rising, it curled away downwind, diminishing into beige haze until finally disappearing. As a draft pulled up the chimney, air sucked into the furnace, fanning the flames into a raging blaze, ever more hungry for the chunks of scrap wood being thrown into it. As the boiler built steam, people became transfixed by the slow creep of needles in the pressure gauges. When he felt sufficient pressure had built, Boyle directed William to a valve, which he duly and ceremoniously opened, charging a pipeline that sent live steam to the new gangsaw. The two sawyers standing by the saw waited until it was up to speed and then fed in a cant that had been saved for this first cut. In less than three minutes, the cant had completed its transit through the blades—incredible speed—and was now sixteen neat planks, bringing cheering and applause from the assembly. One after another, Boyle opened valves at the steam header and then went to the various machines to see them run. To the great disappointment of the doomsayers, nothing exploded—immediately; they would continue to watch, ever-vigilant for latent calamity. William passed out cigars that he had brought from Detroit, and Thomas accepted one, even though he didn't usually smoke.

Surrounded by reciprocating pistons and excited people, Thomas felt apart from the crowd. He reflected on the long winter of building; directing men and materials to form this new mill, an emblem of the new age; struggling in the snow and ice; the cribs—the cribs. And even though they could feel the shuddering scrape of the bottom, a little cash was still left in the bank. With luck, he and William would be able to draw pay once again in August. Watching the smokestack billow, he knew this wasn't his vision; although he felt accomplishment, he couldn't love it the way William did. But pulling against the pier, *Genevieve* sat primly, yards squared with most of her sails bent on, and Thomas knew that in this moment his great wheel had turned.

BOOK THREE
OUTSIDE NEGOTIATIONS

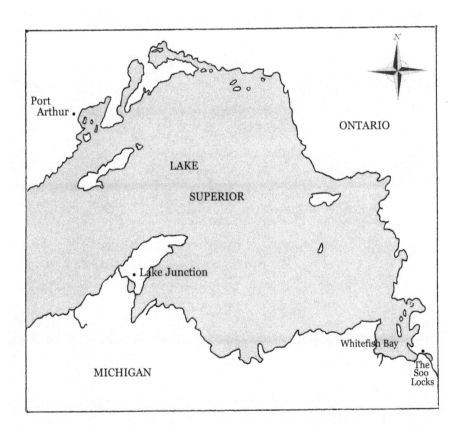

Chapter 1

Late April, 1892

Adding its grace to more hours of the day, the sun carried some warmth to Klara's cheeks and melted the snow at a good pace now. Horses trampled the roads clear, drawing carts and carriages, part of the seasonal swap of sleigh runners for wheels. What snow there was lingered mainly in little rounded piles, mounds that had been shoveled into existence during the winter as walks and lanes were rendered passable.

Klara hung laundry in the backyard behind her house, enjoyed the mild breeze, and considered how quickly it would dry the clothes. The spring wind was youthful, uplifting, and she wondered idly whether the change in season could affect her life with Mateusz in some way. Would the longer sunlit hours and balmy air usher brightness and warmth back into their marriage?

Penitent after revealing his identity to her, Mateusz had become very pleasant—solicitous—and after a short while, she began to appreciate how hard he was trying to regain her favor. He wooed her. She enjoyed his attentions, and one day, when he judged his moment to be right, he had humbly asked her to marry him. With a small group of neighbors, and the few Poles who lived in town as guests, the wedding had been a quiet affair, but it was joyous enough to help Klara banish her remaining qualms about this union. She launched herself into the marriage with exuberance, and for the first couple of weeks, it had been romantic and wonderful. Then—somehow, through the unvaried repetition of daily tasks, or the minor frictions necessary to blend two lives happily, or the satisfaction of initial curiosity—Mateusz lost interest in her. She couldn't bring to mind a single incident or thing she had done that would have brought about this change, but it was there; he rarely spoke and stopped touching her altogether. At first, she hoped this indifference might pass; he could be moody. But as days of coolness stretched into weeks and then months, she wondered whether she had traveled to this land to be a neglected housekeeper. Sometimes, her mind sought out the unknowable: Would life with Anton have been just the same?

Nonetheless, she took pleasure in the day; the clean clothes swung cheerfully in the gentle breeze, and her arm was feeling stronger as she finished hanging them out. She surveyed her small yard, still partially covered in snow, and pictured the vegetables she would plant; she planned the purchase of some seeds before having tea with Felka later in the morning. Picking up her basket, she admired her work and went into the house.

Arriving at Felka's, Klara was met at the door by the lady of the house.

"Klara," Felka smiled, "come in." Felka's home, although sparsely furnished like most miners' houses, provided Klara with all the comforts of sanctuary. Felka had sought out Klara's company in the days after their first meeting, and gradually, the two women had become friends.

"I have a new book for you," Felka announced as she led the way to the kitchen, handing over the novel. The kettle began singing merrily on the stove, and she began the fussy business of making tea.

"It is in English. My sister in New York sent it to me. It is written for children so it is not too hard, but it is a good story."

"Thank you," Klara said, genuinely thankful to have a new book to divert her mind from everyday life.

With the tea made, Felka pulled some oatmeal cookies from a jar on the counter and set it all on the small kitchen table. Taking her seat, she asked with a grin, "Are you scandalized that I have oatmeal cookies and not pierczek?"

Klara laughed. "No, I like American cookies."

"Have you heard the news from the mine?" Felka asked more seriously.

"No. Mateusz doesn't speak of work. He is very quiet," Klara answered.

Felka nodded knowingly, sensing her friend's difficulty, and seemed about to ask something, but she thought better of it and instead followed up on her question: "They have finally found a rich vein of copper in the new shaft at 2,400 feet; there will be plenty of work."

This was plainly a relief for Felka, although Klara had had no idea that Mateusz's job could be in question.

"I didn't know there might be a problem with work," she admitted to Felka.

"Oh, yes, there was talk of temporary layoffs, and Michal had been thinking of going to Red Jacket to see whether they are hiring at Calumet and Hecla, but now he doesn't have to."

Mateusz and Michal both worked as trammers in the mine, filling and pushing heavy carts loaded with copper ore to the skips where the hoist then hauled it to the surface.

Felka risked prying a little bit: "Mateusz doesn't tell you much, does he?"

Klara struggled with the question; although Felka knew about Mateusz's initial deception, an admission like this had a feeling of disloyalty to her husband, but she also yearned to tell her friend the truth and let go of her difficulties for whatever relief it would bring. Her first impulse largely won out.

"He is quiet, as I said, but no."

There was a brief silence, but then encouraged somehow, Felka pried a little more. "Does he ever talk of Anton, about what happened to him?"

Klara now experienced the same grating, icy, horrid feeling she had felt the first time she met Felka in the general store, when Mateusz's real identity had been revealed. What unwelcome bit of news would be doled out from her friend this time? Her anxiety hardened to anger: Why was it that the people she knew kept secrets from her? It was embarrassing at moments like this not to know…not to know what? She decided to close the door on the subject: How could knowing anything more about Anton help in her life today?

"We don't discuss Anton anymore. It is in the past."

Felka once again inhaled quickly, as though ready to say something, but then she nodded her head sagely and poured more tea.

Up, up, up—the smooth vibration told the work-wearied miners they were being drawn toward the surface, by the distant head winch at half speed. When the hoist pulled ore or empty skips, the winch cables fairly sang, but when the man car was being run, the engineer slowed the machinery to three hundred feet per minute from its top speed of seven hundred.

Michal sat in the back row of the car, holding his lunch pail in his lap. Acetylene lamps alight on their helmets, the miners rode the car wordlessly, watching shadows play on the ragged cut rock wall; some thought of their work—chasing conglomerate lode down narrow, angled stopes; most, like Michal, thought of home and dinner. They passed level after level, shooting past tunnels that led to worked out sections of the mine, and periodically stopping when the signal was given to pick up men from the active levels.

Brrrinng! The bell rang out and the hoist slowed to a stop at level 146. Michal watched the crew board, each man paying attention to his feet, crossing the giddy gap between the landing and the car. Missing one's footing when stepping over meant a quick trip to the bottom of the shaft, four thousand two hundred feet below the surface—a longer drop, by far, from the upper levels, than from the tallest peak in the area to the lowest valley. Such falls weren't common, but they were known to happen. Second to the last to board was Mateusz, who took the empty seat in front of Michal. As the hoist resumed its upward journey, Michal found himself looking at the back of Mateusz's helmet and pondering what took place in the head below it. So unlike his gregarious cousin Anton, Mateusz was arrogant, surly, and haphazard in his work. Michal thought back to a day on level 140, during the winter, when he had passed by Mateusz busily thawing out sticks of frozen dynamite that had been brought down from the surface—over an open flame. He had warned Mateusz of the danger, but when Mateusz had snarled back that he knew what he was doing, Michal could think of nothing but to get as far from him as he could.

Michal often thought of Anton's untimely end: Anton went looking for his cousin on level 138, working away from his drilling team, and had been crushed between a runaway tram and a medium-sized puddingstone boulder. Had he been uncharacteristically careless, or had Mateusz made some fatal mistake?

As the great hoist brought red ore up from the earth, warm weather brought the first green tendrils out of the soil, radiating the most vibrant hues of new life.

After a day of weeding and spreading manure, Klara surveyed her back garden, pleasantly excited by the first appearance of her seedlings; it was wonderful to watch things grow, while knowing her own hand was part of their life stories. Farther back in the yard, her eye was also charmed by wildflowers that had sprung up without any effort on her part. Marigolds and pink lady's slippers intermingled with grasses to form a lovely relaxing backdrop to her little garden, staunchly bordered by the woods. It was peaceful and somehow luxurious to have such a view. She sat contentedly on her back porch, soaking in the warmth of the early evening sun, and found where she had left off in the latest book Felka had lent her. It was a novel written for adults in English: *Khaled; a Tale of Arabia*, and she was pleased with herself that she could understand so much of it. Serving Mateusz dinner was the only remaining chore in her day, but as the weather warmed and the days grew longer, he returned later and later, preferring to spend his evenings with some newly hired trammers from the mine rather than with her. His precise activities were unknown to her; on some nights, he had clearly been drinking before arriving home; on many, he had not. Although they continued to share the same bed, and appeared together at church, they lived separate lives. The emptiness of it hurt, but she had stopped expecting him to be a possible source of happiness. She grieved for her lost hopes. Having worked with many disappointed women, she could now see that perhaps this was the way a life was lived—that love, togetherness, and romance were the lacy dreams of young girls, not the stiff fabric of real life. And so, in marriage, she inadvertently leaned toward bitterness, relieved only by the pleasure of her garden, her books, and her improving English.

Chapter 2

May 1892

SUNDAY DINNER—WHAT A stultifying chore. Had it not been for Louise's exceptional French cuisine, Fitzpatrick would have made any excuse to evade the weekly family gathering. At least he no longer suffered through Edgar's long tirades and admonishments, or even the cold disapproval of his rare silences, but even so, he had to admit that these dinners, despite the fine food, had become insipid. Some unique flavor had disappeared with the old man.

Unobserved at the sideboard, Fitzpatrick slopped a few ounces of rye whisky into his glass and downed it quickly before pouring a tall, stiff whisky and soda—his second. The liquor warmed both empty stomach and outlook on the evening as it went down. The fire spread through him, speeding his thoughts, pushing the minutes past, and giving him the facility to endure the foibles and follies of the Standish family.

It was unseasonably warm for May, and the large dining room windows had been opened to their full height, admitting a cooling breeze, billowing the draperies as the family took their places around the long walnut table for dinner. It irked Fitzpatrick pettily that Paul now sat at the head of the table in the walnut armchair that had been Edgar's. Whether Louise had offered her son the chair or he had simply assumed it as heir, the new arrangement stated to Fitzpatrick a continued judgment of his own inferiority within the family. He knocked off the remainder of his whiskey and soda in preparation for the burgundy wine being served with dinner. Louise, still dressed in black, carried a tray bearing a marvelously aromatic roasted beef loin, and took her seat before asking Paul to say the grace.

"Bless us, O Lord and these, thy gifts, which we are about to receive from thy bounty. Through Christ, our Lord. Amen," Paul chanted with his eyes closed.

"Amen," answered the ladies as Fitzpatrick made an early grab for the roasted potatoes. The couple of whiskeys, plus the savory aromas rising out of the china serving bowls before him, put a keen edge on his appetite. When he had piled up enough roast potatoes, he moved on to the glazed carrots and then helped himself to three generous slices of roast beef. After covering his meat with a ladleful of Louise's rich onion gravy, he tore a crusty chunk from the freshly baked loaf of *pain à l'ancienne* and began to butter it. The potatoes were of last year's crop, but had been carefully stored, peeled, cut, and presented. Fitzpatrick cut one piece in half, speared it on the end of his fork, and popped it into his mouth. Surprised by the potato's intolerable heat, Fitzpatrick's tongue batted the scorching spud from one side of his partially open mouth to the other, breathing in and out while he filled his wineglass. He heard a stifled "tut" from Beatrice on his left but ignored her as he quaffed a large gulp from his goblet to put out the fire. An extended silence ensued as the Standish family picked carefully at their plates and pretended not to notice Fitzpatrick's crude appreciation of the dinner. Eventually, Paul assumed the mantle of host and started some conversation: "I bumped into Howard Abernathy down near the opera house yesterday. He said he'll be in on Monday—tomorrow—to start another loan for further expansion." The remarks were clearly directed toward Fitzpatrick since Beatrice and her mother had no involvement with the Abernathies. Fitzpatrick, for his part, didn't care about these people or their loans, so he was irritated that he should be goaded into discussing work on a Sunday. How typically dense of Paul! In times gone by, he would have offered some polite response, but today, he asked himself why he owed Paul any sort of acknowledgment for this banal attempt at conversation. He hadn't the strength of character to be completely rude, though, so a small, "Oh," escaped his lips, instantly supplanted by a large forkful of beef and glazed carrot. Chewing vigorously, Fitzpatrick knew he was spoiling the conviviality of the table, but he didn't really care. In fact, it gave him a small pleasure to have the family work at entertaining him.

"It seems the Abernathy Abrasives Company is just taking flight, orders are piling up, and Howard needs more factory capacity, warehouse space, and workers to meet the growing demand," Paul continued.

"According to him," Fitzpatrick remarked indifferently before draining his wineglass and promptly refilling it.

"Yes, of course, John; we will have to see his numbers and so on, but on the surface, it seems like positive news, for them and for us." Paul smiled conclusively. Louise and Beatrice, with perhaps feminine empathy, sensed intent in the over-tensioning of atmosphere created by Fitzpatrick's lack of engagement, but Paul, either through lack of sensitivity or disregard for slight, simply seemed to turn the page.

"Dinner is wonderful, Maman. I don't know how you can make these carrots so sweet, savory, crunchy, and moist all at the same time—superb." And before she could politely demur, he continued, "Also, as I passed the opera house, I noticed there will be a new performance of *The Marriage of Figaro* starting next month. I think we should all go."

Fitzpatrick momentarily stopped chewing a large wad of beef and took a long pull at his glass of burgundy to help soften the clog. Out of the corner of his eye, he could see Beatrice lapping up this horrid idea of the opera, and Louise across the table was smiling at the thought. Egad, he hated all that caterwauling in Italian, and to be trapped there for a full evening—it would mean two nights with the Standish family in that week. Behind his round spectacles, his eyes narrowed. Had this been an ambush? Was it possible Paul had suggested the opera just to annoy him, at a moment when it would be hard to object? He stabbed another potato and more cautiously bit off a chunk of it from the end of his fork. Paul showed more signs of having Edgar's wiliness with every passing week.

"I'll get the tickets on Thursday," Paul concluded.

Eventually, the dinner was finished, capped by a superb pear and fig pie lightly bathed in sweetened cream. With poor grace, Fitzpatrick took his hat and ambled down the front steps, leaving Beatrice to say good night. He wobbled between the curb and the center of the sidewalk, tipping slowly to his left, then correcting abruptly right. Beatrice skipped forward to catch up and took his arm, perhaps more to steady him than herself.

"You had a fair bit to drink, John," she said reprovingly.

"I was thirsty."

"You know what I mean; you're stumbling," she said.

"How have you become so righteous? I see your brother all week, so is it a wonder I need a drink to look at him on Sunday as well?" he said with rising choler. "Listen." He withdrew his arm from her with an ungentle tug. "I don't need your blessing to have a few drinks, especially if it helps me cope with your nitwit brother. You know your way home. I'm going to play some cards," and so he departed, swallowed shortly by the shadowy indistinctness of hedges, down a narrow side street.

On Monday morning, John Fitzpatrick cursed the stonemason, intermittently chipping away at a long slab of Kentucky bluestone, in the street outside his window. A broken sill was being replaced next door, and although the noise was not exceptionally loud, he found the stop and start nature of it terribly grating, especially since just when he began to believe it had concluded, it would invariably start up again. In his new office, he was free to sit at his desk and squeeze his fingers against the throbbing pain in his temples, unobserved by Paul, tellers, or Charles Savoy, the new chief clerk. It was the burgundy wine, he felt sure, that had given him a sore head. He could manage almost a bottle of whiskey with only a general fatigue to show for it the next day, but the burgundy—he really should have known better.

Clink-clink-clink-clink…chink-clink-clink…clink. The percussion of steel hammer on chisel on stone struck piercing, tympanic notes that assaulted his eardrums perfectly. Stuffing his thumbs into his ears, he continued applying pressure to his temples with his fingers until his vision turned to red in the indulgent suppression of his misery. Last night had turned into a minor disaster: He had been called on every bluff and come away from the table down six hundred dollars. The money he could make back—he had done it before, but arriving home, he had found Beatrice waiting up and they had fought. Considering the night all in all, he would have been better off to have skipped dinner and moved straight on to disappointing his wife, without the unpleasantness of losing at cards or giving himself this pounding headache.

A rap-rap at his door and Charles walked in a few steps.

"How is your paperwork going, sir?" the new clerk asked.

Fitzpatrick had withdrawn his hands from his face at the first knock, repositioning to mimic studious enterprise as he stared at his desk. He took a moment before looking gravely up. Did he detect the merest hint of a smile? He frowned and instantly felt better as he saw a minute sobering in the young man's expression. *Impertinence; Charles wouldn't feel so jovial if he knew how I got to this position*, Fitzpatrick thought.

"Did you come for conversation, or is there something you require?" he asked.

"Er, no, sir. Yes, sir." The clerk answered both questions. "I have some files for you, sir. Mr. Standish sent them over; he's left for a meeting. He asks that you see these loan applicants today."

Fitzpatrick extended his hand, palm upward, for the files and resumed looking at the papers on his desk as a communication of dismissal. In his short tenure as chief clerk, Charles had learned the peccadilloes of his masters and departed without another word. Alone again, Fitzpatrick leaned his ear into his hand, resting his elbow on the desk. Trying to ignore the mason's noise outside, he flipped through the pages of the files with his free hand and nursed a small swelling of indignation; it was an affront that Paul would simply drop these appointments on him without even the minor courtesy of handing them off personally. And where was that pipsqueak off to at eleven in the morning? The thoughts whirled as he turned pages of files unseeingly, until he arrived at a page that stopped him cold. His mouth went dry and the hammering metronome in his head increased in tempo. He checked the front of the file—Abernathy Abrasives—then flipped back to the appalling page. There in large block letters, written out of line and on a slight diagonal across the paper, it said: FITZPATRICK KILLED ME.

His hands trembling, Fitzpatrick slammed the file shut and threw it into his desk drawer. He glanced up quickly to check whether anyone had been looking through his partially open door. Had Paul seen this page? Had Charles? The Abernathy account was one of the files Edgar had been working on the day he died. Obviously, it had been in the vault with him, but which of the other hundreds of files in the bank had he carried that day? Fitzpatrick couldn't remember.

Chapter 3

K LARA WIPED THE rim of the last jar, capped it, and set it with the others. Standing back, she admired the product of her day—twenty jars. When she had started shelling peas in the morning, she hadn't been sure she could get them all shelled, cleaned, packed, processed, and dried by evening, but now, here she was. Dinner was waiting; the hot jars could cool now while she enjoyed some reading in the garden until Mateusz came home. The evenings lasted so long in late June that no matter what time he arrived for dinner, he would find her reading outside.

Just before sunset—very late—Klara heard her husband's booted feet advancing unsteadily through the kitchen toward the back door. She got up to meet him and get his dinner.

"Allo, Mateusz," she began to greet him, but then she was startled by his appearance; his right ear was red and swollen, he had a bad cut over his right eye, and dried blood caked his cheek.

"What happened? How were you hurt?" she asked.

"Never mind. I'm hungry; where's dinner?" he slurred.

He has drank more than usual tonight, Klara thought. She set about the business of serving dinner. She brought the big iron kettle to the boil and made tea, then took a covered dish from the oven. When it was all served out on the table, she sat down silently across from him to eat. Taking his fork in his big thick hand, he tapped on the potatoes sloppily.

"This is all dried out. Didn't you ever learn to cook?"

Klara tried to swallow a little resentment, but instead, she decided to push back. "It was perfectly good when I cooked it, but it has sat here for hours; I didn't expect you to be so late."

His head tottered slightly as he stared at her until finally he taunted, "I guess I'll have to eat it." He took a large forkful but lost most of it on the way to his mouth. The potatoes fell into his lap and he cursed. After a few attempts to catch the fugitive morsels, he only succeeded in smearing them into his already grimy pants. Tiring of the little struggle, he cursed again and returned to his plate.

Klara tried again to discover how he had been injured, although she guessed he had been in a fistfight, obviously against someone with a good left hand. "After dinner, I must clean up your eye. How did it happen?"

His head snapped up angrily. "I told you, never mind. I...." His attention shifted abruptly to the neat rows of jarred peas sitting grand and alien on the kitchen counter. "What's all that?"

"Peas," Klara declared with conflicting feelings of pride and then irritation that Mateusz had not answered her. "I jarred them today."

His lips pressed together and quivered menacingly for a moment before he asked, "Where did those jars come from?"

"I bought them yesterday," Klara replied.

"You bought them? You bought them?" he repeated almost stupidly while working up his anger.

Unaware of any reason why she should be in trouble, Klara ploughed ahead. "Yes, I bought them; I have been saving for them out of the grocery money since I planted the garden. I told you about this idea, but you hardly listen to me." It was irritating for her to have to justify her actions to a man who ignored her except when he wanted something, and who had probably drank the amount of money that the jars had cost since leaving work. How entirely like him to complain now about something that had been planned for months. What did he think a vegetable garden was for? Properly organized, the jars would save the food and plenty of money over time. It was a measure of her inexperience with men that she had missed the warning, for Mateusz had come home a wounded beast—addled, angry, beaten, and vengeful.

"*You bought them!*" he repeated, mocking her. He wobbled to his feet, putting his hand into his dinner plate and upsetting it. Peas rolled lazily off the plate's edge as he shook potato from his fingers. "You bought them! I never asked you to buy them, and I don't want them. You are up here spending money on your fancies while I slave away underground!" Staggering to the counter, he lunged and collided with the jars, sweeping many of them to the floor. Glass smashed and cracked, releasing peas and a minor flood of water that spread in all directions.

"Mateusz!" Klara yelled, angered and horrified by the waste. She jumped in to protect her untouched jars, but he was not done; he got between her and the last jars, knocking her roughly to the floorboards, before completing his sweep. He picked up unbroken jars from the pile and hurled them down again, spattering Klara with bits of broken glass. Then he crushed and mashed all—glass, peas, rubber seals, and metal clasps—into a green slurry under the pounding of his heavy mining boots.

"You will not spend my money this way again!" he screamed. Klara didn't move from the floor. She could see she was no match, physically, against the drunken rage of a brute who moved tons of stone every day. She waited while he performed his mad dance in the peas and glass, until he was spent and fell wasted into his chair. Soon his head tipped back and he was snoring.

She sat silently surveying the mess until darkness concealed it from view. Her mind became quiet as she mourned something greater than the loss of all her lovely peas. She knew that from now on, she must begin doing things differently and be very, very patient.

CHAPTER 4

THE PREDAWN AIR held the warmth of a later hour. Her lips lingered softly on his for a moment, then a moment longer, and he hugged her firmly as they kissed, but it was time to go, and he knew he must break away now. He leaned over and bit her gently on the neck, just below her jawbone.

"Ouch!" she chided playfully.

"Oh, you are scrumptious." He took several more pretend bites in quick succession until she wriggled to free herself from this turn in his attentions.

"Stop, stop!" she giggled as he concluded with a very proper kiss on the cheek. He squeezed her hand gently.

"All right, my sweet; I should be back on Wednesday or Thursday next week," Thomas said. Then he picked up his hat and walked out the front gate. The moment of parting always tore at him; he would like to stay, but two things brought him solace: first, he would return in a week, and secondly, by the time he walked to the mill, his work would displace thoughts of home life until later.

"I wish I could go with you!" Anne called after him. He whirled around and blew her a kiss.

"Someday you will!" he answered back with a grin, then waved and lengthened his stride toward the crest up the road. On his walk, he reminisced on times in the past, before the children, when Anne had shipped out with him. It hadn't been difficult; in fact, it had been only a little complicated, but otherwise very pleasant. He imagined Molly and Curt watching dolphins ride *Genevieve*'s cobalt bow wave in deep water. He wondered whether such times might come to be. "Someday," he said. "Someday...."

An hour and a half later, Thomas felt quite anxious to leave. The mill had become a monster of industry, in his eye, blackening the sky as it gobbled up trees. The incessant screaming of saws reached a different pitch and volume than he had been used to from the water-driven machinery of the old mill, so he found it trying to hold conversation or at times even think. From his place on the pier, he kept an eye on preparations for leaving: Risto and Benjamin cast loose the gaskets that kept the squares furled, prompting Morris to snug up buntlines and clewlines, thereby keeping the sails from flogging around, partially set. Dennis led the securing of deck cargo, and *Genevieve*, facing into the westerly breeze, tugged against her bow lines, eager to be free once more.

While Thomas had been gazing aloft, William had appeared alongside of him. "Well, just about ready?" William asked. This was the second time this question had been put to him.

"Just getting the lumber stacks secured," Thomas replied patiently. William looked down the length of the ship.

"But you're pretty well ready. Can you finish up on your way out?"

Whether it was the noise of the shrieking saws, or the thought that he was being hurried off of his own pier, Thomas gave way to annoyance. "No, I bloody well can't! You will know I'm ready to leave when you see *Genevieve*'s transom as the ship heads through the passage!" he snapped.

William wondered how he had upset his brother. He thought, quite defensively, that he was only being helpful. For the first time today, they were expecting a steamship that he had chartered to take lumber to Chicago. With the mill's new production capacity, there was more lumber than *Genevieve* could carry to market alone. He tried to restore the peace: "I'm sorry, Thomas; I suppose I'm overanxious to make room for the freighter." He tapped Thomas lightly on the shoulder and said cheerily, "This is the load that will actually put money back in the bank."

"Yes, and about time too. I'm ready to draw pay again; Anne is tired of scrimping," Thomas grumbled.

"I know. Me too. But we've made it," William said in a soothing tone.

Forty minutes later, William's wish came to be: *Genevieve*'s main and mizzen shivered in the wind, the square topsails stretched taut, full aback, and the barkentine sat poised for departure. Mill hands slipped the bow lines and the stern line, leaving only a stern spring. *Genevieve* leaned back on the remaining line, and as her stern quarter rested against the pier, her bow swung away until the wind drifted over her beam. Thomas gave a nod to Dennis.

"Brace hard to port," the mate called, bringing the yards around as the stern spring was cast off, and *Genevieve* filled away.

"Time!" Thomas called to Norman, who noted the exact time on the chronometer and wrote it down. The captain then left his spot in *Genevieve*'s bow and walked back to the pilothouse. Once there, he wrote down the degrees, minutes, and seconds from the arm of his sextant and then carefully stowed the instrument. On the lakes, where a ship was never out of sight of land for long, he didn't have much cause to take celestial sights, but to keep in practice, he would shoot a noon-sight or get a fix from the stars at dusk when the ship's demands were not too great.

As he worked out the ship's position from his observation and time, he realized he was enjoying one of those rare spells when everything seemed easy. The crew were working well together, the dry weather continued—it hadn't rained in weeks—and *Genevieve* was ambling south at a steady six knots. While the men enjoyed their lunch on deck under the glorious spread of all sail, he flipped through the tables, found his latitude and longitude, and then plotted his position on the chart. Not bad. Considering DeTour was only ten miles astern, he was sure his line of position was within a half mile.

The ship sailed on quietly all afternoon as Thomas indulged himself in idle thoughts. Anticipating drawing pay for himself again, he planned his first few purchases after the cessation of this long period of austerity; it was time he bought George a bicycle. He looked over the transom while considering bicycles until his roving eye stopped at a new smudge on the horizon. In the clear weather, he could see numerous ships traveling in all directions; the newcomer he registered as another down-bound steamer. In an hour, the approaching ship was visible above the horizon and catching up to *Genevieve* quickly. A further twenty minutes and Thomas could see plainly that he knew the ship: it was Cedric Inch's tug *Hengist*, towing a small scow piled high with lumber.

Inch had bought *Hengist* at an auction several years earlier for a song. She was 110' long and very powerful, having 800 horsepower driving a four-bladed propeller on a five-inch shaft. Built of riveted iron on the Chesapeake Bay, she had begun life as the hardworking oceangoing tug *C+D No.6*, hauling barges as far north as Portland, Maine, and reaching south to Savannah, Georgia. After a lucrative towing contract from New York City to Detroit, the ship had suffered a major fire in her coal bunker, so her owners chose to sell her as is rather than refit her in Detroit. She was put up for auction and so caught the eye of Cedric Inch.

"*Hengist*," Dennis said aloud as he joined Thomas back aft. "We haven't seen her in a long time."

"We've been very lucky," said Thomas, whose enjoyment of the afternoon had soured with the tug's appearance.

"I heard that Inch bought that boat for almost nothing."

"Yes, that's the story. He got her after a fire...which I wouldn't be surprised if he set," Thomas replied, causing Dennis to chuckle. The tug was less than half a mile astern now and still coming up fast.

"He seems to be making straight for us," said the mate.

"I don't think he can navigate; he's probably following us until he sees the shore or someone farther ahead."

Seen from a distance, *Hengist* was pleasing to a seaman's eye; she had a fine long bow, starting in a purposeful plumb stem and running back into a robust beam just abaft the pilothouse. From amidships aft, she tapered very gently, finishing in a broad-rounded stern that provided plenty of deck space for work and steadied the ship from the terrible rolling that plagued many of her more elegant sisters.

When she drew closer, the details of her hard life emerged into prominence, both fascinating and repulsive to behold, since Inch had given the ship nothing more than the barest minimum of effort: the bunker fire had left her hull virtually undamaged but for some blistered paint; its heat, directed upwards, had deformed the deck plating that capped the coal bunker. The pilothouse directly above had caught fire, the conflagration devouring doors, window frames, and all of the paint, leaving warped and tortured, riveted metal as a physical history of its passing. Even the tall smokestack had suffered heat damage, having buckled concave in a section of its port side. It remained bent aft and to port; the angle of tip sufficiently beyond slight as to impart the uneasy feeling that the funnel might soon topple. Behind the stack, Inch had cut away some of the deck house to increase the capacity for loading wood, and then he had added a stubby but sturdy cargo derrick for the heaving aboard of heavy loads.

Closing the distance with *Genevieve*, as she was, all the decrepitude of *Hengist's* hard existence became plain to see. Rusted plate glowed reddish orange everywhere paint had been forced from her superstructure and hull. In places, the rust was merely streaks of dusty metal, whereas elsewhere it bubbled and flaked away in large scabs of crumbly scale. Interspersed among these raddled patches, the original paint clung in blackened and blistered curls, guarding the iron below in a forlorn final stand. Lacking fenders of any kind (Inch had no use for such things), she was a picture book of past mishaps, her dents, scrapes, and scars evidence of rough handling against unforgiving objects. She had been pounded in heavy seas, used as a battering ram, broken ice, flooded, run aground, and set ablaze, and all of her insensate suffering was expressed in the fire and brimstone colors of her textured form. But deep in her battered body, a powerful engine continued turning her four-bladed prop, throbbing out a drone of endurance, with the determination of suppressed rage.

Hengist came on, making almost twice *Genevieve's* speed. Her scow sheered badly from side to side, unwilling to submit to the tug's will but helpless to break free of her captor's relentless drag. Thomas and Dennis started to become uneasy about the remaining space between the ships as *Hengist's* bow came even with *Genevieve's* stern. No one was standing on deck, and the bright sun made seeing into the rusty, twisted pilothouse impossible. Was anyone at the wheel? They wondered. Thomas ordered *Genevieve's* helm to bear away to port slowly; a hard turn would only bring her stern closer to *Hengist*, which by now was a mere twenty feet away. Finally, Thomas could see into *Hengist's*

pilothouse as its doorway drew even with him. Inside was the lone figure of Ralph Inch, Cedric's younger brother. To Thomas's alarm, Ralph
left the wheel to talk out of the doorless portal in the wheelhouse.

"Hey, stand off there. You're far too close!" Thomas shouted.

"Hi there, McGrath. You're still trying to get everywheres with bed-
sheets and broomsticks," Ralph snorted, and as he did so, the scow
behind him reached the end of a long unruly swing to starboard, pulling at an angle on *Hengist*'s stern. Without Ralph's steadying hand at
the wheel, *Hengist* pulled gradually over to port, further crowding
Genevieve, despite Thomas's attempt to make space between them.

"Get control of your ship!" Thomas shouted, but Ralph just laughed
as he passed by.

"Do you want a tow? You sure look like you could use it," the younger Inch yelled, laughing idiotically.

Hengist's bent stack billowed her black breath over *Genevieve*'s sails
and deck, narrowly missing the barkentine's course brace when Ralph
Inch finally returned to his helm. At last, the tug rode clear and ahead
of *Genevieve*, pushing blue-white mounds of water up from her great
propeller, but seeing the wildly sheering scow approach, Thomas ordered the helm to bear away farther to port. The scow, it could now
be seen, was being pulled on a single line coming from one side of her
bow, rather than on a bridle that might have made her a docile tow. She
came up at speed in a hard swing to port, seemingly faster than when
Hengist had approached, and to make matters worse, Thomas could
see that Ralph Inch had altered course to port, purposely hauling his
charge into *Genevieve*'s space. The hulls were drawing together rapidly,
and Thomas knew that, momentarily, the compressed water between
the two would suck them inevitably together.

"Brace hard to starboard!" he shouted forward. The men who had
been idly watching jumped to braces and sheets, quickly hauling the
yards around until the square sails were aback. *Genevieve* immediately
lost way, and the scow, which had been neatly lined up for a sideswip-
ing collision, swung harmlessly into empty space below *Genevieve*'s
bowsprit. With the scow well ahead and *Hengist* growing smaller in
her plume of smoke, *Genevieve* filled away again, allowing Thomas to
sit behind the pilothouse on the broad transom rail alternating between fury at the effrontery of Ralph Inch, and incredulousness that

anyone could be so wantonly reckless. He sat silently, consumed by anger, wishing he had the means to smash *Hengist* and the Inches.

CHAPTER 5

THOMPSON SQUEEZED HARDER with his left hand but was curiously distant for a man engaged as he was. For no specific reason, his mind returned again and again to his line of work and contemplations of his future in it. Using his right hand, he twisted and pulled up, begetting a satisfying shriek that refocused his attention. He clamped even harder around the back of the man's neck, digging his thick fingers into soft spots between the ropy tendons as he stretched his victim's right hand ever farther up his back. The arm was at the breaking point now; he could always feel it, a little more pressure and…pop.

"You have until Thursday to sign up with our union, you and your friends," he wheezed intimately into the man's ear. Then he released his quarry, who jumped beyond his tormentor's physical reach.

"Then we can know each other under the grand umbrella of brotherhood," Thompson smirked. In truth, he cared little for the petty hopes and cares of the members of the Lumber Handlers Association, which was now striving for the respectability of an official Longshoreman's Union. He was here twisting this man's arm because it was a well-paying job compared to many, and it allowed him a freedom of movement in the exercise of his skills. To state that he enjoyed inflicting pain would no longer be accurate; he took satisfaction out of results gained by intimidation. And now he experimented with the limits of his power: How little could he do and still bend a man to his will? In the last year, he had learned to hang back in reserve, saving his energy for "hard cases." Sometimes, he went for a week at a time without actually laying a hand on anyone; his boys could handle such routine persuasion.

"Get lost," he said to the harassed man before him. The poor devil shuffled away at good speed, rubbing his reddened neck.

Lately, there had been more "hard cases" as the independent stevedores who had not already signed up with the union were increasingly more stubborn holdouts.

The afternoon sun boiled away the river's surface, sending up a hot moist layer of warped air. He felt thirsty. His throat often felt dry and scratchy since his injury in the fight the previous year.

"Go get us a jug of beer," he instructed his men, and then he took a seat on the pier to rest from his exertions while he planned his next move. The membership drive for the Longshoremen's Union was providing some extra work, but it would pass, and then he would be dependent on imprudent borrowers to provide him with a consistent living. He had to think of something better, bigger.

As he waited for his beer and contemplated the future, near and far, he saw, emerging from behind the edge of Grosse Isle, a well-remembered set of spars.

"*Genevieve*," he rasped out loud. How he had waited for the reappearance of this ship that had handed him his only defeat in eight years, broken his nose, and ruined his voice.

"*Genevieve*," he repeated to himself as he factored this new development into his week.

Even before the ship came alongside, Thomas could see something was amiss, but he ignored his misgivings as he concentrated on bringing *Genevieve* in with the assistance of a squat, rounded river tug. The little power plant was securely lashed up to *Genevieve*'s starboard hip, between the amidships bitts and the stern.

"Slow astern, please," Thomas called to the tug captain. The little tug huffed out an extra puff of steam into its cloud of coal smoke, the muffled chug of pistons could be heard reciprocating, and the way began coming off of *Genevieve*.

"One quarter astern!" Thomas called over. The chugging pistons increased in tempo, bringing *Genevieve* to a standstill before the current pushed her gently against the pier.

"All stop, thank you," Thomas called, and the mooring lines were dropped easily on waiting bollards.

Ashore, too many restive men loitered around the pier and adjacent quay to signal anything other than trouble. Thomas stood in the waist, one hand holding onto the first main shroud, and coolly observed the gathering. In the mid-afternoon heat, the men glowed red, the more swarthy of them burning a coppery hue as they sweated out a collective inhospitality. A cluster of them led a straggling line to the space alongside *Genevieve* and spread out down the ship's length. Morris and Benjamin began releasing some of the lashings on the deck cargo, prompting one of the men ashore to cry out, "Whoa! Easy there. Nothing is coming or going from this ship."

Thomas was instantly annoyed to have someone off the ship giving orders; nonetheless, he decided to avoid direct conflict. Quite obviously, these were the longshoremen flexing some muscle, but what did they want?

"The boys are just getting ready for when we agree on unloading the cargo," he said while waving Benjamin and Morris back to their work. "Now, what is it you want? Who's in charge here?"

Some of the men cast glances at each other, many wishing to speak up, to be more than members of a large mob, but they clung to their anonymity within the group.

"Fellows like you must have a boss, right?" Thomas asked pointedly, and at last, a voice wheezed from behind the first line of men.

"I'm in charge." A man with a bent nose stepped forward through the quickly parted throng. "There's a longshoreman's strike on; no lumber or anything else will come off this ship until our demands are met," he rasped, and he favored them with an ugly sneering smile.

"What are your demands?" Thomas countered.

Thompson had not prepared for this question. In truth, he had no demands; he had simply assembled this mob of longshoremen because he could, and he hoped to provoke an altercation that would leave *Genevieve*'s crew beaten bloody, especially the tall tow-headed one who had broken his nose. After a moment, he said, "You will be told in due course."

As Thompson delivered this line, a man nudged through the crowd behind him, reached out, and tapped his shoulder. Thompson turned to face one of his men, who stared back at him expectantly.

"Well, what is it? What the blazes do you want now?" Thompson asked.

"Mr. Sullivan has passed the word. He wants to see you immediately," the man answered.

"Oh, he does; did you find out what for?" Thompson looked down his bent nose in a worsening mood.

"No, I was told though—right away."

Thompson clamped his jaw shut and ground his back teeth together. He hated interruptions in his work, and he was especially vexed to be halted on the cusp of inciting violence against a personal enemy. He was sorely tempted to ignore Sullivan's call, but he knew it wouldn't be in his best interests. Rasping, "Awright, we'll go," he turned his back on the ship, the captain, and the crowd, and strode away in bitter frustration.

Arriving at the club, Thompson wound his way to the back office where he knew he would find Sullivan. Upon entering the office, he was surprised to find Mr. O'Shea, the portly owner of the club and president of the coming Longshoremen's Union, sitting behind Sullivan's desk and sliding a ruler down the page of an open ledger. Sullivan stood patiently at his elbow and both men looked up.

"Thompson," Sullivan said as a greeting. O'Shea pulled the ruler aside and closed the ledger, pushing it to one side as though he had completed his work.

"Thompson, you've been a while," O'Shea began abrasively.

Thompson stood quietly accepting the rebuke, even though he had come directly; he knew better than to argue with Mr. O'Shea. Now he had to account, which could go against him.

"I was down at Pier 7, Mr. O'Shea, preparing for some work."

"Ah, that barkentine is in—*Genevieve*. I know you want to settle a score there, but we have more important work for you right now."

Thompson was astonished that Mr. O'Shea should be so well informed; *Genevieve* had only been alongside for an hour.

O'Shea pulled a sheet of paper from a small pile he had in front of him. "Here." He waved it toward Thompson. "This is a list of people who owe me money. I have it on good authority that money is about to become scarce. All of the easy flow out there is about to dry up, and the skunks who presently owe me will owe others as well. So, this is urgent; I want to be first in line to get my money back. Last in line is sure to get nothing, not a shilling. You have shown some talent in getting new members for the union, and the, errr, other odd jobs; now I want you to clean up this list quickly. After this list, there will be another one." He had built some heat and was red in the face after this short speech. He seemed about to say something more when the telephone rang. A look of annoyance passed over his features as he picked up the earpiece.

"Hello, what? Just wait a second," he barked into the mouthpiece. Holding the telephone to his chest, he said, "Thompson, I need quick results. Use whatever means you see as necessary, but don't get caught. Sullivan, show him out."

Among the empty card tables again, Sullivan said, "Well, you will have your hands full for a while."

Thompson looked at him for a moment before responding. "I wonder how he knows these things—the ship being in, the money situation."

"Me as well. He came in a couple of hours ago and said there'll be a panic; we've been looking through the books ever since. It would be nice if he was wrong; it won't be good for business, but I fear he'll be right since he has been before."

"I suppose so," Thompson said indifferently and turned to leave. Before he got to the door, Sullivan called after him, "You'll get another opportunity with that ship."

Thompson grunted something and began looking at the names on his list.

CHAPTER 6

RETURNING EARLY FROM lunch, Paul found his brother-in-law feverishly searching through the filing cabinets. This was the fourth time he had found him so, and while it wasn't such an unusual idea that a man who had been chief clerk should occasionally get his own files, there was something peculiar in Fitzpatrick's frenzied skimming through the folders when he thought himself unobserved. Some of his work had slipped, Paul had noticed, possibly coincident with a lingering smell of whiskey about him. More than once, there had been mistakes in the foreign bond accounts, but thankfully, Mr. Savoy's sharp eyes had caught them. He knew it fell to him to speak to Fitzpatrick, but he couldn't think of the right manner in which to bring the matter up. It occurred to him briefly that foreign bond accounts had a history of errors, so he suppressed a wisp of unworthy misgiving that perhaps these were not mistakes. But then, why would John purposely err?

Noting Paul's arrival, Fitzpatrick picked out a random file and closed the drawer.

"Ah, Mr. Standish," he hummed pleasantly, "how was your lunch?"

"Just fine, Mr. Fitzpatrick; just fine." Paul upheld Edgar's use of surnames at the bank even when they were alone. "Is Mr. Savoy not in?" he asked, referring to Fitzpatrick's search of the file drawers.

"Oh, he's about; sometimes I can't wait the time it takes for him to get me the correct file."

"I've found him capable," Paul defended his new clerk, "but you know his job better than anyone," he said agreeably.

"Yes, well, I must get back to my desk; it will be a busy afternoon," Fitzpatrick replied over his shoulder while effecting his escape.

And the afternoon was busy: it began with a sell-off of foreign bonds and consequently plummeting values. A slide began. The story circulating between banks was that the British had overspeculated in South America and were consequently tightening up everywhere else. As word dribbled out from the financial community to the wider public, the certainty investors had previously enjoyed dwindled with the hours of the day. What was to be done when the assumption of solid footing was found to be weak and undercut? Investors had difficulty deciding the correct action to take because their present poor circumstance was a result of their own preceding judgments. Some cursed circumstance and held on; the less assured looked for prophets to guide them; but many—many, many—did what their friends and neighbors were doing—they ran to the bank to cash out.

When the bank finally closed for the day, Fitzpatrick took to his office and brooded, facing the open window. Outside in the streets, unrest baked in an airlessness that made those indoors swelter as well. The run on the bank had been quite a surprise, but what made it a disaster for him personally was that he had been losing at cards again and had skimmed over a thousand dollars out of the vault to cover himself at the club until he could win back his debt there. The absolute nuisance of it was that Charles had found his "adjustments" in the foreign bond accounts and then corrected the doctored paperwork. Consequently, a visible cash discrepancy would exist when the vault was checked.

If all that wasn't bad enough, Fitzpatrick felt that both Paul and Charles were paying close attention to his movements; he had begun to think one or the other or both may have seen some message of Edgar's in the files. Somehow *they knew*, but they weren't saying anything. He had not found any more incriminating notes from his dead boss, but he still had more than half of the files to check. If only he could have the bank to himself for a day, but Paul had not given him a front door key. Such was the paradox of Fitzpatrick's character that he could feel wounded for not being trusted so far.

Later that night, Fitzpatrick embarked on the only path he could think of to lead him out of his troubles; he set out for the club in the stifling heat to win back his money. Weaving through the various rooms, he was about to settle into a medium stakes table when Sullivan caught his eye and waved him toward a door farther back. Lured on by the thought that perhaps he was being guided to a good game, his hopes were dashed immediately. "Mr. Thompson would like a word."

At the same moment, only a few city blocks away, the little river tug that had put *Genevieve* alongside two days before made up to her once again. The fading light faintly illuminated scenes of vigorous activity on the barkentine's deck: Dennis and a few hands secured the main hatch over a meager cargo of salt; Risto lit the running lights; Benjamin, Morris, and Elliot singled up mooring lines; and through the action, untouched by any sense of urgency, Norman strolled aft with a pot of coffee for the captain. Arriving at the pilothouse, he set pot and coffee cup near the chart table.

"Careful; it just came off of the stove," he said to Thomas.

"Thanks, Norman. I could do with a cup right now."

"You didn't want to get some sleep and go out fresh in the morning?" Norman asked.

Thomas gave a tired grin. "I'd love to sleep and go tomorrow; maybe there would even be a breeze, but no, I don't want to get hung up in this town. We're lucky to have unloaded and taken on this much salt without further difficulty."

In truth, he was astonished to be in this position: the initial strike had mysteriously broken up. Ironically, his agent had engaged a number of the strikers to unload. Despite the heat, the work had progressed well, and then the crew loaded in the salt. Some sour humor hung rank in the damp heavy air, however, and it wasn't only the crotchety aspect of the longshoremen. When Thomas had ventured into the city to purchase a bicycle for George, a palpable sense of unrest had been all around him. It seemed time to leave, and paying for a tow up to Lake Huron seemed well worth the money now that he and the mill were earning again.

The tug whistle blew. He scalded his mouth with an incautious swig of coffee and prepared for a long night of watching the stern of the little riverboat as it hauled him upriver.

Fitzpatrick's first thought as he came to his senses was: *What have I been drinking?* His head hurt abominably, and he had no idea where he was. He couldn't see. He tried to swallow, but there was something—cloth—in his mouth. He wanted to remove it, but he couldn't lift his hand. Still befuddled, he couldn't make sense of his difficulties.

"Fitzpatrick?" A familiar voice wheezed in front of him. Everything was dark and the air smelt tangy. The voice filled him with misgivings.

"Coming around, are we, Fitzpatrick?" the voice prompted. His thoughts were becoming clearer; that was Thompson's voice. Where was he? He sensed motion in front of him; a blindfold was roughly pulled from his head; then the rag was yanked from his mouth. He swallowed quickly, then gasped for air. Thompson pushed his round spectacles onto his face, finally bringing the world into focus: a lantern set on the floor illuminated Thompson in a most sinister fashion, and the walls of the narrow room sparkled in the lamplight. Taking stock, he found himself tied, hand and foot, into an armchair balanced on its rear legs and held that way by a small diameter rope hitched around his upper body. The rope disappeared into the darkness beyond Thompson.

"Where am I? Did you drug me?" he asked.

"You, my friend, are a long way from help; that's the most important thing for you to know."

"What is this place? What do you want?" Fitzpatrick spit out in growing alarm.

"You are in what remains of an abandoned salt mine under the city of Detroit," Thompson wheezed. "Behind you is a disused shaft; I'm not sure how far down it goes—a long way, I guess. They gave up digging here twelve years ago. No one comes down here anymore. As for what I want, you already know I collect on unpaid debts."

Fitzpatrick began to say something, but Thompson made a halt sign with his upraised hand.

"Sshhh, just a moment." He then picked up a glittering ball of rock salt, stepped forward, and tossed it past Fitzpatrick's head into the empty space of the shaft beyond. He then made a show of counting his fingers:

"One, two, three, four, five, six, sev—" A distant thunk rose from the shaft, interrupting the count. "Well, for certain, six, not quite seven—far enough," Thompson smirked.

Fitzpatrick mustered a weak sense of outrage. To think he, a merciless killer, was being threatened this way. If he could only get free, he would put an end to Thompson and his sneering and his threats.

"If you drop me in the pit, you will get nothing more," he said.

Thompson made no reply, but simply twanged the rope like a guitar string. Fitzpatrick flinched, and one of the chair legs shifted in the salty dirt of the floor, increasing his angle backwards. From his altered position, he could see where the tunnel floor ended and became the yawning chasm he was perched over. He attempted to lean his head forward for counterbalance, but he dared not move too much.

"The people you owe money to have occasionally collected from estates of the deceased. It's not difficult," Thompson said. Then he pulled a hunting knife from his belt and tested the blade's keenness with his thumb.

"You won't be alone down there."

Fitzpatrick's little show of bravado melted away; he felt like an impostor before Thompson, who truly was a cold-blooded killer. As beads of sweat rolled down into his eyes, Fitzpatrick felt like crying. Would Thompson notice tears under all the perspiration? The question bothered him absurdly enough that he held himself together.

"Okay, I've been meaning to pay up and I can get some money, but it will take a little time," he said quickly.

"Time. How much time?" Thompson rasped.

"Some in a couple of days, maybe the rest in a week—or thereabouts."

Thompson set the blade against the rope, allowing it to bite into the yarns of one of the three strands. "Be specific; you're a banker. You owe three thousand, two hundred dollars," he said impatiently.

"Okay, okay." Fitzpatrick struggled to remain still as Thompson pushed the knife into more yarns in the rope. The severed fibers cast small lumpy shadows as they curled down the line. "I can get fifteen hundred by Friday and seventeen hundred by the following Friday."

"That's not quite good enough. The people you owe expect better." He began a light sawing action on the strand.

"Stop. Stop. Please, okay," Fitzpatrick squeaked, his marvelous baritone failing him for once. "What do you want? I'll do whatever you wish."

These were the words Thompson had waited to hear; they had only taken ten minutes with the advantages provided by the salt mine. Now it was time to move a pet project of his own ahead while still looking after Mr. O'Shea's business. He sheathed his knife.

"I'll allow you to live and pay seventeen hundred by this Friday. In return for my charity, you will do a small job for me."

The meeting of the Industrial Bank of Detroit's board of directors was suitably somber. Eight well-dressed men, seated around a polished walnut table, sat quietly looking down the summary sheet explaining the bank's position in light of the recent financial panic.

"How recent are these numbers?" asked a pale, fastidious man with impeccably dark curly hair.

"We compiled them this week, Mr. Murray," Paul answered the director.

"So they are accurate," said Murray.

"There have been minor changes in the last day or so—very close."

"Pfooh." Murray blew out his lips in an expression of acknowledged difficulty.

"Well, we're not insolvent," said a white-haired gent at the opposite side of the table as he glanced absentmindedly at his engraved watch fob.

"Perhaps not, Mr. Hobbs, but will we be able to say that at the next meeting?" countered Murray. A silence ensued that Paul felt he must break. "It seems, gentlemen, that although we have had a rapid sell-off of bonds and stocks—particularly railroad stocks—we will, in my estimation remain solvent."

Murray looked clandestinely at the bank's young operating director, ten years his junior, and wondered what great purse of experience the man drew from. He shifted in his chair and studied again the summary sheet. It was a pity not to have old Edgar here at this moment.

"Hahmmn, gentlemen, if I may suggest a course of action?" Fitzpatrick preambled in his warmest expectant baritone. Several sage heads turned his way.

"We have had this run on the bank, and although we are solvent now, it would perhaps be wise to create a new position that will defend us from a second such event as the one we have just survived." When Fitzpatrick saw some slight nodding of heads down the table, he knew he was reaching his audience. Paul, who was next to him, however, seemed tense; his normally generous smile was quite absent from his face.

Fitzpatrick continued, "It seems paramount that we not only guard our cash reserves, but replace what has been lost so far. As the summary sheet indicates, we have some holdings that have lost a great deal of value but are still strong firms. We also hold some stock in companies that will not recover from their recent losses. I'm sure Mr. Standish will know how to deal with these." He nodded cordially at Paul, who looked up at him quite sharply, surprised and perhaps a little pleased; he couldn't be sure. He had the table in the palm of his hand; it was time to strike.

"It will take time to improve our cash position through interest on our normal lending alone; therefore, I suggest we call in some of our smaller loans or any that might be thought of as risky in order to further bolster our position."

Murray spoke up. "I see the sense in that."

Paul shuffled his feet uncomfortably. "Some of our small loans are old customers; we don't want to let down valued clients merely for being small."

Hobbs threw in an oar. "No, no, not at all. We will need to review the makeup of our small loans."

"But we have to move quickly," Murray said. "Stocks are still losing value—particularly the railroads. Who can say if we'll need that money next week?"

"Mr. Murray, I have already made a list," Fitzpatrick said reassuringly.

"Oh. Well then," the directors chuckled, relief and smiles all around. Fitzpatrick smiled as well; it had been child's play.

Chapter 7

Late August, 1892

KLARA WARMED THE bottoms of the old cake pans, setting them over the top of a vigorously boiling pot. When they had steamed for a couple of minutes, she emptied them over a spread newspaper on the table. With some light tapping, the pans released their contents: one, two, three, four…twelve! Twelve big soap cakes—off-white, prim, and sweet-smelling. She admired them briefly, cut them into eighths, and wrapped the resultant bars in precut sheets of butcher paper. Once tied with string, they were packed carefully in the large enameled pot she had previously used for boiling jarred vegetables.

Since Mateusz had put an end to her efforts in food preservation, she now put her long hours alone into a clandestine program of soap-making. Basic brown soap had been easy to produce; she had obtained tallow from the butcher and sifted ash from the corner of the yard, then combined these ingredients with some ground pine bark and pine oil, rendered from needles, for fragrance. Now she was completing a batch of her fancy soap for bathing and washing hair; she had given it a wild-flower fragrance she thought would make it appealing to ladies. The only trick to her work was keeping on schedule; it was imperative that all of her processes be complete and hidden prior to Mateusz's return from work. Thus, she took the pot, tucked it behind a wide loose board that led beneath the back porch, and bumped the nails back into place. Tomorrow, she would carry her stock of soap into Ripley to sell to the general store. They had been very pleased with her products, paying her fairly for them. Her money, likewise, she kept hidden since it was her ticket out, so Mateusz mustn't find out she was saving up. If she could maintain her schedule of soap production and sales, she might have enough money for a train ticket to Montreal before winter.

She had decided to leave him, perhaps even return to Poland if she must. She wouldn't endure a morose life existing next to a man who didn't love her and refused to try. Although Klara had confided in Felka about her troubles with Mateusz, even Felka knew nothing of her grand plan since sometimes it seemed impossible to believe she could heave this entire life into the past by simply packing a bag and walking out. When she thought about standing on the wallowing deck of the sinking schooner, however, she realized she hadn't been spared from a cold drowning only to die here, unnoticed and unloved. Mateusz was mean and hard, and better suited to a life alone. She was just an unnecessary adornment to his preferred bachelor existence, so she couldn't fathom why he had ever thought he wanted a wife.

The next day, she waited until Mateusz's shift had begun at the mine; then she quick-stepped down the road to Ripley, the next town over. She wanted to avoid attracting any attention by selling to the local general store. Laden with a heavy bag of soap cakes, she arrived at Ripley's shop before ten o'clock. The proprietor examined her soap.

"These are very nice," he said as he sniffed the finer scented bars she had made. "I think they're better than your last batch, and those sold very quickly."

Klara beamed inwardly, happy at last to be appreciated by someone, anyone. He paid her a penny a piece for the brown bars and two for the white bars. Putting four dollars and thirty cents into her handbag, she thanked him.

"Can you bring more next week?" he asked. "I'm sure we can sell them."

"Yes," Klara agreed readily, planning to get to work on another big batch tomorrow. If she improved her rate of production, she would be able to travel to Montreal by September.

On her way back into Lake Junction, Klara planned the rest of her day: She had to collect more material for making soap; she would need to make a quick job of some cleaning to keep up appearances in the house; and, of course, have dinner prepared for whatever hour Mateusz came home. She had a letter from Bridget that would be a pleasure to read when all of her tasks were in hand.

Later, she approached her house carrying two large tubs of tallow she had obtained from the butcher. As she walked around to the back of the house, she noticed with a small start that the back door was ajar. Suddenly, Mateusz stepped out, walking with a limp.

"Where have you been?" he demanded.

"What are you doing home so early?" she countered.

"I want to know where you were, and what is that you are carrying?"

Klara's heart sunk. Why was he home early? How could she explain the tallow? If he knew the truth, he would ruin everything and she would have a desperate time getting away.

"I was offered this lard at a very good price, so I bought it to have for our baking. It will last us through next winter," she lied.

"How much was it?" he snorted

"Forty cents."

"How often must I tell you not to spend money on things we don't need?"

Klara knew she must move to a safer topic. "I'm sorry, Mateusz; I might have waited to check with you, but these were the last tubs left at this price. They will save us a few dollars over the winter." She quickly changed the subject. "What has happened to your leg? You are limping," she said as she proceeded past him into the house. Setting her bag on a chair, she went to the sink cabinet to put the offending tallow out of sight. He limped into the kitchen after her.

"There was a small rock slide where I was working; my leg got trapped and the doctor sent me home for the rest of the day—even though I could still work." He sat down heavily at the table, poured a tall glass of forty rod whiskey, and tossed it back. Klara had noticed the low level of whiskey in the bottle and an empty one sitting next to it. Mateusz had been home drinking for a while. Closing the door on the tallow, she breathed a small sigh of relief that her soap operation seemed safe. But as she turned around again, she saw with a start that Mateusz had picked up her bag so he might put his sore foot up on the chair. He swung it idly beside him as he drank.

"I'll put that out of the way," Klara said, reaching to take the bag, but he pulled it back.

"You seem very eager to have this," he commented. "What's in here, more winter supplies?"

"It just has my things. Please, Mateusz," she entreated. He opened the bag and spilled its contents on the table. He tossed aside the letter from Bridget, but when his eyes fell on the money, he looked up and snarled, "Where did you get this money? Have you been holding back from the groceries? Did you take it from my pants?"

She hesitated. How could she explain this away?

"Have you been taking my money?" He belched. "Answer me!"

"I was saving some for a surprise," she said miserably.

"A surprise? Like a big bucket of lard?" He sprang up, ignoring or not feeling his right leg, and clasped her face in his meaty right hand, leaning hard against her, crushing her body against the sink counter. Dull pain probed her jaw as his thumb dug into it, his forefinger squishing her nose to one side while his other three fingers squeezed her left cheek. She was terrified. She tried to break loose from his grasp, but his formidable grip only tightened.

"What have you been doing?" he demanded, although she could not answer, her mouth being covered as it was. His breathing bellowed out of his torso in impassioned gasps; seconds passed as he stared into her bewildered eyes.

"To think that I ever wanted you," he sputtered. Despite her fear, she was hopeful he might at last reveal what was in his mind—perhaps make an end to the strange dull tension that existed in the house. Afraid and desperate as she was, she knew she must be very patient to come out of this situation well. She remained limp in his grasp, smelling whiskey and the rock dust of his hand; she stared back, awaiting what he might finally say about them.

His labored breathing began to catch, trip up, come in short heaves, and, strangely, his face transformed from terrible anger to a mask of quivering misery. Tears appeared and rolled slowly down his flushed cheeks.

"To think of what I have done…what I have done…to have you, and now…you are nothing…nothing like…look at you—like this…it was for nothing."

It came out as inebriated babble, yet there was a sinister enigma in his statement that sent a frisson of horror through her. What had he done? Even as Klara asked herself this question, she wished not to know; she had a sense it must be something truly awful to provoke such deep feeling in him. Without concluding this train of thought, she skipped frenetically to her current jeopardy. Mateusz was quite possibly a very dangerous man. She saw she must get free of him immediately and permanently. She continued to remain still, trying not to upset him further, hoping to find a way out of his malicious embrace without betraying her intent. Her hands, already at her sides, took hold of her skirt and she wriggled in minute movements, slowly hiking it up.

He sobbed lightly as he continued to stare at her. Then his expression gradually changed once again from sadness to puzzlement as the liquor within him subjugated his thinking. His grip eased and Klara had a sense that he might soon pass out. On the other hand, he might easily revert to rage. He had wronged her physically now, and she didn't want to gamble that she had seen the furthest reach of his violence. As his hand released her face, she made her move; she threw her upper body against him, making a small space, then brought her knee up into his groin quite hard and stomped down on his injured foot. He cried out in pain, momentarily unable to respond to her attack. Free now, she reached the stove as he recovered and staggered after her, just about upon her. She grabbed the iron kettle, swung round, and hit him on his left ear. Momentum brought him forward into her, carrying both of them to the floor. He had one hand on her throat, but his other arm was trapped between their bodies. He stared into her face, his eyes blazing with an unfocused whiskey-tempered hate. He was crushing down against her, but she still held the kettle and awkwardly bashed it against his head until he rolled off of her. Shaken, but mostly unhurt, Klara recovered first and was on her feet. As Mateusz rose to his knees, she swung the kettle again with all her might and connected squarely with his left jaw. He went down in a heap at last and lay silent, facedown upon the floor.

For a moment, Klara thought she had killed him, but then with a small measure of relief, she saw the slow rise and fall of his body as he breathed in and out. Before she had caught her breath, she gathered her clothes, letters, and money into a bag. She then set about making one more large batch of soap, keeping the kettle close at hand.

Chapter 8

L ANGUISHING IN THIRD position behind sound and light, aroma is rarely the agent of awakening a slumbering body. Nonetheless, before Thomas was fully awake, he smelled something; it pulled him slowly—smoke. Smoke! The thought shot him from sleep. He leapt from his bunk, donning pants as he did so, and ran up the steps to the deck. Once there, as the cool night air chilled his bare torso, he found *Genevieve* in complete order, broad reaching before the northwest wind toward Whitefish Point. He sniffed skeptically; had he imagined the smell? No—there it was. What could be burning? He hustled aft to the pilothouse.

"Do you smell smoke?" he asked Dennis.

"Yes, sir. It just started to get stronger, but I had the hold checked—no sign of fire."

"Send someone again; let's be sure." The hold was checked again as was the fo'c'sle, salon, and especially the galley, but to Thomas's relief, there was no sign of a smoldering hot pocket anywhere, and the smell of char remained unaccounted for.

The sun beamed brightly down on Whitefish Point astern by the time Thomas took the watch again. Lake Superior's outward flow filled in behind the ship, accelerating her thread through menacing shoals in the Upper St. Mary's River. As the channel's width diminished, Thomas handed the course, upper topsail, and mizzen; burnt air was her constant companion as *Genevieve* crept alongside under bare poles. With a sense of dread, Thomas realized that in one of the hottest, driest summers in living memory, this smoky aroma could mean nothing other than a forest fire.

Klara sat counting her money for the fourth time: $2.80. It was time to make a choice between trying to go farther and finding a place to stay; and in spite of knowing she had only $2.80, she counted once more in the wishful thought that she had perhaps missed the coin that would add to her list of options. But no, there it was: $2.80 was all she had. Having run from Mateusz, the bulk of her soap money had gone to getting the first possible ticket from Hancock train depot to—anywhere. She had ridden the rails to Sault Ste. Marie, feeling that each mile of track left behind increased her safety from the man she had foolishly married. But was she becoming more secure? Confronted now with the paltry handful of coins that represented her life savings, she asked herself whether this had been a good idea, departing shelter and the possibility of earning only to fling herself into complete uncertainty. Good idea? Bad idea? It had been the right idea; she couldn't think anything else now. She wouldn't remain as a victim of Mateusz's violence, and to have stayed even in the same town would have been very dangerous for her. She must make the best of this choice, even though she couldn't see how just yet. One thing she knew: Sitting here recounting her money and feeling sorry for herself wouldn't help things at all. It was time to pick up her few belongings and walk. Looking around town might produce an idea, a job, a friend. Anything was possible.

She left the area around the train station and walked down the main street through the busy part of town until she could see the river. Because the day was hot and the air smelled of smoke, she had the lovely thought of dipping her feet in cool water. Even the sight of the moving river was soothing. Toward the waterfront, businesses began to be devoted to ships and river traffic. Chandleries that sold caulking mallets, tarred marline, twine, and hemp hawsers were neighbors to purveyors of oils and steam engine machine shops that sat alongside victuallers where one could buy anything from raisins and custard to pickled pork. It was from one of these last buildings—a victualler—that Klara saw a familiar figure emerge from the doorway followed by a stock boy pushing a loaded handcart. Could it be? Yes! That confident stride, the wispy white hair; it had to be Norman!

"Norman!" she tried to shout, but her voice faltered in her excitement. "Norman!" she belted the name out solidly the second time and increased her pace to catch up.

Norman turned to see who might be calling him. At first, he couldn't make her face out clearly, but as Klara approached, her bright eyes and heart-shaped face came into focus, causing his weathered visage to crumple into a smile.

"Well, good day to you, my dear." He winked at her and turned to the stock boy. "Take this down to *Genevieve*, the barkentine just past that rust-bucket steamer at the bend."

"Yes, sir," the boy answered and continued on. Norman's face resumed smiling. It wasn't every day that he was chased down by a pretty young woman, and, although he knew he was far too old for her, Norman dallied with thoughts of a past self who wouldn't have been.

"*Genevieve* is here?" Klara asked.

"Just around the bend," he pointed. "I'm on my way back to her." He offered her his arm. "How is your arm now?"

"All better. Strong, thank you," she said and slipped her hand into the crook of his elbow.

"What has brought you to the Soo?" he asked.

"Oh, Norman, trouble." In a surge of relief at seeing someone she knew, Klara quickly blurted out the main points of her story, sometimes peppering her English with Polish exclamations.

"Hold on, hold on." Norman turned to her, unprepared for the verbal onslaught. "Let's get back to the ship and I'll make some tea. Then you can tell the captain."

"Yes, okay," she said, not believing her good luck.

Arriving at *Genevieve*, they saw a small tug alongside preparing to help the ship down through the lock. Thomas spotted Norman climbing over the bulwark and, quite surprised, realized it was Klara whom he had escorted aboard.

"Well, good morning," he said to the two of them.

"Look who I found," said Norman. "She's got a story to tell you."

"I'm afraid it'll have to be quick; we are due to lock down very shortly. They are turning back the lock right now," Thomas answered.

"There should be just enough time for tea. I'll fix it," said Norman.

Thomas showed Klara to the stern rail behind the pilothouse where she sat to tell her story; he settled where he could watch the tug and lock door while listening. After a short while, the lock had refilled, its door beginning to open, and although Klara hadn't finished, Thomas sensed that he knew the ending.

"I'm sorry, my dear, but we have to leave. What can I do for you?"

Klara was dumbfounded. She didn't know what to ask for; it seemed wrong just to ask for money, and even if she got it, she still needed to find a place to stay, or a destination. Now that she was among friends, she desperately wanted to remain so.

"Please, take me with you," she managed to say, knowing it was a lot to ask.

Thomas looked at her and appeared to consider. "To DeTour? All right, but you have to come now, as you are. The ship is leaving, and there's no time to get anything."

"This is all I have," she answered, holding up her small bag.

Thomas nodded; he knew he couldn't leave her here, no matter how her tale might end. "Go see Norman; he'll get you something to eat. We'll get a chance to talk later."

Klara's spirits soared for the first time in months, sitting aboard this great vessel that had saved her life before. As she watched the river tug guide *Genevieve* between the rock cuts and many hazards of the St. Mary's River, she felt *Genevieve*'s strength and solidity carrying her to safety. Borne on a hot westerly breeze, the increasingly pungent smell of smoke dried her throat and stung her eyes, but even that could not dampen her elation. As the air became hazy, the two ships reached somewhat more open water and *Genevieve* made sail while the tug hauled in its towline. Dusk found them approaching Lime Island looking at a glow in the western sky that persisted long past the explanation of sunset.

CHAPTER 9

"I T'S AWFULLY THICK," Norman said to Dennis as they perched back on the rail for an evening smoke.

Dennis laughed. "Do you wonder why we are here burning expensive tobacco when there's all this free smoke around us?"

Norman pulled on his cigarette, momentarily brightening the heater at its tip. "I don't wonder. I want good, clean smoke. It tastes better."

"The fires must be getting closer," Dennis speculated. "If they hit the mill, we might not be able to dock."

"You mean to say you think the old man would leave his family and mill to burn and sail right on by?" the cook asked.

"When you say it that way, I don't suppose he would. It's about time for me to get the lines and fenders up from the lazarette."

Ripping saws dominated the midnight air as *Genevieve* slid into her berth under the smoke-veiled light of a gibbous moon. Thomas had never adjusted to the unending noise of his new mill, running night and day. Leaving Dennis to square away the ship, he escorted Klara up the plank road and over the hill to his house. Anne heard the door and was getting up when Thomas climbed the stairs.

"Hello, Annie; it's me," he said quietly before entering the bedroom.

"I thought so; you're in late tonight."

"Yes, or early for tomorrow. I've brought a house guest," he said prior to planting a kiss on her lips. She was surprised and couldn't quite enjoy the greeting.

"Mmphh," she kissed back. "Who is it?" she asked pulling away from him.

"It's Klara again," he said.

"Did she sink another ship?"

"Something like that; I've only heard part of the story. Norman found her in the Soo, but that can all keep until morning. It's hot and I'm thirsty. I'm going down to the water for a swim, and then I want to drink a glass of ale and go to bed."

"Okay," Anne said as she pulled on a housedress. "I'll get Klara settled. I'm so glad you're home. The fires are getting close."

Thomas renounced sleep in the early morning after a fitful night. He had tossed and turned in the bed as though spitted over the forest fires, his peace roasting away. He discussed with Anne a list of things to pack should evacuation be necessary, and then he made his departure for the mill. Cresting the hill brought forth beads of sweat in the unusual early morning heat, and something seemed strange—missing. It came to him that the customary scream of saws was absent. Looking toward the mill, he couldn't discern whether the tall stack was smoking in the ambient haze created by the forest fires. He hurried on.

Thomas spent some time at the mill looking for William until a teamster pointed him out, pacing the roof of the main building, exuding an air of controlled alarm.

"William, what are you doing?" Thomas called up.

"Checking the water barrels. I'll be down shortly."

As his brother returned to the ground, Thomas noticed that William too was bathed in sweat.

"The fires are close," William said excitedly. "Svensson has been tracking them and reports that they're approaching Carlton Lake."

"Near where we were cutting last winter?"

"Close by; most of the fires are north of us. I'm pushing all of our stock back into the pen until we see how they go. How soon will *Genevieve* be loaded to go?"

"We'll load. We should start as soon as we have the red pine logs out of her. It'll be late today, but I'm not going to depart until I see what happens with these fires."

William looked like he had pinched his fingers in a closing door. "But we need this cargo delivered; we're barely ahead of our bills right now," he prodded.

"The cargo will be delivered, but what I said stands. We'll get loaded as soon as we can," Thomas countered.

With a hot sticky day to look forward to, and as a way not to fret over the forest fires, Anne planned on taking the children to a quiet cove by the river. The smoke haze would be considerably less at the river's surface, and the trip would be good exercise. As Klara was not unknown to her, Anne simply invited her along. Bread was baked, the aforementioned packing was performed, and a snack of venison sausage was bagged so they could camp by the water through the day. It only remained to organize the children. George was prepared, and Molly was busily brushing her hair, but Curt, her youngest, hadn't done a thing to ready himself. An inveterate dawdler, he was found lying on his stomach in the back garden, wearing only his underpants, watching the comings and goings of an anthill.

Once settled in the cove, the children were in high spirits, swimming while Anne and Klara enjoyed wading with their skirts drawn up over their knees, the cool deliciousness of the water caressing their legs.

"Your English has improved, Klara," said Anne.

"Thank you," Klara smiled. "I read much and try meeting English people."

"Well, it's working," Anne replied, also smiling, and then a look of concern came over her face. "Do your bruises hurt?" she asked, indicating Klara's bruised cheeks.

Klara's eyes flitted about uncomfortably as she struggled with a strange embarrassment.

"I'm sorry," Anne said, seeing the younger woman's discomfort. A moment of silence ensued while each surveyed the still waters of the cove and the children's wet frolics. Having only the briefest of explanations from Thomas, Anne said, "Perhaps you could tell me your whole story. Start from the beginning when you left here last fall."

Klara took a deep breath and said, "Yes." Dry-eyed, she began with her arrival in Lake Junction, Mateusz's deception about his identity, and the strained living situation. She brightened visibly talking about the wedding, but then she relapsed into a melancholic recital of Mateusz's disinterest in her and his anger and drinking. Anne listened aghast as Klara recounted the tale of her destroyed peas, and of her ensuing resolve to change the course of her life after the incident.

"And so you did make the change. You are here," Anne said.

"Yes." Klara went on to explain her secret soap-making program that had led to her final altercation with Mateusz. As she described spending the night fabricating soap bars over the unconscious body of her husband, Anne shook her head.

"You are a brave girl," she said solemnly.

Klara nodded. "But now I am married to a bad man—no husband. I am not going back and have nowhere to go," she said glumly. "Who wants me now?"

"Tut, tut—you mustn't say such things," Anne said kindly. "You are not bad; you have been unlucky. This is a common problem, but with a little time some solution will come. Meanwhile, as long as the house doesn't burn down, you can stay with us. Besides, I have an idea; how is your arithmetic?"

Infernally hot, the day wore on as approaching forest fires seemed to suck up the little breathable air, leaving only smothering heat and choking smoke to scald the lungs. Mill hands, faces wrapped in their shirts, pushed pine logs back into the stock pen, ran carts of sawn lumber out to *Genevieve*, and grumbled through satisfying William's wishes in the face of the advancing threat. Working late, they filled *Genevieve*, piling up a considerable deck cargo, until William sought out Thomas.

"Svensson says the fires are past Carlton Lake now. I think they're mainly staying to the north of us," William said.

"I wonder if Inch will get burned. His mill is in that path," Thomas mused.

"I think it might even be north of him," William answered.

Thomas recognized this for what it was—a tickle, the softest of spurs, urging him to get *Genevieve* under way without openly asking.

"I'm going to stay tonight," he said. "I want to be sure before I leave that the fires are past."

William had been afraid of this, but he fettered his tongue before any protest could run loose. If his brother didn't wish to ship out, very little could persuade him to do otherwise. He changed topics: "You made good time returning from Port Arthur; an extra day won't hurt, and," he swallowed visibly, "you've brought Klara back." A sound, distant and muffled, caught the brothers' attention and they fell silent.

"Did you hear something?" William asked, quietly straining to hear. The sound came again—*boom*—a little louder this time. Thomas began to smile.

"What's funny?" William asked during a third louder boom.

"I think it might rain," Thomas replied and gazed west into the inscrutable evening sky.

Having decided against leaving that night, Thomas started up the plank road toward home. Cresting the hill, a slight shift in the wind hurled widely spaced, fat raindrops splatting against his neck—the shock troops of an approaching host. He turned to see the advance of cloud as lightning crackled across the sky. *Boom.* The sound carried, echoing off individual hillsides. The raindrops began to lose individuality, blending into torrents, facilitating a release of all the saved moisture the sky had withheld in the preceding arid months. The landscape was obscured from sight, illuminated only briefly by sharp bolts of lightning if one didn't cringe at the accompanying thunder. As the air turned markedly cooler, Thomas was wet through, but rather than vainly race for shelter, he stretched his arms skyward, tipping back his head to taste the cool water and drink in the marvelous evening.

BOOK FOUR

THE FINAL SQUEEZE

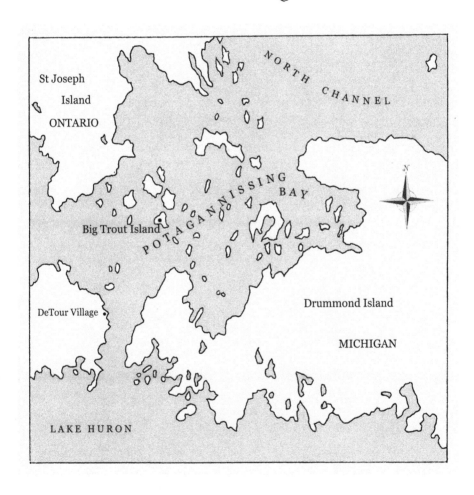

Chapter 1

Late September, 1892

ILLIAM COMMENCED HIS day waiting. Not only waiting, but waiting to the exclusion of all other pursuits. Proud above all of his efficiency, he found it reprehensible to be fully occupied in a solitary, useless activity. "When would *Genevieve* return?" This question pegged him here; the ship was overdue, but the winds had been variable this week and who knew how much extra "sailoring" Thomas would have to do to get her back to DeTour? Hopefully, he wasn't out saving some new unfortunate case. William knew this last thought to be uncharitable, but he was still chafing at having *Genevieve's* last foundling foisted upon him—a runaway no matter her charms.

Pacing his office, William counted the broad pine boards of his floor. At one end of the pattern, he kept a turning point short of the wall in the well-learned measure of his previous office; at the other end, he fetched up close to his rolltop desk and glared at the horrid letter sitting starkly uncompanioned in the center of it. His mind lay manacled to the problem despite the knowledge that fretting brought no profit.

A small knock on the door presaged Klara's entrance. "Good morning, Mr. William," she said.

"Er, yes, good morning," he replied rather stiffly.

She took her seat at the small desk in the corner that had been prepared for her and set about her daily tasks.

Maddening. It was utterly maddening to have her here placidly adding up columns and simultaneously robbing him of the privacy he needed to think and vent. Thomas had brought Klara into the office to provide assistance in coping with the swelling stacks of paper awaiting processing in order to keep their expanded business moving smoothly. William had conceded that he needed help, and he did have to admit that the girl had a head for tallying the various chits and accounts, but he still found it a nuisance to share the office with anyone other than his brother. Somehow, he sensed Anne's hand in this scheme.

His mind returned to the great problem: When would Thomas return? They must discuss the content of this hateful missive before anything else could be undertaken. He composed himself under the imagined surveillance of Klara, sat at his desk, and reread the letter:

The Industrial Bank of Detroit
41 Griswold Street
Detroit, Michigan

McGrath Brothers Lumber Company
Captain Thomas McGrath
Mr. William McGrath
DeTour Village, Michigan
Friday, September 15, 1892

Dear Sirs,

Due to an unexpected decline in financial markets, we at the Industrial Bank of Detroit find it necessary to consolidate our fiscal position at this time. Under the terms of your loan agreement with the bank (specifically clause 11), we reserve the right to recall the loan at our discretion. This letter is to inform you that, regrettably, we must do so now. Please remit to the Bank the remaining balance of your loan: $16,445, no later than November 15 of this year in order to avoid foreclosure proceedings.

Your cooperation in this matter will be greatly appreciated.

Most sincerely,
John Fitzpatrick
Vice President

How could the bank do this to them? It seemed a cruel joke to loan just enough money to start a business going well and then demand it all back at the precise moment when it would be most onerous to repay. Bankruptcy for certain.

A fickle wind brought Thomas alongside in poor humor, frustrated by his three-day passage north from Detroit; for an entire day, *Genevieve* had waited for a breath of air to stir her sails, and in resignation, Thomas had allowed the crew that could to go swimming. The obverse of calm was the heat he enjoyed, lingering surprisingly into September. Watching tall cumulus clouds crowding the landscape around him, he considered regretfully that the heat couldn't last much longer. Soon the great wheel must turn again.

An enervated William caught his eye from the pier, beckoning him off of his ship. En route to the office, William began blurting out the gist of the bank's letter, releasing the burden he had held in wait for Thomas's return. Flinching, Thomas hurried ahead to the office in an effort to throw a blanket over his brother's indiscretion.

Ten minutes later, he was digesting the letter line by line, angered by the jackbooted courtesy of the phrasing, which had no other purpose than to undo them, and the signature of that toad, Fitzpatrick.

"When did this come?" he asked.

"Yesterday. Well, what do you think?"

Outside their door, saws, planers, and edgers screamed as steam-driven iron reciprocated, tirelessly chewing through the log pen's contents. Thomas shot a glance over at Klara, folded the letter into his breast pocket, and said, "Let's take a walk." Thomas led them up the hill to a smooth piece of granite with an upright section rising at an angle from the bottom; partly shaded from the day's sun, it was a superbly comfortable natural chair.

"Why have we come up here?" William asked.

"There are all kinds of ears at the mill; I thought it would be better to have some space. Besides, I can hardly hear myself think in all that noise."

As William sat next to his brother, they each quietly contemplated the mill, all they had built, the effort they had put forth, and the thought that it was all at hazard by the mere stroke of a banker's pen.

"Well, now what do you think?" William asked at last.

"What can I say? I have thought something like this was bound to happen from the beginning," Thomas grumbled.

"Okay, okay. So if you knew it was a foregone conclusion, why did you go along with it? What we need to think of is what to do now."

"Fine," Thomas snapped. "We don't have the money; we can't even suspend payment on anything. The banks are wet with panic, so no one will even lend us the balance, and we probably can't find a buyer for the whole enterprise for the same reason."

"I'm not talking about selling. I won't do it!" William replied.

"So what's your idea?"

William gulped before tendering an idea that he knew Thomas would find odious. "Er, well…I was considering how well our outside shipping arrangements have been going and…." He paused as Thomas sat up straighter, and turned to face him more fully, arms folded across his chest, "and I thought we could continue chartering in the future…. *Genevieve* would be a valuable asset, assuming you would agree to put her value back into the company until it can repay you. It would likely pay back in about a year—the same length of time the loan is set for."

Thomas sat in stony silence, giving his brother an unsettling stare. "You get some great thoughts; you won't consider selling this noisy, smoky, troublesome mill, but you would sell my ship out from under me? Let me tell you something, mister; when I bought *Genevieve*, I did it with cash money and hard work. I didn't put my head in a noose with some greedy banker's itchy fingers holding the lever to the trap door. And I won't sell her—not for you or the bank or anyone else. If we should part company, it will be my idea alone, or an act of nature, so think some more!"

William quietly absorbed the verbal blows his brother laid upon him. He had expected this result, but he still felt disappointed that Thomas didn't feel as committed to the mill as he did. Furious but chastened, he got up and dusted off his pants.

"Well, I'll go think some more," he said with frosty weariness and started down the hill.

Thomas followed him with his eyes, resisting a brief impulse to call him back and have the meeting end better; he had nothing more to say.

A month later, William and Thomas were no closer to paying off the loan or renegotiating with the bank. Return correspondence from their lender simply reiterated that the mill's equipment would be auctioned off if the loan was not repaid promptly. William had selected a lawyer to help them and the brothers were now in Sault Ste. Marie in his office. Seated in a leather armchair, Thomas reflected that the last such chair he had occupied was at the Industrial Bank of Detroit. Mr. DeGere, their lawyer, flitted through a file on his desk, wrote a note on a separate piece of paper, and cleared his throat, "Huhh—hmmm. Hmm. Well, gentlemen, since my first meeting with William, I have written a strongly worded letter to the bank suggesting it would be highly inappropriate for them to call in your loan at this time, and in response, I have received a reply from their counsel stating they are within their rights under the clauses of your loan agreement."

"So where does that leave us? We're no further ahead," William said.

"On the contrary," replied DeGere, "now we know unequivocally that they will not negotiate with you."

"And so?" William asked.

"And so..." DeGere paused to remove and wipe his round spectacles with a white handkerchief, "and so you must consider how you can meet their demands," he said patronizingly.

"That's your advice? The reason we are here is that we can't meet their demands—certainly not in another six weeks or less!" William said.

"I can think of ways to roll over and die without expensive legal help," Thomas put in. "William said you thought we might *do* something about this."

DeGere looked at Thomas blankly for a moment, completed polishing his specs, returned them to his nose, and hooked his thumbs into the pockets of his spun silk waistcoat. "There's not much to be done if they won't negotiate with you, and frankly, I'm surprised they won't. All I can say is do not miss a payment, and perhaps, there might be a chance they will leave well enough alone. Winter is on its way; it's unlikely they can organize repossession of the plant before spring. By that time, you will be only six payments short of completion. Surely, they will take a second look at the situation."

Autumn had finally taken hold. In the early mornings, frost coated *Genevieve's* deck, while ashore hardwood trees commenced a glorious display of ochres and crimson, oranges and vibrant yellows that were the final act for their leaves. Thomas sailed *Genevieve* aggressively at this time of year, trying with each passage to shorten the round trip to Detroit, his only destination. The wind was generally thick and dependable with a greater presence of strong westerlies, but not yet the bitter gales that tore at the rigging in November. Sitting at his desk on one of his brief intervals at home, Thomas was astonished to see Cedric Inch pile in through the office door.

"Gentlemen, good morning," Inch said with a kindly smile that made his watery blue eyes twinkle. He carried in his hand a small leather satchel, roughened beige at its corners, and wore a clean but similarly worn suit. Thomas was the first to recover from the intrusion.

"Inch. What the devil brought you here?" Inch's composure couldn't be rattled apart by Thomas's inhospitable reception.

"Good morning, miss," he nodded toward Klara's corner as he rubbed something from his broad bloodshot nose.

"Good morning." Klara turned to see their visitor and smiled. Inch didn't stretch Thomas's patience any further.

"Gentlemen, I've come to see if you would be interested in a proposition that will benefit us all." Without waiting for assent, he set his satchel on the floor, and not being offered a seat, settled his weight against the edge of Klara's desk.

"I'm sure you're aware that a number of mills have taken losses after August's fires, and we, sadly, had our mill burn to the ground." The McGrath brothers knew this but remained silent, morbidly curious where Inch was headed. Inch, warming to his topic, slid one buttock solidly onto Klara's desk, crowding her inconsiderately. She gathered a few papers and left.

"At the same time, your mill has gone through a massive expansion, and I'm sure, as in any such enterprise, some extra capital wouldn't go astray at this moment." He paused to let this point sink in or perhaps gauge its effect. "I have the remainder of last season's cutting to be milled and no place to do it. What would you say to a partnership? You could saw my timber, I'll take it to market with *Hengist*, and we could split the profits. Maybe it could be a new beginning for us."

Thomas opened his mouth, but William cut in quickly. "Why not just sell us the timber, Cedric? It would be a more direct, clean arrangement."

Inch smiled blandly. "I've been offered money for the stock, but I thought this would be a good time to mend fences, for you as well as for me. I have stock, a little money, and *Hengist* to move cargo. I've heard you're chartering to deliver lumber and might also make use of some extra income."

Thomas saw exactly what Inch was driving at; he had heard somehow that the mill's loan had been called and was hoping to slide into a partnership with little expense at a moment when the operation was desperate for money, and he was gambling, in the same proposal, to save his own business after the wildfire disaster. William was about to ask a follow-up question when Thomas forestalled him with a subtle motion of his hand.

"I don't think we're interested in this, Inch," Thomas said.

For the first time, Inch's face lost its enthusiastic smile as he realized the brothers might not be quite so acutely desperate as he had thought.

"Gentlemen, if you're not interested in partnership," he scrambled, "I do still need to get this timber sawn. It's a long way to Manistique— towing logs on the open lake always involves loss; how about just buying the stock then, as you said, William? I'll give a fair price."

Thomas looked back at him for a long moment and considered what he saw: Inch was every bit as stubborn as he was, so here before him was a man, forced by adversity to swallow his pride in order to save his business. But, he reflected, Inch was also a sneak, a cheat, a liar, and a thief. He gave his one word answer: "No."

Inch's face darkened; he picked up his satchel and left as quickly as he had arrived—an angry sturgeon darting back downriver.

CHAPTER 2

Early December, 1892

K LARA BUNDLED UP for the cold trip down to the mill. A month earlier, there had been at least a glimmer of dawn with which to start her day. But now, as she left the McGrath home, her feet found the path aided by starlight alone.

Walking so, over a barely seen landscape, reinforced within her an elaborate sense of drift, both physical and existential. Her physical drift would end at the mill, stranded upon the bank at her desk, where she would be plunged into the operation's paper organization, but the other drift—where was it taking her?

She had been living with Anne and the children, and sometimes the captain, through what seemed like an endless October that rolled on and on and on. Within that spell, she had begun to ask herself about her plans. She certainly hadn't planned any of this; from a long view, she had planned to be married and perhaps even expecting a baby by now. Instead, she was almost accidentally in DeTour for the second time, keeping books for the McGrath Brothers Lumber Company. Was she still on her way back to Montreal or Poland? With her small pay, she could travel by next summer, but then, life was so pleasant right now, and what would a new plan bring anyway?

She crested the hill and saw the dim finger of the mill's smokestack pointing into a field of clear starry sky. Below the stack, lanterns began to illuminate individual windows as men awoke the sleeping plant. William would be there by now, striding impatiently between stock and machinery, checking quantities and trying to push daylight into the day. How different he was from the captain, who seemed to manage everything so quietly and with a minimum of fuss. It wasn't that the younger brother displayed less confidence, she decided; it was simply that he burned hotter.

Once inside, Klara ascended the steps to the office, sat at her desk, and rubbed the cold from her hands as she waited for live steam to begin coursing through the pipes. The door handle rattled behind her and William bustled in.

"I must adjust that door handle," he muttered to himself. Klara, in the manner of employees everywhere, felt on edge in the boss's company and busied herself arranging a stack of board tallies. William pulled open the middle drawer of his desk, withdrew a small notebook, and immediately left the office. Four minutes later, another rattle of the door handle announced his return, and now began a session of his pacing. She went on with her work in the simple pretense that his movements didn't attract her attention, but she enjoyed quietly speculating on what drove William. These musings led her to consider him not as her boss but as a man; he tried to remain distant—aloof—and yet his face and manner betrayed every tremor of feeling that vibrated through him. He habitually only spoke to her when assigning work, but his instructions were clear and patiently given, which she knew must be a strain for him. Today, inevitably, she came to compare him to Mateusz, the only man other than her father whom she had lived with. William didn't display happiness from day to day, but he was so much more lively and intelligent than her unambitious husband, who in retrospect had seemed trapped beneath a smothering blanket of discontent. But, she concluded, she had not truly known Mateusz.

There was a knock, the door handle rattled again, and Svensson stepped into the rapidly warming office.

"Mr. McGrath, I have the list of equipment still needed for Camp D." And so the morning progressed.

At about eleven o'clock each morning, Klara had the pleasant task of walking over to the general store to meet the incoming mail. The round trip absorbed less than ten minutes (as long as she didn't stop to admire any new items on display), but it broke the day into two pieces and seemingly shortened the hours.

Today, on her return as she climbed the office steps, Klara could hear William vigorously working the floorboards. When upstairs, she was conscious of him watching as she shuffled envelopes into an organized stack, and upon her placing the correspondence on his desk, he fairly pounced on it.

"Thank you," he mumbled and rifled through the pile. At last, he seized one letter, tore it open, and cursed under his breath. Then, as if noticing her for the first time, he looked up, folded the letter into his pocket, and quickly exited the office. Outside as the afternoon turned chilly, William sat on a stack of finished white pine beams in the stockyard and reread the letter he had been dreading:

> The Industrial Bank of Detroit
> 41 Griswold Street
> Detroit, Michigan
>
>
> McGrath Brothers Lumber Company
> Captain Thomas McGrath
> Mr. William McGrath
> DeTour Village, Michigan
> Thursday, November 24, 1892
> Dear Captain and Mr. McGrath,
>
>
> As a result of your failure to repay the balance of funds owed to the Bank by the required date of November 15, 1893, measures will now be taken to repossess for auction any and all machinery necessary to fulfill your obligation to the Bank. Hodge and Roland of Mackinaw City will be our representatives in this matter; they will keep you informed of exact arrangements as they are made.
>
> Most sincerely,
> John Fitzpatrick
> Vice President

"Damn it all to hell!" William beat his fist on the cold pine. Although he had known it might come, the letter tore the bottom out of everything: his mill, his finances, his plans, his future. Mired in self-pitying solitude, an irrational anger scourged him as he thought of Thomas being away at this dire moment, sailing his old nag of a ship.

Sitting next to Norman, smoking at the aft rail, Dennis was the first to notice a thin black cloud in the west, silhouetted by the sun's faltering rays. The wind continued light, warm and easterly, so Dennis dismissed the feature as of no account, but he wondered when it had passed over him all the same.

"This season is so unlike last year. I can't remember a December as nice as this," Dennis said.

"I've seen a couple," Norman said. "By now, I've seen a couple of almost everything."

"I'm sure, you old cruster, but you must admit this is nice; here we are comfortably riding north up Lake Huron under all sail once again."

"You don't have the flying jib up," Norman quibbled.

"You know what I mean," said Dennis. Everyone in the crew had expected snow, heavy weather—turbulence by the end of November—but when it had failed to materialize, the men stopped guessing at its first appearance. The captain had even been bandying about the notion of one more run to Detroit before Christmas. And so, lulled into a belief that good fortune or good weather might carry forward indefinitely, the entire crew of *Genevieve* were taken by surprise when that thin black cloud that Dennis had discounted advanced on them steadily from leeward.

"What's this?" Dennis asked himself aloud as he tapped out and pocketed his pipe.

"Trouble," Norman answered evenly, casting his cigarette into the lake. "I'll get the old man."

The cloud mass was moving quickly, growing in size with every passing moment. As if she were an unwitting victim of a cruel prank, *Genevieve*—braced hard to port—quietly harnessed the balmy east wind, as yet unfazed by the roiling squall to leeward. For a moment, Dennis was undecided about what to do: the wind seemed likely to shift west with the approaching cloud, but if he braced hard to starboard and tacked sail now, he would put *Genevieve* aback and she would be stalled when the squall came; if he did not tack sail, she would be aback with the wind shift—even worse. Time was evaporating; he decided he had better reduce sail in either case and set the watch to that. The cloud had visible features now, textures of black and gray tumbling in one long tube, over and over and over. He realized he should have called all hands and did it now. Better late than never. In a panic, he gave too many commands, and halyards began letting go in chaotic disorder. Risto had successfully lowered the t'gallant into its lifts by the time Thomas reached the deck and took in the situation; the t'gallant was nearly clewed up, but the fisherman stays'l was only part way down when the peak halyard fouled, and the four-sided flying sail—almost free of controlling lines—swung, jerking tight at the ends of broad arcs, twenty-five feet out from the mast head.

The wind held from the east, but the rolling black mass raced in, leaning over them, darkening the evening sky. Thomas felt a great stillness overcome him, humbled by the sight of the cloud's power, and who knew what forces rolled that air so violently?

"Brace hard to starboard!" Thomas shouted, knowing it was too late for the yards to be around before the squall fell upon them. The crew was soon in position at sheets and braces, letting go and hauling. Sails hung slack during a moment of calm as the water blanched greenish gray and...bang, bang, bang—sails flogging everywhere. *Genevieve* heeled hard onto her starboard side, caught almost full aback as the wind smashed into her. The pressure in her square sails pinned her in position, negating drive and laying her over; pushing down, down, and farther down to starboard. The lee deck was awash in torn water, pulsing over the hatch covers, while the wind's war cry screamed through the rigging, declaring a supremacy that wouldn't brook challenge. But challenge it they must, as Thomas well knew, or—or there would be no tomorrow.

Dennis had let the spanker sheet go, and still the wheel would not respond; there was nothing further for Thomas to do aft, and he couldn't simply stand waiting for this situation to undo itself. He began clawing his way forward to better direct and help the crew. As the black cloud rolled past her, *Genevieve* stood up part way, shook madly throughout her fabric, and lay hard over again. The fisherman stays'l, partially caught on the mizzen topmast stay, flogged very hard and began to shred. Thomas felt the wind, like water, flowing over his body; in split second intervals, he noticed Moses scrambling across the tilting deck, losing the purchase of his claws and then digging in again; men at the lee braces were up to their necks in water; and Morris was struggling to free the fouled fisherman halyard. It would be impossible to get the yards around now; he went to help Morris.

If there had been a sound, it didn't register—buried in the atrocious shriek of wind forced through the rigging—but there might have been a quiver or a jolt, felt before the evidence could be seen. Thomas did see a dark, unidentifiable shape plunge into the spume-blown water to leeward. Unseen, a loop of falling mizzen topmast back stay collapsed perversely to weather. It bashed into Thomas's body, broke his grip, and sent him tumbling across the deck into water and darkness.

CHAPTER 3

January 1893

IN CAME THE New Year, glowing but faintly with a lackluster promise that it could not be as disappointing as the year just ended. Since Edgar Standish had founded the Industrial Bank of Detroit, the directors had made a tradition of a New Year's meeting, usually held on the second or third day of January. In prosperous years (most of them), the meeting took the form of a social event, trimmed with a fleeting glance at the balance sheet and congratulations all round on the money being made. But after the panic of the previous year, Paul anticipated a more staid gathering, filled with anxious questions of strategy and standing. Preparatory to the meeting of bank elders then, he called Fitzpatrick into his office to familiarize himself with individual accounts and come up to date with his vice president's dealings.

On the right side of his desk, Paul had a stack of account dossiers to be referred to. At his other elbow was a small but growing pile of folders to be refiled by Mr. Savoy. He leaned forward, making notes across from his brother-in-law, who sat laconically bemused.

"Drummond Seltzer Bottling Company," he prompted Fitzpatrick.

"Yes, payments are up to date. No changes."

Paul continued through the stack. "Garfield Precision Instruments."

"In foreclosure," returned Fitzpatrick, swift and terse.

"I see," grunted Paul unhappily. He couldn't swear to it, but he suspected his brother-in-law of savoring a malicious delight in squeezing and ultimately shuttering some of the smaller companies. He added to his notes.

"McGrath Brothers Lumber Company."

"In arrears; we will have to foreclose in spring," said Fitzpatrick.

"I see they've made all their payments on time, and for the last two months, they have put down extra on the principal. How is it that we have them down as 'in arrears'?" Paul asked pointedly.

"We called in their loan and they haven't paid it back." Fitzpatrick spread his hands and affected a half-shoulder shrug, as if to say, "What should we call it?"

"They are rather far away. What will we do with the property, once foreclosed? Moving heavy machinery won't be worth what we might recover at auction."

"I have a firm that will auction everything at the site. They will handle all aspects, including security."

Paul found this distasteful. "This is a good company, paying extra per month as a show of good faith. Surely, these people, as well as Garfield Precision for that matter, are the companies we are here to loan to."

"We have a mandate from the Board to reduce risk and rebuild capital," Fitzpatrick said, worrying that, of all accounts, this argument should pop up over McGrath Brothers. The tyrannical memory of Thompson's threatening wheeze was never far from his thoughts. Thompson kept it that way with occasional random appearances.

"All the same, the panic has passed and I know my father would have stood by these firms." Paul groaned and passed the file to his left. More files were handled in just this fashion until Paul flipped open a folder titled: "Xavier Garment Manufacture." As Paul scanned the papers, Fitzpatrick blanched; he alone saw his surname, scrawled in Edgar's distinctive hand, across the back of one page.

Chapter 4

March 1893

THE MILL, FOR all its vast dusty energy in summer, was an echoing, slumbering warehouse through the winter. It sat as though some enchantment had stopped time for the pistons and planers, gangsaws and lumber carts, but left Klara and William to witness the hours and days pass unchanged. A pair of cant hooks had been left leaning against a workbench for three months, begging the question, "Will they ever be used again?" In a corner, a small pile of sawdust awaited the ministrations of a dilatory broom sitting next to it. What doings there were largely took place outside the mill; horses were tacked in stables; sledges of timber were dragged into the stockyard and unloaded. Out on the pier, *Genevieve* sat quietly at her heavy moorings in fitful sleep, her broken topmast stumps jagged and sore against the flat winter cloud. Periodically, one of her crew appeared, trudging from the deck over to the main shed of the old mill where they were shaping new topmasts.

William had expanded on Klara's duties as more of his time went to touring the various cuttings and camps. Consequently, though her hours were filled, many of them were spent in solitude, just like her previous winter. She lit the stove in the morning, set about her work, and subconsciously listened for the energetic thump of William's boots ascending the office stairs. She enjoyed those occasional afternoons when he had some questions for her and they reviewed the ledgers together. Of late, however, he had been spending his time at the office staring bleakly at paperwork and stewing at his desk. It was the problem of the bank loan, she knew (having found out about it by simple proximity), and as February turned to March, she could see by his actions that no matter how many trees were felled, the lack of income in winter would leave the situation unchanged. She wished there was more she could do to help, for he bore the problem alone; the captain hadn't been seen at the mill all winter.

Looking out of her parlor window, Anne considered the latest fall of snow; warm, damp, and needy, it clung to everything it touched. *Sometimes,* she thought, *it's the final snowfall of the season that bests a long enduring tree; having stood through the early gales and midwinter's bitter cold, the proud tree gives way to the peaceful, weighty accumulation of a sticky build of snow.*

After such a fine autumn of sailing, it had been a shock for her to have Thomas carried home only partially conscious and with three broken ribs. But the heavy bruising on his face and the tale Norman recounted to her of *Genevieve's* knockdown told her she had been lucky to get him back at all. A tense Christmas had seen her nursing him through delirium, fevers, and agonized breathing in most positions, but her calm through that early trial was rewarded when he eventually regained his composure. In a few weeks, he could sleep lying flat, and his breathing deepened once his ribs had knit.

An exhausting winter went on, but Thomas had passed from crisis to a slow healing that found him physically stronger from week to week. What Anne could see, that perhaps others wouldn't, was that her husband was a shaken man. She didn't believe it was from fear or recollection of the knockdown—similar things had happened in his chosen trade; it was something else she hadn't put her finger on. Abnormally quiet, he held some bad hand of cards to his chest while he considered his draws and discards. He had resumed walking and doing chores, but that had not prompted any talk of returning to work, nor had a visit to *Genevieve,* which she had accompanied him on. But even as he ground away at his core trouble, she knew him to be good right through, and she decided his winter had been long enough. It was time to shake his branches, have him drop his burden of wet snow, and stand straight again.

The breakfast dishes were long finished and a brilliant sun climbed purposefully into the clear sky that followed the previous day's wet snow. Anne had bundled the children off to school and covertly warmed some milk for hot cocoa. Setting another log into the hearth, she opened the curtains and then mixed the cocoa into two mugs, each laced with a healthy shot of black rum.

"What's this?" Thomas asked while gratefully accepting his mug.

"Medicinal," Anne replied with a smile. As she sat beside him on the sofa, they sipped the rich drink in silent appreciation.

"I meant to tell you: a man was hooking up a telephone at the general store yesterday," Anne began.

"More progress has come to DeTour," Thomas replied sardonically.

"Yes," Anne replied neutrally, "and I saw William there; he looked piqued."

"When you say piqued, you mean tired?"

"Yes," she nodded.

"I'm not surprised," he said and sipped again.

"Are you worried about him managing on his own through spring?" she asked.

"Perhaps a little," he said in a detached voice, "but he has what he wanted—a huge mill to run."

Anne steeled herself for her next assertion, which would either open an entire field of discussion or bar a door between her and her husband. "You don't want to go back to the mill?"

He shot a strange look at her—was it surprise, anger, or embarrassment? She couldn't make it out. Whatever the emotion, he let his eyes drop back into the mug. After a lengthy silence, he said, "I know I'm not always forthcoming about my problems or plans: some things are best not to bring up because in the end they melt away like icicles and we see we shouldn't have worried over them at all." He paused for a swig from his mug. "What I worry about now, though, isn't like that. I don't really want to continue with the mill, but in a few months, my wishes are unlikely to matter anymore."

"Because of the bank loan? I thought that problem might resolve by spring."

"We had *hoped* it would resolve by spring, but we have no way of knowing the bank will see it our way." He paused for a silent minute, contemplating his next words. "Even if they do, the new mill—hungry for trees, with its two shifts, and screaming saws, and huge black smoke plume—isn't something I ever wanted for myself, as you know. I'm a bashed-up relic now, part of a past when sawmilling was small and quiet. We took only the trees we needed and left some forest for another day. Out in the cuttings, pretty well everything goes now. I'm not sure what I see for myself next," he finished resignedly.

He saw concern color her features and thought perhaps he had said too much. Dropping his somber manner, he smiled at her. "Whatever the next picture is that I paint for myself, you'll be in the center of the canvas."

Still concerned, she took his big hand into her own. "Well, what about *Genevieve*?" she asked. He was about to answer when they heard the metallic clack of the front door latch lifting.

"Who's this?" Thomas asked aloud.

"One of the children," Anne asserted, but then Klara walked through the door, surprising them both. Before either could speak, Klara said, "Captain, Mr. William asks you to come to the mill: there is a man there from the bank."

CHAPTER 5

IT WAS THE end of dread, at least in its first and most paralyzing form. Each brother knew the gnawing worry that had lay siege to the backs of their minds for the past six months had finally broken through the walls, emerging in their midst. It was something that could no longer be dodged, or suppressed, or unimagined. New worries took hold, but in front of them was an imperative for some kind of action, for it was plain to be seen that pitting mere hope against the weight of dread had not been sound business.

Thomas had sent Klara to the mill ahead of him, and then he had taken his time on the familiar walk to work. Outside the mill, he stopped and smirked as he watched Moses, ears up, sniffing a Pinkerton security man with evident distrust. The watchman, clearly on edge, stood stiff and hopeful that the dog's interest in him might wane. Thomas saw in the two figures the collision of opposing guards: Moses for the establishment, and the newcomer on behalf of the bank, each looking over his charge with a sense of purpose and responsibility. The Pinkerton man began to fidget, eliciting a low growl from Moses. He then made an attempt to kick at the dog to shoo him away, but Moses, with a snarl, ended this line of endeavor with a sharp nip to his calf.

"Ouch! Damn dog!" the man exclaimed as he reached for the billy club at his belt.

"Whoa there, partner!" Thomas intervened. "Moses, come here." The dog came obediently, his tan ears flattened on either side of the black diamond on his forehead, tail wagging low and uncertainly. Thomas crouched and scratched his ears.

"Okay now. Good boy."

"Good boy? That mutt just bit me!" said the guard, rubbing his calf.

"I'll speak with you shortly. In the meantime, leave the dog alone. Moses, come," and with that, Thomas went inside.

Minutes later, Thomas sat at his desk, rereading the letter that had accompanied the watchman. Arriving for the second time at the final paragraph, he understood this to be the beginning of the end.

"Well, what should we do now?" asked William.

"We don't have the money to pay them off; the agreement has us in a pen; the lawyer has been useless as help; what do you think is left?" Thomas replied.

William sat silent. Thomas knew that his brother was thinking the unspeakable: he still wanted to sell *Genevieve* and put the money into saving the mill. The thought rubbed between them, a swollen blister that stung as it chafed, silently irritating them both.

"I'm going home," Thomas announced suddenly.

"Will we talk again tomorrow then?" William asked.

"Probably."

The watchman's arrival created a slow but accelerating new trend in discussion around DeTour Village. As snow melted, so word spread of the stranger's arrival in town, below the soft surface of everything. Teamsters became aware of him first, as they brought loads to the mill— they and the inhabitants of the rooming house. Someone asked the man about his work, and soon they knew his purpose. In the strange way many men have of solemnly delighting in another's misfortune, the talk trickled on into little rivulets of speculation, whispered in the rooming house or saloon, worrying the lumberjacks in their camps. Along the tracks from town to camp, the topic of the guard came up consistently, after a brief, compulsory word about the weather. And when everyone else had heard, silty streams of talk still flowed on and down, into the eager ears of Cedric Inch.

CHAPTER 6

Early April, 1893

WILLIAM BEGAN SQUANDERING twenty minutes of every hour tracking the watchman; he peered surreptitiously around corners or from the edge of his office window, worried that the man might be up to something. One morning, in the middle of a particularly long pacing session, the realization came to him. "I've been looking for that guard most of the day so far," he muttered to himself and turned from the window in time to catch Klara looking away from him. *She's been watching me again*, he thought with a little smile, but instantly his thoughts turned gloomy. *I wonder how she sees me; I must look like a fool pacing and mooning about the window. I watch the guard, she watches me, the guard watches us—it's ridiculous.* He stiffened his back and forced himself to sit at his desk, but ten minutes later, the urge to move became overwhelming.

"I'm going to see how Boyle is coming along with the engines," he declared to Klara and immediately regretted accounting for his movements to an employee. At times, he still felt it was a nuisance having someone in his office, although he grudgingly admitted she did a thorough job with the bookkeeping. And she was pretty.

After a strained chat with Boyle, William climbed the hill to Thomas's granite chair, which was now free of snow, followed by Moses. He had felt Boyle's doubt about the usefulness of firing the boiler to run up the engines and been short with him. Sitting on the sun-warmed granite, William looked down on his mill and reviewed the decisions that brought him to this point. Moses nudged his arm and settled in by William's hip with his head facing downhill. William patted him gently.

"How did I go wrong, Moses?" he asked. Moses wagged his tail twice at the sound of his name and closed his eyes.

Looking down on *Genevieve*, William watched the crew lowering the broken stump of the mizzen topmast toward the deck. Thomas had almost lost his ship last fall, and now they were on the cusp of losing the mill. Indignation surged into his heart—to think of all the effort and sacrifice he and Thomas had made to get this far, only to have it go under the hammer! It was more than unfair; it had to be a crime, moral if not legal. Why should the bank have all of this? What could they do with it? What would he do once the mill was taken away? Would he become a mill hand somewhere else? Or perhaps run a mill for another company? The questions spun round in his mind, each one the spoke of a wheel, blurry and unanswered at each revolution, until a new thought swirled out from where the spokes met the hub. "I won't let them have my mill," he said to the dog. "I will burn it to the ground."

Klara hustled back to the mill. Two noteworthy envelopes were in the day's stack of mail: one was a letter from Hodge and Roland, Attorneys-at-Law; this was sure to be a new development with regard to the bank loan. The other, for her, came from Felka. So rarely did she receive mail that she was on tenterhooks to open the small brown envelope, but she knew it would have to wait until it could be read in the privacy of her room.

Back in the office once again, she tucked the letter into her desk drawer, and had just enough time to array the incoming mail on one side of William's open rolltop desk before he himself rattled the door latch. Sifting through the mail, he selected the Hodges and Roland letter and calmly left the office.

After dinner that evening, Klara was annoyed with herself when she realized her letter was still at work. Working late to finish Svensson's accounting from Camp D, she had left in a hurry and forgotten it, despite reminding herself not to. In any case, she was missing the letter now when she wished to read it so she decided to return to the mill to collect it. As she prepared to leave, Thomas noticed her bundling up for the cool April night.

"Where are you bound, Klara?" he asked cordially. She wasn't sure what the word "bound" meant, so she elongated her neck forward inquisitively.

"Where are you going?" Thomas tried again.

"Ah, back to the mill, Captain. I forgot a letter in my desk," she said.

"I need a walk. I'll come with you," Thomas said, and as soon as he had his coat on, they set off.

From a distance, Thomas noticed a faint glow emanating from two of the ground floor windows at the mill.

"I wonder if William has Boyle working late tonight," Thomas mused; he further wondered what would be urgent enough to warrant the extra hours.

As the guard had gone to the boarding house for the night, they were unchallenged on their approach, and in the faint light, they could see William moving from outside the mill, to inside, and back again. Up close at last, they were standing next to a cart that bore half-a-dozen hay bales from the stable, when William emerged through the big doorway and started at the sight of them.

"Thomas, Klara, what are you doing here?" he asked.

"I think I could ask you the same thing. Are you keeping the horses inside?" Thomas replied.

Unseen in the scant light, William's face glowed with discomfort. He alternated between shame at being caught, particularly by these two people, in an act he would rather not explain; and irritation at being thwarted in his purpose, with the further possibility of an overbearing lecture from his brother. To his surprise, Thomas walked silently past him into the mill. William, now unsure of himself, picked up a hay bale from the cart, returned it, stood up straight flexing his hands, and then followed Thomas inside. Klara pragmatically climbed the office steps to retrieve her letter. From the office, she heard the brothers start to argue.

"Where are the horses, Will?" Thomas asked provocatively.

"Don't be so cute," William retorted.

Thomas took in the hay bales flung against the interior walls. He knew their purpose, but he wanted to hear it from his brother.

"What's the scheme here? Going to warm the place up?"

"So good of you to come in and laugh. All winter I have been racking my brain, trying to find a way out of this bind." He flung a letter at Thomas. "I received that today. The mill will be auctioned as a whole or in pieces on the seventh of May. So here we are...." William's face flushed, his eyes prominent and glistening as they welled up in the lamp light. "Well, I won't be beaten so entirely—they won't have my mill!"

"So this is your idea?" Thomas replied. "It doesn't leave us with a mill either, and the trouble won't end after it's a heap of ashes. Besides, this is my mill too; shouldn't I have a say?"

"Well, what have you done to save it?" William shouted. "You always know better, but what have you done? Besides, arson isn't something you just sit around and chat about; strike a match—and then flames." He popped open his hands, expanding his fingers outward.

"Look; I never wanted all of this, and I certainly don't want to go to jail for it," Thomas snapped back.

As the argument grew more heated and intractable, Klara had gone inside. Now she listened uncomfortably from the office. It distressed her to hear these two good men, whom she respected, pressed to the point of bitter squabble. She wished to slide down the steps unnoticed and make an escape, but then something the captain said caught her attention.

"William, you are sure to be arrested for arson and then you'll rot in prison. You can cut a 'round forty' up here, or even steal a horse and get away with it, but people take a dim view of firebugs—especially after last summer."

That's it! Klara thought. They must not burn the mill, but escape, as she had from Mateusz, and take the good parts of it with them like her bars of soap. Surely, if you could steal someone's horse, there wouldn't be great consequences for walking out with pieces of your own mill. The door handle rattled as she exited the office and the brothers turned to see her. Looking down at William, she saw a mingling of anger, fear, desperation, and need. Yes, William needed the mill. That wasn't true of the captain, she could see; he had his family and his ship. His future without the mill could be imagined. But William? William had tied himself tightly to his work—this place. He needed the mill badly, she realized, and her heart went out to him.

"You must take away the saws," she blurted out from her overlook on the stairs.

"Pardon?" William asked.

"Take the saws away—to home or—another camp," she said. The brothers were quiet, stunned by this suggestion from an unexpected source, but then Thomas shook his head patiently.

"No, no. If they came here and found the saws missing, they would only hunt them down somewhere else."

Emboldened, Klara descended the staircase and pushed her idea. "Can you put away…mm…hide the saws somewhere?"

"It would be hard to keep a secret like that. It would take a number of men, time, and horses. And then there is this guard in the way."

As Thomas listed the difficulties, William calmed down, nodding as his brother made each point. Then all three of them were silent as they followed individual paths through the mill problem. At last, William spoke up. "Okay. I won't burn the mill tonight. But, instead, you have to agree that we will solve these problems and steal it."

CHAPTER 7

AFTER THE DISCUSSION at the mill, Thomas and Klara helped William remove the hay and departed for home. Once at the house, Klara slipped away with her letter, leaving Thomas to settle into the sofa and discuss the evening with Anne.

"We found William getting ready to torch the mill," he began.

"What?"

"Today he received a letter from the auctioneers saying the mill will be put on the block on the seventh of May."

"That's less than a month away!" Anne said.

"Yes, so he thought he would burn the place down rather than give it up."

"Oh, Thomas, what did you do?"

"We talked him out of it, Klara and I, at least I think we did, but if you see a rosy glow over the hill…."

"I think Klara could be a good influence on him," Anne whispered conspiratorially.

"Perhaps, but she has also put some scheme in his mind to steal the mill," Thomas said with a mixture of amusement and resignation. Anne remained silent, considering the merits, flaws, and difficulties of such a scheme while she waited for her husband to elaborate.

"He just won't see that the bank holds all the trump cards. We signed this dirty deal, so according to the letter of the agreement, they can auction our mill. We're finished. They won't negotiate. It isn't fair or right; they didn't work for most of the value they will auction off for almost nothing, but legally, we don't have a leg to stand on."

"And illegally? It's not like you to just give in," Anne said.

Thomas was at first surprised by her question, but it broke the tension and he smiled. "You think I should turn outlaw, become a woodland thief like old Robin Hood?" But then he was serious again. "Let's say we manage to box up the mill and spirit it away; what then? Where will we take it, hide it? What will we do with it?"

"Take it to Canada," Anne said simply. "They won't be able to touch you there, and the Canadians are desperate for sawmills; haven't you always told me so?"

"I have," Thomas said absently, considering the idea. "You have such a brilliant criminal mind." They laughed together at this.

"With the mill in parts, in your own hands, you may still have a way to negotiate with the bank. Once it is auctioned...." She let the sentence dangle, a trapeze swung to the man in mid-air, until he caught the simple truth of it. He looked directly at her.

"It may mean the end of living here," he said. She leaned her head on his shoulder.

"It has been nice here, but we'll find our way wherever we go."

Meanwhile upstairs, Klara leaned on her elbows, lying diagonally across her bed, her stockinged feet crossed up behind her. Her eyes scanned Felka's pragmatic script for the second time in partial disbelief at the news:

Dearest Klara,

I am sorry to be the bearer of bad news, but Mateusz has been killed in an accident in the mine. Even though you had become estranged, I'm sure this will be a blow for you.

Apparently he was working somewhere in the middle levels of the mine. He was hurrying to get to the surface at the end of his shift and tried to catch a moving skip. One of the other trammers saw him miss his jump and he went down the shaft. The company organized a small funeral service for him on Wednesday; I attended with some of the other wives. Klara, my dear, how truly awful; it is the news we wives always fear. I'm so sorry.

Since you have been gone a while, the company emptied your old house and now another trammer is living there.

Your good friend,
Felka

Klara rolled onto her back, trying to absorb the words—Mateusz gone. She had a generous heart, so even for this man who had deceived, spurned, and abused her, she shed a few tears. Soon, however, she began to consider all of the different aspects of this news: she no longer had to fear Mateusz would look for her; she was a widow—imagine being a widow at her age; and she might marry again, but this time, she would know the man first. How foolish to have entrusted your happiness and well-being to an unknown personality. Perhaps not as foolish as taking a running jump at a moving skip over a thousand foot drop, though. She shook her head at the crazy absurdity of it, and then of life in general. Poor strange Mateusz.

CHAPTER 8

SO YOU'RE TELLING me this will take three days?" William asked Boyle.

"It took several months to build, Mr. McGrath," replied the millwright.

"Yes, I know, but we're not trying to make it run; we simply need it removed."

A new sense of purpose inflated William's days at the mill; no longer did he fret time away watching the guard—Thomas had someone assigned to that—instead, he took Boyle into his confidence and they plotted the machinery's removal. Leaning over a low makeshift table in the far-off privacy of his office at the old mill, the two men haggled.

"I'm just thinking over the number of machines, the number of bolts, and the likelihood of losing or damaging pieces," answered Boyle staunchly.

"All right, let's look at it another way: everything that gets left at the mill will be a lost piece. We have to get it all out in one night. That is how long we can hope to divert the guard." Keeping the Pinkerton man out of this business had become Thomas's special province, and despite William's dislike of the guard, he feared what harm might befall him if Norman was involved.

"How much time will we have?" Boyle asked.

"I can't say for sure. Normally, he goes to his lodgings at eight in the evening and is here by seven in the morning. News of the auction is out now—I saw it posted at the general store—and the guard won't be the only tongue in this town to call the marshal down on us."

Boyle considered, knowing Mr. McGrath was correct. Cedric Inch was often seen up at the tavern of late listening in on conversations, eager to glean any news from the mill.

"So, twelve hours—less," Boyle said chewing on a stub of pencil.

"Let's think of what can be broken down ahead of time. Most of the second floor could be dismantled. The man has never seen this mill in full operation. We can keep up appearances with a number of saws on the main floor."

"Yes, I can take most of the planers and jointers out of the line. I can have them unbolted from the floor without looking different, and..." Boyle suddenly had a big smile, "I can turn our big jointer upstairs so that it will send chips firing at the doorway. That will keep unwanted nosiness to a minimum."

"A good thought," said William. "That's the easiest part, but still we will have the engine room, the headsaw, the gangsaws, the edgers, and all of the other heavy equipment on the main floor."

"I'll put some thought into it, sir. All I can say right now is that we'll need every man we have when the time comes."

William saw the conversation had gone as far as it could for one day, but he was thankful to have a man as competent as Boyle working on the problem.

"Very good, Boyle, and remember, not a word to anyone."

Previously that morning, in the cold pre-dawn air, Thomas hitched Arthur to his trap for the first time in months and set off on the long ride to Sault Ste. Marie. He hoped to arrive in the Soo early enough to conduct his business, making return the next day possible. Arthur was ready, the weather was promising, and the road beckoned to man and horse.

By ten o'clock, a ripening sun had still not softened the overnight freeze, leaving the highway quite rutted. The jostle and bump of his trap twinged Thomas's ribs and lower back as his body absorbed the ride's unkindnesses. "I should have put more canvas on the seat," he lamented to Arthur's twitching ears, but he knew it wouldn't have improved his fitness for this ride. A few shorter trips to toughen up would have been the idea, but this journey was unplanned, unprepared for, and quite necessary. Arthur clomped over the ruts, seemingly oblivious to road conditions, and Thomas took in the landscape while trying to ignore his pains. The land he passed through was still heavily forested, but in places, he saw large cut-over tracts, and in a few of these, some misguided attempts at farming; the land was marvelous for trees but hopeless for crops. Passing an intersection at Arthur's best speed, he flinched over bumpy perpendicular tracks and so took no notice of a broad figure astride a chestnut mare ambling toward the junction.

Before he knew why, Inch muttered to himself, "There's McGrath." His mind leapfrogged the evidence and landed solidly upon a conclusion. What brought the words he couldn't say; perhaps long study of his detested rival had imprinted Thomas McGrath's characteristic gestures, traits, and stances onto his mind, or maybe he had just been thinking about the upcoming auction of the McGrath sawmill. How he wanted that mill! But then the meaning of this sighting filtered into his brain. First, McGrath hadn't been seen abroad in quite a long time; his convalescence was a well-known fact. Secondly, he was north of his normal cuttings and, given his circumstances, it was unlikely he would be surveying plats for next winter. Last of all, he had a small bag strapped to his trap, arguing that he was on a longer journey. Suspicion comes easily to the devious thinker, and Inch leapt forward again to the correct conclusion that Thomas had proceeded to the Soo to do something about his problems. Since he was only four miles from home, Inch decided to collect a bag of his own and track McGrath to his destination.

It was four in the afternoon. His back ached mercilessly, and it was with real difficulty that Thomas straightened his spine upon descending from his trap in front of the Upper Lakes Tugboat Company.

"Good afternoon?" He tapped the door uncertainly. In a moment, there was some shuffling inside and a gray-headed man sporting long mutton chops ushered Thomas in. The bare patch between his side-whiskers had been left unshaven for a few days, suggesting a long-awaited bridge between his two cheeks.

"Captain McGrath," he said quite pleasantly, "how nice to see you. Don't tell me you are locking up," he jested.

"No, Captain Harris." Thomas smiled and shook his hand. "*Genevieve* is still iced in at DeTour. She won't be in the locks yet."

"The ice is the very devil this year. I had heard *Genevieve* was knocked down and you injured."

"Yes, but we're both just about mended," Thomas said with a surety he didn't feel.

"Come; take a seat; would you like something to drink? I have an open bottle of tawny port—it won't keep forever."

"Certainly; some port would be nice," Thomas replied.

When Captain Harris had poured and settled into his chair, he asked, "What brings you to the Soo?"

Thomas savored the port and shifted in his chair. "I would like to hire a tug and barge for a week, perhaps more."

"When do you need them?"

"As soon as the ice breaks, the very moment it breaks—and I need this to be kept confidential."

The old captain's eyes brightened as he nodded his head, perhaps avariciously or maybe from a love of intrigue. Despite his best effort, he could not hide from Thomas that he was suppressing a smile. He recovered. "The ice is the very devil this year," he said for the second time.

"Will the tug you have break ice?" Thomas asked.

"Nay; she's good white oak on iron frames—stout, but only wood all the same. We allow bigger vessels to break the thick ice, and she can see her way through small ice."

Thomas had expected this. He moved along to negotiating price and some details of communication to keep the enterprise as clandestine as possible. After an hour, he rose from his chair slowly, thanked the old captain, and ran Arthur to the Old Portage Hotel for the night.

Inch, though he had done his best to catch up with Thomas, arrived in the Soo at five-thirty in the evening. He was barely saved from meeting his quarry by a lucky sighting of his approach far up Portage Street. Inch hurriedly dismounted, turned his horse toward a hitching post, and hid behind her until Thomas's trap had passed by. He shifted position slowly, maintaining his cover, and saw Thomas pull up in front of the Old Portage Hotel. Clearly he had come from the riverfront, but it was too late to check more thoroughly today. Making his way to a tavern where he could get a bed for the night, he considered rewarding himself for the day's effort with spiked ale.

Pale light made his room furnishings discernible the following morning when Inch awoke with a mild headache. His sense of mission returned to him at once, so he stumbled out of bed to pull on his clothes. In half an hour, he had gathered his mare and ridden down Portage Street to the stables of Thomas's hotel where a groom was in attendance.

"Say, young fella, I'm looking for someone with a gray appaloosa that pulls a nice little trap for him. Is he still here?"

"No, sir; he left more'n half an hour ago."

"Any idea where he was headed?"

This question made the young man pause before he said simply, "No, sir."

"Blast," Inch mumbled, but then he realized all was not lost: he would troll the riverfront, and if Thomas were not there, he might still sniff out his doings.

By ten o'clock, using different subterfuges, he had inquired of employees at several maritime businesses whether they had recently seen Thomas McGrath. At last, he thumped on the door of the Upper Lakes Tugboat Company, soon to be answered by old Captain Harris himself.

"Good morning?" the bewhiskered old captain said.

Inch drew himself up to his full height. "Good morning," he said in return. With his eyebrows elevated ever so slightly, Inch's blue eyes glowed with innocence and honesty. "My friend was here yesterday," he smiled. "He thought he might have left his hat and wondered whether I could look in for it on my way by."

Suspicion pinched the old captain's eyes for less than a second before he asked, "Who is your friend?"

"Thomas McGrath," Inch replied warmly, but he didn't have to listen to the response; that look of suspicion had told him all he needed to know.

CHAPTER 9

Late April, 1893

AS THEY WERE for many people, the final few days of the calendar month were a lean and anxious time for John Fitzpatrick. Feeding from an abundantly stocked larder, and never short of whiskey, it was in matters of his gambling that his unease was felt. When he won at cards, optimism propelled him into boldly wagering more, but when the table inevitably turned against him, he became a spectacular maple seed, spiraling from treetops to soil, believing germination and rebirth were no more than one winning hand away. Regardless of his beliefs, hopes, and wishes, toward the end of the month, he often arrived at Sullivan's tables short of a stake.

Entering the club, he scanned the room, checking the quality of the company and keeping his eyes open for Thompson. Sullivan hailed him from the opposite side of a nearby table. "Mr. Fitzpatrick, good evening."

So it's to be "Mr. Fitzpatrick" tonight, Fitzpatrick thought.

"We have a table waiting for another player at the back." Sullivan ushered him toward a corner. The table looked fine; familiar with two of the other players, Fitzpatrick thought his chances good and took the empty seat.

"Would you like a whiskey brought out?" Sullivan asked.

"No, thank you," Fitzpatrick answered as he always did now, "I bring my own." And he drew out a flask to take a nip.

"Of course," Sullivan replied, no doubt concurring that most men who had had their whiskey drugged should do the same.

The night began well, but later on, Fitzpatrick's playing lost its edge as he borrowed too much courage from his flask. At last, it was time to go home, and he saw once again that he had greatly indebted himself to the house. But no matter; his credit was well established, and in a few days, he would be flush again; his only concern was seeing Thompson with regard to his as-yet-unfulfilled promise.

He stepped outside into the darkness, and as he turned right to go home, he stumbled over something round, a bottle possibly, and would have fallen were his right arm not caught by a very strong hand.

"Well, well, Fitzpatrick," came the dreadful wheeze.

Thompson.

"Mr. Thompson," Fitzpatrick said, "I am quite all right; you may unhand me now." He wished to have his hand back, nestled against the new, cold metal in his jacket pocket. Thompson squeezed a little harder.

"You have owed me for a long time now."

"It's coming," Fitzpatrick said. "There's a process; it has to be done with all the appearance of normality."

"I couldn't care less about normality," Thompson wheezed. "Have it done before I see you again." And with that, he dropped Fitzpatrick's arm.

"It will be another week and then…finished."

"I'm out of patience with you," Thompson said and stepped inside the club.

The following morning, Fitzpatrick entered the bank moments behind Paul. Paul had not surrendered the morning opening of the bank to his vice president, but over time, Fitzpatrick began to think of this as inconsequential.

Once inside, he bid his brother-in-law a cheery good morning and then quietly went on to rifle through the thick stack of incoming checks that amassed at Savoy's work station toward the end of each month. For the past few days, he had purposely diverted Savoy from logging these in, allowing himself a chance to peruse them today. Halfway down the stack, he found what he sought: the monthly payment from the McGrath Brothers' sawmill. The stupidity of these brothers was inconceivable; here they were about to lose their mill and yet they were still handing over money as though it weren't happening to them. Even Paul had commented on it. It had become a bone of contention between them with regard to the foreclosure, but now he had removed that obstacle. Pocketing the check, he replaced the remaining stack in the collection tray.

Two days later, a half hour before lunch, Fitzpatrick leaned against the mahogany doorjamb to Paul's office.

"I have to step out early for lunch," he stated.

"Going home?" Paul asked, looking up from his work.

"Er, yes," Fitzpatrick lied, and then admonished himself for committing such a blunder. Paul would talk to Beatrice and it would certainly come up. Now he would have to make a stop at home, however brief.

"Very good; I'll see you at one o'clock," Paul said blandly and returned to his work.

Upon leaving the building, Fitzpatrick considered how his relationship with Paul had changed; the younger man had assumed the mantle and authority of bank president. He was not nearly as forceful as Edgar, but he no longer seemed so lacking in initiative or decision. He had not allowed himself to be swayed by persuasion or flattery as Fitzpatrick had hoped, showing that he possessed some of Edgar's pigheadedness after all. His brother-in-law lacked guile, however, and therein Fitzpatrick held an advantage that allowed his plans to flourish.

It was a short walk to the Third National Bank of Michigan, from where the McGrath Brothers' checks were issued. Entering the bank, Fitzpatrick swallowed his nervousness and strode forward to a portly man behind a teller's wicket.

"I would like to cash this one, please," he stated and then produced the check and his identification as vice president of the Industrial Bank of Detroit.

"Mr. Fitzpatrick, how nice to see you again."

Again? Ugh, he thought. He had meant to use a different teller from last month. "The pleasure is all mine," he crooned amiably.

"This is a fair amount. Would you not be more comfortable handling this through the weekly transfer?" asked the teller.

"I'm afraid we just missed it. These fellows are sometimes late, and this check just missed our usual bundle. I wanted to get it in and credited for them on time."

"How good of you. Oh, could you please sign here?" The teller indicated a line on his paperwork. "I will just need to get a co-signature for an amount this large. One moment."

"Very good," Fitzpatrick said, knowing the procedure.

The heavy man turned from his wicket and went in search of his co-signer. A minute passed. Fitzpatrick felt small beads of perspiration gathering on his upper lip and took out a handkerchief to mop them away. The previous two times he had cashed this check, it had been completed in good time. After he had been standing at the wicket for three minutes, he began to consider walking out; something was wrong. But no, it would do no good to walk out; not only would it look bad, but this was the simplest way to obtain the money he needed and ruin the McGraths. *A man of iron nerve would stay*, he told himself, and stood firm. There was probably a routine reason for the delay. At last, he saw the portly teller returning, followed by a lean gray-haired man, nicely dressed and wearing a silver bow tie. The newcomer addressed him. "Mr. Fitzpatrick? Albert Finch," he stated in a businesslike introduction. "I'm sorry, but we have made a policy decision not to handle checks cashed by other banks in this manner. We won't be able to fulfill your request. We will, of course, put the check in for the next transfer."

Although he had known something was wrong, Fitzpatrick was now flummoxed. The ramifications of not getting the money flooded his mind so that all he could say was, "But, but…but why?"

Albert Finch's expression hardened. "Mr. Fitzpatrick, a man in our profession should understand this; there are simply too many chances for things to go awry. If I were you, I wouldn't wish to carry this amount on my person, even for a short walk. It helps us to avoid… irregularities." The portly teller nodded with a thin embarrassed smile at this explanation.

"Irregularities?" Fitzpatrick asked.

"Yes. When people cash large checks and then some or all of the money gets lost. You understand."

Fitzpatrick looked back at Finch, hating him covertly; this man, his opposite number at this bank, was telling him he didn't think this transaction looked legitimate. He considered arguing further, trying to convince the man, but he decided it was better to make a hasty retreat.

"I'll take the check back and send it with our next bundle," he said pleasantly.

After the necessary side trip home, Fitzpatrick returned to the bank and closed the door, craving the solitude to calm his troubled mind. Cradling his smooth head in his hands, elbows on his desk, he worried through his problems: first and most pressing was his need for cash. He could use house credit once or twice more, but then some sign of repayment would have to be made. He had counted on the McGrath money, but now he would be obligated to fall back on some of his previous tricks. The difficulty of skimming from the vault was that he had little time to doctor the books in an unobtrusive way, and then there was that wretched nuisance, Savoy; that young man was entirely too inquisitive for his own good. Fitzpatrick wished he had gotten him out of the way—somehow. His interview with Albert Finch gave him a crawling discomfort, a spider climbing his spine between the shoulder blades; was it likely that the man suspected him of fraud? Was he the type of fellow to follow up on the idea? It would be a disaster for him if Finch started pulling at this thread or spent time watching for the McGrath check to come through. The lone bright spot in his day was that he hadn't surrendered the check so the McGraths would continue to appear to be in default; there would be no controversy over this most necessary foreclosure. Once the sawmill was shuttered and crushed, who would pay heed to a nugget of accounting difficulty in a slagheap of ruined finance?

A knock at the door broke into his thoughts. "Yes, come in."

Savoy peered in. "Mr. Standish has a telephone call for you in his office," the clerk said in response to his boss's impatient glare. Fitzpatrick wondered when he would get his own telephone; it was worse to be summoned to the big office now than it had been when Edgar ran the bank.

Once in Paul's office, he picked up the waiting receiver and mouthpiece.

"Hello, John Fitzpatrick here," he said pleasantly. "Mm—hm. Yes, I can hear you." The voice on the other end of the line crackled electrically as he passed on his news.

"Mr. Fitzpatrick, this is Robert Hodge calling from Hodge and Roland, attorneys-at-law. We have received word from the Pinkerton agency that there has been some movement of machinery at McGrath Brothers' sawmill."

"What kind of movement?"

"Well, honestly, not much. The Pinkerton man is watching closely. They have been shuffling a few things for cleaning, which sounds odd given their difficulties. We just thought it best to keep you informed. Also…"

"Yes?"

"Also, there is a rumor—not confirmed—that they may be renting a barge."

"Has anything been removed from the mill?" Fitzpatrick asked, his mind in a whirl.

"Not to our knowledge, sir."

"Are you satisfied with security?"

"It's Pinkerton, sir," he said absolutely.

"All right then, Mr. Hodge. Thank you for calling."

Paul caught his eye.

"McGrath Brothers Lumber Company. Pinkerton is suspicious of their doings," Fitzpatrick explained.

Paul smirked. "I've been meaning to speak to you. Close the door and have a seat."

Fitzpatrick worked at keeping a hostile frown from his face; there was something more than annoying in the air. He didn't have time for whatever it was Paul wanted to say; he wondered what the McGraths might be up to; he wondered about Albert Finch; and most of all, he wondered when he could slip some money out of the vault. He dropped into one of the padded leather armchairs in front of his brother-in-law's desk. Paul took a moment to scribble a note in the open file before him.

"I really should be going," Fitzpatrick prompted. Paul held up a finger without taking his eyes from his work, indicating that Fitzpatrick must wait. He closed the file and pulled another one from the side of his desktop.

"I have two matters for your attention: Mr. Savoy has brought this discrepancy in foreign bonds to my notice. You were handling these in January." He slid a small sheaf of papers across the desk. "The top sheet is what I have worked out that the totals should be, and the second sheet is the one you signed and submitted. The difference is nine hundred dollars; a curiously round number, wouldn't you agree? Not nine hundred and twenty-three dollars and seventeen cents, for instance." Paul flashed him a hint of a goading smile.

Fitzpatrick was cornered, and what's more, he knew this was personal. That sniveling Beatrice had most likely been complaining about him to her brother, so Paul had decided to make him uncomfortable.

"I would have to review the paperwork," he said.

"I might observe that we have had a history of difficulty in the foreign bond accounts—oddly difficult to sum correctly. But please, do review the paperwork and see me in the morning when you have. Now, for the second matter." He opened a file labeled "Pritchard and Sons Fine Furniture" and laid it in front of Fitzpatrick.

"What should I make of this?" he asked, laying an elegant finger on the angry scrawl of Fitzpatrick's name in what appeared to be Edgar's hand. "Papa loved to use his ballpoint pen, so he must have thought of you often," he prodded.

The panic was hard to suppress; his hand sought out his jacket pocket, for the reassurance of gunmetal there, only to find he had left his jacket in the office. Saliva and a bitter taste filled Fitzpatrick's mouth. He knew he had not been as careful with his last pull from foreign bonds, but he had felt sure no one was looking. Also, he had a sense that if he was truly caught red-handed stealing from the vault, there would likely be almost no consequences; the scandal of a bank officer pilfering money would be more than any of the directors could stomach. At worst, he would be told to leave quietly. But if suspicion should fall upon him with regard to Edgar's death, that would be a matter that could lead to a long, sorry stay in prison. He swallowed, tongue-tied, and made an attempt to comment, but the words caught in his throat. Swallowing again, he became indignant: Why was he allowing this tenderfoot to intimidate him? What could he really know? His voice returned to him.

"I have little idea what your father spent his time on," he croaked, closing the file and pushing it back forcefully.

"Well, it is a curiosity nonetheless, in much the same way it is curious that we are short exactly nine hundred dollars in the January foreign bonds," Paul stared at him.

"I have things to do, and then I'm going home," Fitzpatrick replied. Paul made no move to stop him as he stood up.

Later that evening, Fitzpatrick examined his shave in the mirror, knotted his tie, and began adjusting his shirt cuffs. Between cuffs, he unlocked what he thought of as his medicine drawer, pulled forth a half-full bottle of rye whiskey and a small tumbler, and poured himself a shot. Preparation was the key to solving his problems, he was learning: so far he had been lucky not to have experienced greater consequences for the bold actions he had taken, but no more would he run such risks. His eyes drifted to the revolver he had sitting on the dresser, bought to be a tangible part of his low-risk policy. Carrying the weapon brought him a sense of security; there were even moments when he felt the cool weight of it in his hand that he wanted Thompson and his minions to show up, but prevailing wisdom dictated that peaceable dealings carried less risk. He slipped the gun into his evening jacket, hanging in his open wardrobe.

Tonight, he had to win at the card tables, and he wanted to display the confident air of a conqueror. When his opponents saw him sit down, he wanted them to wilt. While pinning on his cuff links, he thought briefly of Thompson. Shaking his head, he tried to clear it of the image of the bent nose and contempt-filled sneer that haunted him. He tossed back the shot prior to filling his silver flask. The sound of his wife climbing the stairs prompted a swift return of his whiskey bottle to the dresser drawer; there was no need to stir up another conversation about his drinking. The door opened.

"John?"

He didn't look in her direction but twitched his shirt collar fastidiously in front of the mirror. "What?" he asked.

"Are you going out again tonight?"

"What does it seem like?"

"You are going out," she said flatly, disappointed.

"Well, what of it?"

"I'm alone so often now; you're out almost every night," she said quietly, almost to herself.

"Why not go see your mother?" he said in an attempt to brush her off gently. He didn't want a conflict while he puffed up his mood for the evening ahead.

"We used to talk in the evenings. How long has it been since we played gin-rummy? Would it be so dull to play cards with me?" His silence stretched on. "I suppose so," she answered her own question hollowly.

He hated explaining himself to her. Angrily, he picked up his suit jacket and swung it over his shoulders, the gun in his right pocket thudding heavily against his ribs as he stuffed his arms through the sleeves. "Uumph," he grunted, surprised by the blow.

"What is it, John? What's wrong?"

Was she asking why he had grunted, or was the question about the two of them? Either way, it was too much. There were times lately when he wished he could just push her out the window.

"Beatrice, I'm going out. I am a vice president; I have people to meet. I can't sit around and gab all night with you or play boring games of gin rummy. Now, will you let me alone so I can complete dressing?"

"Papa was a president and managed to be home most nights," she persisted.

The ghost of Edgar once again.

"Papa," he mimicked in a falsetto. "I haven't missed him that much. Why do you bother bringing him up?" he asked, not expecting an answer.

Beatrice flushed angrily and stormed out of the room. "You haven't got a heart," she threw over her shoulder from the hallway.

Fitzpatrick knew he had said too much, especially given Paul's suspicions. It pricked momentarily at his feelings that she thought him unkind, but at least she was gone. He tucked the flask into the inside breast of his jacket and patted the gun in his right pocket.

The very next morning, Fitzpatrick felt he was rebounding, having won a small amount at cards the previous night. He had concocted a likely excuse for the foreign bond discrepancy, and he hoped simply to ignore any more talk about Edgar's scribblings. Relieved on all fronts, his mind was free to conduct the actual work of the bank. Savoy knocked on his door.

"Another telephone call, Mr. Fitzpatrick."

To Fitzpatrick's relief, Paul was away from his desk as he picked up the receiver and mouthpiece.

"John Fitzpatrick speaking."

"Mr. Fitzpatrick, Robert Hodge here," crackled the voice. "Today, news has come from Pinkerton that a tug and barge have arrived at the McGrath Brothers' sawmill."

"Well, what are you doing about it?" Fitzpatrick asked, his stomach flip-flopping.

"We can contact the marshal, but at present, they haven't done anything wrong." Yesterday's panic was not far away. Fitzpatrick had forgotten his worry over Albert Finch and was summarily reminded of it. This mill had to be crushed; he had to make sure.

"I'm certain they're thinking about it. Can you get more security up there?"

"We can try," Hodge replied.

"All right then; good day to you," Fitzpatrick rang off, not quite satisfied with Hodge's promise to try. He returned to his office with the idea of collecting his hat and taking a walk to think things over. Since he had only been absent for two minutes, it came as a surprise to find a small cloth bundle sitting squarely in the middle of his desk. A gift? It was a bag, improvised from a sheet of burlap, tied at the neck with a bow of white cotton butcher's twine. Tucked into a loop of the bow was a note.

"Mr. Savoy?" he summoned his clerk in almost the same way as he used to hear Edgar call for him. "Mr. Savoy, did you put this here? Do you know what it is?" he asked the young man when he arrived.

"No, sir," replied the clerk.

"Was someone in my office?"

"I haven't seen anyone, sir."

"Oh, all right then," he frowned, shooing away Savoy with a backward wave of his hand. He pulled apart the bow.

The bag fell open, and cascading slowly, overspilling his blotter, across the polished surface of his desk was rough, unrefined rock salt. His heart beat wildly, the contained panic spilling out in all directions in the same fashion as the salt. With a trembling hand, he unfolded the note to read a single word, handwritten in small letters:

Time

Chapter 10

THE McGRATH BROTHERS, Boyle, and especially Klara, each in his or her own way, contemplated what a chancy building material deception was. The continued preparation for transport of the mill machinery, as well as all of their current hopes for the future, were founded upon the uncertain elasticity of a guard's mistaken belief in their subterfuge: How much longer could the man be placated by explanations of cleaning or repair work? When would his naturally complacent suspicion snap into an active sounding of alarms? As at last the ice broke, a new race commenced, assuring them these questions would soon find their answers.

Shards of the great ice sheet drifted in broad packs on the river as *Genevieve* was warped away from the pier to swing to her own anchors. In late afternoon, Thomas stood with William on the company pier, watching the slow approach of the tug *Avenger* and her barge.

"It won't be a secret any longer," Thomas remarked. "Not that I'm sure it is now; have a look by the road." He jerked his head in that direction.

"Inch." William scowled as he recognized their adversary. "How did he know?"

"He has big eyes and ears and watches us closely."

"We'll just have to move quickly and hope for the best," said William.

In truth, it would have been hard to conceal from the public eye the small army of men standing by to begin their labor of loading the hired vessels. The official word being broadcast was that some machinery was being sent out for repair, but every man hired knew a different story was in play. The arrival of tug and barge finally brought the Pinkerton man out of his torpor. "You must stop this loading at once," he declared, approaching the brothers on the pier. Nothing was moving as yet, but the brothers didn't argue that point.

"Or?" Thomas asked.

"Or?" the guard was astounded. "There is no *or*. I'm telling you that you must cease and desist," he said with furious self-importance.

The dream of hustling everything out of the mill in one night had been impossible, William had already conceded, but he had hoped for a small headstart before the whistle was blown on them. Now, however, the deception was past and everything would depend on speed. There was no point in pretending further, and William couldn't hide his dislike for the guard any longer. "You have done your duty now, but you are not welcome here. It would be best not to get in the way. Why not go report to whoever sent you and be gone?"

Enraged by his impotence, the guard turned abruptly and left.

"This may put the cat among the pigeons," Thomas said.

Having completed her work for the day, Klara was started on her way home when she was overtaken by the Pinkerton man. Observing his hurried pace and distressed mien, she knew the little bubble of fiction they had all been working in had finally burst. She followed him to the general store, which he entered, in all likelihood to telephone his superiors.

Stepping quietly between display items on the store's covered porch, Klara looked in the window and had her suspicions confirmed as the guard picked up the telephone earpiece. She withdrew from the window. If she could only stop that call, she might buy some valuable time.

"Hello, Mr. Hodges?" the Pinkerton man fell silent. "Yes, sir, I'm calling to tell you there's a barge alongside the McGrath Brothers' sawmill. I believe they're about to load it with machinery."

"Yes, sir.... Yes, sir.... Yes, sir, I will telephone the marshal in Sault Ste. Marie...."

Klara could see the telephone line connected to the side of the store and thought of ways to pull it down: A horse stood tied to the hitching post, patiently awaiting its owner, but its reins wouldn't reach as high as the wire—she discarded the idea. Then her eyes fell on a long-handled hoe, displayed on the porch with some galvanized washtubs, brooms, and spades; it would have to do. Stealing another glance in the window, she grabbed the tool and returned to the telephone wire. It was high, but she felt sure she could reach it. She swung, narrowly missing her legs in the follow-through. Jumping as she swung again, she connected with a loud pop and a few sparks as the line dropped to the ground. She ran down the length of it for about forty feet and hacked again, once, twice—through. She dropped the hoe and picked up the dead end of the severed section, dragging it behind her as she hurried away.

Inside the store, the guard swore an oath that earned him a sharp look from the proprietor.

"I beg your pardon," he said, "but this telephone has stopped working, and I have an urgent call to put through to Sault Ste. Marie!"

The shopkeeper tried the receiver. "I see your problem," he said.

Brisk, purposeful lines of men commenced shifting machinery at first light the next day, following Boyle and William's plan. Small tools and previously disassembled planers, edgers, and saws were carefully stowed in the barge while Boyle dismantled the main engine. Driven ice chunks worried Thomas over the difficulties they could pose to ship travel; schedule, lost minutes, and the possibility that a marshal or other authority might show up to stop them furrowed William's brow; and Boyle, at moments when his attention could be in two places, watched the machinery being carried out, agonizing over the possibility of losing essential parts. As the day came to a close, the brothers felt optimistic; the upper floor had been cleared of machinery, the ground floor was emptied of lighter equipment, and it only remained to load the headsaw and main engine, both of which sat broken into their constituent parts. Moving the heavy pieces would require the morning, and then they could be lifted onto the aft deck of *Avenger* with her derrick and steam winch.

Soon night crept over the mill, bringing the work to a shuddering stop. The buildings and sheds, mostly empty now, echoed with the last few voices before falling completely silent. Out on the tug, the crew enjoyed a final cup of coffee and a smoke before turning in. Some time after all motion had ceased and the dim lights had been snuffed, a dark figure stepped quietly aboard *Avenger*, carefully turned the four dogs sealing the engine room door, opened it up, and slid inside.

The following morning, Thomas hefted his sea bag and stepped over to the door.

"Please be careful," Anne entreated, a lock of dark hair hiding her left eye. It was unlike her to say such things, but he couldn't deny the difference in circumstances from previous departures.

"I won't be gone long. Just enough time for the fuss to die down; then we'll see what to do next. You mustn't worry." He kissed her and began his walk up the lane. His plan was to sail *Genevieve*, in company with *Avenger* and her barge, to Spanish River in order to keep himself and his ship beyond the frustrated reach of what pursuers they might have. Having spent nearly five months ashore now, Thomas felt a peculiar mingling of feelings on this strangest of first sails; with her new topmasts up and stayed, the anticipated pleasure of taking *Genevieve* out again was countered by knowledge of the awaiting fog and ice. Underlying these pragmatic concerns was also a mild tingling of nerves over having been brought ashore unconscious from his last passage. He hoped *Avenger* would complete loading on time to facilitate a clean getaway.

As Thomas considered matters in DeTour, not terribly far away in St. Ignace, Fitzpatrick boarded a surrey driven by Robert Hodge and departed town, heading east. He had left Detroit, clear in his mind that the pressures surrounding him in the city could only be released by the successful auction of the mill. Lancing that boil would rid him of Thompson, Albert Finch would cease to be a worry, and he could then manage Paul's questions, having saved the day by halting any movement by the McGraths. He touched the gun in his pocket; they would bend to his will one way or another. He spoiled for the redemptive conflict to come.

Thomas saw confusion on the deck of *Avenger*; parts of the headsaw and the enormous components of the main engine and its boiler were stopped on their tortuous route to the tug.

"What's the holdup?" he asked the tug captain.

"We've had a sabotage," came the reply. "Someone stole aboard last night and has made off with the governor flyweights and mangled a number of the copper steam lines." William joined them, and when the difficulty was repeated, he sent for Boyle, who went below to look the damage over with *Avenger*'s engineer. When Boyle emerged again, William pounced on him. "Well, Boyle, can you fix it? Can you adapt a governor from our engine?"

Boyle shook his head sadly. "There's a lot of very cunning damage down there. Someone knew how to injure an engine all right. I'm sorry, sir, but it will take a couple of days to get her running again. Some parts will need to be made."

Thomas and William exchanged glances. This could be the end. The mere fact that *Avenger* had been sabotaged showed that unknown ruthless forces were arrayed against them, playing for time. If they couldn't get away today, they might never.

"Can the deck winch be operated?" Thomas asked *Avenger*'s engineer.

"Yes, sir. I have to replace one condenser line. I think we could have steam up to the winch in an hour."

Thomas arrived at a sudden decision. "I'll warp *Genevieve* alongside *Avenger*. We'll transfer machinery across her deck, and I'll tow away the barge."

"That's a lot of extra work; you said yourself that *Genevieve* isn't a towboat, and what about the ice?" William fired off objections in no specific order.

"All we have to do is get to Canada—about fifteen miles depending on which islands we go around. We're out of time and choices," Thomas replied, hoping he could truly accomplish what he had proposed.

William looked wistfully at all the parts and pieces, the levers and wheels of his once mighty mill, loaded in manageably sized chunks on the barge and *Genevieve*. He was sad to see all of their building undone. When the final piece of the power plant, the boiler, was nestled onto *Genevieve's* deck and lashed down, the ship was very suddenly ready to leave. Following all of the action of the preceding days, the moment everyone had toiled toward arrived as something of a surprise, dispelling the final geographical illusion of the mill's permanence. When William spied Moses sniffing around *Genevieve's* deck, cataloging the new cargo, he realized his dog was far more prepared than himself for departure.

He ran up the steps to his office, for what he realized would likely be the last time, to collect his suitcase and the company's books. Opening the door, he was startled to find Klara at his desk. She brushed a loose strand of blonde hair behind her ear.

"Mr. William, I have your books," she said calmly.

Incongruous to his situation, William gave way to an element of charm in the air. Was it something in Klara's tone, or the elongated exoticism in her pronunciation of "books," or the fact that she was here, where he needed her, completing something he had meant to do himself? He was stalled in the doorway.

"Your books?" she said inquisitively, wondering how he had not understood. She had packed his recent records, ledgers, and the address book into his satchel for him.

"Klara." He smiled, touched. "Without these, I can't do business; thank you." He was suddenly overcome by the thought that there was more than one way that this event, leaving, might end their association—an idea he found as unpalatable as leaving the mill itself. He had seen her every day for months, and for half of that time, he had been noticing her more and more. Why had he not done anything about it? He could have, he realized, but instead, he had buried attraction beneath his work; what time he had wasted! Coming forward, he took the closed satchel from her, setting it down next to his desk.

"What are you still doing here?" he asked.

"I am closing up. Put things away for when you are back." They looked at each other, each wondering whether such a time was no more than a fantasy. His natural impulsiveness took over—reaching for Klara's hand, he pulled her toward him and kissed her gently on the forehead. She leaned into him, putting her hands on his hips, sliding them up his back beneath his coat as he kissed her lips. She drew back smiling and surprised. "Mr. William. You are tickling." She stroked playfully at his red whiskers.

"I'm sorry." He looked crestfallen.

"Hmm, maybe again," she said and embraced him a second time. Their second kiss lasted, filled as it was by all the longing that two people, spurned in their pasts, stored away in chests of daily wanting.

Feet pounded the stairs on the way up to the office, splitting Klara away from William. A perfunctory knock accompanied the door's opening.

"Captain's ready to cast off, Mr. McGrath," Dennis Ringle stated peremptorily.

"I'm coming," William replied, but Dennis remained in the doorway.

"Oh, very well," William said. Giving Klara a brave wink, he picked up his suitcase and satchel, and trailed the mate down the stairs.

Outside, Thomas had not been waiting idly for his brother: *Genevieve* had connected towlines to the barge and was hanging against the mild southwest wind by a single bow line from the pier and a stern spring made up on *Avenger*'s amidships bitts. She sat as usual, facing west, the breeze sighing in fine on her port bow; with yards squared, her topsails set aback, surging against the remaining lines, she was restiveness personified. William clambered over the bulwarks, bags in hand.

"Let go the bow line." The bow slid out slowly as the weight of the ship pivoted around the stern spring. *Genevieve* turned and turned, her bow pulling away faster until it looked as though her square sails might fill.

"Brace hard to port." The yards came around. "Let go the stern spring." Free of moorings, the ship gathered way and the barge's mooring lines were cast loose. Morris and Risto surged small amounts of slack into the tow lines, allowing them to take the heavy strain of the barge slowly and without snapping. An awkward couple of minutes ensued as the full load was taken and the tail wagged the dog: *Genevieve* would not answer her helm at first, but by holding one tow line tighter than the other, she began to turn predictably, if slowly, and at last, she was under way.

Fitzpatrick was disgusted. He and Robert Hodge had arrived in DeTour Village only in time to witness the ship and barge's disappearance into a low layer of fog that left only *Genevieve's* rig visible.

"Is that the ship?" he asked.

"I am told it is," answered the lawyer.

"And where is our security man?"

"I told you, sir, he went to fetch the marshal. He reported from the Soo; they should be along shortly."

"Well, of what use will that be?" Fitzpatrick's baritone, ragged with annoyance, rasped faintly. "The ship is gone, stuffed with our property, and according to you, they only have to make it to Canadian waters! What will stop them?" he groused.

"There's a lot of ice out there still," Hodge offered uncertainly.

"There might be another way to stop them," offered a helpful voice behind the men.

CHAPTER 11

THOMAS WAS GAINING a greater respect for tugboat captains. He now found himself maneuvering two ships instead of one, which called for an elevated level of forethought if he hoped to alter course. Added to the complexities of his work were the dual tasks of finding open leads in the ice to make progress northeast, while reminding himself of his proximity to the rocks and islands that dotted the path to freedom. The wind had dropped off, allowing a sea smoke fog, born of the ice, to lay thick and dreary over the deck, broken only by fitful chill gasps of air. Add in the adverse river current and the sum of these difficulties was that, by nightfall, his progress was no more than three miles from the mill, leaving something like twelve more to go before entering Canadian waters. Virtually becalmed and losing ground to the current, he dropped anchor for the night and allowed the men to stand watches in the galley's warm shelter, listening to ice chunks grind competitively against one another out in the darkness.

By ten o'clock the next morning, conditions were becoming more promising; a light north-northwest wind set up, dissipating the fog and shifting the diminishing ice south. Thomas weighed anchor and commenced the tedious process of turning *Genevieve* and her tow onto the desirable heading of northeast. In order to access the open and relatively safe expansiveness of the North Channel, he would first have to negotiate the rock-strewn waters of Potaganissing Bay. A string of islands stretching north to south guarded the bay's entrances, and with the barge in tow, Thomas wanted to get to weather of Little Trout Island so he might beam reach safely into the bay. After their second heartbreakingly slow tack, they were almost north of Squaw Island.

The men were coiling down lines when a smudge was noticed, charcoal on sapphire, against the western sky.

"Do you see that, Thomas?" William gestured excitedly toward Lime Island.

"I do. Don't fret yet; it might be any number of down-bound ships, or even a fire on shore," Thomas replied, but in the pit of his stomach, he felt the premonitory nibble of anxiety. Currently headed toward the smudge of smoke, he was on the wrong tack for flight should it turn out to be an unfriendly ship sent to find them. Knowing it would take twenty minutes to tack, he decided against waiting to identify the newcomer.

"Ready about."

Men went to braces and sheets, and also to the towlines since adjustments to them would help *Genevieve* to turn.

"Helm's a lee." Around she came slowly, slowly in a long painful arc that suddenly collapsed as the square sails went aback and the ship sagged off to leeward. After what seemed an interminable time, she was rotated around enough.

"Let go and haul." The yards came around and she filled away again—the determined plough horse straining against the harrow. Norman came aft and watched the advancing ship. After a while, he gave a low whistle.

"What is it?" William asked, his apprehensiveness overcoming his usual disdain of the cook. Norman waited a long moment, purposely tormenting the younger McGrath brother.

"*Hengist*," he finally replied.

"Inch's boat?" William asked.

"Yes," Thomas said. "Good old Cedric. It wouldn't be like him to miss an opportunity to get in our way."

Fitzpatrick boiled with impatience, ranging fore and aft between the hired men who loafed about *Hengist*'s rusty, neglected deck. Marshal Griffiths's tardiness had delayed the tug's departure until fog had made it impractical. Robert Hodge then declined joining the expedition in favor of remaining as "shore support" when he had laid eyes on the charred, battered tug. In Cedric Inch, Fitzpatrick recognized kindred qualities of cunning and duplicity, leaving him less than assured they would find the McGrath ship stuck in the ice as the tug's owner had promised. And sure enough, little ice was to be seen as *Hengist* finally cleared away from her berth in Raber that morning. But as the sun approached zenith, the white sails of a distant ship came into view—approaching them absurdly enough. Fitzpatrick climbed the flaking iron ladder to the pilothouse.

"What are they doing? I thought they were heading for Canada," he asked of the Inch brothers. Cedric smiled pleasantly, but it was Ralph who answered. "You wouldn't catch me on an old rag boat like that—can never go wheres you want—hoping for the right wind to get you anywheres. He ain't got the wind he wants, that's all."

"I see," Fitzpatrick replied, drawing out the second word knowledgeably, and descended to resume prowling the scaly deck. In short order, the ship and barge had turned toward Canadian waters, he realized, and seeing no change on board *Hengist*, he ran back up to the pilothouse.

"They've turned, they've turned; they are running for it!" he exclaimed.

"Of course," replied Cedric Inch. "But they'll never get that barge through Potaganissing Bay. We'll be up to them before the start of another hour."

Aboard *Genevieve*, Thomas and William discussed *Hengist*'s approach.

"Do you think Inch is operating alone?" William asked.

"Unlikely," replied Thomas. "He would have no authority to try to turn us around. He might come out just to bother us for sport. On the other hand, he has mentioned wanting our mill more than once." On balance, Thomas reflected that anything could happen.

"They are catching up," William said. "Isn't there any way you can make this old boat go faster?"

Thomas sucked in a breath and held it, curbing his tongue. He was unused to being questioned on the deck of his ship. He looked back at the barge, the enormous deadweight of the mill fastened to him, dragging along behind. In this gentle breeze, *Genevieve* would easily make five knots without it. The wind was picking up now, but it would take a gale to make real progress towing the barge. Why had he done this? At least the ice had thinned out. He exhaled.

"We can drop the tow; that's about it," he said.

"And lose everything?"

"We still have the main engine and the headsaw. That's the makings of a good mill right there. But listen; we'll stick it out. It might only be Ralph Inch trying to be a nuisance."

Looking ahead, Thomas could see he only had three miles to go to reach the northern tip of Little Trout Island and enter Potaganissing Bay, but their current speed was a mere three knots. *Hengist* was overtaking them easily, her bent stack leisurely wafting a smoky steam downwind. She would soon be abeam of them, some four hundred feet to windward.

"Hey, take a gander at who is up in the bow," Thomas said.

"Fitzpatrick," William said. "And I think I see Marshal Griffiths. Where are they going? It looks as though they are passing by."

"I think they might try to block the passage north of the island. They're a little far out to talk."

Just then, the marshal did cup his hands around his mouth and called over, but his words were carried away in the rising wind. Thomas looked aloft to consider his press of sail.

"What are they doing now?" William drew his brother's attention back to *Hengist*, for a new burst of steam and cinders erupted from her bent funnel as the tug's corroded, peeling profile turned into an oblique perspective of her plumb iron stem's menacing wedge.

"He's going to ram us!" William answered his own question.

"Morris, Risto, let go of the towlines!" Thomas shouted. *Hengist* was closing fast, the sharp metal of her bow cleaving pale blue water into rolling curls of white foam. It was too late, Thomas realized; they were about to get hit somewhere back aft.

"Everyone get forward!" he commanded. "You too, William," he said as he took the wheel and spun it as fast as he could to starboard in a last ditch effort to mitigate the coming collision. The port towline was released, but Morris had not yet freed the last wraps of the starboard towline.

"Forget it, Morris. Go!" he shouted, watching the hampered turn of his ship.

On *Hengist's* bow, Fitzpatrick couldn't master his exhilaration. Seeing his prey running from him hopelessly was one of the most exciting scenes he had ever witnessed. He capered about from foot to foot, thrusting his hands in and out of his pockets. As *Hengist's* tall bow loomed over *Genevieve's* lower transom, he foolishly climbed onto the bulwark to watch the exact moment of collision take place.

In a fury of flying splinters, *Hengist* drove hard against the barkentine's name board, on the slightest of angles, between the third "E" and the second "V." The starboard bulwark burst its fastenings and separated, the ends of deckboards crackled as they sprung up, and a great hunk of the starboard transom itself broke loose and hung gruesomely from a few very tenacious, splintered fibers. Both ships rattled with the shock, toppling many to the deck from their feet as the colossal timbers of *Genevieve's* framing stopped the tug. Fitzpatrick, in *Hengist's* bow, catapulted from his delicate perch, landing on all fours atop *Genevieve's* popping starboard deck, his gun clattering forward as it escaped his pocket.

Aboard *Hengist*, Marshal Griffiths, in a real show of enterprise, rattled up the ladder to the pilothouse.

"That was not necessary," he said to the Inch brothers. Cedric Inch's face was an innocent blank, his eyebrows faintly elevated, his eyes and mouth passing the impression that he could possibly, in the next moment, smile or break into tears.

"We don't want her sunk," the marshal fed into the silence. Inch knew this better than anyone. He needed this machinery badly, and he wanted to be certain there was no resistance when he hauled it all back to DeTour. What better way than to cripple *Genevieve*? "I'm sorry, Marshal," he said. "They weren't stopping when you hailed them, and Ralph here didn't know what else to do."

"Well, pull back. I want to get alongside, collect Mr. Fitzpatrick, and talk to them." Inch opened his mouth but his words went unheard, drowned out by staccato cracks of gunfire.

As Fitzpatrick scurried after his elusive pistol down *Genevieve's* quarterdeck, peripheral images of sailors, armed with belaying pins and recovering from the impact, advanced upon him. Highly excited, scared, and alone as he now found himself, he picked up the revolver and came up firing.

BAM! BAM! Peoww! He shot twice, once missing Morris, the second round ricocheting off the boiler as he tracked William, who dove for cover. He spotted Norman, forty feet away, carrying a skillet and caught in the open, also ducking toward the big boiler's shelter. He pulled the trigger: BAM!

"Great turds, I'm hit!" Norman shouted as the bullet sent him sprawling to the deck. Fitzpatrick displayed a wicked grin, but his exultation at dropping a man was cut short as he was outflanked by a new adversary.

Although he was generally a friendly mongrel, it was not by accident that Moses had risen to the top of the drowning cage in the Detroit River two years previously. Possessed of a latent ferocity, he could mount a savage attack when called to battle. His barking had gone unnoticed in the pandemonium of grinding hulls and gunshots, but a fierce canine loyalty swelled his heart as he now entered the fray. Launching himself at Fitzpatrick's left leg, he sank his teeth deep into the hamstring and thigh muscles just above the knee.

"Waaaahuuhghhh!" Fitzpatrick wailed as he fell against the mizzen pinrail, trying to comprehend the pain. He grasped it all too clearly in the next second as Moses shook with all the might his sixty-pound body could provide, gouging in deeper with his teeth, showing this violent intruder he was most unwelcome.

Fitzpatrick, wracking pain quivering his body from within, and shaken by the dog's mauling without, beat ineffectively at his assailant with panicky swings of his left hand. He fired a shot into the deck as he struggled to position the gun against the tan blur of Moses's wrenching form. While preparing to squeeze the trigger again, a ten-inch cast iron skillet smashed the bridge of his nose, shattering his glasses and dropping him to the deck unconscious. Farther forward, Norman clamped a hand over his bleeding left shoulder, staggered to the amidships bitts, sat down, and said, "Bull's-eye."

Moses resumed barking at his vanquished foe, stopping periodically to sniff him suspiciously.

Only seconds had elapsed from the moment of collision until Fitzpatrick's incapacitation. Thomas, reeling from *Hengist's* impact, had just registered the fight with the gunman when it was suddenly over. *Hengist* was reversing her engine, loosening *Genevieve's* wooden grasp of her iron stem. If he didn't get free, Thomas felt certain he would be rammed again. He stepped with doleful caution across deckboards, sprung up and down like a keyboard in play, to drop the starboard towline. Once relieved of the barge's crippling drag, *Genevieve* parted from *Hengist* and was free. Thomas returned to the wheel and tried a tentative pull at the spokes. *Very stiff*, he thought, *but workable.* He put the helm over to port and brought *Genevieve* back up to the wind.

Genevieve heeled, shooting forward at an easy seven knots, and at the helm—legs braced to the incline of the deck—Thomas knew his own power once again. It flowed between him and the ship beneath his feet, between them and the primordial crying wind, and he determined in that moment that he would not be bested, not by these bullies, but would see his ship avenged for the wrong they had done to her.

"Mr. Ringle, get below quickly; check the bilges and look at the damage aft. Also, send Benjamin to me," he said.

William came aft. "Norman's been shot."

"I saw. How bad is it?" replied Thomas.

"It's in the shoulder; Risto's slowing the bleeding. Norman won't let me touch him." Thomas gave a wry smile at the final statement, and then Dennis was back to see him.

"We have a number of weeping planks and two streamers in the lazarette, but we're not flooding. I can stuff the leaks aft with oakum," Dennis offered.

"Not yet; I'll need everyone just now."

"You've let the barge go," William stated.

"Had to, Will; you can see that, but the mischief's not over yet."

On *Hengist's* bridge, Ralph Inch was still in reverse when *Genevieve* dropped the towline and shot away.

"What are you doing?" Cedric asked him.

"We're picking up the barge, right?" Ralph asked.

"No, you fool!" Cedric slapped him on the back of the head in a rare show of temper. "We want to catch them."

Ralph, grumbling, rang the telegraph down to the engine room to stop the engine and then rang for full ahead.

"Get the three-inch hawser on deck. I want some short lengths of chain and four big shackles—also, about one hundred feet of three-quarter-inch line," Thomas said to Benjamin. "Get it out of the hatch without showing it off; feed it along the deck to the port amidships bitts." His plan was to foul the tug's propeller; he was presently to weather of *Hengist* and she was pursuing from *Genevieve's* leeward quarter, slightly off to starboard. If the hawser could be lowered into the water unseen, they might have a good chance of tripping her up. The hawser was fed out, weighed down by chains and shackles periodically along its length, and then secured by an inconspicuous three-quarter-inch line to the port amidships bitts. The only remaining difficulty was that their trap must be sprung shortly, as the little archipelago barring Potaganissing Bay lay a mile and a half ahead.

The two ships cut forward, nearly matched for speed; *Hengist* at a pace of nine knots, and *Genevieve* going almost as fast in the fresh breeze now blowing. Thomas feared the tug might not catch him in time, so he began to pinch up, sailing slightly too close to the wind to give the sails full pressure and truly drive the barkentine. Looking over *Genevieve's* ruined stern to the baleful promise of *Hengist's* freshly scarred bow, he considered that if his gambit didn't work, he might lose his ship—and more. *Too late to think about it*, he told himself. Given half a chance, Inch would hammer him again anyway. He could hear *Hengist's* bow wave. *She must be close enough*, he thought, and eased his helm to starboard, putting *Genevieve* directly before the tug.

Cedric and Ralph Inch, uninhibited by the marshal's presence, engaged in some anticipatory gloating.

"She's between us and the rocks now," Ralph said brightly. "There's only another mile and she'll have to turn; then we'll have her." He grinned savagely. Cedric smiled despite himself.

"I don't want her rammed again this time. You understand?" said Marshal Griffiths vehemently.

"Marshal," Cedric said, opening his pale blue eyes wide and showing the lawman his palms, "we'll do everything possible to avoid that. Isn't that right, Ralph?"

"Ooh, I think she is starting to turn," said Ralph just before a sudden banging noise began hammering up through the ship's iron structure.

"What the devil is that?" snapped Cedric.

"Dunno," said Ralph, stricken, as more hammering noises joined in and *Hengist* began to lose speed.

Staggered cheers broke out in pockets across *Genevieve's* deck as the crew saw *Hengist* falter, her bow slewing suddenly downwind. A sharp twang reported the three-quarter-inch line's parting as *Hengist's* hungry four-bladed propeller ate up all the line it could.

"Ready about!" Thomas shouted, bringing order back to the deck. Less than half a mile remained to the islands, so he had to get *Genevieve* clear.

"Helm's a lee!" he called when the pinrails were all manned. As the ship came into the wind and was committed to the tack, he left the wheel momentarily to take a quick look at the transom. It was in sorry shape, but the mizzen sheet staple looked as though it would hold, and so would the rest of it, he decided. Back at the helm, he called, "Let go and haul." The yards came around and *Genevieve* settled on a new course.

"Mr. Ringle, clew up the course and hand the t'gallant, quick as you can." He had one more piece of business to attend to.

The hammering sound from beneath *Hengist's* stern was merciless in the engine room. Unaware that the propeller had sucked in and bitten down on three hundred feet of hawser, several shackles, and some chain, the engineer wisely cut off the steam for the sole purpose of stopping the noise. As it happened, the ship had lost her drive in any case.

"What the devil is happening?" Inch asked.

"Something caught on the prop, I'll wager," replied Ralph, who had done this to himself numerous times.

"McGrath," Inch stated acidly in a bitter acknowledgment of the plain truth. "Well, get it fixed."

"I'll have to drop anchor and get the boys over the side," Ralph said, knowing it would take hours, especially in this icy water.

Inch's veiny nose turned purple with frustration as he pulled at his hair.

Thomas had put Risto on the wheel and conned the helmsman from a vantage point at the port rail, just abaft the mizzen shrouds.

"A little more to port; good, steady there!" he called. He felt *Genevieve* was handling smoothly under reduced sail, now that the course and t'gallant were taken in. He wanted finesse rather than speed for what he had in mind.

The neglect on *Hengist* extended beyond her platework, decks, and pilothouse; her rarely used ground tackle had not seen a lick of effort in years, and as the men rushed to prepare an anchor for dropping, they found the item fastened securely into the bulwarks by three recalcitrant rusty bolts. They halted cursing, looking up from their labor to find, in a strange turning of tables, the gray barkentine rushing at them.

"William, Morris...are you ready?" Thomas asked.

"Um-buh, yes, sir," Morris answered, and William dropped a quick nod. *Genevieve*, even under reduced canvas, was still making six knots. Thomas aimed her at *Hengist*'s bow, which lay just a little more downwind than her stern.

"A little more to port," he called to Risto as the distance shortened. "Good, steady." They were only a ship-length from the tug now, so men on *Hengist*'s deck seemed to scatter in all directions at once, uncertain of what to expect or where to run.

"Four turns to starboard now, Risto, quick," Thomas ordered.

"Aye, sir," said Risto, pushing the stiff wheel around as fast as he could.

Thomas watched *Genevieve* swing from her beam reach up to starboard, her bows arcing clear of *Hengist*'s stern. She clawed to windward, pinching, pinching, as the gap between the two hulls closed. He could see the marshal waving to him and shouting, but he had no time for that now. The topsails began to luff as *Genevieve*'s speed fell away to three knots and the two hulls were divided by mere yards.

"Hard a port!" he roared over the din. "Mr. Ringle, set the course!" The moment he had called these orders, *Genevieve* touched against *Hengist*'s low counter with her port stern.

"Now!" Thomas shouted, giving William and Morris their cue to fling the inert Fitzpatrick aboard the tug. As the bow fell away again and her topsails filled, *Genevieve* pulled clear.

Thomas could now devote some attention to addressing the marshal. "Marshal Griffiths, I've brought your little killer back." But the lawman stood dumbfounded.

Inch called after him instead, "Hold up, McGrath; it's still not too late for us to work out a deal."

Thomas laughed out loud. "Good bye, Inch," he said plainly and turned his back on them. He had a barge to catch.

As the great belly of the course filled, accelerating *Genevieve* toward the orphaned barge, William joined his brother at the rail.

"I must say, well done," William said. Thomas received the compliment quietly.

"What will happen to *Hengist* now?" William asked.

Thomas gazed back at the helplessly drifting tug and said, "They'll have to unwind that huge propeller, but it looks like the rocks of Little Trout Island will have her for company tonight." After a ruminative pause, he asked with a smile, "Can you think of a more terrible time to be unable to spread a little sail?"

June 15, 1893

IF ITZPATRICK STIRRED HIS thin mutton stew and searched for the will to eat it. After a prolonged interval considering the dish, he forced in a spoonful. *Gamier than usual, an exceptionally old ram no doubt*, he thought, but even had it been good tasting, he had no appetite. After three more slurps, he wrinkled his still-swollen nose and put the tin pot near the edge of his cell for collection.

The only window to admit light into the hallway—if that was the proper term for the space between rows of cages—showed him that the evening was far advanced. The light faded away, and thus far, no lamps had been lit.

With an officious rattle of keys, the jailer approached, causing the few incarcerated men to wonder what was coming—soup pails were generally collected in the morning. He stopped in front of Fitzpatrick's cell.

"Well, Fitzpatrick, it might be your lucky day." The guard smirked as he inserted a key and clanked open the lock's heavy tumbler. With a metallic groan, the door swung open. "You are free to go."

"I made bail?" Fitzpatrick asked, astonished that someone had posted a bond for him. Perhaps Beatrice had come to her senses and persuaded Paul to drop the fraud charges.

"Something like that," was the guard's response. His smirk broadened into a grin. Fitzpatrick was ushered through the innards of the city jail, given his few belongings, and shoved out the side door. It was a shock to be outside after spending five weeks in the lockup; it made it hard to formulate a plan. He had never had a chance to replace his smashed spectacles after being rescued from that awful tugboat. The world beyond the jail was just a blurry dusk filled with improbabilities and difficulty. He blamed blurry eyesight for his capture. *There's no way they would have caught me if I could've seen the wanted posters at the train station.* For deep down, despite arrest and imprisonment, Fitzpatrick believed in a fantastic image of himself: a resourceful, cunning, iron-willed thinker—strong and predatory.

All of that was about to change.

"Fitzpatrick," came the dreadful wheeze. A pungent rag smothered his nose and mouth, ushering in an interval of blackness.

Hours later, Fitzpatrick began to regain consciousness, noting first the numb prick of pins and needles in his hands. *Manacled? No*—an exploration with his thumb told him that his hands were lashed behind his back with rope. A lump of dry cloth filled his mouth—fear filled his heart. Dim lantern light sparkled off of the walls, and although he couldn't focus, he immediately recognized his surroundings.

"Fitzpatrick? Ah, Fitzpatrick, we meet again," Thompson said in a horrid, almost jovial rasp. Moving closer, he set his lantern on the floor. "Yes, here we are again. Can't say I love it here, but this old salt mine has been very useful to me over time."

Fitzpatrick wriggled slightly, testing his bonds in the familiar chair. Both his hands and his feet were bound, but mercifully, the chair sat on all four legs this time. He decided to remain motionless, knowing what lay behind him. Thompson picked up the lantern and moved closer still, the dim light illuminating his cruel lips and bent nose as they came within Fitzpatrick's focus.

"You'll be wondering how you got here—a common concern of visitors to this place. First of all, you'll be reported as escaped from the jail." Thompson gave a short nasty laugh. "It will be a big mystery. Friends of mine can sometimes arrange such things. But the essence of why you are here is failure—your failure: We had a deal, and now I find that the McGrath brothers are not out of business at all, but are selling lumber as usual. Worse yet, you get yourself arrested and are being asked some nosy questions—questions that might involve me." Thompson reached out and picked at an edge of the cloth in Fitzpatrick's mouth, causing the bound man to hope. He hoped he might be getting a chance to respond—beg; perhaps he would get a chance to explain how he had made every effort.

"I might need this later," Thompson said as he yanked out the cloth and kicked the chair leg closest to him. The chair wobbled, nearly stabilized, and then a single rear leg slipped over the crumbling edge of the forgotten mineshaft. Fitzpatrick screamed out a piercing "Nooo!" as he tried to counterbalance, but the villainy had been done and he was consigned to complete his long tumble.

Six weeks later

Genevieve, with her crew mostly away on leave, sat quietly unattended at a small stub pier in Spanish River, enduring the heat of mid-afternoon alone, until her master, with a horse-drawn cart, pulled alongside of her.

Thomas had forgotten just how much dunnage came with a woman and children. As sweat trickled into his eyes and down his back, he hauled what he hoped would be the last load below. It seemed as though he had been shifting the contents of his entire house around for weeks now, only to have it arrive in a heap in *Genevieve*'s salon. Unburdening himself at the bottom of the companionway stairs, Thomas looked at what he had wrought: an enormous pile of bags, books, and boxes dominated the middle of the salon, awaiting designation to new homes and hiding places. Shaking his head, he wondered how all this extra gear would be blended into the order that had been *Genevieve*. No doubt Anne would be instrumental in organizing half of it, and he could foresee jettisoning some items as time went by.

Returning to the deck, he spotted William walking down the road, his hat shading his eyes from the bright sunlight as he approached the mill. "Well, my brother, how are you?" he called and advanced to meet him.

"Thomas." William came forward and the two men embraced.

"How did it go?" Thomas asked.

"The journey was fine—no complications and the divorce will be finalized in October." William had been to Indiana on the advice of his lawyer as divorces were obtained more expeditiously there.

"That sounds good," said Thomas.

"*Genevieve* looks whole again," William remarked, admiring the fresh paint on the barkentine's elegant transom.

The brothers hadn't seen each other in almost two months. After the initial fuss had died down, Thomas had returned to DeTour in order to collect the contents of their homes and other small equipment. Immediately after their delivery to Spanish River, *Genevieve* had sailed for Collingwood, in Georgian Bay, to be dry-docked and repaired. In the time since her return, William had been gone to Indiana.

"Yes, it was a fair amount of work: new planks, new deckboards, some new framing—but she is sound again. Come below; I'll show you the cabin improvements," Thomas said proudly.

After the brothers had descended the companionway steps, William said: "You have a fine collection of boxes there."

"Don't I now? Nothing comes without compromise. Tomorrow, I am going to wheel George's bicycle down here and somehow keep a straight face as I tell Benjamin to find a home for it in the lazarette."

"But anyhow, here we are; we rebuilt my cabin; the cabinetry is changed and my little desk is gone, in exchange for a more er—matrimonial bunk. I'll do my paperwork out on the salon table."

"Very nice," observed William, admiring the craftsmanship and clever use of space in the new layout.

"And we have refit the other cabins to accommodate Molly here"—Thomas opened the door to a very small cabin on the starboard side, just forward of the lazarette—"and Curt and George"—He opened the next door immediately forward—"will share this one. The salon stores that used to be here will be kept up forward where Norman can keep an eye on them."

"How is Norman?" William asked.

"Better and better. His arm is still building strength, but I see improvement every week. He's been back in the galley for about a month now, and he's practicing throwing a skillet with his left hand."

William laughed. "I'll stay out of the line of fire while he's perfecting his aim." He changed the subject. "And how about the rest of the ship? Are you happy with the repairs?"

"Yes, the yard had some very good shipwrights; they did a fine job of getting everything fitted correctly and realigning the rudder. As I said, *Genevieve* is as good as ever."

"Good, good." William paused for a moment, then said, "I have some news, and I wonder if it might affect your plan to ship out for Europe?"

Thomas gave his brother his full attention, awaiting the momentous news silently.

"On my way home, I passed through Detroit and, through our agent there, I have found out that John Fitzpatrick was arrested for embezzlement and fraudulent bookkeeping. There was also some talk that he might have had a hand in the demise of poor old Edgar Standish."

"Really? In a way, I'm not surprised. And so?" Thomas asked.

"And so here the story gets interesting in two ways," replied William. "About six weeks ago, it seems that Fitzpatrick escaped the city jail and has so far evaded recapture. What is particularly interesting for us is that I have had a telephone call with Paul Standish, who has reviewed our situation and apologized for the bank's treatment of our loan. As things stand, we are now paid in full and free to return to DeTour when we wish. If you like, we can move some of our equipment back and set up to run both operations. Life could go on much as it was," William said happily.

Life could go on much as it was. Thomas considered and realized that "much as it was" was the part he didn't want; he and the mill had been on divergent paths for several years. A side of him wished he could stay and be content with the work and the life they had built here, but he knew a wide world of possibilities and sights were just waiting for him and his family. He currently had a good order from Glasgow, Scotland, for number one white pine beams. He chose his words carefully. "Will, the idea is very tempting, but I'm far along in my plans now; I have to give my scheme a try. Maybe I'll be back looking for work in a year, but for now, I must ship out."

William nodded since he had expected this, but nevertheless, Thomas read disappointment on his face. He picked a new topic to cheer him up. "It's Klara's birthday on Friday; you made it back just in time."

"I didn't want to miss it. I'm not sure she'd forgive me," William said in return.

In Friday's long summer evening, the mill was silenced and swept clean. Returned members of *Genevieve's* crew set up benches and picnic tables outside from the ready material of planks over sawhorses. Morris set a cauldron boiling above a bonfire fueled by bark and offcuts. Curt and George shucked corn for the great pot while Anne and several other women laid dishes of potato salad, tomatoes, sausages, pasties, and pies around the table's centerpiece: an enormous, two-layered, frosted lemon cake. William had learned that lemon was a favorite flavor of Klara's so he had brought the tangy fruit with him from Detroit's Eastern Market.

Mill workers and sailors, friends and family all showed up for the event. Norman tapped a new keg of lager, and as the sun disappeared behind the trees, the fledgling mill hummed with the entirely different note of human enthusiasm. A fiddle was produced and William took Klara's hand to lead the dancing. Klara's face, her eyes, positively glowed in the firelight. Her radiance emanated not from the single beer she drank with her dinner, but from an elevated sense of being appreciated. She had come far since her last birthday—which had been ignored—to now being the guest of honor, dancing with a good man she could love and respect.

Standing on his own, Thomas watched the couple dance, William's face reflecting Klara's happiness. At last, he felt his brother would be all right. Looking aloft, he was in time to see a falling star, its long tail blazing through space. Where would it land? Where would he land? It was going to be different for him to blend his two selves: the master mariner with the husband and father—he had always been conscious of the shift he made between roles. The future was more uncertain than ever, but for the first time in a long while, it truly beckoned. Soon he would be harnessing a wholesome west wind, running *Genevieve* toward a distant continent. He was still gazing into the sky, trying to make out all of the Pleiades, when Anne surprised him, slipping an arm around his waist.

"You look lonesome over here, Captain," she said.

"I was," he smiled and looked from her, back to the revelry as he put an arm around her shoulders. "It's a great night, though; a fine party."

"It is." Her brow knit. "It got to be rather large, though—extravagant," she said.

He heard in this her apprehension over the future; she knew their funds, as well as William's, would be limited for some time to come. "It's also our send-off," he said.

"That cake was a square yard, two layers thick," she quibbled.

"A thing of beauty, and look how happy they are." He gestured to Klara and William. "They're almost as happy as we are." He grinned and kissed her cheek. As he held her hand in the flickering firelight and took in the party, he watched Morris and Risto feast on cobs of corn, dancers tapping toes, drinkers and storytellers throwing crazy shadows far into the surrounding darkness of the magical northern night.

Someone moved, revealing Curt to Thomas. His youngest stood beside the food table, pushing an extra large piece of lemon cake into his mouth, attended by Moses, who sat drooling on the boy's feet, patiently awaiting the drop of some stray morsel. Thomas pointed inconspicuously so that Anne might see the spectacle and said, "One should always keep some money aside for birthday cake."

A Dream of Steam

Fact and Fiction

A TRUE STORY INSPIRED me to write this novel. Family connections to Michigan brought me out sailing with my father-in-law years ago in Lake Huron's North Channel. While there, I stumbled upon the story of the Moiles brothers who, in 1889, executed the heist of their own sawmill to save it from being taken by creditors. I subsequently found two versions of the event, prompting me to write a thoroughly fictionalized third version of the basic fact of the heist. I bumped the timing of the heist forward to the early 1890s; so much was happening in Detroit, Michigan, and the nation that it was a rich period to develop storylines in. Even so, in a few places I have fudged history slightly to serve the tale I've told:

Stray dogs were a big problem in nineteenth century Detroit, as they are today. By the 1880s stray dogs were rounded up by professional dogcatchers and often drowned. The Detroit Humane Society was set up in 1877, and I can imagine they made the effort to stop the drownings, but it is likely the practice lingered on as people were slowly converted to more humane treatment of animals.

The Panic of 1893 took place in the winter of that year, not in the previous summer as I've rendered it.

In researching the formation of the International Longshoreman's Union, I did not find a long rap sheet of murder and mayhem. The struggle to organize, however, was often witness to brutal contests, and certainly, the Detroit docks were notoriously violent at that time—even the police avoided going there. It is likely that a character such as Thompson worked those docks.

By the 1890s, train lines were in rapid expansion; every year saw many towns across the country newly connected by rail. DeTour, at the eastern tip of Michigan's Upper Peninsula, did not enjoy that development. Timber ports were serviced mainly by ship, leaving them somewhat isolated in deep winter. Historically, Ojibwa (Chippewa) Indians delivered mail. I have found anecdotal evidence of them bringing the mail across lake ice in the 1890s, but I don't claim to know how common the practice was or how it was dispatched.

Despite a few historical licenses, I hope you have enjoyed *A Dream of Steam,* and that the story has given you a glimpse of a possible past.

Thank you for reading.

James W. Barry

Glossary

Mill and Logging

Cant: Large timber, squared in a sawmill.

Cant hook: A hinged metal hook at the end of a long handle used for gripping and rolling logs or cants.

Edger: A saw dedicated to giving boards a straight edge.

Flyweights: Twin metal balls that spin on the governor of a steam engine.

Gangsaw: A saw with a series of parallel blades for cutting a cant into planks in one passage.

Governor: The mechanism on a steam engine that regulates speed through centrifugal force.

Headsaw: A very large circular saw blade primarily used for cutting logs into cants.

Limber: A person who cuts the branches away from fallen trees

Millwright: A person who maintains mill machinery.

Peavey: Similar to a cant hook but fitted with a sharp spike at its hook end used for rolling logs.

Planer: A machine with a set of rotating horizontal blades for smoothing the surface of rough sawn boards.

Plat: A plot of land.

River hog: A man working on the driving of logs downriver.

Slashboard: A small dropleaf gate in a dam to control water flow beneath it.

Undershot waterwheel: A wheel powering a mill driven by water flowing against its bottom side.

Ship

Abaft: Toward the stern from another object on a ship.

Abeam: At right angles to the ship's length.

Aft: Near or toward the stern of a ship.

Amidships: In the middle of the ship, either fore to aft or side to side.

Athwartships: Across a ship's length.

Backstay: A wire connected to the top of a mast that leads downward and holds it aft.

Belaying pin: A thick pin set in the railing of a ship for the purpose of securing ropes around it.

Beam reach: Sailing with the wind coming at 90 degrees to the ship's length.

Block: A sheave or pulley mounted in a case for redirecting rope.

Brace: A tackle attached to the yardarm for controlling the orientation of a square sail.

Broad reach: Sailing with the wind coming from behind 90 degrees to the ship's length.

Boom topping lift: A tackle attached to the aft end of the boom to control its height.

Bowsprit: A spar running forward from the ship's bow.

Bulwark: The extension of a ship's side above deck level.

Buntline: A control line of a square sail used for gathering in its middle.

Clew: The aft lower corner of a sail or both lower corners of a square sail.

Clewline: A control line of a square sail used for hauling up its lower corner.

Course: The lowest square sail on a square-rigged ship.

Eye of the Wind: The direction from which the wind is coming.

Fo'c'sle: A corruption of forecastle: the accommodation area for the crew in the bow of a ship.

Fore: The mast closest to the bow.

Freeing ports: Small openings in a ship's bulwarks for releasing water from the deck.

Gybe: To maneuver a ship turning the stern through the eye of the wind.

Halyard: A rope or tackle attached to the top of a sail for raising or lowering it.

Leeward: On or toward the side sheltered from the wind.

Leeway: Sideways motion or sideslip in a ship's progress.

Lift: A wire connected to a yardarm, balancing and suspending it from the masthead above.

Masthead: The top of the mast.

Main: The center and usually principal mast of a ship.

Mizzen: The mast aft of the ship's mainmast.

Parcelling: Cloth wrapping applied to wire to prevent corrosion.

Pinrail: A section of railing fitted with belaying pins.

Port: The left side of a ship when facing forward.

Sheet: The line or tackle attached to control the clew of a sail.

Shrouds: Wire rigging that secures a mast from side to side.

Spar: A thick, strong pole used for a mast, yard, or boom on a ship.

Spiderband: An iron ring fitted to hold belaying pins, clamped around the mast.

Sternway: Reverse motion of a ship.

Tack: 1) The forward lower corner of a sail. 2) To maneuver a ship by bringing the bow through the eye of the wind.

Tackle: An assembly of blocks and rope used to build mechanical advantage.

T'Gallant Mast (Topgallant): The third and uppermost vertical spar on a square-rigged mast.

T'Gallant: The square sail attached to the t'gallant mast.

Topmast: The second or middle vertical spar on a square-rigged mast.

Tops'l (Topsail): The square sail attached to the topmast.

Waist: The middle of the ship from fore to aft, often where it is widest.

Warp: A very heavy line used for pulling a ship or anchoring.

Way: The forward motion of a ship.

Windward: Facing the wind or on the side facing the wind.

Yard: A cylindrical spar, tapered at each end, slung across a ship's mast for a sail to hang from.

Yardarm: The outward extremity of a yard.

About the Author

James W. Barry has been a career sailor and is a rigger of traditional ships. He spent many years sailing small square-riggers on the Great Lakes before his voyages took him to bigger (and smaller) ships on the open sea.

As a master rigger, James has re-rigged historic ships for museums, and developed set pieces for Hollywood, notably for the films *Master and Commander*, and *Pirates of the Caribbean* 2, 3, and 4.

Never home for very long, James divides his time between ports along the Eastern Seaboard, the Caribbean Sea, and Michigan.

A Dream of Steam is his first novel.

You can learn more about James at:

www.JamesW.Barry.com.

CPSIA information can be obtained
at www.ICGtesting.com
Printed in the USA
LVHW052049060220
646086LV00013B/1336